ALL WE HAVE LEFT

EMILY PAXMAN

TITAN BOOKS

*Also by Emily Paxman
and available from Titan Books*

Death on the Caldera

All We Have Left
Print edition ISBN: 9781835417591
E-book edition ISBN: 9781835417607

Published by Titan Books
A division of Titan Publishing Group Ltd
144 Southwark Street, London SE1 0UP
www.titanbooks.com

First edition: June 2026
10 9 8 7 6 5 4 3 2 1

This is a work of fiction. All of the characters, organizations, and events portrayed in this novel are either products of the author's imagination or are used fictitiously. Any resemblance to actual persons, living or dead (except for satirical purposes), is entirely coincidental.

A CIP catalogue record for this title is available from the British Library.

EU RP (for authorities only)
eucomply OÜ, Pärnu mnt. 139b-14, 11317 Tallinn, Estonia
hello@eucompliancepartner.com, +3375690241

Designed and typeset in Sabon LT by Richard Mason.

Printed and bound by CPI Group (UK) Ltd, Croydon, CR0 4YY.

to the islands that raised me;
may your shores always be a safe harbour.

ONE

BLACKBERRIES SHOULD BE out of season by now, but I find a bramble still dotted with plump fruit, soaking up the autumn sun. Some are mouldering on the vine, but enough look edible that I take off my jacket and use it to cradle the berries, sling style. I should have brought a bucket, but I wasn't expecting luck this late in the year. It's a testament to the blackberry itself—a resilient plant, growing where it shouldn't, when it shouldn't. In the pre-Quake days, people spent a lot of time and money cutting back the canes, but I'm glad they never managed to get rid of them. Not all of humanity's failures are for the worst.

My stomach rumbles as a berry bruises against my fingers. Juice runs down my thumb, but I don't give into temptation. A hungry forager is a slow, selfish one. I'll wait until I'm with April. She needs them more than I do, anyway.

Once my jacket is full, I retrace my path. The sun is noonday high. I'm expecting to find April re-reading our copy of *And Then There Were None*, which is her favourite, for reasons I can't fathom. Something about horrible people dying horrible deaths comforts her.

But when I push back the branches of the oak tree we hid our tarp behind, I spot my little sister crumpled over like a leaf, the book fallen from her hands.

"April?" I drop the jacket and rush to her side. She was awake when I left her. She doesn't respond to my voice, so I roll her onto her back. "Hey! April! You okay?"

She takes a shuddering breath, and my pulse slows. Still alive, though her cheeks are stark white. She manages to shoot me a withering look as she blinks awake. "What?"

"Are you okay? Did you pass out again?" I press two fingers against her forehead, which is always too warm these days, but she swats me away, growing more pissed by the second.

"No." She rubs one of her eyes. "Kayla, I took a nap. On purpose."

"Oh." The problem is *sleeping* and *fainting* and *dead* all look an awful lot alike. I swear, one of these days, I'm going to come back and she won't wake up. We're so close to Crofton, but that only winds me tighter. Nothing would be worse than losing my sister now, when we're within spitting distance of help. "Sorry."

"Now that *that's* cleared up, I'm going back to sleep," she says.

"No can do, actually."

She turns her morning bitch face to me, clearly expecting orders to start hiking. It's most of what we do these days. I nag her until she walks. She walks until she collapses. Repeat cycle. I hope it's a welcome surprise when I grin and say, "I brought breakfast."

"You... what?" She rubs her eyes. "I thought you were scouting for TNS."

"Well, I found something much bet—" I stop, realizing the berries are scattered over the forest floor, thanks to my earlier panic. Whatever. It's fine. Birds shit all over those bushes anyway. Dirt isn't going to hurt anyone.

I hold a hand up to April. "One second."

She groans and lies back down. "Kayla..."

I hastily stack them in the centre of my jacket. "You're going to be excited for this. I want you preparing your excited voice."

"Yaaaaay..." April feigns enthusiasm with all the conviction of a cat learning to swim.

"Ta-da!" I lay the jacket out between us.

She props herself on her elbows. "Oh!"

"See? What did I tell you?"

"I thought you just found mushrooms or something," she says, taking a handful.

"No, the kitchen staff realized you always send the mushrooms back, your highness. Only the best for you."

She rolls her eyes but doesn't bother sassing me, too focused on the berries. April would have squealed at a treat like this a few years ago. I miss the little girl she used to be sometimes. But that tiny *oh* when she saw what I brought her? From a fifteen-year-old, that's a standing ovation.

After she's taken a couple of handfuls, I treat myself to a few. I eat slowly, savouring every ripple of juice over my tongue. It's been weeks since we had fresh fruit. I could wolf the whole pile down in an instant, but I pace myself so she can have the majority. Even eating twice the rations I do, she's losing weight.

A whisper of dread curls around my lungs, but I shove it away. There's no point in wondering exactly how close we are to Crofton. We should be within a few kilometres, but pre-Quake maps provide estimations at best. So many roads and landforms are a jumbled mess of their former selves. All we can do is hug the coast and head north.

"So you didn't see any sign of TNS?" she asks, between mouthfuls. Anyone with half a brain fears True North

Strong—TNS for short—the paramilitary group that runs our region. After the Quake, they gathered up most of the firearms from Victoria to Calgary.

"No, and I don't expect to. Those berries were right on the main road."

"So?"

"So, no one's around. They would have picked them." It's a good and a bad sign. No people means no one to hurt us, but what if it also means no one to help? "I guess... I guess it isn't worth it to the islanders to come over, just for blackberries."

April nods, doubtless doing the same mental arithmetic. "They must have their own bushes."

"That must be it."

As a rule, we don't talk about the possibility that Salt Spring Island *won't* be able to help us. For the past eight years, I've led us to countless places only to find the things that should have been there were missing. Houses we used to shelter in? Stripped down for firewood by someone else. Spinach patches I planted in the fall would be picked over by the time we returned in spring. But this is more important than having to spend another night under the tarp or miss a meal. For April, it's life or death, which means it is for me, too.

I pull out the pre-Quake map I use to navigate Vancouver Island and measure our route again. Usually, we spend this time of year living off the salmon run at the Goldstream estuary. It's the perfect place to gather the fat and protein we need to sustain us through the winter, before hunkering down in an abandoned neighbourhood and praying TNS doesn't finds us.

But April fell ill at the end of the summer. At first, it didn't seem like much: headaches, dry mouth, dizziness. I've pushed through worse. But April has never had my stamina, so we stopped to rest for a week. I waited for her to get better. And waited. And waited.

Eventually, we had to talk about options. We both knew there was only one.

Back when our mum was alive, we met another group of survivors when we went to fill our water bottles out of the Cowichan River. They didn't try to shank us right away, so that was a good sign they weren't TNS. Still, that didn't guarantee they were safe either. Mum eventually approached and offered to trade for some of their food. We'd grabbed some jewellery and a wind-up watch from an abandoned house earlier that year. We had no use for them, but the people by the river were interested.

"You could come with us," one of them said, his eyes roving to me and April. I would have been fifteen; she was just five. "It would be a better place to raise your girls. We've got a school, a hospital—"

"Thanks, but we've taken enough chances with colonies already," said Mum, and I certainly agreed with that assessment. I started to drag April away, knowing it would be my job to carry her if things turned violent. Most people don't like it when you refuse to join their cult.

"Suit yourself." He shrugged and turned back to his companions. "We're on Salt Spring, if you change your mind."

"Salt Spring?" Mum's eyes narrowed.

She didn't say it, but we *had* heard of them before. The leader of our last colony used to tell us harrowing stories of the way the Gulf Islands hunted down anyone who opposed them. They were as bad as TNS. Probably worse, considering they'd been able to fight TNS off. He warned us, if we ever met anyone from Salt Spring Island, to get the hell away while we were still alive.

As we stood there on the riverside, I remember

wondering if we'd already lost our chance to run. Though if we had, why weren't they shooting yet?

The man from Salt Spring nodded. "You can get to the island from Crofton. Provided you come unarmed, the guards will let you in."

Mum thanked him, but once her back was to the group, she rolled her eyes.

"Unarmed, my *ass*," she muttered to me. We both heard the same subtext. Maybe they didn't want to kill us. But they'd only take us into their colony if we were helpless and easy to control. We'd been down that road before and knew better than to trust strangers to protect us.

Even though it's been years, his words still haunt me. A *hospital*. I've got a vague idea of what that is, thanks to the books we find lying around in abandoned houses. In all likelihood, it's a myth, like Santa Claus and a dozen other things from the pre-Quake days that only exist in picture books now.

But April needs a fairy tale. Nothing else is going to save her.

We finish the last of the blackberries, and I fold up the map. I shutter the memories; bring myself back to the present, so that I can focus on keeping both of us alive.

"We should get going. I think we'll make it today. I smell the ocean." I offer her a hand up and she wobbles. I wish I could carry her pack for her, but I've already got most of our gear. Pots and pans clatter against the outside of my bag.

I use all the pep I can muster as we strike camp. We can't hike long distances like we used to when she was healthy, but the few surviving street signs I've spotted place us tantalizingly close to the Crofton Ferry Terminal.

The thought makes me more uneasy than I dare admit out loud. The last thing April needs is doubt, but Salt

Spring could have been invaded by TNS in the past ten years. TNS gets to everyone eventually, especially decent people. Or the island could be a creepy ass cult like the last colony we sheltered in.

I don't think I'm a paranoid person by nature, but I know better than to take chances. Yes, there are people out there who claim they want to protect us. But in these population-depressed, fractured remains of the world, any colony's motive for saving us is pretty obvious. I'm a female of peak breeding age. April isn't far behind. So yeah, Salt Spring might want us. But what if the cure is worse than the sickness?

I try not to think about that option. This is our only solution, so we're going for it, and I'm telling myself every lie I need to so I can make peace with the decision. Once we get there, we'll be safe, April will get better, and life will be all rainbows. The world is a messed-up pile of broken buildings and thorny vines, but that doesn't mean all the good is gone, right? There are still blackberries growing between the prickles. One small miracle is all we need.

TWO

LIKE MOST PLACES this far north, Crofton is a small town. Or was. Now, it's nothing but shattered houses. Not every building fell during the mega-quake that levelled the Pacific Northwest thirty-two years ago, though some days, it feels that way. The epicentre hit Seattle, but the Quake was powerful enough to throw unbolted homes off their foundations past the northern tip of Vancouver Island.

More than Crofton's fair share of buildings were destroyed. That probably happened during the chaotic aftermath. It was everyone for themselves, once people realized no relief was coming. In a better scenario, the Canadian government would have helped. Sadly, a host of foreign powers saw the Quake as the perfect opportunity to strike a weakened USA. Canada got dragged in, like a remora going down with the shark it's suctioned to.

Before the Quake, my mum wanted to be a high school science teacher, but she joined the Red Cross when images of Vancouver Island's flattened cities made the news. She flew out of Ontario with one of the only shipments of relief supplies that made it here before everything went to shit and she had no way home. Not that it mattered. She would have died if she'd stayed out East, so I guess her bleeding heart saved her.

Well, she would have died *sooner*. The world might not have ended all at once. But end it did.

Since the houses of Crofton have been reduced to frames, there's little to block my view of the beach. Beyond a stretch of blue Pacific waters rises an island. It looks massive from here, but I know from maps that it's small compared to Vancouver Island. I can't imagine it taking more than a couple of days to walk Salt Spring end to end—less, if the roads are in good repair. Most of the shoreline is reinforced by a wooden stockade. The only gaps are at points where the coast is so steep, there's no chance TNS could scale the cliffs, even if they wanted to. I can't decide if the sight makes me feel better or worse about our prospects. Fences are great for keeping TNS out—but also for locking people inside.

Finally, we find a fallen metal sign announcing the ferry terminal. The dock is collapsing into the ocean, lack of repair and rising sea levels doing their part to wash this place away. There's no sign of any boats. I'm starting to wonder if I'll need to carve a canoe and paddle, when April shouts.

"Look!"

At the water's edge stands a large, metal barrel with holes drilled into the bottom. It's chained to a crudely constructed post, a rough sign affixed to the top. Painted in a thick, tarry substance, the sign reads:

**WELCOME TO HISTORIC CROFTON FERRY TERMINAL.
FOR PASSAGE TO SALT SPRING, LIGHT FIRE.
PREPARE ALL DOCUMENTS FOR IMMIGRATION.**

"Do we have documents?" April asks.

"Of course not." I know what the word means, but again, I get that Santa Claus feeling of stumbling upon something that only exists in legends. At least a hospital is something I can understand bringing back from the pre-Quake days, but paperwork? Who are these people? I was born in Port Alberni, which was relatively civilized, but even they never bothered with shit like this. At least, I don't think they did. I was only nine when it fell to TNS.

"Should we make some?" April asks.

"No." How would we? Rip pages out of one of the few books we carry, then write over them with a piece of charcoal? "We're going to build a fire."

By that, I mean I'm going to build a fire and April will set up the tarp, then rest. It takes me the remainder of the day, scrounging enough wood and dry moss to get a bonfire going in the metal bin. Now I understand why the buildings here have been stripped to ruins. It's easier harvesting wood from the suburbs south of the terminal than trying to chop down any of the massive trees to the north. I saw off a few lower branches, but like so many before me, end up filling the barrel with Crofton's bones. I scrape as much of the house paint off the wood as possible, but April and I still sit upwind so we don't inhale the fumes.

If TNS is nearby, they'll be on us in our sleep. But the bonfire needs to be visible across the water.

April, at least, seems encouraged as we take shelter from the mounting rain. "They've got, like, a *system*," she says, relishing the word. "They're already prepared for us to come. Well, not *us*, but people like us."

"It's great," I say, though I hear something ominous in her words. We're going somewhere that has a host of rules we've never dealt with before. And with no documents, we're starting off by doing something wrong.

Maybe more than one thing.

Provided you come unarmed.

No chance in hell. I've got my slingshot in my pocket and a knife strapped to my leg, like always.

Dinner is deer jerky and dried blackberries we gathered earlier in the summer. As the sun sets, I pull out *Anne of Green Gables*. I've read it so many times, the spine is falling apart. I want to swap this one for a new copy the next time we're looting a house with books. It was super popular before the Quake, so I can almost always find it.

Although… maybe I won't get the chance. Some colonies don't allow books.

I read aloud as Anne slams Gilbert over the head with her slate and get a faint smile from my little sister. She's heard it almost as many times as I have. The people in books are safe and predictable in a way real strangers never are, and so they're our one source of company, aside from each other.

April falls asleep with her head lolling onto my shoulder and I don't have the heart to move her so I can get comfortable too. As the night closes in, I sit awake, braced for any sound of rescue or attack.

JUST AFTER DAWN, a boat approaches, canvas sails billowing as it works against a headwind. It looks nothing like the photos of BC ferries I've seen on brochures from the pre-Quake days, but that's to be expected. Those ran on oil, which is long gone.

April screeches with glee. The boat fills her with energy I haven't seen in ages, like hope itself might cure her, and she flies out of the protective cover of the tarp. On her way, she knocks free a torrent of water droplets and my ankle gets an icy *good morning*.

"April!"

"We're here!" She waves her arms at the approaching ship. "We're here! And we're…"

Her arms drop to her sides. "Kayla?"

"Yeah?" I get up carefully, not interested in another barrage of rainwater from the tarp.

"Is he holding a gun?"

Sure enough, the posture of the figure at the bow suggests he's carrying a sizable rifle. Two more men flank him. Shit, I knew it. The whole smoke signal thing was a trap, and we fell right into it.

"Start running."

"But we need—"

"I said run!" I shove her towards the north, where there's some tree cover, and she finally gets her ass moving. By the time she reaches the trees, I've shoved our tarp and *Anne of Green Gables* into my bag. I'm just a few feet behind her, but the boat is already coming ashore. April is barely sheltered within the grove when she collapses, struggling for breath. I duck behind a Douglas fir and lock eyes with her, trying to will strength back into her limbs.

"April, run!" I hiss. "I'll buy you some time and then—"

"I'm not… leaving you." Her breathing is laboured.

"I'll catch up. Get a head start."

"Can't."

Her cheeks are ghastly white. I can feel our chance of escape slipping away. The men with the guns are going to come and drag us away to their island and after that…

My mind sputters out. The people Mum met at the river didn't seem dangerous. But clever people hide their true intentions. They said we could go to the island if we showed up unarmed, so why are these guys carrying guns? They don't want to meet as equals, which means we can't trust them. On instinct, my hand goes for the slingshot in my pocket.

April takes a steadying gulp of air, the colour starting to return to her face. "I think I'm ready to—"

Before she can say more, gravel crunches as someone disembarks the boat. The boots have a heavy tread and surely belong to one of the armed men. I track the sound of footsteps as the man walks towards the barrel where the remains of our fire are smouldering.

A deep grunt reaches my ears. "Not this shit again." Then there's a strange crackly noise. "We've got an empty beach."

"Do you need back up?" Another distorted voice joins the conversation, though how I can't guess. I haven't heard anyone else come ashore.

"No, stay on the boat. I'm coming back." He takes a few steps. It's almost too good to be true. He's going to leave without looking in the woods, because he doesn't want to get caught in a trap either. We're going to survive to see another day.

Except, now how are we going to get April medical treatment?

Doubt nags at me, as in the background his voice retreats. "There's signs of a small camp, but I don't see enough footprints for TNS or—wait." And then I hear the tell-tale sound of a gun sliding off his shoulder and the mechanical click of hands taking their position. "You the one who lit the fire, kid?"

April. He's seen April.

There's no time for carefully weighing my options. I dart out from between the trees, firing the moment I get a clear view. My stone flies true and hits him squarely in the back of the hand.

"Shit!" He cries out as he loses his grip on the rifle.

"April, RUN!"

We've got seconds before he gets that gun up and takes

aim. All I could do was draw his fire onto me instead of her. But as I dive into the protection of the trees, she's just gaping at him like a wide-mouthed toad. Every animal has a fight, flight or freeze response. And lucky me, my precious baby sister defaults to the worst possible option. Really, it's a miracle we've survived this long.

"Backup! Yes, get down here!" he yells into a small black box, wasting a few more seconds he could have spent shooting us. "And you! Sally Slingshot! Stop running. Don't give my guys something worth putting a bullet in."

I press my back against one of the trees, teeth gritted in anger. I don't want to obey. If this was just about my survival, running would still be my best bet. Like he said, bullets are expensive. I don't know of anybody who can make new ones these days, so it's not worth spending one on an enemy who just wants to get away from you.

But April has crawled out from behind the protection of her cedar and stepped blatantly into the open. I would ask who raised her, except this failure is entirely on me.

"Is that a walkie-talkie?" she asks, her voice strangely bright. "I've seen pictures, but I've never—"

She breaks off as two more men jump off the boat, both with guns. One heads straight for me.

"Drop the slingshot," he says. He's tall and wiry, with a few whisps of dark hair coming loose from a bandana. There's a hard line to his frown—and I wouldn't bet on me if the two of us ended up in a fist fight. So, I drop the slingshot, and raise my hands above my head for good measure. He notices the knife strapped to my thigh and pulls that out, before directing me towards the clearing around the smoking signal fire.

The third guy has April, leading her forward by the hand. We all gather around the one who must be their leader, wrapping a piece of cloth around his bleeding hand.

As I come within a couple feet of him, his eyes flick up to me, and I stagger backward.

It might sound odd, considering I already shot him, but I never properly *looked* at him. Now, he's all I can see. My own, personal *oh shit* moment manifested in human form.

To start with, he's massive—taller than Bandana Man with shoulders twice as wide. Honestly, why did he bother bringing a gun? A guy like this could pop my head off with one hand. Right now, he looks like he wants to. He glowers at me, and I stare mutely, stupidly back. He's blonde haired and blue eyed, with a full mouth that belongs more in a pre-Quake magazine than on someone who presumably wants to kill me. But there's a slight twist to his features. His nose has clearly been broken and reset at least once. A scar cuts across his pale skin from the back of his jaw to a couple inches down his neck. They're potent reminders of where we really are. *When* we are.

I break away from his glare, only to see the blood blooming through the bandage on his hand. As the adrenaline ebbs away, what I did comes crashing in on me.

"I... I..." I stammer, unsure if I'm planning to apologize or skip straight to begging for mercy.

"You lit the signal fire?" he asks through clenched teeth.

I manage a nod.

"Just the two of you?"

Another nod.

"We'll see about that." He slings his rifle back over his shoulder. "Silas, you take the south. James, you're checking the treeline. If you see any sign of additional parties, wire immediately. Do not engage alone."

The two men snap to their orders without another word, leaving me and April to their leader. As ever, I do the mental calculus that keeps us alive. There's room to run now, but while I might be able to outpace this behemoth,

April won't. He's not aiming the gun at us anymore, but if I made a play to grab it, he could throw me off him like a ragdoll. Plus, he's wearing an old RCMP vest, so a bullet wouldn't do much to him if I did manage to fire the gun.

He is, no doubt, running his own calculations. He spares April a glance but is considerably more preoccupied with scowling at me. I stand like a dead bug pinned in a collection, limbs splayed out for science. He hasn't said I can lower my hands yet, and I don't dare make any sudden movements. Not when he's clearly deciding if I deserve to be stepped on.

I can't imagine I impresses him. None of my clothes are in good condition, all worn and stitched over a thousand times. I'm decked out in cargo pants and a T-shirt with a rip in the centre that I haven't had time to mend yet. I've tied a polar fleece sweater around my waist—the kind that holds onto every stray twig it encounters. My short, dark curls are an unholy mess, so I'm guessing I won't appeal to his mercy through my feminine wiles or anything like that.

April, however, reaches up to tuck a piece of hair behind her ear, her eyes on one of his biceps. Which, I will grant her, are substantial.

"Do you want to explain to me why the hell you lit the signal fire and then attacked our team with nothing besides a slingshot?" he finally asks.

"You had guns," I say.

"We have guns. You have a slingshot. And you thought firing on us would *help* in that situation?"

"I thought it would give her a chance to get away." I gesture towards April. "And I mean, if we ran, what's in it for you if you shoot at us? Dead women won't do you any good. Not worth the bullet."

"Dead *women*?" The furrow in his brow deepens. "So, you saw me come ashore with a gun and immediately thought we wanted to... do something to you?"

He doesn't say it out loud, so neither do I. Nobody has to, because we all know there's more than one kind of violence to fear in this world. In our shared silence, his expression shifts. He's still scowling, but it feels less personal, like he's pissed, but not necessarily at me.

He breaks the silence. "Okay. Here's what we're going to do. You two are going to take off your bags. Set them down, then step five paces away. We're going to wait for my guys to come back, and if your story checks out, *that's* when we'll talk."

"Thank you!" April drops her bag eagerly. I'm more hesitant, but I do follow suit, because what other choice do I have?

"Everything all right down there, Charles?"

I jump at the crackling of the little black box strapped to our guard's RCMP vest. He pulls it out and speaks into it again, confirming April's suspicion that it's a walkie-talkie. "Situation under control for now. James and Silas are checking for hostiles. Stand by."

"Roger."

"So…" I watch as he clips the box back onto his vest. "Is your name Roger or Charles?"

The question catches him off guard for a second. His face breaks into a smile, as if I've said something funny or stupid. Probably both. "Sid, actually. Sid Charles."

"Then who's Roger?"

"No one. It's just a thing people say in walkie-talkies. Means *okay* or *gotcha*."

"Why don't you just say that, then?"

"I dunno. Some kind of pre-Quake thing. Why does anyone do anything anymore?"

He reaches into his pocket and pulls out a bit of rolled up paper. He crouches down next to the barrel so he can reach the holes at the bottom and sticks his paper tube deep enough in to catch on the smouldering embers. When he draws it back up, I realize I'm staring at a lit cigarette.

What the hell?

I'm transfixed as he threads it between his teeth. Cigarettes ran out years ago, or so I thought. Granted, I also thought walkie-talkies were a thing of the past. The implications of both are staggering. Salt Spring must have some way of generating electricity. They must have stockpiles of old cigarettes.

For the first time, it really hits me that this man—Sid Charles, was it?—might come from somewhere that can help April. It might all be true.

"We need a hospital," I say abruptly.

"No shit." He takes a drag on the cigarette. "You look like a good meal would kill you."

"No, I don't mean both of us. I mean my sister—"

"How about we wait for my guys to come back, then we can start talking about whatever it is you want from us. Okay?"

"We can talk now. We'll cooperate. I'll do anything you want if you can help her." I say and April nods. Her earlier eagerness all makes sense now. She'd picked up on the signs that I was too survival-brained to notice. "I'll tell you whatever you want to know."

His eyes flick over me again. Now that he's no longer scowling, they are so, *so* blue. "No."

"Why not?"

"Because on the off chance you two *are* some TNS ploy to get us to drop our guards..." He gestures vaguely towards the trees and all the imaginary people he's worried about. "I would rather not be distracted."

"Oh, come on! You're smoking a cigarette."

"I can smoke and fire a gun at the same time."

"You're not even holding it."

"Would you like me to?"

"Kayla, it's fine." April waves her hands, pleading for me not to screw this up any worse than my slingshot did. "We can wait. I don't mind."

"It's still pointless. There's no one else out there and when he finally believes us, he's going to realize he wasted his time," I say.

"So... Kayla." He repeats my name. "Got a last name?"

"I thought you said you didn't want to talk. Because I'm *too distracting*." I toss my head back dramatically and make sure my voice drips with sarcasm. It would work better if I had long, flowing hair, but he clearly gets the idea, because my performance draws a laugh.

"Now you're getting it."

"Yeah, well..." My stomach clenches as this big, blue-eyed man smiles a lopsided grin at me around his cigarette. "Fine. We'll wait."

"Thank you." He turns his gaze toward the horizon, which I take as an opportunity to sit down. April joins me and I hold her hand, trying to steady both our nerves. We could be here for a while. It's difficult to prove someone *isn't* there, so who knows at what point his men will stop looking?

I sit with my back to Sid Charles, who seems happy to scan the area for danger and ignore me, too. Typically, I don't turn my back to strangers, but I can't look at him right now. Our conversation still has my stomach in knots, and not in a way that has anything to do with the gun on his back or the intimidating size of his muscles.

Okay, it might have a little to do with that second one.

I was making fun of him. That's what I was doing, wasn't it? Pointing out his paranoia and mocking him for it. That all seemed obvious in the moment, but the way he responded to me has made me wonder... was I flirting with him? Just a little?

As he stands watch, I sneak a glance at him. He seems even taller from this angle and my eyes sweep up his legs, to his waist, his chest.

I duck my head away, feeling the back of my neck flush. This is so wrong and stupid.

April and I sometimes run into other people in the wasteland of Vancouver Island, but the interactions are always tense and brief, long enough only to barter items before everyone backs away, never wanting to be the first to offer their backside as a target. Honestly, if I met Sid Charles in the woods, even without the gun, I would avoid him. I only deal with people who pose the same threat I do. I mean, I would approach someone weaker—but *those* people typically run away from me.

All this is to say, I haven't met someone who's my type in a very long time. If I even have a type. But if I had to make one up on the spot, Sid is composed of the things that I value most in a person: calm under pressure, big enough to scare the shit out of anyone dangerous, no rotten teeth when he smiles. Even his busted nose recommends him. Clearly, he's survived getting hit in the face before.

Sitting here with that realization is terrifying in a way I wasn't prepared for. I can't remember the last time thoughts like this even occurred to me, which means I've let my guard drop. Even if I hadn't shot him with my slingshot— even if he didn't wield an absurd amount of power over my life right now—I have no interest in going down that path again with anyone. Not after what happened to Curtis.

Curtis.

I usually avoid thinking about him, so I squeeze April's hand tighter, forcing my mind back to the present. Trusting these people goes against every impulse I have, but if it means saving April, I've got to try.

I have no idea how long we sit around waiting. It feels

like forever, but the sun stays in about the same place in the sky. Eventually Bandana Man comes back, looking less angry than before.

"Well?" says Sid.

Bandana Man shrugs. "I found their trail easily. Followed it back a kilometre or so. Just two sets of tracks. If anyone is following them, they're way back and we should get out of here before they catch up."

"Great." Sid pulls his walkie-talkie from his vest and clicks the button. "James, you found anything?"

"*Haven't seen shite*," comes the crackly voice.

"Then get back here. Silas found their trail. We're leaving as soon as you're back."

"*Brilliant.*"

"On your feet." It takes me a second, but I eventually realize that Sid Charles is addressing us. As April and I stand, Bandana Man passes him a clipboard from one of his bags. Sid thanks him, clicks a pen, then turns a grim, approximation of a smile on me. "Welcome to Salt Spring Island and her Gulf Island Territories, a legacy nation of the Dominion of Canada. What is the purpose of your visit?"

"What?" That was far too many words for such a small island.

"Why do you want to come to Salt Spring?"

"Oh. We told you that. The hospital."

"Great." He marks something off on the clipboard. I go up on my toes, trying to see what he's doing, but he's so damn tall, he can easily hold it beyond me. He eyes me warily, then continues his spiel. "The hospital is open to all Salt Spring Island nationals and members of allied nations. If you are not currently a member of an allied nation, you are eligible for Sanctuary Seeker status, granting you provisional access to the hospital. Are you a member of an allied nation or are you seeking sanctuary?"

"We're just trying to go to the hospital."

"I got that. Where are you from?" The way he switches between legal babble and more ordinary speech makes it clear he's done this before.

"Well… nowhere, really. We're nomads." Some of his earlier words about allied nations start to click into place. "Is that a problem? Do we have to be allies already to use the hospital?"

"Not necessarily. Are you seeking sanctuary?"

"What the hell does *that* mean?"

"Are you looking for a safe place to live?"

April mutters a tentative "*yes*". I snort at the question. I mean, who isn't? Unfortunately, safe places don't exist anymore. But I think I'm getting the idea of what he—or rather, the authority he represents—wants from us, so I force myself to smile.

"Yes, Sid Charles. We are sanctuary seekers. We would like *sanctuary* at your hospital."

"Okay, great." He checks off more things on the clipboard. Some of the tension I'm carrying in my shoulders eases as I realize that it's happening. We're getting what we want. "You'll be required to wear masks until the doctor is certain you aren't contagious. There's one on board, and he'll perform an initial assessment."

"Really?" That sounds too good to be true. "You brought one?"

"Yeah, they come on all these immigration calls," he says, packing the clipboard away. "Mostly because you nomads always come with a shitload of health problems. But also, in case someone tries to kill the guards. So I guess we both get to see the doctor today."

"I wasn't trying to—never mind."

"Once we reach port, I'll arrange for an immigration officer to meet you and sort out your sanctuary case." Sid's eyes snap to something in the distance. When I turn, it's to see the third guy jogging toward us. "Right, time to go. I'll need you to surrender any weapons now. Failure to do so will result in your sanctuary case being denied."

This time I don't need him to clarify.

"That isn't fair. You have guns."

Like he said earlier, my slingshot and knives don't count for much against guns, but I'm loath to give them up all the same.

"No, it isn't fair." He stubs his cigarette out on the side of the barrel. "But you want to visit our hospital, so you're going to do what makes *us* feel safe."

I want to argue further, but April is already opening her bag and handing over everything right down to the kitchen knives.

"Be quick about it." He chides me when I take too long admiring the etching on my mum's old knife. I have a few other pieces of her: a pair of pearl earrings; a tiny glass perfume bottle, scent faint, but lingering. Even with those mementos, I'm hesitant to let the knife go.

"Will we ever see these again?" I ask.

"No. But their value will count towards any fees you rack up at the hospital," says Sid, passing us some cloth masks to fit over our mouths and noses.

When I finally drop that last knife, Bandana Man gathers them up. My lungs tighten and I'm sure it's got nothing to do with the flimsy mask I'm wearing. We're helpless now. True, these men don't want us dead. And Sid Charles has been remarkably forgiving, considering his hand is still bleeding. But plenty of colonies play the long game. They gain your trust, then they strike.

I haven't gone unarmed for a single day since we left Astolia. The only reason my family got out of that compound was because once we were beyond the gates, it was easy to run. That's not an option on an island.

But April's eyes are fixed on Salt Spring's looming form. It's our last hope. So, I follow her up the ladder that leads onto the sailboat deck, Sid and his men trailing behind me.

"James, get your ass up here." Sid calls. At that, I turn to see one of the guys lingering on the shore.

"Right. Just making sure no one's coming," he says, but there's a hint of sadness in his voice, as if he wanted to stay outside of Salt Spring's fences a little longer. Or maybe I'm just projecting. There is a definite chance I'm projecting.

The final guy climbs aboard, and the three of them take up posts at the front of the ship, guns trained on the shore. The captain calls out and someone casts off. As the ship pulls away from the broken-down dock, the world wobbles beneath us. I grab onto a bench, trying to feel secure, but it's no use. Everything is shifting, carried by the sea.

As the nose of the boat swings away from Vancouver Island and towards Salt Spring, I shift on my bench, not wanting to lose sight of my old island. The shore retreats slowly, never far enough to vanish beyond the horizon. Home—such as it is—will always be across the water. Tantalizingly out of reach.

Then there are footsteps, and my view is obscured by the guards walking around to keep their guns aimed at the Crofton beach. Sid Charles looms ahead of me, casting his shadow over the past I'm leaving behind.

THREE

ONCE WE'RE UNDERWAY, a man comes up from below deck and introduces himself as the doctor. I'm slightly annoyed when he tends to Sid's hand before checking on April, but that's a problem of my own making, so I don't complain out loud. He changes the bandage and applies some ointment to the site that makes Sid wince.

"Keep an eye on it for any sign of infection."

"You got it." Sid flexes his hand against the bandage and a lump of guilt forms in my throat. Just now, I realize that I spent our entire conversation on the beach so caught up in saving April, I never apologized for hitting him with my slingshot. I want to call out a *sorry*, but before I work up the nerve, he strides back to his post next to the other guards, pulling out another cigarette as he goes.

"Thought you were trying to quit," one of them says.

"Shut up, James."

"Okay, so what's the story here?" The doctor's voice pulls me away from watching them.

"It's my sister, April. She got sick." I place a hand on her shoulder, giving her permission to take over explaining.

Usually, I do most of the talking around strangers, like Mum did when she was alive. But April knows her symptoms better than anyone, so she might as well take the lead.

She talks the doctor through how for the past several weeks, she's struggled with dizzy spells and fatigue. They go over the weight loss and the dehydration. The doctor points out this could all be explained by malnutrition, which is when I speak up again.

"We wouldn't be here if this wasn't different. Something is *wrong*. Something new," I insist. "Maybe we haven't been eating the best, but we're always good about water. Why's she so thirsty all the time if something isn't wrong?"

"Perhaps you caught a stomach bug? Untreated water can—"

"We boil *everything*."

It's like he assumes I don't know how to take care of her, but my Mum loved science. We have a decent grasp on what's safe and what isn't, which is why we're still alive. He still goes through a host of other questions, asking about any other symptoms she might have—a raised temperature, congestion, headaches, vomiting, the list goes on. Some of them she has, like the headaches, others she doesn't. (We are thankfully vomit free.)

"You can take your mask off," he says finally. "I want to check your ears, nose and throat."

With that, he pulls out a small case of instruments that look reassuringly like the ones in old picture books. It's almost fun, watching him use this old tech to examine April, right up until he checks her throat and goes, "Oh."

"What is it?" I ask. Poor April can only make a concerned wheezing sound, since she still has the stick thing pushing her tongue down.

"She's got the beginnings of oral thrush," he says, indicating a white patch towards the back of her tongue. "How old did you say you were?"

"Fifteen," she says, once the stick is out the way.

"Hmm." The doctor pulls out his own walkie-talkie and clicks it on. "I've got two young females, both malnourished. Ages twenty-five and fifteen. Have a wagon ready when we arrive and notify the hospital. The kid needs immediate intervention. Immigration should meet us there."

"*Roger that*," someone calls back through the speaker. They must have the ability to reach all the way to Salt Spring's shore, which is frighteningly powerful.

I grab April's hand, feeling vindicated now that the doctor is taking her symptoms seriously, but also nervous. *Immediate intervention* makes it sound like we barely made it here on time.

He gives us a smile. "Don't worry. Things are about to get a lot better for you two."

That would be very comforting, if it wasn't the type of thing someone says right before springing a trap.

THE HOSPITAL STINKS of alcohol. It's antiseptic, they say, and I do have memories of that. Back in Port Alberni, they used to brew a powerful bathtub spirit for rubbing on cuts or sewing up wounds after surgeries. But my eyes water as if to say *this can't be healthy*, and I almost drag April from the place. Except I wouldn't have a clue where to go. After we got to the dock, they transferred us into a covered wagon with the doctor. I know we travelled vaguely northeast, but that's not enough information to formulate an escape plan.

April gives me a helpless look when the doctor insists on taking her into one of the examination rooms alone.

I try to sneak past the nurses. "Why can't I come?"

"*You* need to fill out paperwork," says the woman managing the front desk. She presses a clipboard into my hands. "Also, you're supposed to eat this. Doctor wants to make sure you get a square meal today."

She passes me a sandwich—something I only recognize because once upon a time, they were the culinary preference of children ages three to eight and feature heavily in picture books. Is this wheat bread? Wheat is such a pill to grow on rocky terrain, I can't comprehend why anyone would bother. I set the strange food and clipboard aside.

"I can do that later." I take another step toward April, but the woman throws an arm out, barring me.

"I'm sorry, hon. You're not going back there. Not to Emergency." She gives me a sad smile. "You've gotta let Doctor Tremblay do his part. He'll take good care of your sister."

"This is Emergency?"

Hospitals don't feature heavily in lifestyle magazines or storybook illustrations, so I've never known how to picture one. From this view, it's mostly hallways. Behind us there are a few chairs and a potted plant. There's a young woman seated in the corner, regarding me with interest, a ball of yarn lying forgotten in her lap. Nothing like what my mind conjured when I heard the word *hospital*, let alone *emergency*. What did I expect? Blood squirting out of bodies?

"Why don't you take a seat?" The Desk Lady guides me towards the seating area and the one other occupant snaps back to her crochet, as if she hadn't been gawking. "Tom should be here soon. He'll get you sorted."

"Who's Tom?"

"Your immigration officer. He's a peach, dear. He'll take good care of you and—oh! Here he comes now!"

A bell tinkles above the door and I turn. In walks a man older than anyone I've seen since leaving Astolia. He's at least sixty, judging by the amount of grey in his beard and the lines etched into his skin. His hair has more colour left, enough to make it clear it used to be red. He uses a cane to support his left leg, which means that if we ran into each other out in the wilds, I wouldn't need to run away from him.

And yet, his arrival makes my stomach clench. Perhaps it's the shrewd look in his eyes as he scans me—a look I would never associate with someone who is *just a peach*. I know instantly who he reminds me of.

The Grand Astrologue. The son of a bitch who ran the colony my parents and I fled to after Port Alberni fell. The markers of power are different—the Grand Astrologue dressed in long robes, whereas this Tom guy just carries a briefcase—but they're there. He must be someone important; how else would he still be alive at his age?

"It's good to meet you. I'm Tom Sullivan." He gives me a slight nod. "I'm assuming you're either Kayla or April?"

I don't say anything, fighting my impulse to kick him in his bad leg and run.

He lets out a laboured sigh. "I'm sorry. Do you speak English? There weren't any notes from the border guard about primary language—"

"Oh, she can talk plenty. Lots of questions about that sweet little sister of hers." Desk Lady steps forward, smiling enough for the three of us. "Tom, meet Kayla. Why don't I set you two up in one of our other rooms? We'll come find you when your sister is ready for visitors."

"Thank you, Pat," says Tom. He winces as he steps

forward on his bad leg. Okay, I *might* be reading too much into his grim expressions.

"Go on, dear." Pat nudges me forward, and it's only because of her that I finally relent and follow him. At least they're letting me past the front desk. Maybe I'll be able to sneak off and find April once Tom's back is turned.

Pat escorts us to a room with long, electric light fixtures hanging overhead which, naturally, are not on. The one window is small, and there are no candles, making it a dark, dingy place. Tom takes the desk below the window so that he can use what little light we have. He sets his briefcase on the desk, pops open the latches and removes some papers.

"Please, take a seat." He gestures to the chair on the other side of the desk. My eyes flick around, trying to work out if this room was used by patients or for doctor meetings thirty-two years ago when the lights still worked. "Take a seat, *please*."

"Do I have to?" I would rather be close to the door, where I might get a sense of what's happening to April.

This question produces a huff from Tom Sullivan. "You're not used to trusting strangers, are you?"

"Excuse me?" The answer to that is obvious, but I'm not going to give him the satisfaction of saying *yes*.

"It's perfectly normal. Your reactions are typical for a Wildling."

"Wildling?"

"It's a legal term for a nationless individual, like yourself."

"They should come up with a better word."

He rubs his eyes, as if to say he's been through a thousand conversations like this and doesn't have much patience for doing it yet again with me. "I'll be sure to pass your complaints along. But if you could please sit down?

This process will be far more successful for you and your sister if you cooperate. I'm here to help you."

"Sure."

"The border guard gave me your basic information. You and your sister are seeking sanctuary?"

"Sure."

"A definitive yes or no would be more useful," he says. "And *please*. Sit down."

I could take Tom Sullivan in a fight. I'm sure of it. But I'm not sure what the point would be when I'm already stuck on this damn island. Plus, there's April. Despite my misgivings, one thing he said rings true. If I want them to heal her, I need to play along. We can worry about escaping once she's better.

Tom looks oddly pleased when I finally pull out the chair and slide into my seat. "Wonderful. The guard marked *hospital* as one of the purposes of your visit. Am I right in assuming that's the reason you're seeking sanctuary?"

"Sure—I mean, yes."

"Well, we all start somewhere." He makes a few more notes. "I have given names for you and your sister. Do you have any family names or previous affiliations?"

"You mean a last name, right?"

"Exactly."

"Hollins. Kayla and April Hollins."

"Any other living family?"

"No."

"Sorry to hear that. If you know your parents' names, we like to record those details, too. Sometimes we're able to link up missing family members or—"

"No one is going to link up with us. They're dead."

"Even so—"

"I saw their bodies."

He looks up from the forms, a sad smile on his face.

"Again, my condolences. But perhaps they had friends or other relations? Please, Ms. Hollins."

I seriously consider stonewalling him. My dead aren't his business. But the mention of friends has made me wonder if someone we knew back in Port Alberni might have ended up here after TNS sacked the settlement. "Andy Hollins and Genevieve Laclerc."

"Wonderful. Now, I understand if you don't have all the information regarding my next questions. But do you know your and your sister's birthdates and birthplaces?"

"I'm twenty-five. Born in Port Alberni. Septemberish, I think."

"Ah. Happy birthday to you, then."

"Oh… thanks?" Shit, is it September? Am I twenty-six? It doesn't matter. I press on. "April is about fifteen. Born in, well… spring. We didn't really know, because—"

"Yes, that would be after Port Alberni fell. Sad day, that."

It's strange, hearing him talk casually about the day any semblance of safety was ripped from my life. I'm more comfortable saying nothing about it at all, and since April has no memories of the place, I can usually get away with that. Unfortunately, this guy is old enough to know the post-Quake history of the region.

The Quake damaged every city on Vancouver Island, but nowhere got the shit knocked out of it quite like my hometown. Most other cities in the region were relatively protected in the Strait of Georgia, but not Alberni. It sits on an inlet facing the whole Pacific Ocean. After the Quake, the inlet funnelled the tsunami waters into a fifty-metre plume that wiped out everything. Ironically, the damage saved the community, at least for a time. TNS didn't target us, because they assumed there was nothing left to steal. For several years, survivors in the area were able to rebuild. We had farms and houses, even a small school where my mum taught about thirty kids. It's strange to think how normal it all felt. I was too young then to know how lucky I was.

When I was nine, TNS found out we were functional and attacked our colony. Death or cult. Those are the options.

"If you don't mind my saying, you've been living in the woods a long time," he says. "There wasn't anywhere else between your time in Port Alberni and now?"

"Nope." It's a flat-out lie, but I have plenty of reasons to keep my mouth shut about Astolia. First, there's that story the Grand Astrologue told us about getting attacked by people in Salt Spring. Granted, he was a real piece of shit, so I can't blame the islanders for going after him, but I lived in his colony for over four years. I don't want to be painted with the same stripes as him if they are enemies.

But more important than that, my life isn't Tom's—or his government's—business.

"Extraordinary. You're quite the survivor."

"Thanks."

"So, you've had some time in civilization with traditional schooling, but your sister hasn't?" asks Tom. "That's a pity. I'm sorry you didn't find us sooner."

"She's had schooling. My mum and I taught her stuff."

"Of course, of course," he says with a patronizing smile. "Well, she'll have ample opportunity to catch up here. We require that all minors attend school."

"Okay."

"Our hope with all sanctuary cases is that they successfully integrate into life on the island. Sanctuary seekers are entitled to a ration card and housing. You and your sister will be placed with a host family, typically for a few months, who will show you how we do things here. Once you've had a chance to learn the ropes, you'll be able to apply for your own housing and employment. Then, provided every other step of the process goes well, you'll be able to apply for citizenship in as little as a year. How does that sound?"

It sounds like more paperwork. Hopefully, April and I will be long gone before we have to deal with that circus. But that's not the response this man is expecting, so I give him a thumbs up and say, "Great."

"Now, I do have to inform you that while free health care is provided to citizens, we can't offer that to sanctuary seekers," he continues in the same officious tone he's used for this entire meeting. "We try to make the first visit to the hospital as affordable as possible, but you must understand, we've had too many cases of sanctuary seekers who take advantage of the hospital, then leave without providing value back to the community. Much as we would like to help everyone, medicine is scarce these days, and we can't afford to—"

"You want payment. I get it. We brought goods to trade. Pearl earrings." I came prepared. The people at the riverside who told us about Salt Spring traded away food for a few shiny bits and bobs, so hopefully the same will go for medicine.

My answer pleases Tom, who nods. "Wonderful. We understand each other."

"Can I see April now?"

"I'll speak to the hospital staff. I just need the doctor's evaluation, then we can complete this process." He reaches out a hand. "Welcome to Salt Spring, Ms. Hollins."

I accept the handshake, because why not? Between all the sanctuary seeker gibberish, he finally said something that makes sense. He's the first person to mention payment. Sure, he coats his words in layers of bullshit, but he knows how the world really works.

He asks me to wait in this room, which I agree to. Playing along is working out well enough. I pace the dark room, wondering what's going on with April. How long does it take to diagnose a condition? If only I had some idea how hospitals work.

A chorus of raised voices fills the hallway just beyond my door. The sound sends my pulse rocketing. It can't be to do with April, can it?

Forget waiting around. I throw open the door without a second thought. But just as I'm stepping through, one of those frantic voices becomes crystal clear.

"See? Now she's escaping!" It's Tom Sullivan, his eyes wide and wild. The calm, slightly bored man of before is gone. The change startles me so badly, I don't react with the speed I should. "Apprehend her!"

"Tom, this is a hospital!" Desk Lady shouts from somewhere behind him.

My reflexes kick into gear and I dive down the hall, looking for an escape. The problem is, they're blocking off the exit. All I have access to is a maze of hospital hallways, which April may or may not be at the end of. She could be in a totally different wing for all I know. I grab a doorhandle at random and try to open it, only to find it locked. As I'm wrenching on it, the click of a gun sounds behind me.

"Let go of the door, Ms. Hollins." Tom Sullivan hurries forward as fast as his bad leg will allow, gun-toting lacky not far behind. "We need to have a discussion."

I reel toward them and throw my hands in the air. I *knew* it. So much for promises of safety. "But why—"

"Medical records." Tom holds up a sheaf of papers. "Doctor Tremblay's report includes *all* medical interventions performed at the border. You're going to tell me why he treated a slingshot wound on the back of our guard's hand."

"Oh."

He gives me an insincere smile that lets me know I really am in deep shit. "I see we once again understand each other."

FOUR

I WANT TO scream.

I want to run.

I want to throw up on the tile floor.

Maybe that last one would be a good idea. If I vomit, it will look like I'm sick too, and they'll take me into Emergency. I'll find April and we'll run away.

We don't actually have much of a discussion. Tom asks me if I attacked the border guard and my "technically, yes" is all he's willing to listen to. He sets me up with a guard and leaves.

"Keep her here while I find Mr. Charles. This is a bloody mess."

And just like that, I'm back in the dark room, only this time no one is pretending to be friendly. I sit in silence with the armed guard, watching the sun shift across the lone window. More than once, I consider fighting him for his gun, but I know he's not the only person who could attack me while I look for April. Plus, I've never fired a gun.

So, against my every impulse, I wait.

Finally, there's a commotion and the door flies open.

Desk Lady's voice rings out, "You can't *all* go back there," along with Tom's rough reply of, "Do you want me to bring the judiciary down, too?"

My guard straightens to attention, getting his gun in position.

Three people burst inside. Tom leads them, limping on his bad leg, face red as his hair. After him comes Pat, flapping her hands in dismay. At the back of the pack, barely fitting through the low frame of the door, is Sid Charles. And he looks *pissed*.

"So Charles, is this the girl?" Tom asks.

Sid looks me over, a muscle twitching in his jaw. "Yeah. I guess that's her."

"And you didn't apprehend her?" Tom barks. "A hostile party attacked you, and you didn't—"

"It was a slingshot. She posed no threat to us."

"There could always be more than a slingshot. People *plan* things out there." Tom gives me a sideways glance. "Did you check the area? There could have been an ambush, or—"

"Of course we checked the area! They were alone."

"Well, if you had written a report, I would have known that!" Tom fires back. The more they argue, the less room there seems to be between the walls. Everything constricts around their rising voices. "What were you thinking?"

"I was thinking that leaving it out was the only way to avoid this bullshit!" Sid thunders. "Look at her, Tom! She's starving. Are you seriously going to throw her in jail when her kid sister is sick?"

"People are more than their appearances, Mr. Charles," growls Tom. "Maybe you saw a damsel in distress, but the moment we turned our back on her, she started running around the hospital. She is *dangerous*. And leaving that out of your report was reckless."

"It's a scrape on the hand," says Sid. "I'm fine."

"I'm not worried about you! How am I supposed to place her with a sanctuary host if the moment she's left unattended, she starts firing projectiles or running away? You might be willing to risk someone else in our community, but I'm not. It isn't safe, and I won't do it!"

There's silence. I can't look at these men anymore. I'm a cornered animal. There's no hope of escape. I'm already on their island. Guns behind me. Guns ahead. And somehow, they've convinced themselves that *I'm* the dangerous one? The level of delusion is staggering.

An ugly gasp works its way out of my mouth as I struggle to breathe. My lungs are nothing but filmy bubbles, popping as they crash into my ribs. My throat is salt. The waves of their words won't stop pounding against my head.

I'm a hostile party. Sid was supposed to apprehend me, but he didn't. He just fudged some paperwork and figured that would be enough, but he should have told me. He should have left me safely in Crofton, where they couldn't do this to me. Now, this bearded bastard wants to send me to jail while they've got April helpless in a hospital room and won't let me see her.

I have to run. There's no other choice. Who cares if a bullet comes with it? But when I take a step, my knees buckle, and I barely make it onto a chair without falling over.

Panic attack. I haven't had one since my mother's death. There were things Mum used to get me to do to stop them, but I'm already inside the storm, a trembling mess struggling for air or even to hold myself upright.

Through the haze, I feel hands against me. I swat them away instinctively, but a soft voice manages to cut through my terror. "It's okay, hon. You're okay. You want a sandwich? Doctor said you're supposed to eat."

Pat. The Desk Lady is attempting to shove a sandwich

into my hands. I gulp for air, coming to enough to murmur, "I don't want it."

"It's not poisoned. We don't execute people here," says Sid.

"Why in Hell's name are you putting *that* idea in her head?" Tom shouts, except he's wrong. Sid didn't; it's exactly what I was worried about.

I dry my eyes and meet the flinty gaze of the man I once struck with my slingshot. Despite our bad start, he seems to be the closest thing I have to an ally.

"Please…" I don't know what I'm begging for. I don't even know what he can do for me. Tom is the immigration officer, not him, but I realize now just how lucky I was that he ever listened to me. "My sister is sick. I'll do *anything*."

His eyes are as clear and blue as the summer sky. When his gaze falls away from mine, that sky clouds over.

That's it, then. I'm going to jail, all because I did what anyone would in the wilds. These people are nuts, just like my mother knew they would be.

Sid Charles clears his throat. "I'll take her."

Take me *where*? I almost blurt this out loud, but so long as it's not jail, it's probably an improvement, so I manage to shut up for once.

"Come again?" says Tom.

"You said you aren't worried about me. If this is about finding a sanctuary host who will take her, then I will. Me and the boys will be fine."

There's a beat of silence, thick and uncomfortable.

"Pat, would you excuse us? You can leave, too." Tom gestures at the armed guard, who seems eager to get out of this situation. Pat, for her part, lingers by the door, as if this has finally gotten interesting. "Both of you. *Out*."

I'm not sure if I feel better or worse watching them leave. Obviously, I'm glad the gun is gone, but whatever is happening now is something Tom wants as few witnesses to as possible. That thought freaks me the hell out.

Once the door is shut, Tom straightens and serves Sid a commanding look. "I won't allow it. You have a minor living on your property."

"Carlos is a tough kid. He'll be fine. Besides, it might be nice for the sister if there's someone her age who can show her around school," Sid argues. "I can talk to my guys, but I know they'll agree. And if the major objection is placing her with a willing sanctuary host—"

"Look, Mr. Charles—*Sid*." Tom sets down his briefcase, as if this will help make his point better. He places a hand on Sid's shoulder. "As a friend—"

Sid snorts in a way that suggests Tom is stretching the definition of that word.

"As a *mentor*, then. I would highly recommend you reconsider. There will be other sanctuary cases you can take. Better ones. If this is a matter of optics—"

"It's a matter of not losing our shit over something that wasn't that serious," says Sid.

"I'm not being unreasonable! Attacking a guard posted at a foreign border would have been cause for arrest during the pre-Quake days, too. There's precedent."

"Well, I didn't report an incident. And the hand injury could have been from anywhere. The doctor didn't see the shot," says Sid. "So unless you want to turn this into a drawn-out legal process? I mean, if we're talking *optics* here…"

"You wouldn't." Tom's face blanches. To my amazement, it seems Sid has leverage over him, though I can't guess what kind. "You have just as much to lose. More, even."

Sid shrugs.

Tom glances between the pair of us. He's clearly still furious, but eventually, he grabs his suitcase. "To hell with both of you, then. If you can't make rational decisions, that's no fault of mine. Very well, Mr. Charles. Congratulations on obtaining your first sanctuary case."

"Thank you, I…" Wait. I'll admit, I was only half paying attention during Tom's bafflegab a while ago, but I think I understand where this is going. "Does this mean you expect me to live with *him*?"

"If you would prefer the penitentiary, I am more than happy to—"

"No! No, of course not, but…" I look at Sid, who for the first time since this started is regarding me as if I'm insane. Maybe I am, starting an argument over lodgings so soon after getting out of jail time. "Thank you?"

Tom cocks an eyebrow. "Still sure you want to take her, Mr. Charles?"

"Uh… yes." The word almost doesn't sound like a question.

"Your funeral," says Tom, opening his briefcase. "With that, why don't I get your papers? Ms. Hollins, as a sanctuary seeker, you are entitled to temporary lodgings, rations, and a path to citizenship, should you choose to pursue it. Your application will be evaluated after two years."

"Two years?" Sid repeats. "It should only be—"

"*Two* years," Tom continues, "due to a first demerit that we must award you due to lengthy unknown affiliation."

"That's bullshit," Sid barks.

"I have to make judgments where I can. It's been sixteen years since TNS destroyed Port Alberni," says Tom, glaring at him. "She could have fallen in with any number of aggressive factions during that time. The Denman Dogs. Red-Whites. TNS themselves. I'm being incredibly generous here."

"It's fine," I say. For one thing, I bet Astolia is on that list too, so I'm getting off easy. Besides, why should I care that I can't apply for citizenship right away? We're leaving this island as soon as April is well.

"Good. One demerit." Tom scribbles that on the head of the page with enthusiasm. "In your care is a dependent, fifteen-year-old April Hollins. Per Sanctuary Law, she is entitled to enrollment in the Gulf Islands Secondary School. I suggest you see to it that she gets there. Otherwise, you'll be awarded another demerit."

"Okay." For now, I'll agree to everything. All I want is out of this room.

"I'll check in every three months, though either of you may reach out if there are problems." Tom shoulders his bag and heads for the door. I'm once again struck by the desire to rush forward and kick him in his bad leg.

There's a drawn-out silence after he's gone, during which I stare at Sid as he picks up the sanctuary papers Tom left behind. Even in those simple motions, the tendons in his wrist flex in a way that's equal parts mesmerizing and terrifying. He may have defended me, but as I consider living with this man, it strikes me all over again that he is *not* someone I would approach at a watering hole. He could do anything to me. Once we're alone, who's to say what he might try?

"Sorry about Tom." Sid breaks the silence. "He's a grumpy piece of shit, but he means well. If that makes sense."

It does not. I say nothing.

Sid forces a smile. "All right. Looks like you're coming with me."

"Now? But my sister is still in there. I haven't seen her since—"

"Right. Sorry. Of course." Sid grabs both the hiking packs April and I carried in with us, swinging one up onto his shoulder. "Go check with the front desk. I'll wait for you."

I stare at him, blood hammering in my ears. I don't get the impression he likes me much, but he's better than prison, isn't he?

Unless I'm only being sent to a different cage.

It doesn't matter. Like it or not, I'm stuck with Sid Charles for the foreseeable future.

FIVE

 it's a straightforward diagnosis."

Doctor Tremblay breaks the news with a smile. We're seated inside a room that looks more like how I pictured hospitals. A curtain has been pulled across the middle to give the illusion of privacy on one side. April is wearing a loose gown and sitting on a metal bed. She's attached to an IV tube, but otherwise looks like herself and the doctor says not to worry. The IV is to rehydrate her; she'll come off it in a couple hours.

A steady hum emanates from the IV, like a beehive. Odds are, that's the sound of electricity. It's surreal to know that somewhere, there's a solar cell or turbine that April is hooked up to, pumping her body back to life. She has colour in her cheeks and a grin on her face. After all the agony of getting here, it's worth it. One look at her, and it's clearly worth it.

"I gave her an emergency dose of insulin when she came in and she's responded well. Given that, I feel confident making a diagnosis," says Doctor Tremblay. "We're still running tests to confirm, but I don't foresee any complications. Sadly, procedures that used to be simple take time now. We're waiting for the liquid from her urine sample to evaporate."

"Urine sample?" I repeat.

"They made me pee in a cup when I came in. Said there might be sugar in it." April's face puckers up, like she wants to laugh.

"I'm sorry... *what*?"

"Sugar crystals can form in the urine of those with untreated diabetes. It's not the best verification method, but one of the few we still have," says the doctor.

He keeps making these apologetic statements, clearly aware of what medicine used to be before the Quake, but from my perspective, he's a magician. April was dying, and now she's not. It's that simple.

"But the medicine is working? The... what did you call it?"

"Insulin. Yes, it is."

"Great. So she's better? We can go?" I still need to pay them, but hopefully my mother's earrings will cover that, and we can get off this damn island. If we can, I will scream, dance, throw myself into the ocean and swim across the Salish Sea.

The doctor's welcoming smile fades, as if I've said something pitifully stupid. "I would like to keep her for observation tonight."

"Good. Sure, let's do that." I can wait one night. I'll crash at Sid's place and sleep with the largest stick I can find tucked under my pillow.

"But that isn't the heart of the matter, Ms. Hollins. Your sister's condition is treatable, but persistent. I assume you've never heard of type 1 diabetes before?"

"I haven't heard of any type of diabetes."

"Then we need to have a talk."

The doctor pulls out a diagram of the human body

that's far more sophisticated than any April and I have found in abandoned picture books. Once or twice, I've come across an old medical textbook while scavenging, but they were always too heavy to take with us. With a nasty lurch, I realize my understanding of the human body is no better than a child's.

He points to a small spot on the torso that I've never seen labelled before called the pancreas. Apparently, there's a substance it secretes, which tells the body how to handle the energy we get from food. *Insulin.* The word pops up again and again. It's essential for living a normal, healthy life and for whatever reason—environment, genetics, who knows—April's body attacked her pancreas and now it has fully crapped out on her. She can't make insulin on her own. The only reason Doctor Tremblay was able to save her was because even without pre-Quake medicine, it's still possible to get insulin by boiling down pig pancreases.

A shit load of pig pancreases.

"She'll need regular injections for the rest of her life. You're in luck, though. Our hog population is high enough that we can process enough insulin to sustain up to thirty patients, and there are currently only nineteen other insulin replacement-dependent people living in the Gulf Island Nations. Your sister can lead a long, healthy life."

"So... If she needs it for the rest of her life, then how much insulin do we need to take with us?"

His eyes crinkle with another mournful, pitying smile. "Ms. Hollins, insulin isn't shelf stable. It lasts a month before it spoils. This hospital is one of the few places that spends the resources to maintain consistent refrigeration. She'll need to live on Salt Spring."

I feel myself nod, as if this is no big deal, but I can't unstick words from my throat. Back when we lit the fire, I knew there was a chance we could get trapped here. Maybe this place would expect indentured servitude in exchange for medical care. But I always held onto a glimmering hope that at some point, we could break out. But refrigeration?

I hadn't realized there might be parts of living that were inescapable.

"It's okay, Kayla. I wouldn't want to live somewhere without a doctor again, anyway. I mean, it's more than just the insulin, right? What if something else goes wrong?" says April.

"It's true. You'll need to manage your condition carefully to avoid long-term complications." The doctor turns back to April and it hits me what a useless, selfish bitch I'm being, panicking right now. This isn't even happening to *me*.

They must have talked this out already, because nothing he says surprises her. It's more like they're picking up the thread of an old conversation. She's stoic as he tells her how to watch out for issues with her eyes or lightness in her limbs. Monitoring symptoms matters so much now because it's too difficult to regularly test blood.

She takes it all in, then asks if this will be written up for her, so she can read over it. I don't absorb Doctor Tremblay's answer.

She *has* to stay here. Anything else is a death sentence.

When I find my voice, they're talking about dose size and frequency, but I'm too agitated to listen. "So what's this going to cost us, long term?"

"Well, that depends," says Doctor Tremblay.

"On what?"

"How quickly you obtain citizenship. Did someone have you fill out sanctuary papers?"

"Sure, sure." And there's already a demerit on them.

"Good, that's the first step. Full citizens of our nation have a right to free healthcare. Until you qualify, you can expect to pay about a thousand dollars a year out of pocket," he says.

"Okay." I have no idea how much money that is. Nothing in books from the pre-Quake days is particularly helpful in explaining how money works now. It's easy to find copies of popular ancient books, like *Pride and Prejudice*, where the characters lose their shit over someone having ten thousand pounds a year. It's also easy to find sailing magazines where a single yacht sells for a million dollars. Nowadays, most colonies don't bother with money. Turned out to be nothing but useless paper when society collapsed.

But society has reared its ugly head on Salt Spring, so maybe it's necessary here. It's probably easier than maintaining a running tally of the going rate of pig pancreases versus the cost of a new axe or whatever else someone might want.

"We subsidize it as much as we can," the doctor says, reading the dread on my face. "And there is another option, if you're willing to explore it."

"We'll do anything," I say.

"Well... your sister is only fifteen. Sanctuary laws are different for children." He's no longer meeting my eye; something horrible must be coming. "If you surrender custody of her to the state, she'll be eligible for free care."

"No fucking way." I push back my chair.

"Kayla, I *need* the medicine," April says. I almost kick her for even acting like this is an option. Does she have so little faith in me?

"I know. You're going to have it and *I'm* going to get it for you. I'm not letting them take you away. We're a *family*. These assholes aren't taking that from us."

"I understand your feelings completely," Doctor Tremblay says. Liar. "I'm sure you'll figure something out."

"I will."

If only I had a single clue how.

# SIX

I'M SO CONSUMED by thoughts of money and custody and citizenship that I'm completely caught off guard when I spot Sid Charles brooding next to the potted plant. He doesn't bother sitting, preferring to loom over the waiting room like an ill-tempered gargoyle

I'm supposed to go to *that* man's home.

For someone who takes up so much physical space, the stillness of his posture is disconcerting. I want him to fit neatly into some category so that I can anticipate his next move, but his brutish size doesn't match the calculating man I met on the beach. It's difficult to trust someone who is clearly capable of violence, if it suits him—but this is also the same man who stood up to Tom for me. I grab hold of that fact and step forward.

At my movement, his head whips away from the window. "You ready to go?"

"Right. Go…" I clear my throat, looking for some excuse to delay the inevitable. "Where are we going, again?"

"My place. I'm putting you up." He moves towards the door, obviously ready to be done with everything that's happened today. When I don't move, he gives an exasperated grunt. "You don't have to worry about *that*. No one's going to bother you. You'll have a separate room. Maybe even a separate unit, if I can talk some of the guys into sharing."

"We will?" Despite the circumstances, hope flickers in me.

"Oh, yeah. We're making sure this is down the line, above board, all that shit. Can't give Tom more to make a stink over."

"Uh… thanks?" So the thought *has* crossed his mind. But he's done the calculus and decided endangering me isn't worth the potential blowback. This guy is ruthlessly logical.

"You need any help carrying your stuff? Is it just the two packs?" Sid asks.

"Only the packs, but—" Before I can make any further objection, he turns the door handle. The cheeky tinkle of the bell over the door is the final straw as my good humour boils away. "Can you wait for just a *second*? My sister is back there."

"Is she coming with us?" He is undeterrable. Clearly, patience isn't his strong suit.

I turn my back on him. "Give me five seconds." Ignoring the frustrated huff behind me, I flash Desk Lady the biggest smile I can muster. "Hi! Pat, was it?"

"That's me, hon."

"Great. Are there any forms or papers I should be taking with me?"

"Oh, don't you worry. I gave those to Mr. Charles."

Of course. "Well… thank you. And when can I see April tomorrow?"

She goes over visitation hours, including a tangent where she exhaustively describes what time she takes her lunch break, in case I come in and there's no one to help me at the front desk.

"Okay, great," I say, when there's a break in her ramblings. My next words are whispered. "And… where do I go if I want to trade something for cash? I've got some valuables I don't need anymore."

"The exchange. It's right next to City Hall," she answers at full volume.

"Perfect." I want to ask where City Hall is, but she doesn't seem to understand my need for secrecy.

When I turn back to Sid, his brow is furrowed. I walk toward the door, trying to hide the tremor of my limbs. Outside, I'm relieved to see there aren't any men with guns around, though I suppose they would be redundant. Sid Charles is holding all my worldly possessions hostage and I'm no better equipped to fight him than a bear.

As we walk beyond the hospital, I get my first real look at Salt Spring Island. The hospital is on a paved street, the cracks in the concrete recently repaired. Across the road, small wood cottages sit stuffed between the old stucco homes of pre-Quake days. I spot one man riding a horse, but most people speed by on bicycles.

"Careful." Sid pulls my arm when I wander too close to their path.

I shake him off with a scowl. "I can tell when they're coming."

"Sorry. You just seem preoccupied. Why do you want to go to the exchange?"

"What do you mean?"

"Pat told you to go to the exchange. What are you trading?"

"It doesn't matter."

"Does your sister's treatment cost a lot?"

"Do you think maybe I don't want to talk about this

with you?" I whirl towards him. "That maybe this is personal and has nothing to do with you?"

A muscle strains in his neck as, for a beat, we engage in a staring contest. I don't know why I want to push back against everything he says, but I can't help it. The people I want to lash out at, like Tom, are far away, but this poor sucker is here and so, *so* easy to yell at.

Right now, he's not so much menacing as confused, as if I'm a bit of sap stuck to his fingers that he can't rub off. I notice new details—like how neatly his pale hair is combed backward and the fact he's clean shaven. It's a style I've seen in pre-Quake magazines more often than on real men. My father always wore a beard. It's as if Sid Charles is trying to resemble the respectable gentlemen of yesteryear, but it's not a look he can pull off. He's too hulking. His nose is too crooked. No matter how perfectly he tucks his shirt, he radiates wildness. Something about his earnest attempt to appear unthreatening, coupled with such abject failure, makes my chest hitch with pity.

I wonder what he sees when he stares back at me. *Look at her, Tom.* What about looking at me did he think would change Tom's mind? My unbrushed curls? A body that is unavoidably female?

He clears his throat, and I blink, unsure how long we've been glowering at each other. "The exchange," he says slowly, "will give you the government rate for any items you want to trade. It's a decent option, but they always take a cut. You might have better luck using other channels, if you're trying to get the best value for whatever you're trading."

I blink. "Excuse me?"

"But... well, we can talk about how legal those buyers are when we get home. Just please, stop walking so close to the bikes. You're freaking me out."

"Really? You scare easy."

He rolls his eyes. "Turn here. I need to grab my bike before we head to the bus."

"Bus? Where are we—"

"A few kilometres outside town. On an acreage. Most people do."

"Do what?"

"Live."

Acreage. Living on an acreage. It sounds pleasant. Unbelievably so.

It's probably more cult propaganda. Though I have to admit, this place doesn't look like a cult. I haven't seen any signs with slogans plastered on them. And since leaving the hospital, no one has been openly carrying firearms. Not even Sid.

"Hey. Where's your gun?" I ask.

"Back at the ferry terminal."

"You—you just *left* it?" I can't imagine having the power of a gun—or ever giving it up if I did.

He laughs. "It belongs to the base. Whoever's on guard duty will be using it."

"Then how is—where…" As I continue to look around, I still don't see any signs of surveillance. In fairness, I can't imagine it's easy to keep everyone under constant supervision here like they did in Astolia. The compound there was small enough that we were never out of sight of one of the watchtowers. What do the people here do with all this space? What do they do while no one is looking?

"Everything okay?"

"I… sure." I force myself to walk normally. "Everything's great."

I follow Sid east, and a view of the ocean opens up in front of us. Wisps of this morning's clouds blow overhead, taking their rain to a distant island. It must be another of the Gulf Islands, though I don't know which one.

At the centre of town is a long, narrow harbor. Numerous sail boats are anchored along the pier and beyond them, massive iron barges have been rafted together to block the entrance to the inlet. Along one, the words BC FERRIES are written in faded blue paint. The stockade must pick up somewhere beyond there, but the walls are so far away, it's tempting to forget they exist.

"If you want, you can check the rate at the exchange tomorrow," he says suddenly. "Then I'll see what my guys can find for you, and you can pick your best option."

"You don't have to solve this for me. I can take care of myself."

"Sure, but it's my job to help you. That's the whole point of a sanctuary host."

"It isn't help I wanted or asked for."

"Actually, you kind of did. When you applied for sanctuary—"

"Look, I know!" I'm so tired of people reframing what I did or didn't do today, I can't take his know-it-all tone anymore. "I said what I had to. My sister was sick so I said yes to whatever the hell would get her through those hospital doors. You *know* that's true, so don't be an ass and act like it isn't!"

"Fine! You're right, but... can you maybe try *not* to make this any more difficult than it already is?" We've arrived at his bike lock-up; he wrestles it open with far more aggression than a little key like that needs.

"Oh, sorry. I forgot." I clasp my hands together and put on the most obnoxious, high-pitched voice I can muster. "Thank you, thank you, Sid Charles! You have saved me! Without you I would never—"

"I'm not asking for thanks! I get that you're scared as shit right now, but this place has rules. Ignoring them doesn't make them go away. It just makes guys like Tom think you're going to lash out and kill everyone. He's your immigration officer. He can ruin your life. Mine too, actually." He locks me in place with a pleading look that is undeniably arresting, thanks to his sharp blue eyes. "So chill out. *Please.* You want to help your sister, don't you? Can you play along for her?"

"I... fine. Whatever." Bringing up April is a dick move, not least of all because it makes me realize how often I've had some form of this conversation with her. *Yes, April. Those are wolves you hear howling. But can you stop freaking out? Can you fall asleep anyway?* The predators aren't going away, but it's better not to let them know where to find easy prey.

"Thank you," he sighs.

I lean against an old lamp post that no longer has lightbulbs in it and watch him wheel the bike a few feet to where there's a wooden sign with Bus painted on it.

"I *am* grateful, by the way." I say suddenly. He gapes at me, as stunned by this admission as I am. "You didn't have to defend me to Tom, but you did anyway. I'm very, *very* grateful. Without you, things could have..." I take a shaky breath. "I could be—"

"It's gonna be fine. We'll get you through this."

We. He says it so easily. What's it like, being able to trust a stranger? I haven't given him a single reason to help me. In fact, I've made his life demonstrably worse.

Maybe this is just the sort of man he is. Maybe he's just... kind?

"Oh, and... I'm sorry about the slingshot." Should have said that ages ago, too. "Did it hurt?"

He snorts. "Of course, it hurt. Rocks hurt."

"So why didn't you arrest me? If there was a law and it hurt..."

He gives me another long stare. I wish I could read his

emotions, but unfortunately, all his expressions seem to be some variation on a scowl. "Honestly? It just seemed like a shitty thing to do. And you only shot at me because you were trying to protect your sister. To me, that means you aren't dangerous. Not really."

"Not really?"

"Well, you obviously could be if you wanted."

"Damn right. I could mess you up *good*, Sid Charles." At that, his eyes go wide and my heart sinks. Oh, shit. Does he think I'm being serious? "That's a joke, by the way. You can tell that's a joke, right?"

"Yes. I can tell." He collects himself and even gives a faint smile. Okay, maybe he isn't *always* scowling. All too quickly, it vanishes, like the real world has just caved in on him. "I'm sorry I didn't warn you about Tom. I thought if I didn't report it, it would be like it never happened. But now..."

A wave of shame hits me as he trails off. He deserves this crappy situation even less than I do.

"I'll get out of your hair. I promise. I'll figure out this medicine thing, then April and I won't bother you again. It will be like you said. Like it never happened."

He shrugs. "Sure."

I have to admit—well-intentioned as my promises are— they sound incredibly naïve.

SEVEN

THE BUS TURNS out to be another covered wagon, nothing at all like the illustrations in the *Let's Go to School!* picture book I used to read to April back when she was learning her alphabet. But it does have enough space for Sid to lift his bike in, dump my bags, and carry us. There are other people riding too, so I suppose it counts as public transport. Everyone sits in polite silence for the duration of the ride, which suits me fine. I'm already scrubbed raw from everything that's happened today.

Eventually, Sid signals for the driver to stop. He offers me a hand as I hop down from the wagon, easily dwarfing mine. Hard callouses support me as I try to find solid ground. But the nerves of reaching our destination—this man's home—make me shaky and so ironically, I have to hold onto him for longer than I want to as I steady myself.

We walk down a gravel drive flanked by evergreens that eventually opens into a field of cultivated grain, golden and ripe. Closer to the homestead are several raised garden beds, most laden with mature summer crops, but some showing new plantings of onions, broccoli, and carrots.

The building at the centre of the acreage is larger than I expected, more like the duplexes April and I sometimes scavenged than a single-family home. On the upper landing, a young man leans against the railing, nursing a cigarette. He does a double take when he sees us approaching.

"Holy shit! Is that her?"

"Carlos, you shouldn't be smoking." Sid ignores the question, heading for a shed where several bikes are parked.

"It is. That's totally her." The kid tamps the cigarette out on the wooden railing.

Sid rolls his eyes and says, "Kayla, meet Carlos Dominguez."

"Hi!" Carlos rushes down the stairs, at my side before I can muster up a reply. "James told us all about it. I thought he was full of shit, but then Mr. Sullivan came and—"

"Give that here." Sid plucks the cigarette out of the boy's hand.

The kid keeps talking as if this has happened a hundred times before. "Did you actually shoot Sid? With a rock?"

"Um…" I have no idea how to answer this.

"Yeah. She did."

"That's amazing!" The kid starts laughing. "I'd be in so much trouble if I did that. Wow. He won't even let me get a slingshot."

"And now you know why."

"Welcome to the farm!" Carlos grabs my hand and shakes it so violently, it's impossible not to be charmed. "Where's the other girl? Tom said you had a sister, right?"

"She's still at the hospital," I say.

"Oh, shit." He drops my hand, eyes wide. "Is that why you're here? Shit, that *sucks*. That sucks big time."

"Yes, thank you, Carlos," says Sid. "She doesn't want to talk about it."

"No, it's fine. April's going to be okay, but… yeah, it

does suck." And it's nice to hear someone say it out loud.

"Okay, cool. I'll tell the other guys you need space," says Carlos. "We're super chill, so you don't have to worry about anyone giving you crap for keeping your shit to yourself."

"*Thank you*, Carlos." Sid places one of his hands over Carlos's face, covering almost his entire head, then shoves him away. "Get out of here."

"Are you *staying* here, Kayla?" he asks, stumbling towards the stairs.

"I think so?" I look over at Sid, who gives a sharp nod.

"Tom appointed me her sanctuary host."

"He did? Dude, that's awesome! How'd you talk him into that?"

"Just good luck!" I say with a bright chirrup. No need to tell people it's because Tom thinks I'm a menace to society and only Sid was willing to risk my company.

"Are you gonna stay forever?" Carlos asks. "It would be cool, having girls on the farm."

"Carlos." Sid gives him a warning look.

"I just mean because it would be different! Like, *cool*." When my mouth pops open in alarm, he helpfully adds, "The acreage is supposed to house a few more people, so we figured if we could get some sanctuary seekers, that would beef up our numbers. And it would be cool if it wasn't such a sausage fest, too. Like, what's a community without any women?"

"I..." My chest seizes up. Sid mentioned his "guys" when he was talking to Tom, but how many exactly are there? "We're not staying. Tom said we didn't have to stay. We're just here until—"

"She's going to want to go somewhere else eventually," says Sid.

"What! Why?" Carlos looks positively wounded.

"Well... even I can admit, this isn't the most hospitable environment," says Sid, disappearing into the bike shed.

"Bullshit! Kayla? So you know, we are, like... *so* hospibbible," says Carlos, with utmost sincerity.

I bite hard on the inside of my cheek. "Thank you."

"I'm gonna go tell the guys. First sanctuary case! Woo!" He punches the air, not as ready to give up as Sid. "We're gonna be the friendliest place you could possibly live. Just you wait."

He means well—in the same way a puppy eating its own poop means well—but as Carlos dashes towards the homestead, bile rises in my throat. Overt friendliness is not what I'm looking for. Especially from a group of... how many guys?

Sid comes back from locking up his bike. "He's a lot, but he's a good kid."

"No kidding. So... it's all men? No women at all?"

Sid winces. "None."

"How many of you are there?"

"Eight."

"And none of you are married or—or..." I stammer.

"Silas is dating a guy who lives by the docks and James usually has a girl or two hanging off him but... no. Not yet."

"Oh." I'm not sure how to react to that. Astolia didn't allow men to date other men. Maybe that's a good sign? But seven straight, lonely men is still too many.

"You know how the end of the world was. Crazy guys with guns."

Unfortunately, I do know. Men owned more of the weapons and tools that kept people alive after the Quake.

"But that's not why we want sanctuary cases," Sid hurries to explain, but I'm distracted by the drama unfolding behind him. Carlos darts between doors, knocking on them, gesturing enthusiastically as he communicates with one man, then another, that I'm here.

The long-fabled woman has arrived. A figure steps out who I recognize as one of the guards from the beach. Not Bandana Man, but the other one. James? He grins a smile as wide as a watermelon and my nerve fails me yet again.

I try to slide beyond their view, using Sid's massive frame as a shield. He keeps talking. "We were approved to take over this acreage when the former occupants got too old to work it. That was a year ago. Before that, we were working full-time for the border patrol, but we're mostly here now. They only called us in today because the signal fire was lit and they were short staffed. My old boss asked if I could do him a favour. Ironic, right?"

I nod, as if I any of this is making an impact on me, but I'm rather distracted by the sight of one man leaning over the railing to get a better look. "Damn, she's skinny," he mutters, sounding disappointed.

"I think the only reason we were granted the acreage is because we've got the young guys needed to work the farm, but we are underpopulated," Sid continues. "These places are supposed to be for families, so yeah. Council might take the acreage back if we don't meet occupancy expectations within a few years. That's why we want sanctuary cases. The whole *point* is to take the pressure off any of the guys needing to marry, or—"

"That's great. It's perfect." Nowhere else is going to take me, so he doesn't really need to explain. At some point, I can apply for my own housing and get out of here. "You said we could have our own room? Or unit? I think I'd like that."

As many doors as possible between me and the tiny army living in the rest of this house, please and thank you. Even without guns, they're an intimidating group. Every single one of them is taller than average, beefier than average, scarier than average. How do they know each other? Is this a sports team? Do they have sports on Salt Spring?

"Yeah, let's set that up." Sid turns towards the gaggle at the railing. "All right guys! Kayla and her sister need a unit to live in, so someone needs to give theirs up for a bit. Dom? Albert? Maybe you could—"

"That isn't fair!" shouts one of the men. "Just because we're related—"

"I'll do it!" Carlos throws his arm in the air. "I can room with you, Sid."

"No."

"Why not?"

"You just want to steal my cigarettes."

"That's not fair! I promise, I won't—"

"Anyone else?" Sid drowns him out. "I'm fine with being one of the people sharing, but we need someone other than Carlos."

"I said I promise!"

"Me." A quiet voice materializes from behind the crowd. Bandana Man has stepped out from where he was lurking in the shadows, though he isn't wearing the bandana anymore. I should learn his name. Still, I would recognize him anywhere. I'm not one to forget a face that has aimed a gun at me. "I'm at Roger's place half the time, anyway. She can use my unit."

"Perfect. Thank you, Silas."

"Yes, th—" I sputter to a halt when I see the scowl on Silas's face. The one man willing to give up his space for me also seems furious about my very existence.

"This way." Silas gestures for me to follow him, so I take a wobbly step towards the middle-left unit on the upper level. Sid follows along—in fact, nearly the whole crew does, but a bark of annoyance from Sid sends them scattering for their own rooms. I'm still not sure what the full dynamic is here, but one thing is clear: Sid is in charge.

Inside, I'm greeted by a seating area cobbled together

from odds and ends. The table is missing half a leg, steadied by a large block of wood beneath it and there's a large hole exposing the stuffing in the couch. But there are also blankets piled around in a way that makes the space feel comfortable. On a small shelf, there's even a collection of handmade clay figurines, most depicting animals. They aren't glazed, which makes me think they were made post-Quake, possibly by Silas himself.

"All of this is yours?" I have camped in fancier houses before, but never could have carried so much stuff.

"Yeah. Two bedrooms. Only one of them has a bed, though," says Silas.

"That's fine. April and I are used to sharing." I reach for the door handle of one of the bedrooms. "Is it okay? May I?"

Silas nods. I open it and discover that he's filled the spare room with gardening equipment. Shovels, rakes, pruners, bags of seed and a host of other tools I can't identify.

"We might need to grab something from here occasionally. But most of the stuff we use everyday is in the shed," says Silas.

"Okay."

"I'll make sure the boys knock first."

It isn't great news, but we're lucky to have any privacy at all living with eight men.

Next, we go to the bedroom, which has a queen-sized mattress lying on the ground, also buried in blankets. Silas mumbles about needing to get his stuff, crossing to a coat rack in the corner where he's hung everything from hoodies to jeans and belts.

Sid clears his throat. "There's one kitchen serving the whole acreage. It's downstairs. Helps keep the place warm in the winter. You're free to join us for dinner, if you want." He sets my bags down. "There's a washhouse upstairs and down. Pump is out back by the fire pit."

"Oh." Their own pump? That's a luxury.

He nods. "Dinner should be in an hour. Carlos made—"

"Actually, I think I'll just… unpack." It's the most tactful way I can find to say *please leave me alone*. I need time with my thoughts so I can come up with a plan for how I'm going to rescue April and me from this rapidly unravelling situation.

"Right. Okay." His head dips, disappointed.

"Sorry, do you *need* me at dinner?" I ask. "Is this a sanctuary host thing, or—"

"No, it's fine. Take all the time you need."

Silas shoulders past me with an armload of clothes, the coat rack now empty.

"I'll send you a plate," Sid says.

"No need. I've got food in my bag."

"Okay."

He still sends someone. By then, I've closed every door I can and dragged the broken table in front of the main door so it can't swing open. Better safe than sorry.

A knock comes to the door and a voice I don't recognize says. "Kayla? You in there?"

I don't move a muscle. Whoever it is jiggles the door handle. When it won't budge, something scrapes against the floor. "I'll just leave it out here, if you want it."

The scent of garlic and rosemary wafts under the door. I wait until the delivery boy is long gone before I give into temptation. A bowl of stewed beans is waiting for me. I barricade the door again before I tuck in. The beans burst easily against my tongue, creamier than I've ever managed to cook them, and a small sigh escapes my lips.

As I chew, I listen to the men who share this home. Their laughter travels through the thin walls—and as the sun sets, a startling new sound fills the air. Twangy vibrations layer together to form something hauntingly, indescribably beautiful. It must be an instrument. I almost sneak out to see what it is—a flute? A violin? It's not a piano, at least. I've found a few of those, and while they were usually broken, I've got some idea how they're supposed to sound.

A voice joins in, deep and resonant. Sid. He sings softly, but I can make out a refrain that loops over the delicate music. *Ain't No Sunshine*. Over and over, the song laments.

My fingers close around one of Silas's many blankets. I think I remember my dad once singing the same tune. But I can't be sure. I've never heard it with music before.

EIGHT

THAT NIGHT, MEMORIES of a different colony haunt my dreams.

After Port Alberni fell, we had to find somewhere that would take us. Mum was pregnant with April, making life in the woods a terrifying prospect. We hiked for months, until we reached the Cambell River Valley, where a choir of disharmonious bleating greeted us. Goats. They might as well have been angels to our ears.

Mum insisted on approaching the people herding the goats first, even though she was six months along. "I'm the one they're least likely to shoot. I'll go down, surrender to them—"

"They're least likely to shoot *me*," I retorted. Even at age ten, I knew it was true. Mum had explained the birds and the bees to me and why that mattered to the people who'd survived the end of the world. Even if I couldn't have babies yet, I had a great deal of untapped potential.

"And the promise of meeting *you* is how I'm going to get them to agree to take all of us, including your father." What Mum didn't say out loud was that the opposite was also true. If these people proved hostile, then she wanted me with Dad, the more able-bodied of the pair.

The gambit worked. The Astolians trained their guns on her at first, but no one shoots a pregnant woman on sight. When they approached Dad and me, they were carrying one of Mum's pearl earrings as a token to assure us she was safe. Just one. Before she went down, she'd given us strict orders to run if they brought both.

The man I would later come to know as the Grand Astrologue approached me and pressed the earring into my hand. "Well, aren't you a pretty little thing?"

I gave a faint smile. There was tension in my father's shoulders. I couldn't guess whether he wanted me to thank the man, so that these people would like us better, or if he wanted me to tell this stranger to step away. We both settled for doing nothing.

They didn't bother with anything so cumbersome as paperwork, but like Salt Spring, there were plenty of rules governing Astolia. The Grand Astrologue gave us a lecture about every stricture we needed to obey as we followed the shepherds back to the compound. We would have to attend the nightly heart-gather and listen to his preaching. I wasn't allowed to wear men's trousers anymore. My pants were pink and clearly had *Girls Size 12* printed in the waistband by their pre-Quake creators, but apparently, they weren't appropriate.

Astolia housed twice the number of people as Port Alberni—around six hundred—but the footprint of the compound was much smaller. The walls were built from abandoned shipping containers, stacked three high, with a man in a crow's nest at each corner. Between those guards and the ones escorting the goats back to the compound, there were more firearms than I had ever seen in my life. Against all odds, I felt hopeful. How could somewhere with so many guns be unsafe?

The compound was crowded, especially with hundreds of goats stuffed into the central pen. The whole place stank. Even on a starved stomach, the stew they fed us tasted off. But they let me have as much as I wanted and for the first time in months, I ate until I felt full.

After supper, they sent me to meet another girl my age, who was instructed to hand over one of her skirts. She seemed to be holding back tears.

"I'm Beth-Anne." She wouldn't look me in the face as she passed the stained, goat-hair skirt to me. "And I guess... well, I *guess* you can have this one."

I thought of the few books my mum had saved in her grab bag when we fled Port Alberni, including a copy of *Peter Rabbit*. I would be heartbroken if someone made me give it to a stranger.

I threw my arms around Beth-Anne. "Thank you. I'll give it back when I get my own."

Her arms slowly found their place around my back. "Oh... no. You don't have to worry about—"

"Do you like *Peter Rabbit*?"

"Who?"

"It's a story." I set my bag down and began digging it out. "I could read it to you."

Beth-Anne's eyes widened. Blue and open, like a fresh summer sky. She nodded, and we tucked ourselves into a corner of her family's hut. She loved the story, but once we were done, she didn't want to linger on the illustrations. Instead, she shoved the book into my bag.

"We'll keep it safe," she said.

"Safe from who?"

"They only like us reading certain things at school. *Important* things."

"My mum's a teacher. She says this book is okay. They read it to little kids."

"Well... still." Beth-Anne buried it under a sweater. "To be safe."

"Sure. I guess." After losing Port Alberni, I was willing to do anything to be safe. I've never felt safer than I did that day, unaware that the wolves were inside the flock.

Maybe I should feel lucky that on Salt Spring, I'm treated like a wild animal. Sometimes, it's safer to be hated than wanted.

AS SOON AS I wake up, I pack my things and head out. April and I have been separated for long enough and that damn doctor better let me take her away tonight. The sun isn't fully up when I leave, but I've only walked a few paces when I hear someone yell, "She's awake!"

Eight heads turn toward me. The guys are scattered across the farm, working together to harvest their fall crop.

"Hold up!" calls the one voice I know well enough to recognize, and I slow my gait. A horse whinnies as Sid pulls the reins of a mule attached to some kind of reaper. He hops off and one of the other men takes over, driving the mule through the fields, breaking down a line of grain. My nose twitches at the dust.

Sid hurries to catch up with me before I can escape down the gravel drive. "Did you get anything to eat?"

"I'm fine." I try to ignore him, pressing forward down the path.

"Wait—why are you carrying all that shit?" He's noticed both the pack on my back and that I have April's in my arms. "You know you don't have to cart that stuff every-where, right? That's what the apartment is for. Living in."

I sigh, turning toward him to explain that once again, I am fine. I would rather not leave all my worldly goods on a strange man's property without anyone to monitor them. But as he draws closer, my tongue lodges in the back of my throat.

He's dressed in jeans and a worn white T-shirt, chaff sticking to the spots where his sweat has leeched through the cotton. There's a hint of the shape of his nipples pressing against the fabric. My eyes dart around for something else to focus on. But there's so much of him to notice and nothing to obscure my view. Farmwork has rendered him slick, so his shirt clings to every angle of his body. His piney cologne hits me in the same wave as the natural musk of hard work.

I'm only used to seeing men this bare in magazines. April found one that compared the *beach bods* of every guy who ever played Spider-Man and has religiously carried it around ever since, but those pictures never thrilled me the way they did her. They had muscles so sculpted, the veins were visible. To me, they looked dehydrated, their bodies seconds away from digesting those pretty little muscles. I never understood the appeal.

Sid does not have the body of some fictional Spider-Man. His shoulders are rounded, and while there's a definite narrowing of his frame from his muscular chest down to his hips, there's still a healthy layer of flesh puckering over his hip bone. I try not to notice how low his jeans are riding. He needs a belt, but maybe that felt too restrictive, working in the sun. At any rate, he needs *something* to distract me from the thought that keeps circling inside my head, that if I reached out to touch his stomach, it would feel soft and warm.

"So you're heading out?" he asks. The only response I can muster is a formless gurgle. His brow pinches. "What was that?"

"Oh! Just saying thanks for... thanks." I blink myself

back to sanity, determined to look at his face. Work and sweat have rumpled his hair so some falls forward into his eyes, but if I focus on his broken nose, I can convince myself that this man is not making my stomach spin.

It's got to be the sweaty shirt. I've been starved for male contact, and now my hormones are latching onto the first flash of masculinity they find.

"Sure," he shakes his head, clearly not believing I'm sincere.

Guilt and anger prickle through me. "No, I mean it. *Thanks*."

"Whatever." He's clearly taking the bags as a sign I don't trust him. Which, to be fair, I don't. But it's not *personal*. I don't trust anyone, so he could stop being pissy about it. I nearly say so, but he swings his arms, agitated, and my eyes are pulled to the roll of his shoulders instead. "I need to get back to work. You know where you're headed?"

"Yup."

"And you know how to get there?"

"Yes. The bus… does it cost money?"

"No, it's a basic service. Comes by every hour."

"Thank you." With that, I resolutely put one foot in front of the other, walking away.

The gravel crunches behind me. Relief hits me as the tension severs between us. He let me go. I'm not being held hostage on the farm.

As I ride the wagon into town, the polite silence isn't nearly so comforting as it was yesterday. It gives me too much time with my thoughts. I know what I should be focused on—April, in the hospital, waiting for me. April, who needs medicine. But no matter how hard I try to stay on task, my mind wanders to eight years ago and a boy with hair that stood up straight on end, a gap between his front teeth.

Curtis.

Curtis, leading me beyond the protection of our camp once my mother was asleep. Curtis, pressing me against an oak tree, his mouth working across mine. Curtis, peeling off my blouse as he whispered that he loved me. And *me*, whispering the same words back. I can almost feel the pressure of his chest against my ribs, stringy and lean.

I don't know why I'm thinking of him now, except that I keep returning to the same cold truth. He never got the chance to grow into a man the size of Sid Charles. The boy I loved *never* looked like that.

My hands shake as I open my bag, digging around for something I usually keep buried, for fear it will stir up dark memories. For a second, I worry I've lost it, before my hand closes around the small, weathered surface of a carved cedar heart.

I pull it out and press the token to my lips.

NINE

"SERIOUSLY? THAT'S IT? A hundred dollars?"

"A hundred dollars is a lot, miss. You're lucky the rate for gold is so high," says the man at the counter. Behind his desk, the exchange is filled with bags of vegetables, a couple of bicycles, broken hockey sticks and just about every other random piece of garbage you could imagine. Workers pull crates using everything from wagons to proper pallet jacks. All these goods are headed for the resale store down the hall, including my mother's earrings.

If I agree to sell them.

Sid mentioned something about *other avenues*, but I need money now. I can't bring April home without medicine and this will cover it for a month. Hopefully, in that time I can find a job. Tom said something about sanctuary seekers being allowed to apply for jobs, so it doesn't seem impossible.

"Okay, I'll take it."

The man counts out five twenty-dollar bills, all emblazoned with the signifiers of the long-fallen Canadian government. The plastic-coated banknotes outlasted the empire that printed them. I'm flexing one back and forth when he sweeps the earrings behind the counter. With that, another piece of my mother disappears. I'm almost relieved the perfume bottle turned out to be worthless.

"Can I help you with anything else?" he asks, his tone suggesting I've stood here too long and am holding up the line.

"Oh. No… well, maybe?" I point at the people pushing around palettes and wagons. That looks like the kind of thing I could be competent at—walking back and forth carrying heavy goods. "How do people get jobs here?"

"We hire periodically. Usually, we run an ad in the weekly newspaper, letting people know we're open to applications."

Applications. More paperwork, then. This damn island has a love affair with the stuff. Still, it might be worth it if it means I can afford April's medication. "And do people get paid money for working here?"

"Of course. Standard wage."

"Standard wage? How much is that?"

The man cocks his head, putting the information together. "You must be new to the island."

"Sure." I'm surprised it wasn't obvious sooner.

"Standard wage is ten dollars a week."

"Ten dollars a—are you *shitting* me? That little?"

"Well…" The man looks deeply uncomfortable. There are people muttering behind me, but what do I care? There's no way this is ruining their days more than mine. "It's in line with local standards. No one uses cash for essentials anymore."

The words Tom spoke to me when he issued my papers come back. As a sanctuary seeker, I'm entitled to housing and rations. How is medicine not essential? If you have the power to save someone's life, why wouldn't you? Of course, Tom had a line for that, too. Medicine is scarce. To him, April and I look like opportunistic leeches.

"Is there anything else I can help you with, ma'am?" asks the man.

"What kinds of jobs make more money? Like, a lot more?" Twice as much would be the bare minimum. Unless April and I both work—but no, Tom already made it clear that she has to go to school and if she doesn't, we'll be in trouble all over again. I can't imagine what a fifteen-year-old as clever as April could possibly need more education for.

The clerk's answer sheds some light on the situation. "Doctors. Scientists. Government officials, maybe? Perhaps you should have this conversation with your sanctuary host?"

"Thank you. Yes. I will." But I've got the gist. Fancy jobs. The kind that require a lot more know-how than schlepping heavy boxes around a warehouse. I haven't attended school since Astolia and even then, it was nothing but basic reading and writing. Maybe it's a good thing April is being forced to go to school. If only her future self could pay for her current ailing body.

I've taken up more than my share of time. With the money in hand, I head out of the exchange, then trudge uphill toward the hospital. I don't know if I'm supposed to use the Emergency entrance now that April is already inside, but if I'm in the wrong place, the Desk Lady doesn't make a fuss of it. She gives me a cheerful *hello*. "Doctor Tremblay was about to send news to the acreage that your sister is ready for discharge, but look at you! Here already." She scribbles notes on some paper. "Now, there are some costs we need to resolve before we send her anywhere."

"I brought money."

"So prepared! Let's get you sorted, hon."

The knives, axes, and other weapons I surrendered at the border count towards payment for April's hospital visit, so that's good news. Still, by the time I've covered the cost of an IV, a night of observation, and Doctor Tremblay's time, plus enough medication to last April a month, I've barely got ten dollars left.

Doctor Tremblay comes out to meet me. When Pat tells him I managed to cough up the cash for April's first supply of insulin, his face breaks into a surprised smile. Of course, I don't say that I have no idea where the money for next month's dose is going to come from, but why sow doubts in his mind?

He leads me to her, giving a long lecture about all the ways she'll need to monitor her condition. I try to pay attention, I really do. But all that helpful information vanishes from my brain the moment we enter April's room and I see I'm not her only visitor.

Tom Sullivan sits in front of my sister, scribbling away in a folder, interviewing her without me to oversee the interaction. That son of a bitch.

"Get away from her!" I fly to April, who goes rigid in my arms.

Tom straightens in his seat. "Pardon me?"

"You don't talk to him without me. Understand? Don't talk to this man!"

"Kayla, what are you doing?" April tries to shove me off, but that only makes me tighten my grip.

"He's trying to get us in trouble—"

"He's our immigration officer!" April shouts. I knew it. He's already getting his hooks in her. "It's his job to help us!"

"It's his *job* to protect this island from people like us. Don't let him lie to you."

Tom snaps his folder closed and rises from his seat, his usual hard scowl in place. "Two things can be true at once, Ms. Hollins. For instance, this meeting has been both surprising and entirely predictable."

"So you admit it? You're trying to get rid of us?"

"No, I am not." He slides his folder into a bag, the calm of his movements all the more enraging than yelling would be. "This sorry state of affairs requires no effort on my part. It's a shame, Ms. Hollins. Upon meeting your sister, I wondered if I was mistaken in my estimation of your character. She's been raised well, by some miracle. However..." He gestures at me. "It would seem my years of experience haven't failed me. The fact that you rushed in here, assuming an adversarial situation when—"

"You locked me in a hospital room yesterday! You threatened to send me to jail! Don't you bullshit me that you're the good guy—"

"I don't care what you think of me. I truly wish I knew how to help you, Ms. Hollins. But while some people are built for civilization..." He nods toward April, before looking back at me. "Some, tragic as it is, are not."

"Fuck off! You have no idea who I am."

"Please. This kind of stress isn't good for your sister," says Doctor Tremblay, rushing in belatedly. I glower at him. Yeah, *I'm* the problem here. Raising a fuss, trying to protect April, that's the problem. Not the bastard undermining us at every chance he gets.

"Please be aware that every demerit you receive will elongate the citizenship process by one year, Ms. Hollins," says Tom. "And that should you obtain a third, your sanctuary status will be suspended and subject to review."

"A third?"

"A third." Tom puts his hat on and heads for the door, limping against his bad leg. "This conversation counts as your second."

TEN

AT FIRST, APRIL is furious with me. She doesn't understand what I was reacting to, having spent her time on the island cocooned in the hospital. Once we're outside, I explain demerits and how Tom penalized me for shooting Sid's hand. At that, her indignation shifts.

"We can't be citizens for a whole extra year because of a *slingshot*? That's bullshit!"

I'm so relieved her allegiance is swinging back to my side. "Right?"

"Does that apply to both of us or just to you?" she asks.

"Um…" I dig our papers out of our bags to find an answer.

Until now, I hadn't even realized that we each had a set—one for April, and one for myself. Both have the same column marked: *lengthy unknown affiliation*. A host of other reasons for possible demerits are listed, including *hoarding/unlawful possession of public resources and aggressive behaviour*. That last must be what Tom is slapping me with now.

"Well, at least it will only be two years for me," says April.

"Assuming he doesn't stick us both with aggressive behaviour."

"Why would he? I didn't fire the slingshot. I didn't yell at anyone in the hospital."

"Because he's a power drunk asshole." Even as I say it, I'm not sure it's true. Tom called April *well-raised*. He might be pissed with me, but would he want to ruin her life, too?

"It doesn't matter. We've got the medicine, right? We'll figure this out. Once you get a job, none of this will matter," says April.

She carries herself with a chin-forward air. It's so like the April of several months ago, I could cry. My sister is back. Sure, there are bags under her eyes and this new verve would vanish without her drugs, but it's all I wanted. I don't dare ruin it. I can't steal hope from her when she's finally caught hold of it.

So I don't tell her about the measly pay of any job I can hope to get. She'll find out soon enough and then…

And then maybe she'll ask me to give up custody, too.

"By the way, what did you say to Tom?" I ask.

"Same as you. Told him I was born in the woods. All that stuff."

Then she kept our story straight. We settled on what we planned to tell people once we reached Salt Spring ages ago, but it's still a relief to know we didn't botch it. "Good."

As we ride the bus back to Sid's, April leans out the back so she can see the surrounding hills.

"Are those farms?" Her voice is breathy with wonder. "They are. They're farms."

"I guess." There's farmland all around Sid's place. Some ruined suburban architecture remains, but most of it seems to have been torn down in favour of agriculture or higher density housing.

"And that's where we're going, right?" she says. "I hadn't really thought about it until now but… we're going to live on a *farm*. With a bunch of other people."

"A bunch of *men*. You need to be on your guard."

"Of course," she says, but my warning seems to have the opposite effect, because she smooths down her ponytail. I'm regretting giving April that stack of fashion magazines filled with "the summer's hottest looks" we found in an abandoned beauty salon two years ago. I should have burned them instead.

The bus lets us off a short walk from Sid's acreage. We walk past the hedge and April gasps with delight. The big field, the garden plots, the bike shed, the pump—everything earns a squeal and pointing fingers.

It doesn't take long for us to attract attention. One of the younger boys is splitting wood in front of the house. Immediately, he zips up to Sid's unit and hammers on the door so loudly, someone downstairs opens up, too.

"They're back! They came back!"

What if Sid's still wearing the same thin T-shirt from this morning? April shouldn't see him in *that*. But when the door opens, he looks ready for the cool autumn night—same pair of jeans, paired with a plaid button-down, rolled up at the elbows.

I'm fairly certain I'm not disappointed.

He walks towards us slowly and deliberately. A handful of the other guys outpace him. The boy who was splitting wood leads the pack, but he's followed by more shouts, more doors opening, and soon, the entire household is making their way toward us. It's like harvesting a fish weir, everyone clamouring to jump into the net first.

Arms reach out, and April and I are drowned in a cacophony of voices. Sid might have held them back yesterday, but the dogs are off their ropes now.

"You came back! I thought for sure you were gonna wig out and—"

"Hey! You're the sister, right? I'm Carlos and—"

"Suck it, Albert! They're back! You owe me two bucks and—"

"I'm Wendell. Do you like potatoes?"

We both stumble backward, suffocating. April's cheeks, ruddy with excitement a moment ago, blanch white, like she's about to keel over.

Before it comes to that, a pair of large hands cuts through the crowd, grabbing each of us by the shoulder. "Back off, guys. They don't need all of you at once."

I curl toward Sid, trying to use his body to block out the commotion. April takes hold of me, her fingers digging into my arm. I latch onto the only thing from the deluge that stuck.

"What was that about potatoes?"

"Oh! Yeah, we got lots of them. Making up a chowder now," says one of the men. He steps into my line of vision, wielding a long object. Without thinking, I slap it out of his hand—only to realize it was a wooden spoon.

"Uhhhh…" He stares at where it's lying on the ground. "I mean, if you don't like potatoes—"

"Potatoes sound great!" I shout. *Pull it together, Kayla. They're all going to think I'm batshit.*

"Wendell, why don't you help Carlos get things ready and we'll eat outside? The kitchen is a little cramped," says Sid.

"Yeah, okay." He picks up the spoon, then leads the others away. They seem less inclined to crowd us now that they know I might attack their cutlery.

Once there's space, I push away from Sid. "I'm so sorry. I didn't mean to—"

"It's no big deal. I'll talk to Wendell."

"But you guys *can't* say anything! Not to the hospital

or Tom or… They think I'm crazy." Or dangerous. I don't know. But I can't imagine this helping my case.

Sid meets my eye, then nods. "Like I said, I'll talk to Wendell."

"Thanks."

"If it makes you feel any better, no one here gives a rat's ass about Tom. He was our case worker too and—"

"Your case worker? Like, for immigration?" I repeat. "You're not from the island?"

Sid cocks his head to the side. "What made you think we were?"

"I…" I haven't given it much thought. Looking back, it should have been obvious. There's a practiced niceness about most people here, masking their real intentions. The doctor, Pat, even Tom—they all coat their words in a layer of politeness Sid doesn't bother with. "But you know how everything works here. I assumed that meant…"

He shrugs. "You don't really have to question a place if it's all you've ever known. C'mon. Soup's on."

Before I can ask him anything else, he strides ahead, leading us to the back of the house where a collection of bricks and flat stones have been cobbled together to make a ramshackle patio. There are old plastic patio chairs, a carved lounger, and a collection of logs nailed together into rough benches. A fire pit has been dug in the centre of the configuration, but it isn't lit right now.

The smell of something herby and warm emanates from the indoor kitchen. My stomach turns over in eager anticipation. April and I actually did cook good meals most of the time in the woods. We had dozens of foraging spots we rotated between throughout the year, eating everything from morels to wild salmon, and even tended plenty of self-seeding patches of domesticated vegetables, like lettuces, onions, and runner beans.

The trick was never to stay too long. Before TNS could notice us building anything, we would be off to our next hotspot, ready to gather another harvest. We're only in such rough shape now because April got sick. The forced hike meant surviving on nothing but dried rations and that's…

That's why this soup smells *so* damn good. What must it be like, having a permanent garden to tend to all year round?

April and I take seats on one of the benches. Across from us are the two men who helped Sid bring us to the island. Silas acknowledges us with nothing but a nod, his dark, shoulder-length hair all but obscuring his thin face. The other lounges in one of the plastic chairs, head leaning back so that I can see the shape of his Adam's apple puckering against his throat. He looks more like the cover of the cheap paperback romance novels April and I used to dig out of people's attics than he does an actual human man. The moment he notices me staring, he flashes a perfect grin.

"I don't think I ever properly introduced myself. James DeLuca," he says, without further prompting. "Glad to see you found your way to our door again."

"Thanks." I go back to staring at the garden beds, which do me the courtesy of not talking back.

"Of course, you've met our Silas. He's not one for chit-chat." He gestures to the lanky man. There's something strange about the way James talks that I can't place my finger on, like he's skipping over the letter "r" in some of his words. Is that an… *accent*? Do accents still exist? And if so, where did his come from?

"Unless you've got questions about plants," James adds, holding the "a" in plants for too long. *Plaaahnts.* "If you like, he can give you a tour of the gardens tomorrow." *Gaaahdens.*

"Shut up, James," Silas says, still staring at the pit. "Anyone want a fire?"

"Sure. It's cold enough." Sid leans forward and at his word, Silas heads for a woodpile a few feet away.

I'm trying to piece together the dynamic here. Plenty of cues have suggested that Sid is in charge, as he was at the border, but I sense a further pecking order. Most of the group is inside, getting the meal ready, but these three, gathered together, share something else besides a desire to shaft someone else with the cooking duties.

The younger ones seem to fall in a range—Carlos is at the bottom, another has the beginnings of a beard—but the gap between them and these three is more pronounced. The five inside are boys. Sid, Silas, and James are men. There's some history here that I don't know enough about to intuit the details. Sid even said it himself; Tom was their immigration officer. Not just his. *Theirs.* Did they all come here together?

Eventually, Carlos comes out with the soup and someone else passes out wooden bowls. There's a clamour of hands and ladles, punctuated by gruff calls from Sid to not horse around and spill anything. Guilt pinches at my stomach as I realize this is what I walked out on yesterday when I refused dinner. This group of boys and their... fathers? Brothers? When one of the younger boys starts needling Silas with his spoon and he has to swat the kid away, I realize who they remind me of: me and April. A few years later. A few more people. But the dynamic is startlingly similar.

I bury my nose in my bowl. The potato chowder has been blended with sage, oregano, and a smoky animal fat to give the soup body. I've already wolfed down half my bowl when I notice April hasn't touched her food. I'm about to tell her to hurry up and eat while there's still leftovers when I notice that she's diligently taking something out of her paper bag. A jar of insulin. A needle. She lines up a shot on her leg and stabs herself without a single complaint. I look away, blinking furiously.

"Is the soup too hot?" Carlos asks, his voice anxious.

"No, just smoke in my eyes." I shift to another angle on the bench, trying to make my explanation convincing. "The soup is great."

Unfortunately, my new position has put me in Sid's direct line of sight. I see him making the calculation, eyes roving between April, packing her used needle into a separate bag, and me, too weak to watch her do it.

"So I was saying to the guys," Sid says, in that flat, direct way of his. "While you're here, the upstairs washhouse should be just for you two."

"What?" I like the idea of privacy but hate the thought of owing him more than I already do. "You don't need to do that."

"No, I think it's a good idea," says Sid. "This place is supposed to house eight families, anyway. We're under capacity. It will be good practice, in case anyone else moves in."

At that, James snorts. Silas smacks him across the back of the head, but it doesn't stop the other boys from breaking out in snickers. Just what I need. More attention being drawn to our obvious gender discrepancy.

"Sid, that's very… *gallant*, but not necessary. We'll be fine."

"Speak for yourself. *I* want a washhouse." April finds the craziest times to regain her confidence, I swear.

"April, we're two people. There's eight of them."

"Kayla doesn't like accepting help, but I would be more than happy to—"

"*April!*"

"Why don't we talk about it later tonight?" Sid's eyes lock with mine. "We've got a few things to go over."

"Will I be there when you're talking about it?" asks April. "Because I have opinions."

"No, you will not. You're going to bed once you've finished that chowder."

She pushes her lower lip out. "Then I'll eat very slowly."

April makes good on her promise, but even so, the time slips by too fast. I spend the evening trying to learn the names of the last few boys but get hung up when one of them is *also* named Tom. The conversation devolves into talking about what a dick Tom at City Hall is. No one asks for the details of my encounter with him today, but Young Tom makes a show of saying that the reason Tom has the last name Sullivan is because he *sullies* the good name of Toms everywhere.

Then a wasp starts circling April's food and Carlos announces he's going to "ninja slap" all the bugs pestering us out of the air. I'm too busy watching him flail around to ask who the last couple of boys are, especially since James is subtly sticking his feet in places that might make Carlos trip the entire time.

Overall, the dinner time conversation is loud, obnoxious, juvenile. And harmless. These boys are wonderfully harmless.

Too soon, April finishes her meal. Despite her protestations, she's rubbing her eyes, so I guide her away from the bonfire to the unit Silas leant us.

"This isn't fair. I'm missing out on stuff. Being sick sucks." She collapses onto the bed.

"But... you're not sick anymore, right?"

"Well, depends on how you look at it. Maybe I'm always sick now." She sighs. "They seem nice. Sure are a lot of them, though."

"Do you mind?" I don't know what I could do about the situation at this point, but I ask anyway.

She shrugs. "It's all right. I'll feel great about it if we have our own washhouse."

"April."

"Is it so bad to want space?" she asks. "I think... I think I liked the *idea* of living with a bunch of guys better than... well, this."

I snort. "Oh, yeah?"

"I'll get used to it. It doesn't feel bad, but..." A shiver steals down her back. "It's still *different*."

"Very different." I sit next to her on the bed and squeeze her hand. She leans her cheek into my shoulder and for a while, we let ourselves sit in companionable silence. The hum of crickets starts up outside and I can almost make myself believe we're somewhere in the woods, far away from all of this.

"I want to be good at this." April's face is set in a determined frown and I know she means far more than living with men; there's managing her illness and who knows what else ahead of her. "I'm *going* to be good at this. Doctor Tremblay said I need to catch up on school. I'm going to be good at that, too. All of it."

"You don't have to be brave with me," I say, but she doesn't respond. Instead, she releases my hand and stretches out on the bed. I open her pack and pass her the cedar strips she's been weaving into a bracelet, so she has something to fiddle with tonight. I blow her a kiss as I head out, which makes her roll her eyes in that predictable teenaged way.

She's back. I really have my sister back. And a month from now, we're going to run out of the only thing keeping her alive.

Finally, once I've shut the bedroom door firmly behind myself, I release the tears I've been choking back all day.

ELEVEN

"**SO, YOUR SISTER.**" Sid blows on the liquid inside his clay mug, sending steam curling up into the inky night air. "She needs injections?"

I don't bother answering that. We're seated on a bench on the eastern side of the acreage, the other guys far enough away that their noise around the firepit is nothing but a murmur. Once I had my emotions under control, I came outside and told Sid we could talk if he wanted, and this was the spot he chose. I try not to feel paranoid, sitting next to this relative stranger without a single tree to give cover around us. Despite my spiking pulse, logic tells me this probably isn't a deadly situation. It's just so brazenly *open*.

I'm not sure what the exact size of the acreage is, but it feels like a lot. Astolia never had a farm of this size. It's difficult to defend open space, and so we suffered through low crop yields instead. There certainly wasn't any land like where we sit now—at the edge of the property, across from a pond filled with sleeping mallard ducks.

"Is it… diabetes?" he asks.

I nod.

"Shit."

"Yeah."

"They had to run a bunch of tests on Wendell a few years ago. Thought he might have it. Turned out to be a lingering case of pneumonia, but it was scary as shit. I'm sorry."

"It's better to have an answer. She's going to be okay." But my voice wobbles. After so many years of living just with April, I'm not great at sharing my emotions with people. I'm also realizing I'm not great at hiding them, either. I've had no practice.

"Totally. It's treatable, right?"

"Yeah."

"So it might take some time to get used to. But you're both gonna be okay."

"For sure."

Sid is letting the pauses between us linger long enough that if I wanted to, I could say far more. He's my sanctuary host. It's his job to be friendly and listen to me. But maybe the label is why I don't go on. No matter how nice he tries to be, he still represents the Salt Spring government on some level. He could report anything I say to Tom Sullivan.

Though Tom was his immigration officer, too. That *does* pique my curiosity.

"How long ago did you come to the island?" I ask.

"Me?"

"You. And the other guys. Did you all come over together or—"

"Um, yeah. All of us."

"Where did you guys come from?"

He takes a long drink from his mug, staring out at the ducks rather than me. "A shitty situation. Like you."

"Okay. Fair enough." I know a request to kindly fuck off when I hear it. But if I'm not going to talk about my shit and he's not going to talk about his, I can't see the point in this discussion. Plus, I'm exhausted, which is weird since I hardly hiked anywhere today.

But as I stand to leave, Sid rallies. "Hold on. I wanted to talk to you about next steps. You know, so you aren't blindsided by anything."

"Oh. Right." I sit back down. "Like what?"

"You need to get April registered for school. She'll need to take a placement test. Carlos can help her get there every day."

"Every day?" It makes me sick thinking about it.

"They get weekends off."

"Weekends?"

"Saturdays and Sundays. You'll get used to it. They're big on dates and months and shit here."

"Right." I nod, pretending this is what has me worried and not the idea of April going to a school. On the one hand, school was great when I was a kid in Port Alberni. My mum taught us real things about the world, plus math and spelling. Astolia was another matter. It was ground zero for the Grand Astrologue to indoctrinate kids with whatever nonsense he wanted.

"We're in the middle of harvest right now, which kinda sucks for you. Busy time of the year. But I can try to take some time off and show you around town, too."

"No, don't go out of your way for me." I already owe this man too much and even now, I keep wondering when the act will drop and he'll demand something in exchange for all the trouble I've caused him. I think of April and her grand dreams about being good at life on this island and in a way, I get it. We have to figure out how to exist on our own terms here, rather than constantly being in debt to everyone. I need to get a job and our own place to live and the hell out of here before we end up trapped.

Unfortunately, that does mean asking Sid for one more small favour. "There is one thing I could use your help with."

"Of course," he says, perking up.

"I need a job. Maybe two. Where do people get jobs?"

"Really?" His eyes flick over me in a way that makes me uneasy. "I thought you didn't plan on staying on the island."

"Diabetes."

"Oh! Oh, shit. Right. It's permanent." He blinks. "Sorry. I should have realized."

"It's okay." It's not like the average person is an expert on health matters these days.

"And you aren't citizens yet, so... *damn*." He rubs his hand across his chin, which shows a faint prickle of beard growth against his pale skin. He must have missed shaving this morning. I quickly avert my eyes before he can notice me staring. It doesn't take long for him to put the final pieces together. "I guess you need a paycheque soon."

"Bingo."

"Normally, I would tell someone who just arrived on the island to wait a few months before worrying about job hunting. You've got enough on your plate already," he says, which is a very nice way of calling me a weakling. "But if you need something quick, there's ads in the newspaper. Can you read?"

"Of course, I can read! Why does everyone keep assuming I'm some kind of wild animal?"

"Sorry!" He raises his hands defensively. "I only meant... sorry."

"It's fine," I say. His opinion doesn't matter. So why does it sting that he thinks just as little of me as Tom does? "I'm tired. I'm heading in."

"Yeah. Me too."

We walk up the slope toward the homestead side by side,

not speaking. Sid doesn't actually head for his apartment. Instead, he turns toward the firepit where the other guys are gathered.

"Ah, you're back," says James, sliding a large wooden object into his lap, left hand gripping the narrow neck. As Sid sits, James starts plucking at the strings and the same magical sound that filled the night yesterday takes up again.

Country Roads, he sings. I feel like a small child, sliding her finger over a page in a picture book until it lines up with the right image.

Guitar. The music is coming from a guitar.

For a second, I'm motionless, entranced by the warmth of the music and smouldering fire. But then Sid looks up and catches me staring. He gestures for me to join them.

I bolt.

These aren't my people and he shouldn't have to keep pretending to want me around.

Inside the apartment, I slide into the bed I share with April.

"I promise," I whisper, careful not to wake her up. "I'm going to solve this. No one is taking you from me."

THE GUITAR IS only the first of many things I try to make sense of through books. Books are my only context for concepts like months, days of the week, and—by far the strangest thing to care about—hours of the day. But people here *do* care. April's school placement test can only happen during "regular working hours" or some shit. In fact, it also needs an official *appointment* like we're meeting with a barrister from a Charles Dickens novel or going to the dentist like the Berenstain Bears.

See? Books. I *can* read, thank you very much, Sid Charles.

All this is to say that it's over a week before we're able to set up the appointment. April and I ride the bus into town and ask to be let off outside City Hall. Inside, the smell of so many people in close quarters is overwhelming. It's a cramped, weaving warren of a building. The signage hangs from the ceiling, nailed over what used to be grocery store aisles. Sid says the old market was one of the few buildings in town large enough to accommodate a full-scale government. The regional offices that used to service the island weren't enough once Salt Spring needed to operate as an independent entity, so now aisle four is where you meet the Minister of Economics instead of grabbing a can of soup.

We find the aisle labelled EDUCATION – SOCIAL DEVELOPMENT where a pleasant looking woman is seated at a desk. Behind her, the old store shelves are filled with boxes of files. She sets April up with a registration at the local high school—effective next week—and then pulls out the test.

"Since you're coming to us as an older student, we'll have to assess your literacy and mathematics skills, to see if they're in-line with expectations for your grade," she says.

"Totally on it." April tosses her ponytail over her shoulder with a flourish. We spent the days leading up to her appointment drilling spelling and grammar, so she's going in confident. Unfortunately, the last time I was in a school of any kind, I was a year younger than she is now. But she's a better speller than I am. Hopefully, that will be enough.

"Wonderful." The woman gestures for April to step past a curtain partition that's been added to the aisle to give her some privacy. "You can pick her up in a couple of hours."

"Great!" I say, as if I have any sense how long an hour is, let alone two of them.

But I do have my own errand to run, so I scan the aisles until I find number twelve is labelled: HOUSING – IMMIGRATION – PUBLIC SAFETY – HOMELAND SECURITY. I draw up short when I see those departments grouped together. Two desks are located in this aisle, candles burning on each one. And at the one closest to me is my nemesis—Tom Sullivan, hunched over a stack of papers. A small placard hangs from his desk that says *Minister of Immigration and Housing*. A wave of relief hits me when I realize I won't need to talk to him after all. I skirt around the entire complex, so that I can enter the aisle from the other side and approach the man seated at the far desk.

"Hi!" I put on my brightest voice. I even brushed my hair and put on the one sweater I own that doesn't have any holes. Dress to impress! That's what book characters do when they want a job. "I saw the ad in the paper. It said you're looking for border guards?"

"Oh!" The minister gestures for me to step forward. "That's wonderful. Take a seat. We never can find enough willing volunteers."

That's what I'm counting on. The paper said this position offers twenty-five dollars a week—way higher than anything else I qualify for. I asked Sid how dangerous these border guard jobs are, and he said it's mostly marching along the shoreline, monitoring the fence and doing—to quote him—jack shit. But the mere idea that TNS could be out there is enough to scare most applicants off. Apparently, me and my slingshot were the most exciting thing to happen at the border in a couple of years, which is laughable. I've survived far scarier situations, so this should be a breeze. I might even get to carry a gun.

"Tell me a little about yourself," says the minister.

"Um, I'm Kayla Hollins. And…." If only the Berenstain Bears had been old enough to go job hunting. Then I might have some script to work from. "… and I haven't fired a gun before, but I've got good aim with a slingshot and a bow. I used to feed myself with them, so I had to be good at sneaking up on stuff. I can hike for long distances and—"

He straightens. "Feed yourself? Are you a Wildling?"

There's that awful term again. "I'm a sanctuary seeker."

"Right. Of course." He makes a note on a piece of paper. "Kayla Hollins. That was your name?"

"Yeah."

"Wonderful. Perfect. Go on." He smiles, and yet I sense something has slid off course. "You were saying something about hiking?"

The whole discussion, he's incredibly polite. He asks about the places I've visited on Vancouver Island and seems impressed when I tell him my family survived the Port Alberni massacre. I chalk up the earlier awkwardness to nerves. By the end of our conversation, he's even laughed at a few of my jokes. He finishes our discussion with a handshake and assures me he's so very glad I came in to ask for a position.

"You'll hear from me soon."

"Great." Did I do enough? I know so little about landing jobs, but I don't think I embarrassed myself.

April is still busy, so I'm left to pace the building, stewing over my attempts at gainful employment. At one point, I pause to read a bulletin board that has a poster up announcing an upcoming election, but my mind is elsewhere. They take sanctuary seekers as border guards, don't they? They hired Sid and his guys. Granted, Sid is roughly two times my body weight, but that doesn't matter when weapons come into the picture. I've taken down elk bigger than him.

Finally, April completes her test. I'm hoping we both

got lucky today, but when she's released, she's got a scowl on her face and bright red cheeks.

"We'll have your results soon," says the Minister.

"Thank you! April's really looking forward to going to—" Before I can finish, my sister shoves past me with an aggressive thrust of her shoulder.

"Let's just *go*," she snaps.

I give the woman a helpless shrug, then chase after my raging sister. Once we're outside, away from the prying eyes of others, I tap her shoulder. "Slow down! You okay?"

"No! They're going to think I'm stupid, even though I'm *not*! The reading and writing section went okay. But the math—I hadn't seen half of it before! Like, look at this." She pulls a piece of scrap paper out of her pocket. They must have provided it to her. "Have you ever seen *this*?" She points at a symbol that looks like the letter "V" attached to a flat line.

"Isn't that the sign for long division?" I did my best to teach her basic arithmetic, but naturally, she knows nothing that I never learned. Mum tried to keep teaching me after we left Astolia but once she got to stuff like calculating the length of triangle sides, I couldn't see the point.

Apparently, the point was to teach April so that she wouldn't have a temper tantrum outside a government agency.

"Then why does it have that little tag on the front, hm? And why didn't they put the number you were supposed to divide by next to it? It was just this symbol on top of a number! No other hints!" She turns the paper around so she can scowl at it again. "It was over numbers like four and sixteen and eighty-one so… maybe it has something to do with the product you get when you multiply a number by itself? But I don't know! It isn't fair. I'm not stupid!"

"So you didn't recognize one symbol. So what? That doesn't mean—"

"There was an entire section called geometry!" she shrieks. "What's geometry?"

"Oh… that's like, studying shapes and stuff."

Her eyes narrow. "You mean you knew?"

"I… sorta?"

"You knew about geometry! And you never warned me. Don't even look at me, Kayla!" She marches toward the bus stop and all I can do is follow her, biting down on my cheek to keep from laughing.

That night, April spends dinner quizzing each of the boys about whether they have anything that resembles a geometry textbook, but the only boy currently enrolled in school is Carlos, who is no help.

"Oh, I'm not taking math this year," he says.

"You—what?" April sounds scandalized.

"Yeah, I suck at that shit. I'm doing this cool program, actually! It's like, half regular school, half work placement. I'm doing the agriculture focus, so working on the farm half the year, doing English or whatever the other half. You should look into it! Then you won't have to give a crap about the math thing."

"*Won't have to give a crap?*" April sets her bowl of stewed beans down, as if she needs her full body to yell at him properly. "You mean you gave up? On the entire concept of math?"

"Uh… sort of?"

"Carlos chose something different," Sid interjects, more defensive than Carlos himself. "The school system has to be practical. Most people are needed in agriculture or trades these days. He's doing something valuable. But it's great if you want to do high level academics—"

"Want to? It's the principle of the thing! Proving that I *can*."

"April, that's not the best reason for doing something,"

I point out, still fighting laughter.

She throws me a withering look. "Well, of course *you* wouldn't understand. You're happy just surviving."

I'm so taken aback by the accusation; I don't have a rebuttal. Does she have any idea how difficult *just surviving* is? Things might seem easier now that we're on this island, but our position is still precarious. We're living in someone else's apartment, eating someone else's food and have no guarantee that we'll be able to pay for her insulin when she runs out in a couple of weeks. Her life hangs in the balance more than anyone's. She should be thrilled with survival.

"I'm going to bed," she announces.

I make a move to follow her, but Sid places a hand on my shoulder, halting me. "Hey, do you have a minute?"

"Um… sure." My eyes are fixed on April as she marches away with her nose in the air.

"Great. Duck pond?"

I sigh, annoyed to be pulled in the opposite direction, but it's better than hanging around the fire with all the other guys. They seem like nice enough boys, but there are so many of them. Two of them—Dominick and Albert— are brothers and they look so damn similar I still can't keep straight which is which.

The bench is wet tonight, having soaked up the rain that fell earlier this morning. Still, Sid sits on it, silent as he takes out a cigarette. I see him most evenings at dinner, but this is the first time we've been alone together since when I first arrived. I hesitate, telling myself it's because I don't want a wet butt and not because I still feel uneasy next to him.

"So how did the interview go?" he asks.

"Oh! Fine. Maybe?" I decide to sit and while the damp does seep through my pants, it's not as cold as I thought it would be. Probably because Sid radiates nearly as much heat as the firepit through pure body mass.

"Maybe?"

"He called me a Wildling."

Sid rolls his eyes. "Asshole."

"Exactly. But you got a job guarding the border, didn't you? Don't they take Wildlings?"

"Yeah, you've got rights. Employers can't discriminate against sanctuary seekers due to citizenship status," says Sid. "There was a big court case about it a few years ago. *Hawkins vs. Cuthbert Composting*. It set a precedent and now everyone appeals to it."

I snort. "That's oddly specific. Do you sit around reading court decisions for fun, Sid Charles?"

His cheeks flush. "Sometimes."

"You're just a big nerd under all those muscles, aren't you?"

His brow furrows. "I can't tell if I'm being insulted or not."

"Hmmm. Not as smart as I thought, then."

At that, he descends into a scowl and I grin like a feral cat. Then, as if reluctantly taken in by my antics, the corner of his mouth lifts. Soon, we're both laughing. I can't remember the last time I harassed someone like this other than April and there's something delicious about it. My chest warms as a strange thought seizes me. I could do it. I could be friends with this man.

That realization is terrifying. I've lost everyone I've ever cared about, aside from April. My mother, my father, and Curtis were the most gutting, but the list is far longer. Unbidden, someone comes to mind who I hate dwelling on even more than Mum or Curtis. Beth-Anne Reed— my best friend during the years we lived in Astolia. She and Sid have a lot in common: blonde hair, blue eyes, far more serious than me. But most unsettling? Both were "assigned" to make me feel welcome in the community.

"Anyhow, I'm sure it's fine." I switch the topic back to safer ground, unwilling to probe the feelings he roused in me—good and bad. "He seemed to warm up to me by the end of our conversation."

"I'm sure it went great. They're pretty desperate for hires right now. I can put in a word for you."

"Thanks." I give Sid a genuine smile. I don't like owing him, but this also matters so incredibly much. I need it to work out. "Was there anything else we needed to talk about?"

"No, I just wanted to check in," he says.

"Then I better get back to April." I hop off the bench, dusting my pants, though it doesn't do much to get rid of the wet patches.

"You sure? I got the impression she wanted to be alone."

"Why would she want that?"

"Well, everyone does sometimes."

"No, they don't. Nobody wants to be alone."

Sid laughs outright. "That's bullshit, and you know it. You avoid people all the time."

"Not the people I trust," I say. "Nobody *likes* to be alone."

His smile vanishes. "Kayla, you don't have to live that way anymore. You're safe here."

"Sure."

Easy for him to say. He's the size of an ox and has seven people he can rely on. That's probably the closest anyone comes to the villages and cities of earlier generations. Community building was wired into us by our ancestors, who lived during a time when it was still safe to reach out to other people. Evolution is a slow process, which is why humans managed to outrun it, right into our own destruction. Now, we survivors have got all these left over inclinations that make us join cults.

Sid Charles might have started his life in Salt Spring as a sanctuary seeker, but he's one of *them* now. He's bought into whatever dream it is they're selling.

"Good night, Sid. It was nice chatting with you."

And it was. It hurts more than usual to walk away, safe in the solitude that protects me.

TWELVE

A WEEK LATER, I spend the day pacing the farm as I await April's return from her first day of school. By now, the sights are familiar. Most of the acreage is fields of oats. The stalks have been broken down and the men have moved on to later steps in the harvest. Today, they sit in a circle, talking while they swish the grain around in baskets. They toss the contents just high enough for the breeze to catch the chaff and carry it away. I give them a wide berth, not wanting to intrude, though Sid's words from the other night echo in my ear.

You don't have to live that way anymore. You're safe here.

It's so tempting to believe him. Most of the guys are comfortable ignoring me now, which is wonderful. Indifference is one of the safest emotions to inspire in a man. Aside from small talk at dinner each night, they expect nothing from me. I doubt they'll even notice once we're gone, aside from Silas who will be relieved to have his apartment back.

Well, Sid might notice too. Any time I pace near their

group, his eyes flick up. It only lasts a second and I wouldn't know he'd done it at all if I wasn't watching for the gesture. We're both guilty of… what, exactly? Curiosity?

I turn away rather than dwell on the thought for too long and keep walking.

It rained last night, but the sun has broken through the clouds to illuminate the dew that clings to every surface. The cedars at the edge of the farm shimmer with heavy mist, their scent lifting into the air. These have always been my favourite mornings. Nothing feels better than rolling back a wet tarp to find the world filmy and bright.

My walk takes me to the far edge of the property, where Silas keeps a small clutch of chickens (they're almost far enough away not to wake us up in the morning) and a beehive that everyone says is a huge pain in the ass to keep alive through the winter. I skirt by the duck pond, my boots sinking through the sodden grass into the muddy layer below. Closer to the farmstead, I pass a few rows of vegetable gardens. So long as Sid's guys meet their assigned grain quotas, they're free to use the remaining land how they wish. It's late enough in the season that many of the plants have started to die back. Yesterday's rain did the tomato vines no favours. They're greying, though fruit still ripens along a tangled trellis and it takes all my self control not to run off with a handful of cherry tomatoes.

And that's it. I can circle the whole acreage dozens of times in a day, going nowhere. Forget April's medicine, I better get that border job just so I know what the hell to do with all my pent up energy.

Late in the afternoon, April comes home, a massive stack of papers in her arms. "They put me in Grade 10," she says before I can even ask how it went. "Mostly because my English scores were high. I'm in a remedial math class for kids who've fallen behind, but I am *not* staying there."

"And what are these?" I reach to take some of her load and realize the papers are math workbooks going all the way back to Grade 6. They aren't bound with spines, like pre-Quake books, but crudely made with stapled printer paper.

"My ticket out of the stupid kid class."

"April, we do *not* call ourselves or other children stupid." I should have taught her this a while ago, but it never came up in our old lives. She had no one to compare herself to other than me and I had a ten-year head start on everything. How was I to know she's so competitive?

She grabs the workbooks roughly back from me. "I've got a lot of studying to do."

"Be careful about rushing yourself. You just finished your first day and—holy shit! There's *more*?"

Carlos has turned the corner into the gravel drive. He's loaded up with twice the stack April carries. He peeks around the pile, eyebrows raised as if to say *don't ask me how I got roped into this.*

April tosses her ponytail over her shoulder. "Social Studies and Science. Come, Carlos."

He follows obediently into the apartment. Behind me, several of the guys bust up with laughter.

"Ah, young love," says Wendell and next to him, one of the DomBert brothers swoons dramatically.

I throw them a scowl. "That is *not* what is going on."

"Oh, don't worry about it. Carlos is a coward," says James, refilling his basket with another scoop of grain. "No reason to think he'll ever make a move."

Sid even joins in. "She could do a lot worse."

"It's not personal. She just isn't interested."

"She told you that?" Sid's icy blue eyes flick up to meet mine. I should be firing back something about how we're sisters. She doesn't have to say she isn't interested because

I can *tell*. But it's also the type of thing I know he'll push against. How am I supposed to really know, when April hasn't had the chance to live around kids her own age before? I have no clue what she's attracted to, other than guys who once played Spider-Man. Real life attraction doesn't play out the same way it does in magazine photos.

Luckily, I'm saved having to answer by Carlos running back towards us. I resist pointing at him and saying *see*? He didn't bother staying with her! Nothing going on.

"We stopped by the mailbox and—" he starts, but Sid is already standing, hand outstretched.

"It came?" asks Sid.

"Yeah." Carlos passes him a pile that includes the newspaper and another paper, folded over and sealed with wax.

Sid rips the seal open and spends a couple seconds reading it silently. Both James and Silas are on their feet next to him. "Holy shit, it's official."

"Hell yes!" Silas, usually the group's sullen, silent shadow, thumps Sid on the back. The younger guys jump up, asking to see the letter too. I'm on the verge of joining in when Carlos side-steps the group to get to me.

"And this one has your name on it." He passes me another letter.

"Really? Oh!" The wax seal has a maple leaf imprint in the centre and around it, the words *Government of Salt Spring*. It brings a smile to my face. Someone has gone to the trouble of making an official seal, probably because it's easier to get beeswax now than it is to manufacture paper envelopes like people used in the pre-Quake days.

Government of Salt Spring. Heh. That long, stupid-ass name the government officials usually use must not fit.

I dart away, grateful now for the commotion around Sid, so that I don't have any attention on me. My first letter! I'm not sure what I'm expecting. Something from April's school? Tom Sullivan being his obnoxious self, but now by post? I open it carefully, not wanting to wreck the seal.

Dear Ms. Hollins,

Thank you for visiting the Ministry of Public Safety and Homeland Security. It is with deepest regrets that I must inform you that your application to the border guard has been unsuccessful. While we welcome applications from all members of Salt Spring Island's community, the presence of two demerits on your sanctuary papers unfortunately means—

I go back to the beginning and reread it, not quite believing the words. He can't be serious. Sid said sanctuary seekers have a legal right to employment and there was a court case about it. Except... he didn't say anything about demerits. I must be the exception. I am so horrible, Salt Spring doesn't even want me to die for them in their border guard.

Letters, I realize now, are the coward's tool. That weaselly bastard. At least Tom Sullivan has the guts to tell me he hates me to my face.

Blood pumps in my ears as I read the rest of it.

Should you resolve your file with the Department of Immigration to a state in which you have no demerits, we would welcome your reapplication—

I don't have any idea how to do that. Besides which, there isn't time. April is running out of insulin and this border guard idea was the only one I had that provided any hope of supporting us. I'm angry—at this shitty government, but also at myself. Why the hell did I think they would trust me? Of course they weren't going to give me a gun. If I were them, I wouldn't give me a gun either.

For the first time, I think I understand Tom's point. *Some people aren't made for civilization.* That was the gist of what he said. I am too dangerous and untrustworthy for this colony to take a chance on. The only way I can save April is by giving her up.

The thought makes me physically ill. I stumble away from the people chattering happily behind me. Whatever news Sid got, it's good. Isn't he lucky? No one is asking him to give up his sister.

At least they don't notice me sneaking away. Once I reach the open road, I start running. The direction doesn't matter. All I can hope is that the slap of my feet will drown out my thrashing heart.

She's all I have. She'll die if she stays with me. I'll die if I lose her.

I push myself harder, muscles responding as if there's a cougar on my trail. I picture April inside Silas's apartment, pouring over a dozen Math workbooks and my chest feels as though it could split in two. She has no idea what deep shit we're in. More than anything, I would love to grab her and tell her it's time to go. We never stay in the same place for too long and once again, this one isn't safe. The people here want to rip us apart.

What a clever tactic. Astolia used guns to keep everyone in line, but here, it's all paperwork. Letters are a lot cheaper than bullets. They'll cut us up and remake us. They'll decide where we live, who gets to be a family and what kind of work we're expected to do, all without firing a single shot. The Grand Astrologue could take some notes.

My legs grow weak and I stumble to a halt, grasping my knees for support. I have no idea how far I've gone, but at some point the sun set and the wind picked up. It catches all the hot, sore spots on my body, knifing me further. I suddenly become aware of the balled-up paper in my left hand, which has grown soft and crinkled from sweat. So much for treasuring my very first letter. I start ripping it. With each tear, my breath comes faster until the only way I can fight my mounting panic attack is by screaming. I howl like the wild animal these people take me for.

Finally, there's nothing left but shreds on the gravel road. I crash to my knees, fighting to regain my breath. When the lightness in my head subsides, I hear a raven cawing from a distant tree. All at once, I'm alert and listening for danger. Did someone see me? Am I going to get another demerit? But no one answers me besides the crow. This damn island. There's somehow too many people and too much space. How am I supposed to know whether I'm being watched?

I don't know where I am, but I ran in a straight shot. I might as well turn around. Much as I don't want to return to the acreage, April is there. I tell myself as I walk that I'll think of something. I've protected April all by myself for nine years. Something will come to me. I get nothing but mounting darkness for my efforts as a thin moon rises overhead.

It's about an hour (I'm starting to figure out how long those are) before I reach the acreage. I'm greeted by an intense pinprick of light that stops me in my tracks. The beam is a perfect circle, otherworldly and ethereal. I stare at it, stupefied. What's causing it? For all I know, it could be an angel.

Then it swings around onto me and I am blinded. I reach up to shield my eyes, and someone sighs from behind the glow.

"Fucking finally." Angels, it turns out, have dirty mouths.

"Sid?"

"Where the hell did you go?" He lowers the beam, striding forward.

"I went for a run." My eyes follow his hand, still curious about the light. As he nears, I recognize the shape of the tool he's holding. It's just a flashlight. I've found dozens over the years in abandoned houses, but never one that works.

"You got a letter and then you went for a run? Without telling anyone?"

"I'm sorry, were you worried?" I look up as he comes within a couple feet of me. Even in the gloom I can make out the stitch in his brow and the rapid rise and fall of his chest, as if he's been frantically running around for the past hour himself.

"No shit! Carlos said you got a letter from the government and then you disappeared! Of course I was—"

He's cut short by my body colliding with his. The tears I've been too angry to cry all day leak down my cheeks. Piney notes, mingled with cigarette smoke, fill my head as I breath him in. "Thank you."

Slowly, his arms wrap around me. I bury my ear into his chest, treasuring the thrum of an anxious heart. I should apologize for freaking him out, but it's the most beautiful sound I've ever heard. I know its rhythm so well. It beats with the same urgency mine has always given to April.

For the first time since my mother died, someone was worried about *me*.

THIRTEEN

SID IS SO damn practical. We clearly need to talk. I should explain myself after that little display, but while I would prefer to blurt everything out and be done with it, he insists I need to eat first. Everyone else has already finished dinner, but there are leftovers. It's only the usual stewed beans and potatoes that make up so many of our meals, but even if the food here is growing familiar, I'll never stop being amazed at how abundant it is.

"Where's April?" I ask.

"Already back to studying," says Wendell as he ladles the stew into a bowl. "Where *were* you?"

"Nowhere. Just went for a run."

"Told you it was nothing. You're paranoid, man," Young Tom tells Sid, with all the confidence of a nineteen-year-old boy. Sid only shrugs.

And that, right there, is why I trust him. He could have said, "*Actually, she showed up a sobbing mess, so suck it,*" but he doesn't.

Trust. The thought is freeing, and terrifying.

Once I've finished wolfing down my portion, Sid and I

"

head for the duck pond. The bench creaks as his bulk settles next to me. The scent of him hits me again and heat floods my cheeks, so I look away. It's silly, because there wasn't any special meaning to the hug we shared. Sometimes, a person just needs to crash out on the first friend they can find. And that, I realize, is what I have started thinking of him as. For all I've fought it, Sid Charles is my friend.

"So." His voice is a low rumble.

"So." I swing my legs, not ready to meet his eye.

"What was the letter about?"

"I didn't get the job." With every word, I can feel my world collapsing like a rotted-out building.

"The border guard one?"

"That's the one."

"Shit, I'm sorry. But there will be others, right? You'll find—" When I let out a sharp laugh, he cuts himself off. "No?"

"April's got days left before she runs out of insulin. I need to find almost a hundred dollars before then. Anything less is a death sentence."

His eyes about burst out of his head. "One hundred bucks?"

"Yep."

"How're you supposed to—how is *anyone* supposed to do that?"

"Well, getting a job would have helped."

"But nowhere is going to pay you that kind of money other than… Kayla, I'm sorry. I am *so* sorry." At that, he pulls a cigarette out of his pocket. "Maybe I can talk to Bill again."

"Who's—"

"Minister of Homeland Security and all that other stuff. He's a reasonable guy. I don't know why—"

"The letter said it was because of my demerits."

"That's bullshit," he says, striking a match aggressively. "You've only got one. I'll talk to Bill and—"

"Two. I've got two, Sid."

The match goes out as he stares at me, dumbfounded. "What?"

"I got a second one."

"How did you… Why didn't you tell me about this?!"

"I didn't think it was a big deal."

"It's a demerit! Of course it's a big deal."

"Well, I didn't know! How was I supposed to know?"

"It's in the word. *Demerit!* That's a bad word!"

Despite the situation, I can't help laughing. "You are such a goody-two shoes."

"Yeah, it's hilarious. So funny!" Sid shouts. "Now would you like to tell me what you did to get yourself written up again?"

"I… may have told Tom to fuck off."

For a beat, Sid stares at me, like he's in awe of what a shitshow I've created in so little time. Then, the shock abates, and he lets out the deepest, sincerest belly laugh I've ever heard. It's so loud, it's vaguely terrifying, like all Sid's big emotions. I've met quieter moose. But a grin spreads across my face all the same.

"Wow. At least you spent it on something good."

"Did he do this kind of shit to you when you were in immigration?" I ask.

"Yeah—well… no, actually. I was well behaved. James got written up once because, like you, he hasn't got a clue when to shut his mouth."

"Rude."

"Rude, but true. Tom likes me. Even stuck his neck out for me a few times. But it took a few years before he was willing to do that. It was like with you. I had to prove myself before he would trust me."

His words are ambiguous in a way I don't think he intends. Am I like Sid in that scenario, or Tom? I almost ask which he means, except the answer doesn't matter. Both are true. I'm untrustworthy *and* untrusting. I hate that I have anything in common with Tom Sullivan, even though it shouldn't surprise me. Sometimes, it feels like he's the only person on this island who's properly paranoid about outsiders.

"Enough about me. When did he give you the extra demerit?"

I tuck my legs into my chest. "He was at the hospital when I went to pick up April."

"Damn, that was weeks ago. Too late to appeal it." Sid pulls another match from his pocket. This time, he manages to light his cigarette. "Though he probably wrote you up for aggression, which is tough to dispute. It's your word against his. Court almost always sides with Tom."

"Honestly, if I had to argue with Tom in front of a court, I would probably end up strangling him right there," I say. "But he *would* deserve it."

"Just don't let him hear you say that." Sid takes a drag on the cigarette.

"I'm sorry I didn't tell you about the demerit. Will it get you in trouble? As my sanctuary host?"

He exhales smoke, clearly mulling over the question. "I won't lie. It's not *great* for optics. We might have a harder time getting future sanctuary cases. But overall, it's fine. Lots of newcomers get demerits."

"Still. I *am* sorry." I get the sense he's minimizing the situation, trying to protect my feelings. He probably doesn't want me sobbing all over him again. "If I ever can do anything for, um, optics? You just tell me."

"You don't need to worry about me."

"Maybe not, but I'd like to," I say. "I mean… you worry about me."

"I worry about *everything*. Just ask the guys."

"You broke the rules for me." I reach out and touch the scar on the back of his hand. His fingers tighten around the cigarette, as if he's startled by this tiny gesture. "And I'm beginning to realize that's a pretty big deal for you."

For a beat, we hold each other's eyes. I think he feels the shift between us. Ever since I came, he's been diligently offering his help, and I've thrown up walls every time. I've certainly never offered anything back before. My cheeks grow warm, so I speak out of a need to break the spell.

"You're a citizen, right? If I surrendered April, could *you* adopt her?" I ask.

"*Surrender* her? Why would you want to do that?" Sid straightens in his seat.

"Well, wouldn't that mean she would belong to Salt Spring? They would have to give her medicine."

"What? Did Tom tell you that?" Sid thunders, and I wince. Even if he's angry on my behalf, it's more than I can handle. "That piece of shit! He knows better! If he's playing me—"

"Woah! No, it wasn't Tom. It was the doctor."

Sid falls silent as he takes a long drag from his cigarette. When he blows out the smoke, his voice is calmer, but a hint of rage still shimmers beneath the surface. "Right. Okay, *new* piece of shit. The doctor shouldn't have said that to you, Kayla. That's *not* how safe surrender laws are supposed to work."

"Safe surrender?"

"It's a law that allows Salt Spring to accept unaccompanied minors as citizens. Or—just as important—kids whose guardians want to drop them off with us."

"*Want to drop them off*? What does that mean?"

"So, imagine this not-so-hypothetical scenario." Sid's gaze grows distant. "Lots of people out in the wilds don't trust us. They don't want to live with us. That's fine. That's their choice. Now, imagine someone out there gets pregnant. It's not what she wants. No safe way of terminating it out in the bush. She ends up carrying the child to term, and instead of abandoning it after birth, she comes to Crofton and lights the signal fire. We show up. We let her surrender the baby. No questions asked. She leaves. The baby grows up here, a full citizen."

"That's happened to you, hasn't it? You've taken babies at the border?"

He nods; his eyes still fixed on the inky darkness beyond the duck pond. "And I've brought over a pregnant girl who gave birth in the hospital a week later. She left on the next ferry off the island. It's a shitty situation. But the whole end-of-the world thing *is* kind of shit. That law isn't supposed to be for fifteen-year-olds with diabetes. He shouldn't have said that to you."

"Maybe," I say. "Or maybe he's right. I mean, it's not like I can take care of her."

"Don't say that."

"I don't even *want* to be here. At least April does." A part of me understands the women who made the choice to leave. There's something tempting in the idea of letting April live her life here, while I'm free to go back to Vancouver Island and everything I know. But what would be the point? With no one to love, why bother clinging to survival?

"I'm sorry, Kayla. You're caught in a stupid government oversight," says Sid. "Most of the laws about the hospital and citizenship are designed that way because we can't hand over our stash of pain meds to any random person coming from off the islands. But April isn't going anywhere. The legal framework should be different for chronic conditions. If you talk to Tom about it, maybe he could raise the issue with Council."

"I'm not talking to that son of a bitch about anything."

"Fair enough," says Sid. "It wouldn't solve the problem soon enough, anyway. You need citizenship *now*."

"So if I surrender her, then you take custody of her—"

He shakes his head. "No. You shouldn't have to do that. Plus, there's a good chance they wouldn't pick me. I've never hosted a sanctuary case before, and I've got no blood relation. They'll send her to someone with a stronger track record. Children's immigration is super strict. The only way you could legally share custody with me would be—oh, shit."

He stops so suddenly, I'm sure he's spotted something on the pond, but when I look, there's nothing but the moon's dim light reflecting off the surface. Yet Sid—pale as he always is—has somehow gone translucent.

"There's a way I could share legal custody?"

"It's two demerits, right?" Sid asks. "So, three years until you can apply for citizenship?"

"Yeah."

"Shit." He sets down the cigarette so he can crack his fingers against each other. "You could share legal custody with a citizen, get access to the medical system, all that garbage, if..."

"Just spit it out." I grab his arm, amazed he's thought of something. "I'll do anything."

He laughs, though not like when he found out I cussed out Tom. This laugh is chilling and hollow.

"We could share custody if you married me."

FOURTEEN

THE LAST TIME I thought about marriage, it was with Curtis.

We were going to get married one day. Or maybe we already were. Who knows what counts as legal authority when you're living in the woods? If there was an officialness we were waiting for, it was working up the nerve to tell my mum, because in our heads, it was a done deal. We were teenagers and we were married and we were idiots.

This proposal—if it is one—is just as reckless.

What would be the best reaction right now? Laugh it off? Punch Sid in the arm? The face? I keep waiting for the bubble to pop. This can't be real—so why is he still wearing that stricken expression? And why haven't I said anything?

I clear my throat, my voice startlingly calm. "But... but Tom wouldn't let that slide, would he? He'll give me another demerit or—"

Sid shrugs. "Demerits measure how much of a flight risk you are. You would actually *lose* a demerit if we got married."

"You're kidding."

"You would lose the second one if you got pregnant."

My body launches into the air. By the time Sid has a chance to react, I've put a couple metres between us.

"I'm not suggesting it! These are the legal facts. Do you want to know the legal facts of your situation?" He gestures wildly, face burning red. "They take it as a sign that you're integrating into the nation if you settle down and have kids with another citizen. Salt Spring still needs people, it's just... they expect gratitude. They need people who can prove they *want* to be here. Which, by your own admission, you don't."

"I'm not sleeping with you." I meant to say marrying. I'm not *marrying* him.

"Obviously not! It's fine, Kayla. You've clearly got a lot of trauma around sex or—or something. Frankly, I have *no* interest in dealing with—"

"*Excuse me?*" I fold my arms. "I do not have—"

"You shot me *on sight* at the border"—Sid holds up his scarred hand—"just for talking to your sister! Like I was trying to cart you two off like a pair of virgin sacrifices. If that isn't some post-sex cult bullshit—"

"Whatever! Fine, it doesn't matter. We're in agreement. We're not going to sleep together so—so what's the point of all this?" I take a step closer, not because I want to be near him, but because I would rather only the crickets eavesdrop on us. "I'd do a lot of stupid shit to save April. But *you* can't want to marry me. Why are we even talking about this?"

He's silent. I let out a sigh, because at last, something I've said has killed this foolishness. I was almost starting to consider it. Losing a demerit *and* getting insulin for April? Doesn't sound half bad.

"I'm not a virgin, by the way," I blurt out.

Sid's eyebrows lift. "Oh?"

"And it wasn't what you're thinking. He was a nice boy. I loved him."

"You're still not telling me everything."

"He was the only one," I say resolutely, and it's true. We got out of Astolia before I could be bartered off. "But I've got a right to protect myself, haven't I?"

"You do. Of course, you do."

I breathe in the cold night air, trying to clear my head. If we can think of one solution—well, more like fever dream—we can come up with another.

I sit next to him on the log bench. "Is there anything else I should know about my legal situation?" When he remains quiet, I try to butter him up with a compliment, to make up for the fact that I screamed for all the world that I never want to have sex with him. "You know a lot about that stuff. It's really helpful."

It doesn't work. He gives a snort and shakes his head.

I sigh. "Sid…"

He turns to look at me, eyes steely with sincerity. "I would do it."

"What?"

"Marry you. With whatever boundaries you needed. I would do it."

A claw closes around my heart. The chance for this to be a joke passed a long time ago. "But… why?"

He hesitates for a second, as if he knows that sharing this might send us down a path we can't escape. But ultimately, he pulls something from his pocket—the letter Carlos brought him earlier this afternoon. "This is why."

I know even less what to expect than I did with my own letter. The stamp in the corner resembles the one that adorned mine, only this one comes from the Office of Elections.

Dear Mr. Charles,

This letter is to inform you that your application to run in the upcoming general election of Salt Spring Island and her Gulf Island Territories has been approved. Per your request, your name will be eligible for a position on the general council. Constituents will have the opportunity to select your name from a ranked ballot—

The letter goes on, but it's more detail than I care about. "Holy shit, Sid!"

"Yeah."

"So you don't just read court cases for fun. You want to be in government."

"I really do."

"But why?" I'm not sure if this is a stupid question or not. Clearly the people in control of the colony wield a lot of power—look at Tom Sullivan—but with all the paperwork, most of the job seems like miserable pencil pushing to me.

"I've told you that the boys and I are outsiders, right?"

"Yes."

He takes another drag on his cigarette. "We weren't that different from you and April when we got here. The kids were young back then, so Silas, James and I applied to foster them together, but we weren't technically their guardians when we arrived, and we weren't citizens, so it was a flat *no*. Even when we got citizenship, it took forever to get the crew back together. Tom was willing to work with us, but the boys had their own host families and half of them disputed our case. The court decision was that we had to prove we had secure housing and a bunch of other shit before we could take them. So, we worked that border job for years, trying to scrape enough money together to apply for an acreage. But this place? It's still better than most. It survived the end of the world and has the human decency to give people a chance."

He gestures at the pond, but I'm sure he means more than that. The whole island. A quiet, peaceful place that, for all my protesting, is the safest I've felt in years. We're so removed from the problems on the mainland and larger islands. Barricaded into paradise.

"Last year, we finally got the acreage, and everyone moved in. It's all we wanted, but I still broke my back for years to get what this place promised me when I first came."

There's an undercurrent of anger in his voice, and yet I don't think he regrets it. He's fiercely protective, if anything, and it makes me want to lean in closer. I shift so that my body faces his, even though he's still fixated on some abstract point in the distance. "And that's why you want to get into government?"

"Yeah. I spent years fighting with red tape and people's preconceptions. And obviously, I'm not unique." He uses his cigarette to indicate me. "Salt Spring is the best place I've ever lived, but it could be better. It *should* be. So now that I've been a citizen for long enough, I'm running for office."

I've never heard someone sound so pissed off and so hopeful at the same time. It's not a combination I know how to parse. "And you think they'll actually let you join the government?"

"If I get elected, they have to."

"But people in power don't just give that up."

He laughs, which seems an odd reaction. But maybe I'm showing my ignorance about how this place works yet again.

"No, but if I run a good enough campaign, I might stand a chance. Tom's even been giving me some pointers." He rolls his eyes. "He considers me one of his great *success* stories."

"Seriously?" I snort. "Honestly, I think I would rather just have him hate me."

"It's not all bad. He's been on council since the Quake, so he knows how to get elected," says Sid. "And he figures the biggest thing in my way is optics. I'm a big, scary dude and by most people's standards, still a newcomer. I could use something that softens my image." And then he winces, as if the next words are painful. "I could use a wife."

"Oh." And so we arrive at the heart of the matter.

"You and your sister? You're kind of perfect. I would get a wife and kid in a two-for-one deal. Even the fact that she's sick is helpful. People eat that shit up."

"That's terrible!"

"I know. But it's true. You would be very, *very* good for optics."

It's the least sexy thing a man has ever said to me, yet my cheeks flush. "And... there's no one you would rather marry?"

"No one who wants me."

"Shit." So that's why he's willing to settle for my frigid company. I'm also curious how this can even be true, because Sid is a decent man. Even if he wasn't, he's a tall, jacked, blonde-haired, blue-eyed specimen. Women have settled for far less. There *should* be someone out there willing to marry him. But she isn't here. Instead, his earnest eyes are fixed on someone who only wants to use him for his citizenship.

I falter from his gaze. "But won't people be suspicious? Could we get in trouble?"

"Hypothetically, yes. But you've lived here a month already. It's the end of the world. People get married fast all the time. Once you find someone, what's the point in waiting?"

Like me and Curtis. If we'd waited, we never would have had any of the happiness we got to share.

I shove the thought of him away. It only makes this conversation more painful.

"So we'd need to make people believe we're actually in love with each other."

"Yeah. I guess we would."

I swallow, terrified at how seriously I'm considering his offer. "You've studied this legal stuff, right?"

"Basically since the moment I got here."

"So… you would tell me if there was some other way? A different loophole? Something easier than…"

"There's nothing." His gaze drops away. "Well… you *could* marry someone else. James might be willing. But the sex thing would be a sticking point."

"Very funny." It would be for most people. Even if there are other lonely men on the island, I don't fancy the idea of turning up at the local watering hole and auctioning myself off to the highest bidder. Like Sid said, most men would want sex out of the deal. So it's him or…

It's him. My only option.

"Kiss me." Who said that? Oh yeah. Me. The words are out so fast, it's more like an intrusive thought than a well-considered request.

Unsurprisingly, Sid startles backwards. "*Excuse me?*"

"Kiss me right now, Sid Charles, or I won't marry you." When he only gapes at me, I let out an exasperated huff. "We have to convince people! I want some proof you can be convincing before I say yes. Otherwise, I'll just end up in *more* trouble, with *more* demerits and then I'll have to give up April—"

"Right. Fair. Very fair." His eyes flick up and down, taking all of me in. The fact that he's got a look of outright horror on his face is *not* encouraging. But I hold my ground, though not for the reason I gave him. I'm far less worried about his performance than my own.

I haven't touched a man since Curtis died. What if I recoil at his touch? What if I start crying? Fake or not, being with someone could trigger me in a way that sends the whole charade crashing down.

He scootches closer to me on the bench. I close my eyes and tip my chin, a desperate refrain circling my mind. *He's just a body. Just a body. Just a body with free healthcare.* The heartbeat in my ears is at a fever pitch but he's clearly too nervous to get it over with, so I sit there, awkwardly waiting. I open my eyes, about to tell him to forget about it. We've already failed. But my scowl seems to be the kick in the ass he needs. Before I can call it off, his arm scoops me up by the waist.

It happens so abruptly, I let out a startled gasp, which means my mouth is slightly open when we meet. Pine and cigarette smoke flood my senses. We never discussed tongue, but he seems to take my parted lips to mean that he's supposed to test those waters, too. His crooked nose slides against my cheek as he deepens the kiss. At that, an avalanche cracks open inside my skull, drowning me in a deafening chorus of shrieks and screams; a massive, continental shift that is so profound, it obliterates everything that comes after it.

I don't know how long I spin inside the aftershocks. I'm barely sensible of myself. There's nothing to guide my body other than instinct and without mental intervention, my physical form just keeps kissing him. My hands tighten around the collar of his shirt as his tongue curls against mine. A soft *mmm* comes out of me. I press in further, brain gloriously blank. Even my legs are moving on their own, climbing towards his lap.

That's when he breaks away, shoving me back to my own side of the bench. Cold air rushes in where he used to be and with it, my conscience.

What the hell was that? In a weird way, it doesn't even feel like I was there for it. As I catch my breath, my mind's eye scans over the rubble left behind by the mental avalanche. It's a jumbled mess, the scattered boulders made up of worry over April, guilt on behalf of Curtis, and horror at how easily my body remembered how to kiss a man. But also... relief. We could pull this off. My experiment was a success.

I've got a lifetime of bad memories to get in the way of another relationship. But rather than overwhelming me, the cacophony renders me numb. It's perfect. I could go to town on him without feeling a thing.

"So... what do you think?" he asks.

I touch my mouth, analyzing the sensations of the past minute. "Sid?"

"Yeah?"

"You said you're trying to quit smoking?"

"Oh shit." He hides his face in his hands. "I am so sorry. I didn't think—"

"No, it's fine, just... keep working on it, I guess." I feel like an asshole, but what am I supposed to say? Tell him he's a good kisser? Even if it's true, what a weird thing to say to a friend! "Maybe we try for no aftertaste next time?"

"Next time?" He straightens to attention. Even seated on a bench, his height is intimidating. My heart hasn't stopped hammering since he kissed me, but it grows even more frantic as another instinct takes hold—the same part of my brain that fired a slingshot at him a month ago. But that version of Kayla wasn't the one who surfaced during the kiss. The paranoid side of me is weaker than the part that trusts him.

I nod, before I lose my nerve. "I think we could do this, if you still want to."

"I do."

What an ominous phrase.

"April runs out of insulin in a few days," I say. "How fast can we get this done?"

"We can go to City Hall tomorrow," he says. "I can ask Silas and James to serve as witnesses."

"Tomorrow, then. Great." Now that it's decided, I can't get away from him fast enough. I hop off the log and dust bits of bark from my pants, hoping it hides how much my hands are shaking. "And then… maybe we can stop by the hospital? Get Doctor Tremblay to put April's care in your name?"

"Sounds like a plan."

"Great. Thank you." I stare at him, knowing I should say more. Words should be easier with the man who will be my husband tomorrow. "You're… You're a really good friend."

"I wouldn't be so sure about that."

We both make laughing noises. Ha ha ha. This is so funny. What a quirky friendship we have!

At that I salute him. (Yes, a salute. What are my hands doing? My body is clearly still confused.) Then I take off towards the unit I share with April. Though… that probably is about to change, too. If I marry Sid, that means I'm staying long-term, and Silas will want his place back.

If I were braver, I would have stayed with Sid and started hashing those details out. For another thing, what's expected of me as a politician's wife? But whatever it is, I'll do it. It's not a lot to ask, if it means I can take care of my sister.

FIFTEEN

"**DO YOU REMEMBER** how to do factoring?" April asks over a bowl of oatmeal the next morning, notebook propped open in front of her.

"They've got you going to a factory at school?" I ask which prompts April to heave a laborious sigh. "No?"

"Kayla, it's a *math* thing. I'll just ask a teacher."

"Yeah… that's probably for the best." I'm not in the right condition for a long conversation, anyway. If April finds out what I'm planning, she will have opinions and I'm not interested in making this a committee decision. Luckily, she's so consumed with worries about school that she doesn't notice my hands shaking as I eat.

As we finish our food, Carlos knocks on the door, saying they need to catch the bus. I follow her out, under the pretext that I want to wave goodbye. The whole time, I can feel Sid's eyes on me, even though he's on the other side of the acreage, scattering feed for the chickens. I avoid looking at him, only to find James and Silas also staring at me; Silas with a scowl and James with all fifty million shark teeth on display. At least no one says anything until

April and Carlos are gone. Once the school wagon rolls past the drive, our younger charges aboard, all bets are off. James throws his arms wide.

"Salutations to you upon this most blessed of days!"

"Eat a brick, James," I snap.

"Oh, good. She's already learned how to communicate with you." Sid swings the empty feed bucket as he marches up the slope that leads down to the chicken coop.

"I wouldn't expect anything less from the woman who captured your heart."

Captured his heart? What did Sid say to them last night? Did he tell them about the kiss? Oh, *please* don't tell me he mentioned the kiss.

Then Silas whispers, "You sure you want to do this?" and it becomes clear James is full of shit.

"If Kayla's on board, then I am."

"*I'm* not the one who's going to back out." So that's how it's going to go, is it? We'll just goad each other to the altar.

Silas sighs heavily but doesn't argue. Together, the four of us head to the road. Wendell is out splitting wood and notices us leaving, but aside from the curious tilt of his head, he makes no attempt to stop us. All too soon, another wagon rolls up and we climb aboard. As we trundle off, the last moments of my freedom wilt away.

One more hour.

The bus kicks up dust, horses trotting past idyllic farms. James yawns and stretches in the seat across from me. Sid and Silas avoid looking at anyone.

The irony of what I'm doing isn't lost on me. What would my parents think if they saw me riding into town with a man I've known for barely a month, ready to become his legal wife? We fled Astolia precisely because they didn't want me forced into marriage.

Thirty minutes.

The bus stops a block away from City Hall. When I hop down, Sid catches me by the waist. I know he does it to be helpful, but my stomach seizes.

Twenty-five minutes.

We enter City Hall, and I can't help but notice that Sid automatically leads us in a path that avoids proximity with Tom's section of aisle twelve. The aisle that functions as the legal department is split in two between criminal courts and civic matters.

I'm getting married in a remodelled grocery store. This is not the illustration that picture books use at the end of their stories when Cinderella ties the knot with the prince. Is this what Curtis and I would have done, if we'd found a place that officiated marriages? Maybe it's fine that we never got to have a real wedding.

Twenty minutes.

We stand in line. A clock ticks in the corner. James yawns again.

Really, this is fine. I haven't wanted another partner since Curtis died, so I'm not giving anything up.

Ten minutes

We reach the counter. Sid makes our request for a marriage license and the first available judge to officiate. They check to make sure we've got our witnesses in order, go over my sanctuary papers and blot out one demerit.

See? I'm reaping the benefits already. This is so reasonable.

Two minutes.

Apparently, the courts can decide our matter quickly. No reason to dilly-dally. The aisle has been partitioned into numerous smaller rooms, for privacy, and we're called into one of them. Sid's hand slides into mine. I don't know if I need it to stay steady, but I hold on anyway. I should look like I'm in love with him, after all. Thinking this, I smile and hope any tears strike the officiant as those of a happy, blushing bride.

No, nothing I do will convince them of that. A happy bride would have worn something other than the shirt she slept in and muddy boots to her wedding.

One minute.

Once we're inside, a woman in a neat pantsuit smiles at us. We pass her the paperwork; I imagine her going over it and getting enraged when she sees the demerit I still have. But it doesn't faze her. Soon, she's grinning at the pair of us.

"Well, these days are the best part of my job." She steps behind a podium, where she can spread out her papers and ready a pen. "Are there any special words you prepared?"

"Ummm…" Obviously not.

"I, Sid Charles, take Kayla Hollins to protect and to care for. Both her and her family." He says it like he's rehearsed it and I feel awful that I don't have anything to return.

So I parrot his vow back at him. "I, Kayla Hollins, take Sid Charles to protect and to care for. For always."

Well, there's a flourish that's mine, I guess. Sid's brow pinches in surprise.

The judge murmurs a lot of legalese while we stand there, holding hands. Yadda yadda power vested yadda yadda Salt Spring and her Gulf Island Territories yadda yadda in memory of the Crown of Canada yadda yadda husband and wife.

Husband and wife.

There's a pause, but neither of us makes a move. Husband and wife. Someone has to make it official. I go up on my toes and pull him by the neck toward me to peck a kiss against his closed mouth. It is significantly less tumultuous than our kiss last night and for that, I'm incredibly grateful. He also smells slightly less like cigarettes. I don't think he's had one since last night so… progress.

James and Silas sign their names on the witness papers, then clap Sid on the shoulders. Sid turns toward the judge. "How long until our copy of the records is ready?"

"The legal department will mail them to you in a day or two."

Sid squeezes my shoulder. "We'll need to wait before setting things up with the doctor."

I nod, fighting the lump in my throat.

"Do you want to go home?" he asks.

"No." April and I need to move out of Silas's place, and I need a distraction. "It's my honeymoon. You're buying me shit."

SIXTEEN

"**HOW DO YOU** even know what honeymoons are? Did people go on honeymoons up in Port Alberni?"

Sid leans against a pallet jack, waiting as I examine a table full of rugs, towels, dish cloths and a host of other household linens. Every single one of them is beautiful: a fuzzy bathmat shaped like a fish with only one hole near the tail; an embroidered tablecloth that would be perfect, if not for a wine stain over one of the delicate roses. The prices aren't bad—a dollar for the bathmat, two for the tablecloth. Or to be more accurate: I am now learning how expensive April's insulin is. Pig pancreases don't come easy, I guess.

I put the tablecloth back, deciding I can do better, and hand a loonie over for the bathmat. "You're going to give this to April." I press it into Sid's arms. "Tell her it's for *her* washhouse."

"Oh, you've finally come around on that?" He looks ridiculous, clutching a teal striped fish to his chest, bits of fluff sticking to the hair on his forearms. That alone pleases me.

"Well, it's my house too, now." I stroll down the tables, relishing being on the buying end of the exchange. Sid already paid for a bed, plus a few more blankets and pillows, but I've got a small amount of spending money of my own. We agreed that the only thing that makes sense is if I move into his place. It will look suspicious otherwise, and Tom will still have to visit the acreage on occasion to oversee my sanctuary case. It's better if he finds us living together. Luckily, Sid says his spare room is devoid of gardening tools. We talked about maybe getting two beds, but that could tip someone off, too. Plus, April and I are used to sharing, so it's no big deal.

I currently have thirteen dollars to my name left over from when I bought April's first round of insulin. I know what my mother would say about it. Buy something that keeps me alive or makes me happy. Nothing else matters.

Besides, if I stop shopping, there's no excuse to avoid going home. And once we do that, I'll have to tell April.

"You're really in a mood." Behind me, there's a crunch as Sid pushes the pallet forward, following me over to a display of earthenware.

"Am I? You probably should have gotten to know me better before marrying me." Honestly, I'm surprised by the lightness in my voice. Not because I'm a morose, depressive person, but because I wasn't able to leave survival mode until now. The weight that has drifted off my shoulders is tremendous. It's done. The hard part is over.

Now some part of me is curious if it's possible to enjoy this situation.

The rows of tables at the exchange are a perfect place to start. I've lived in two separate colonies, raided countless pre-Quake buildings, and I've still never seen this much *stuff* in one place. Anything I could want is here. Bicycles, wool socks, bits of irrigation hose, even solar cells. A big sign sits next to them with the words *good as new* emblazoned on it.

"*That* is a scam," Sid says, annoyed. "Council repossesses all high-quality electrical equipment. You'd be lucky to charge a night light with those things."

"You should report them to Tom."

"He doesn't manage the exchange. It should be Leah Perry. She's Minister of Economics. Though, I think the exchange is a joint venture with the Ministry of Agriculture, so that would involve Adam Tilney."

My attention wanders as he rattles off names and offices of people on the island council, until I realize this might be the sort of thing I'm supposed to know as his politically-minded wife. Shit, does this position come with homework? Maybe April isn't the only one who needs to study up.

A table at the far end of the hall catches my eye and I gasp. Books. Hundreds of books.

"Sid!" I run to the booth. He follows at a leisurely pace. "Look at all of these!"

Many of the covers are damaged, the spines cracked, but there are *books*. It always broke my heart when I found a stash of books. In a kinder world, I would have filled my whole pack with them. April and I would read through the picture books at least and—I'm ashamed to say it—sometimes rip out our favourite pages to take with us.

All the usual suspects are here. Leatherbound classics that held up better against mould in unattended houses. Worn-out paperbacks for the voracious readers of romance, thrillers, and mysteries. Most exciting is a collection of comics, sleeved in plastic, that have barely faded. I would buy every one of them in a heartbeat if not for the price— five dollars an issue.

"Damn." Maybe I can afford one? April loves comics.

Even though the stories are usually disjointed due to missing issues, the pictures are lively and exciting. I'm admiring an issue of *Spider-Man Loves Mary Jane* when Sid reaches me.

"You should check out the library before you commit to any of those."

My hands go limp, dropping the comic. "You have a library? A real, current, working *library*?"

"Yeah, it's…" He startles when he notices that I'm on the verge of tears. "You really like books, huh?"

Like books? For years, they were the only access I had to people other than myself or April. The only part of the world that was ever new or changing. There's no way to express it, but I try all the same. "It's where I learned about honeymoons."

Sid's mouth quirks into a smile. "Well, then we *have* to go visit."

He probably only wants me to stop wasting time shopping for junk, but I don't care. Last night he spent so much time going on about all the ways Salt Spring was better than the rest of the world, but this is the first time I believe it could be true. This is the first real proof of paradise.

Even now, I expect it to be a joke. The books won't be free. My demerit will mean I'm not allowed to get a card. But when we arrive, Sid walks me to the desk and helps me talk through the process with the librarian. We've got my sanctuary papers with us because of the wedding, so the librarian has my address recorded in her ledger within a few minutes. I can take ten, for three weeks at a time, before they start asking for the books back, and it's so wonderful, I actually do start crying. I've been holding in a mountain of emotions today, and this is one too many, bringing the whole rockslide rushing down. At least it's a positive feeling.

The book limit turns out to be the only terrible thing

about the library. There are so many more than ten books that I want to read. I try to think of authors I've enjoyed and skim the shelves for their titles. I fill my arms with Lucy Maud Montgomery, Jane Austen, and—because I'm feeling brave—Agatha Christie. That's more for April than me, though I do plan on reading everything I've picked up.

I heft my pile onto the counter. If this doesn't make up for having to live here, nothing will. As the librarian stamps each book, I turn to Sid. "You going to get anything?"

He shrugs. "Nah, I don't think so."

"Really?" Apparently, I should have gotten to know my husband better before marrying him, too. "Why not?"

"I can carry those for you." He picks up the stack, ignoring my question.

"Those are due back on November third." The librarian hands me a slip of paper with both today's date and the one I have to return the books by. I stare at it for a beat. October thirteenth. I guess that's my wedding anniversary. I stuff the paper into my pocket and hurry to catch up with Sid, who is already outside with everything we purchased from the exchange.

"Do you like books?" I ask him.

"Sure."

"Why don't you like books? I thought—"

"I literally just said I do like them."

Nice try, Sid.

"I *thought*," I drag the word out. "That you would be into, like... non-fiction or something. I mean, you're really smart."

The compliment only draws a surly, "Oh yeah?"

"Yes. Obviously. You've got the whole bloody Council memorized. You read court cases for fun, so of course you're—"

"You don't have to do this." He shoves the pallet to the bus stop, his movements brusque.

"Do *what*?" Are we having a fight? I'm not opposed to yelling at him when necessary, but I don't understand what's set him off.

"*This*. Whatever it is you're trying to do right now." He grabs the bed frame and dumps it next to me. "Connecting! Trying to make this special or *mean* something. You don't have to. Like that kiss back in the court office—"

"Woah, is *that* what this is about? I'm sorry if I crossed a line, but it was our wedding and the judge was staring at us. We're supposed to be in love, in case you've forgotten."

"It's fine. It doesn't matter. It was barely a kiss. I'm just saying, you don't *have* to do it." He flails his arms like a willow in a windstorm. "This isn't real. You don't have to pretend like it is. It'll be over in three years and—"

"Wait, *three years*?"

"It's okay, it will probably be less."

"*Less*? What are you talking about?" None of this is making a lick of sense.

"April's medication. She's fifteen, right? So she'll be legally an adult in three years. But you'll both be citizens before then, so I'm guessing it will be more like two."

"But we're married."

"Yeah, but that's when we would get divorced. Because what's in it for you after that?"

"I…" *Divorced*. I've read the word before. I know what it means, or should mean, but I've never seen it in practice. The Grand Astrologue sure as hell didn't allow divorce to wreck his perfect community. "I don't know."

"Right, exactly."

He keeps talking as if we're agreeing on everything. I'm not sure Sid has looked me in the eye once during this conversation. If he did, he would notice how stunned I am.

"But what about you?" I say. "Are you going to want to get divorced in two years?"

He shrugs. "Hopefully, by then I'll be on Council. The election is scheduled for March."

"Oh."

Finally, it twigs. His eyes fly wide. "Holy shit! Did you think this was forever? Shit! I am so sorry, Kayla."

"No, no. It's okay." It's great news, right? The husband I don't want also wants to divorce me. We're just waiting for a convenient time. "I didn't know divorce was legal here."

"Yeah, totally legal. And you don't need my consent. You can leave whenever we're done with this. *Shit!* No wonder you were so freaked out this morning!"

I don't know what to say. I should be relieved, but something about this smacks of rejection. How stupid is that? Of course he doesn't want to stay married to me. Why should he give up the possibility of a life with someone he loves?

"All I'm saying is that this is temporary, right?" he says.

"Right."

"So…" He looks over his shoulder, as if to make sure none of the people who could get us in trouble for cheating the law are listening. But the city is filled with strangers who are all distracted with their own lives. Still, he leans closer so that he can whisper, the intimacy of his voice at odds with his words. "We shouldn't have to perform for each other. When it's just us, you don't have to kiss me or pretend you like me or anything like that. Okay?"

Pretend I like him? This time, I know why the words cut. He is the closest thing I've had to a friend in years, but apparently, he thinks I'm even faking that. Now I do want to yell at him. Except, we're out in public and I would rather the masses stay uninterested in us.

I reach for a safer objection, where I know logic is

indisputably on my side. "It was our *wedding*. Did you want that judge to report us to Tom?"

"You're right. I know you're right. Forget about it, okay? I don't know what's wrong with me."

"It's gonna be weird for a while," I say, hoping this will make him stop freaking out. "We've just... gotta get used to each other."

"Sure. I need to return the pallet and the jack to the exchange. If the bus comes by, hold them for me, okay? Then I'll help load everything."

"Okay."

When he leaves, I perch on the edge of the mattress, like a bird ready to take flight. There isn't any sign of the bus so I reach into my pocket in search of something to fiddle with. My hands close around the library receipt.

Due date.

I guess other things expire here, too.

SEVENTEEN

I'M STARTING TO suspect that it's not *people* who are silent on the bus, but me and Sid. Now that we've set up our imminent divorce, it's like he's satisfied with the terms of our agreement and has nothing to discuss. He stares out the back of the wagon, eyes unfocused. I'm not brave enough to ask what he's thinking about.

My nose is buried in a copy of *The Murder of Roger Ackroyd*. So far, they're talking about marrows, which is a British word for some vegetable. I haven't a clue which kind, but it doesn't matter. I'm not absorbing the story anyway.

Even with divorce on the table, we still have to live together for two years. Two years is a long time. People die in two years. Babies are born. Birth control being what it is, if Sid and I were actually married, within two years we would probably...

I pull the book tight to my face—too close to focus on the words, but I need to hide the heat in my cheeks. There's nothing to worry about. He's counting down the days to our divorce just as much as I am. But what are April and I going to do when the two years is up? Take the bathmat and leave? Find a home somewhere else? I guess I'll have a job by then.

Shit, I need to get a job. I need to find *something* to do with myself, so we don't land on our asses when this is over. But the only things I know how to do are foraging and hunting. Neither skill is relevant in a place with full-scale agriculture. And I already know the government has no interest in letting me handle a weapon.

If I'm going to keep living here, I need to find some new version of myself that provides value to this island. *Some people aren't made for civilization.* Tom's voice rattles in my skull. Who do I think I'm kidding?

We reach the acreage and unload everything we bought. Sid runs ahead to get the guys to help with carting furniture into the house, while I guard the pile. After a minute, a chorus of shouts reaches my ears, indistinct but excited. Sid's sharp bark punctuates them, *not* matching the jovial tone of the others. I take a few steps to the right and crane my neck so I can see down the hedge row that leads into the acreage. James is running towards me, waving what looks like a flag in in one hand and wearing something on his head. Horns? Yes, that's exactly what they are. Bright red, bedazzled devil horns, attached to a hairband.

"There's the lady of the hour! I've brought your headdress." James holds out the item I mistook for a flag, though I still can't tell what it is. Not until James pushes back my curls and ties the white fabric behind my ears.

A veil. He cut up a pillowcase to make me a wedding veil.

And running after him, roaring like an avalanche, is Sid, trailed by Wendell, who's trying to force him to put on a plastic top hat. Behind them are the other boys, dying with laughter.

"Leave her alone! She doesn't want to deal with you!" Sid yells.

"Oh, come on. You two can't do something so brazenly stupid and expect us not to celebrate it." James spins me around, grabbing each of my shoulders so that all I can see is his magazine-worthy smile. "What do you say, Kayla? Silas splurged for a couple bottles of real wine. Carlos even attempted to bake a cake."

"It's not an attempt, it's a cake! A pound cake," Carlos protests, his indignation a little less effective since he's sporting a baseball cap with a spinner on it.

"A real, honest-to-goodness cake. I think we've got ourselves a wedding!" James throws his arms out and the boys cheer. Every one of them is wearing some sort of ridiculous headgear: Silas has a Santa hat, Wendell is in a pink fedora, and Young Tom has a pair of ears I recognize as belonging to Mickey Mouse, thanks to picture books. The brothers DomBert are in a spikey green crown and a foam maple leaf.

"She hasn't even had a chance to tell her sister!" Sid yells.

"Well, it's a little late for that." James shrugs, like he knows he technically screwed up, but doesn't care.

"April knows?" Shit. I'd been hoping she was still at school and I would have a chance to gather my thoughts before confronting her. How much time did Sid and I spend dicking around at the exchange? I really need to learn how to tell time.

"Yeah, sorry about that. Didn't know it was a big secret."

"Then where is she?" Not in the… wedding party?

"Back at the house. I think she wants to talk to you about it," says James, as if this is all perfectly normal. Nothing to worry about. "But she *did* accept a flower crown."

"Well… at least I don't have to think of a way to bring it up."

"See? That's the attitude! You are going to be so good for him."

"*James*. Leave her alone." Sid is still fending off the

hat, which bears the words *HAPPY NEW YEAR* in gold lettering. Seriously, this is so—wait.

A grin springs onto my face as I catch onto the vision. "This was so thoughtful of you!"

Sid's rage shifts to pale-faced terror as he realizes what's about to happen. "Don't you dare gang up on—"

"Are you going to play your guitar for our first dance?" I ask James.

"I will serenade your love until the stars fall from the heavens." He bows and plants a kiss on my wrist. I have never been so thrilled to see Sid's face burning with irritation, a feeling which grows sweeter when he lets Wendell cap him with the top hat. Really, he should thank me. Someday, when we're divorced, he'll look back on this moment and feel nothing but sweet relief that I'm out of his life.

But I'm here now. I've got two years to leave my mark.

"All right, groomsmen! We need to haul the bride's dowry into the building. Hup, two!" James claps his hands and the younger boys holler, rushing to help.

I take this as a cue to lace my arm through Sid's, so he can escort me. "Shall we, husband?"

"I thought we just talked about this. Not performing for each other?"

"*You* talked about it. Besides, we're doing it for your boys. If they want to throw a party, I say why not?" I turn a cheeky grin up to him. "In fact, it would be far more unnatural for me to pretend not to want this."

"You *want* this?"

"Of course I do! There's cake. I've never had cake! You aren't going to deny me my very first cake, are you Sid Charles? On my wedding day?"

"Fine!" He falls into step next to me. "How long are you expecting me to wear this thing?"

"Oh, you better keep it on all night." I toss my head, so

that the veil flutters. "I'm not taking mine off."

He scowls. "Yours isn't plastic."

"Then you need to allocate more of your budget to James's silly hats."

"Are you kidding? This isn't even the whole collection. He has a problem."

"I think it's delightful."

"You haven't had to live with him for twelve years."

Twelve years. Was that when they immigrated? There are still so many things I don't know about Sid. Even if our marriage is fake, I should know them. Not that I haven't tried asking, but I could try harder. I run my free hand along his bicep and smile. "How did you meet everyone? Where did you guys come from?"

His eyes slide over my hand, then back to my face. The muscles in his arms are tense against my fingers, but he softens the longer I smile at him. This ridiculous veil is proof that I'm being nice to his friends, which makes it harder for him to brush me off. He can make fun of James all he wants, but his crew are family to him.

"Vancouver," he says at last.

"Really? But that's so far away!"

"I know. That's where James came in. He was the only guy Silas and I knew who could sail a boat."

"A *boat*? How'd you get your hands on a boat?"

"Yeah, it's a long story. And I want to tell you. You deserve to know, but... we've got other things we need to focus on." He inclines his head down the gravel path.

That's when I see her. April sits on the front steps, determinedly looking at no one, plastic flowers tucked into a braid that wraps around her head.

"Right." I give Sid's arm a parting squeeze and walk toward her, hoping the cloth headdress doesn't make me look too ridiculous for a serious conversation.

"Hey, wanna talk?" I try to keep my expression light, not a small feat given the sharp pucker of her mouth.

"Oh, *now* you want to talk." April rises, sticking her nose in the air as she heads into Silas's apartment. At first, I think she's trying to walk out on me, but she tosses a look over her shoulder. "Well, are you coming?"

"Fine." I would rather talk to April without an audience, anyway. Once I'm inside, she locks the door. I take a deep breath. "First off, I'm sorry I didn't say anything this morning. But I wanted—woah! What are you doing?"

April shoves a towel into my arms. "I'm taking you to the wash house. You need a bath. Then, we're fixing your hair."

"Excuse me?" I try to fight her, but she's surprisingly forceful.

"And you're wearing this." She presses a flimsy dress covered in sunflowers into my arms.

"April, it's too cold for this." I only wear it at the height of summer. Half the time, I swim in it.

"I told James you would say that. But seeing as it's the only dress you own, it's what you're wearing." April pushes me down the hall towards the washhouse. "Don't worry, they're making Sid do this, too."

"Fine," I say. "But only because I'm so relieved you're not pissed with me."

"Pissed? Kayla, I could *murder* you! How could you do something like this without telling me?"

"Then why are you playing along with this whole wedding thing?"

"Because James let me have some makeup an old girlfriend left behind. He said so long as I dolled you up tonight, I could keep it." She pulls two tiny tins and some thin brushes out of her pocket. "This one's made with charcoal. And I think this is beetroot?"

"Why are you so easy to buy off?"

She shuts the washhouse door. "Get in the tub. We can argue while I untangle your hair."

I grunt and pull off my T-shirt. The tub has already been filled; James really did think of everything. It's not warm, but I've rinsed off in colder streams. I sud up with a bar of lye soap, occasionally bracing my hands on either side of the tub as April mercilessly yanks a comb through my curls.

"Are you trying to make this hurt more?"

"I don't know. *Maybe.*" April tugs again. "You married a stranger."

"C'mon, Sid isn't really—"

"You married a stranger! You couldn't think of some other way to get a bit of stupid money and so you—"

"I didn't have a choice. We need his citizenship."

"But what about when we become citizens? This whole problem is temporary, but now you've run off and married him—"

"The marriage is temporary, too." I twist my head to try to see her. She's clutching the comb so hard her knuckles are white. "Sid says we can get divorced once we're covered."

"Divorced?"

"That's what he says."

"Kayla! What if he's tricking you? Is that why you went along with it?"

"No." I fix her with a firm eye. "I agreed to it before I knew about the divorce thing. He didn't trick me. He doesn't even want to have sex."

"That doesn't make sense."

I sigh, sinking deeper into the soapy water. "It's still true."

April doesn't have a response to that, but she does go back to untangling my hair. Her hands are gentler now as she mulls this over instead of taking out her anger on my scalp.

"I guess a place with a hospital and a school might have divorce too," she says at last.

"Right? Oh! And guess what? Downtown, they have a library!"

That brings out a gasp. "Yes! Did you see it? A girl in my English class told me about it. She says it's even bigger than the one at school."

"It's *amazing*. Sid took me after the wedding."

"You've got to take me with you next time!"

"Oh, absolutely."

She tries to laugh, only for it to catch in her throat. "Kayla... I thought you were stuck forever."

"No. Just a couple of years."

"Well... that's not too bad, then." She blinks, the relief so intense on her face, she's obviously struggling not to burst into tears. "You should have told me first, but... I guess it's better than the government splitting us up."

"Definitely better."

"I ... I was so worried. I couldn't handle it if you ruined your life over me." She rubs her eyes.

"April, if it was for you, it wouldn't be ruining my life."

"Shut up and face forward." She sniffs back the last of her tears. "I need to get this hair tamed."

She's in a much better mood after that, chattering about how excited she is to try the makeup on me. Once she's finished with the matts in my hair, we do our best to squeeze out the excess water and I dry off.

Apparently, this occasion calls for every frilly thing we own. April lends me a seashell necklace of hers we picked up ages ago, and despite my reservations, I don the sunflower dress. April flips to a page in one of her favourite magazines and does her best to recreate something called a cat eye. What this means is she spends an exorbitant amount of time, painting, wiping away, then repainting the charcoal cream on my eyelids. Finally, she's satisfied and blends a small amount of the beetroot into my cheeks before painting my lips a deep red.

"You know, James is right. Now that I know you've got your divorce planned, this is hilarious," she says, pinning the veil securely to my head. "Fun, even."

"Right?"

But all April's words have done is highlight how strange my own reaction was when Sid told me the news. She heard about my impending freedom and was immediately happy. So why do I still have this unsettled bubble in my stomach?

Once I'm trussed up to April's satisfaction, she unlocks the door, though doesn't let me through. There's a lot of whispering and sniggering. She reappears, clutching a bundle of heather tied up with—I suspect—another piece of the pillowcase on my head. The ends of the bow are frayed, but it's undeniably a bouquet.

"We're ready." She beams at me. "Just walk down the stairs. James took care of the rest."

This is so ridiculous. I only agreed because it annoyed Sid. I bet he didn't let James pressure him into dressing up. There's no way his lips taste weirdly of beets right now. But I step out, because Carlos made a cake, damn it.

Sid isn't wearing makeup, but he does look different. The five o'clock shadow is gone from his jaw and he sports a black jacket to match the top hat. Very smart.

I grin and close the door behind me. At the sound of the latch, he turns to look at me. And swallows.

For a second, I'm frozen. James starts strumming his guitar as the other boys cheer. One wolf whistles, but I don't see who, because Sid has not blinked since locking eyes with me.

My whole body explodes with heat. What idiot said it

was too cold for a sundress? I'm burning up. Unfortunately, that means I'm flushed across my boobs, which he's never seen so prominently displayed before. Or my shoulders. Or my arms. Or my calves. Shit, there is a lot of me available and he cannot stop staring.

"Go on, Kayla." April prods me in the ribs and I stumble gracelessly down the first step. Automatically, Sid reaches out, and instead of catching myself on the railing, it's his hand that guides me down the stairs. I'm shaking as I draw in front of him, like we did in the courthouse. Only now, Silas is officiating, still decked out in the Santa hat.

He's wearing the only serious expression in the entire party. Well, him and Sid, who is putting a lot of work into breathing right now.

Silas doesn't bother with most of the ceremony. He simply raises his arms like a preacher and says, "By the power vested in me as Lord of all Christmas, I pronounce you man and wife. Now, kiss the bride."

"Kiss the bride! Kiss the bride!" everyone chants, including April. James even changes the rhythm of the chords he's strumming to keep time. "Kiss the bride! Kiss the bride!"

"Sid," I whisper. "You know you have to."

Another swallow. But he nods and leans in. I reach for his neck and his hand closes around my waist, lifting me towards him. I've barely registered the surprise at his touch—warm through the thin cotton dress—when our mouths meet. The boys erupt into cheers, but the din is nothing next to the blood pounding in my ears.

It isn't a long kiss. Why should it be? Just long enough for his lips to part against mine. Long enough that I twist my head to get a better angle. My tongue brushes against his and my belly swirls. He nips softly at my lip.

Just a short kiss. And as I land back on my heels, I

could almost kiss James, too, because Sid tastes of mint instead of the cigarettes. Well, that and…

Sid reaches up, touches his mouth. "You… had this sweet flavor? Like…"

"Beetroot?" I supply.

"Oh, that's it." He laughs, and the tension in my chest releases. Maybe that whole rabbit in a snare act he gave me on the stairwell was nerves. James probably told him he had to kiss me and as Sid made clear earlier, he doesn't want to do that.

But that *swallow*.

I'm overthinking this. Sid isn't attracted to me—the woman who fired a slingshot at him. And why would I want him to be? I've got no interest in pursuing him because I'm never risking what happened with Curtis again and—

Curtis.

It truly hits me that I've kissed another man three times now. Even if there were good reasons every time, I'm a traitor.

"As the lady requested, a first dance!" James starts a tune with a slow, plucked accompaniment. "Please enjoy *The First Time Ever I Saw Your Face*, arrangement courtesy of the Gordon Lightfoot songbook I snagged at the exchange last week."

His tenor is a perfect, folksy warble. It's not a song I've heard before, but immediately, I love it.

"Come on." Sid tugs my hand. I follow him to a spot beyond the ring of plastic chairs and overturned logs. The field of grain sways gently behind us, dancing along in the faint autumn breeze. It's beautiful—romantic, even. More than I ever dreamed of getting in a wedding. Except…

Sid puts his hand on my back. It's everything I could wish for—but with the wrong man. My legs are leaden, and he shifts his grip so that my spine bends the direction he wants me to go in. "Just follow my lead."

"You know how to dance?"

He smiles, extra roguish with that broken nose. My skin tingles where his thumb presses above the dress's neckline. "Stay here long enough, and you get to learn a lot of things."

I laugh as he twists his wrist in a way that sets me spinning. How did my body know what he wanted from me?

When I finish the full circle, he's there. I land in his arms, closer than before, and he lets us sway. "You look beautiful, by the way."

"Thanks. You aren't half bad yourself."

He grins, and my pulse flutters. I'm in two places at once. My mind wants to go to the place where I grieve my dead, heart locked tight against another loss. But my body won't follow. It's too busy being *here*, basking in the warmth of his chest pressed against mine; tightening my grip over his hand, so that he knows to keep holding me close. My tongue teases at my lip, searching for something.

In response, Sid clears his throat. "I should apologize," he says. "I didn't realize you wanted a real wedding. If I let you down—"

"No! It's okay. I thought I didn't." How could I have known? Nothing like this was ever an option with Curtis.

"So you're happy, then? This is good enough?"

"Sid, it's..." I almost say *perfect*. But it can't be. "I mean, I could use a slice of cake."

He grins from ear to ear. This is the most I've seen him smile in one night. "Yeah, me too."

THE CAKE IS delicious. Sweet, dense, with just a hint of lavender to cut through the thick crumb. Carlos even drizzled honey over the top so the rose petals would stick.

I don't think April's magazines could do better. Sid reverts to his curmudgeonly self when he finds out Carlos used a whole pound each of butter and eggs, but all I have to do is smack him and say, "It's our wedding and I'm *worth* it!" for the mood to recover.

What can I say? The wine is working.

There isn't more than one glass per person, but that's enough to give an inexperienced drinker like me a pleasant buzz. James points out that Carlos and April are too young to have any; since it's our wedding, Sid and I get their servings. That's enough to make everyone's jokes hilarious for the rest of the evening.

We spend hours singing along to James's guitar, and every one of the guys takes a turn dancing with me and April. By the end of the night, my feet are aching, my skin prickling with cold. I curl toward Sid, seeking body heat.

A second later I'm waking up with a gasp, my head sliding off his arm. Sid takes that as our cue to leave and helps me teeter my way up the steps to our apartment.

"May you be blessed with a son in nine months!" James calls, and the other boys howl.

I grab the railing, staggering with some mixture of wine and exhaustion. "Does he know we're not…" I can't remember how to finish that sentence, so I make a thrusting motion with my hips.

"James? Oh, yeah. He knows. But that's never gonna stop him."

"But you know, it was good practice," I say.

"Dry humping the air?"

"No! The kiss. That was good practice."

Sid gives a disbelieving laugh. "For what?"

"For like, your election stuff." I'm not explaining this as well as I mean to. It all makes sense in my head, but Sid is staring at me like I've got crickets between my ears.

Which... maybe I do. Wow, the crickets are loud tonight.

"I think we've gotten more than enough practice at this point," he says as we reach the top of the stairs.

"No!" I slap him on the chest. "I mean, yes. Like, we got it right that time. You smelled good! And I was pretty good too, right?" I rock my shoulders up and down, so that the straps of my dress tug against the triangles covering my boobs.

"Sure?"

"Yeah... Curtis thought I was a good kisser." I yawn so deeply, my jaw aches. "When do we start doing all the politics wifey stuff?"

"Really looking forward to that?"

"Well, I need to know when I'm supposed to kiss you. Psych myself up for it."

"Wow. Okay, time to get you in bed."

A hand sweeps under my knees and I fall into his arms, laughing and kicking my feet. He hauls me upstairs to his apartment, which I guess is my apartment now too.

"You are a wiggly drunk."

"Ha!" I loop an arm around his neck. He smells *so* good, and I burrow my face into him.

He sets me down inside the room I plan to share with April, on the new mattress. Someone must have carted it inside while I wasn't paying attention.

"For the record, Sid," I say as he moves to shut the door, "you're a good kisser, too."

He smiles, giving no hint as to what he's thinking. "Good night, Kayla."

EIGHTEEN

IN THE MORNING, I desperately want to fling my traitorous body into the Pacific Ocean.

"Oh, shit…" I press my face into my pillow as memories of yesterday flood back.

"Are you hungover?" April is awake, one of the library books in her lap.

"I don't think so? We didn't have that much."

"Still more than I got."

"Believe me, you didn't need it." I reach for my pack, digging out a sweater and pair of pants, since there's no way I'm flouncing around in this dress for another minute. Still, my hand lingers as I stuff it into the bag. My wedding dress.

I don't fancy meeting Sid after I ended last night as a giggling mess in his arms, but when I open the door, he's nowhere to be seen. In fact, there's *nothing* to be seen. In terms of layout, the apartment is identical to Silas's but the couches and blankets are gone. The only sign of human habitation is a pair of work boots next to the front door. There's nowhere to sit, nothing on the walls, not even dirt on the floor. If the place wasn't so clean, I would assume it was abandoned.

"What the hell?"

"Yeah. Weird, isn't it?" says April behind me.

"Did I marry a psychopath yesterday?"

"Maybe. Maybe he's married lots of women before. Maybe he murders them in the living room, scrubs it, then hides the bodies under the floorboards."

"Oh, shut up."

"Of course, if that's the case, then it's *too* clean. Draws suspicion."

"You read too many murder mysteries."

Still, I hesitate in the doorframe. Why is this bothering me so much? I don't care how much crap Sid owns, do I? Even if this is abnormal—which based on Silas's place, it probably is—it's not a crime. Maybe he likes sliding around the wooden floors in his socks. But that unnerved feeling doesn't go away. Staring me in the face is hard evidence that I know absolutely nothing about my husband.

"He must eat breakfast in the kitchen," I say at last. "We might as well try going there, too."

April sighs, picking up one of her notebooks. "I guess."

Up until now, we'd been avoiding most of the shared spaces around the acreage. Our rations come with oats and those are easy enough to cold soak overnight, so no need for the kitchen. We usually eat dinner at the firepit outside. It feels safer than going into confined quarters with a whole bunch of strange men. But if we're going to live here long term, maybe it's time to explore our new home.

I lead the way downstairs, only to stop in my tracks once I push the kitchen door open. April bumps into me, but once she sees what's in front of us, she's equally awestruck.

"Wow…" April says.

I've been inside of big kitchens before, back when April

and I squatted in abandoned houses. But what makes this one impressive is that it's fully stocked. Drying herbs hang from the rafters, the shelves piled high with bags of beans, oats, wheat, potatoes, carrots, and onions. A haunch of smoked meat rests on the counter, wrapped in wax paper, and a bouquet of salad greens is stored with a glass of water beneath them, to slow wilting.

I haven't seen a store of food this size since... have I ever? I wish I remembered Port Alberni better, then maybe I wouldn't feel so small. I wander past the stove to a storage unit and pull open drawers to find bowls, spoons, and wooden cups. When I happen upon the knife block, I'm tempted to take the butcher knife and stash it in my bag, but I'm guessing they'd notice if it went missing. A washtub has a collection of dishes stacked inside of it, their surface still damp. Above it is a chart marking everyone's dish duty day. That's got to be Sid's doing.

"I'm totally studying here from now on," says April, spreading her books out on the massive oak table at the centre of the room.

"Eat up. You've got school," I say, passing her a mason jar filled with our overnight oats.

"It's Saturday."

"Oh. Right." Damn it, not this nonsense again. "So... what do you want to do today?"

"More factoring," says April, sharpening a pencil. "My teacher says it's the key to solving polynomials."

Whatever that means.

"Cool. Maybe I'll help on the farm, then."

Outside, Silas is leading the guys as they pack grain into government-issued bags destined for the Ministry of Agriculture. When I ask him if there's anything I can do to help, he only shrugs.

"We've already got this under control." He gestures at

the two assembly lines of guys filling, tying and stacking bags. "But maybe you could clean up the garden beds? We haven't had much time to deal with them lately and now the weeds are taking over—"

"That sounds perfect."

I'm more used to working on my own, anyway.

The raised beds do shown signs of neglect. Quite a few green tomatoes are rotting from the wet weather, so I start by gathering any that are still in decent shape to ripen indoors. We're not wasting tomatoes on my watch. Once I'm done harvesting, I push the leaf litter around so that it isn't smothering any of the lettuces. In the process, I unearth several slugs which I have the satisfaction of tossing to the chickens. Finally, I tackle the weeds.

I don't recognize all the cultivated plants. Most, like the potatoes, shelling beans and dent corn, are things I tried to keep going in the little plots April and I circled each year. But there are also rows of something with frilly leaves that looks like carrot tops without carrots attached, and another plant that clearly belongs to the cabbage family, but instead of forming large heads, there are knobby bulges up and down the central stalk.

What I do know well are the weeds. I rip up patches of chickweed and deadnettle, depositing them in a large basket. By the time I'm done, my muscles are aching pleasantly. I find myself thinking that if this is what it means to be married to Sid, I'll survive. Two years of working with plants sounds nice. What will these beds look like over the course of a year?

Once I'm done, I have a substantial basket of greens. A few are too sun-scorched to make for good eating, so I drop the detritus off at the compost pile. The rest, I carry into the kitchen.

April is still chewing her lip over the math workbook,

so I let her be and hunt through the kitchen drawers until I find a cutting board. It feels incredible to wield a knife again. Natural. I chop the greens until I've got a large salad, then touch it up with a few dried blackberries. The noon sun is shining overhead, so I call into the fields that I've made lunch, if anyone wants it. Carlos, James, Wendell, and Dominick are the first to abandon grain packing duty and run inside, but they're less thrilled when they see what I'm serving.

"What the hell is that?" Dominick asks.

"I think we usually compost these?" says Wendell.

"Compost?" Who knew Salt Spring Islanders could afford to be so wasteful? "You guys are throwing out perfectly good food!"

"Is there dressing?" asks James.

"Hold on, I'll make some." Carlos opens a cupboard and pulls a few bottles out—one filled with golden liquid, the other slightly pink.

"You are such babies. It's food!" April comes to my defence, taking a forkful without ever lifting her eyes from her textbook.

But no one else touches it until Carlos drizzles a mixture of the two liquids over the leaves. Finally, they tuck in.

"This isn't too bad."

Thanks a lot, James.

Dominick winces. "Do we have any dill?"

"No, I want to taste this as is." Carlos chews thoughtfully, not at all put off by my creation. "Yeah, this works. I could use this. What did you say this was, Kayla?"

"Chickweed and deadnettle."

At that, Dominick spits a leaf out. I smack him on the shoulder. "The names make it sound worse than it is!"

"How many years were you living out there without dressing?" James asks, awestruck. At least he's finishing his bowl. "Tragic."

"It's good! What is wrong with you guys?" I mean, it's better when I serve it over salmon or something else with a bit of fat. I grab a leaf and taste it, wondering if the sun scald was worse than I thought. "*Oh.*"

It's exquisite. Carlos's additions have done what the salmon always had to, upping the robustness of the flavor. But there's something else. A fruity pucker that sears my tongue yet leaves me wishing for more.

"What did you do to this?" I round on Carlos. "What was in that—what did you call it? Dressing?"

His eyes widen, afraid I'm about to bludgeon him like I did Dominick. "Canola oil and apple cider vinegar?"

"*Vinegar.*" I slap a hand on the table. "That's what it is!"

"Don't take too long, guys." Sid's voice echoes in the kitchen as the last four come in from the field to grab a bowl.

"Your wife made weed salad," says James, turning to him with a grin. "Isn't that nice?"

His brow furrows. "What?"

"Sid!" I call, a new hope seizing me. "Can I take cooking lessons from Carlos? Please?"

"We need Carlos for harvest," says Sid. "Plus, he's at school half the time."

"Damn it." I want to know Carlos's tricks. Food is life. It's always been my guiding drive, and unlike everything else on this island, I can understand why this is valuable. Food that only existed in books seems possible now. Vinegar. Cakes, even!

"I mean... it would be good to have someone other than me who knows how to cook on the farm, right? And I still have to make dinner every night. You could follow me around while I do it." Carlos blushes so deeply it shows even on his dark skin. "If you want."

"Yes! Yes, I would like that."

"And I wouldn't mind if you showed me what else you

used to eat in the woods. In case we're missing things," he adds. "Like, I never know what mushrooms are safe."

"I can totally do that!"

"But so you know, I'm not *that* good."

"Carlos, you're a god for all I know. Thank you!" I wrap my arms around him. The poor kid looks like he's seconds away from bursting into flames.

All day, I shake with excitement, anxious for them to finish work so I can pester Carlos with questions. While I wait, I open drawers and cupboards over and over, taking stock of all the ingredients we might use tonight. It's strange to think that such a young boy knows things I don't, but I guess that's the advantage of growing up here, rather than out in the wilds.

Eventually, April tells me that I'm *ruining the vibe* for her, so she heads upstairs to the empty apartment.

"At least there won't be any distractions," she says dolefully.

When Carlos finally finishes work for the day, he comes bearing eggs recently collected from the farm hens.

"We're having huevos rancheros," he says, setting the basket on the counter. "Well. White people huevos rancheros."

"But you aren't white though, are you?"

"No, but a white lady taught me how to cook." He shrugs. "We do the best we can with what we've got."

We start by crushing chilis and garlic together, and rendering pig fat so we can fry everything once the chili sauce is ready. From one of the cupboards, he pulls out a pot of beans left to soak overnight and gets them on to boil, so we can have them on the side. That will help make what traditionally used to be a breakfast meal more filling and dinner appropriate. And tomatoes! He pulls a jar of canned tomatoes out of the cupboard and adds them to the sauce.

"Do they have jobs where you do this all day? Just cook for people?" I ask.

"Sure. There are a couple of restaurants in town. It's hard to get those jobs, though." He cracks the eggs carefully into the pan, so not a single yolk breaks. "The woman who hosted me when I first came here ran a café. She taught me all this shit."

That explains why the others defer to him in the kitchen. I remember Sid saying the group was split up when they sought sanctuary, but I hadn't thought about how that would shape them all into different people.

"How old were you when you came over?"

"I was five."

"Wow! That's pretty young. Why didn't you stay with your sanctuary host?" Working in a café, cooking food all day sounds amazing to me.

"I thought about it. My host liked me." He washes his knife slowly, eyes dropping away from mine as the question sends him back to earlier memories. "But... she liked me because I was useful. We got here, and I was scared as shit they would do something to us, so I behaved. Never felt like myself there."

"Yeah... I know that feeling." I envy him, that he managed to please the people around him, instead of making a thousand enemies.

"But Sid and Silas would come visit. They'd check in on me, and I knew they would want me around no matter what I did. Plus, they saved our lives, so..."

"They did?"

"Totally. I mean, I was a good soldier. But who would want that for a life, y'know?" he says. "They saved us."

"Soldier?" An icy prickle travels down my spine. Sid said the way he met the guys was *a long story*. "You were a soldier when you were five?"

"No joke. TNS is screwed up. Who gives a kid that little a gun? It only had blanks in, but that's still dangerous, man." Carlos is too busy dicing green onions to notice I'm missing the context. Or should I say, *was*.

I should have seen it coming. A group of boys who came here on a boat. There's only one group besides Salt Spring that controls boats. True North Strong. TNS.

No wonder Sid skimped on the details.

"Totally!" I busy myself with picking leaves off cilantro so that he won't realise I'm freaking out. Shit shit shit. I am married to a member of TNS. I am in a house stacked to the gills with those *build a new and purified Canada, shoot first, ask later* gun nuts and—

No.

No, I can't let my mind go there. Just because they lived in TNS once doesn't make them mindless drones. I know how I feel about people learning I lived in a cult. I was eager to please the Grand Astrologue, because he was going to decide who I'd marry one day. He used to say I was beautiful and healthy; that I would make the perfect mother for the babies needed to repopulate the world.

He made it all sound so… natural. I spent a lot of time tending April, even back when my parents were alive. Dad was busy running a woodshop and Mum just wasn't herself. She and Dad called it post-partum depression, though when I asked what that was at school in Astolia, the teachers insisted it was made up. The Grand Astrologue even talked to me about it. He came by the school, pulled me aside and gave this long lecture about how some people were born weak and unfortunately, my mother was one of them. But I was different.

"Look at you! Ten years old, and already you know how to raise a child. The stars have told me you're going to be a wonderful mother one day," he said with confidence.

"You're such an important part of the work we're doing here."

How was I supposed to argue with that? How was any kid? He wasn't even totally wrong. I did enjoy caring for my baby sister. But he twisted that love against me and made it seem like it was the whole reason I existed. It was easier to believe him than I dare admit.

When I was fourteen, my teachers made all the girls in my age group strip down to our underwear so they could measure our chests and hips. All part of assessing our reproductive fitness. They gave Beth-Anne an *A* and me a *B+*, as if we had any control over the angles of our curves. I was terrified and confused, especially when they told us not to tell our parents. It was an important part of showing our loyalty to the Grand Astrologue's mission. But my mother always knew when something was wrong. She prodded. I told her. That was the final straw. We started planning our escape.

So yes, there are skeletons in my closet, too. As Sid put it, we both had to leave a shitty situation. But all I can think about is April's offhand joke about bodies underneath the floorboards. It sure seems less funny now.

"That's enough cilantro," Carlos says, noticing the massive pile of plucked leaves.

"Oh. Great. I'll wash up." What I really want is to retreat. To get my head together so that I don't accidentally suffocate Carlos with the ghosts of my past.

"Yeah, we're about done. I'll round up the guys," he says.

I intend to come back. All I've found out is that we have more things in common—we all grew up brainwashed. How nice is that?

But once I'm inside the washhouse, my composure breaks. Instead of cleaning myself up, I double over, retching into the drain next to the pump. Hands shaking,

I move the fish bathmat out of the way so I don't stain it. My fingernails scrape against the floorboards as I heave, again and again, until my stomach is empty, my whole body trembling.

Because as much as I want to be understanding, one key difference divides me from these men.

My cult never murdered *their* families.

NINETEEN

I MADE DAMN sure April didn't see the attack that killed Mum and Curtis. We were away gathering berries when it happened. I heard the guns, grabbed her, and ran. Only a few days later did I head back to pick over what was left of our camp. I didn't bring her with me. She didn't need to see the bodies.

I sit in the washhouse, waiting for my stomach and brain to settle. How many panic attacks have I had since coming to this damn island? I can't remember the last time they were this debilitating. All while watching after April in the wilds, I kept going. Now, without the threat of starvation hanging over my head, I can't seem to make my knees hold my weight. Shouldn't it be the other way around? Isn't life supposed to be easier now?

Half an hour later, I'm steady enough to sneak out of the washhouse and head for my room. No one bothers me all evening. I bundle myself inside a blanket and hide until long after the sun sets. When April comes in, I try to pretend I'm asleep, but she shakes my leg.

"You missed dinner."

"I wasn't hungry." Which is actually true. I lost all appetite after puking up lunch.

"You helped *make* it."

When I don't say anything, April sighs. "Sid says if you're feeling up to it, he'd like to talk to you. He said I should tell you he talked to Carlos."

Oh great. He knows.

I push the blanket back and head out. He must hear me, because at the sound of the door shutting, the one that leads into his room pops open. The narrow door frame barely contains the bulk of him, and I'm reminded of the day we met. Fearing him was a very, *very* logical reaction.

"Hey," he says.

"Duck pond?"

"Started raining an hour ago. We can talk in the kitchen." He moves toward the front door, but I don't follow. He turns back toward me with a wan smile. "It will be empty. The guys know we need to talk."

"Do they know why?"

"Carlos does. So we should probably assume they all do, too," says Sid. "I told him not to mention it to April so that you can decide how to break the news and—Kayla, I'm so sorry."

His voice quakes like he's about to come apart right in front of me. I don't know how I want April to find out about his history, but this isn't it.

"Fine. Kitchen, then." I stride past him, not meeting his eye. He's not the only one at risk of falling to pieces right now.

The kitchen is warm with the smell of tomato sauce, though the surfaces have been scrubbed clean. The stove is still hot, with a pot of mint tea simmering on the burner. Sid offers me a cup and I say yes, if only because mint is good for upset stomachs. All the physical trappings of comfort are here, but as Sid passes me a mug, I'm careful not to let my knuckles brush against his. Yesterday, I kissed this man. Not out of desire, obviously, but I felt safe enough to do it. Now, I sit at the far end of the table, putting as much distance between us as I can.

Neither of us wants to start the conversation, so we sit in silence for a long time, watching steam curl up from tea that's too hot to touch. As far as I'm concerned, this story isn't mine to tell, so I wait for him to work up the nerve. Even now, he's putting this off.

Finally, he takes a deep breath. "You didn't deserve to find out this way."

No. I really didn't. If there's any reason to feel justified in my anger right now, that's the one. I wonder how long it would have taken him to spit it out if Carlos hadn't blown things up. He made overtures when he mentioned James knowing how to sail a boat. There have been enough hints that I sort of believe he was going to tell me. But damn, it sure would have been nice to know before I married him.

My eyes flick up from my mug. His pale face is splotched with red, as if he's been in tears himself. When our gaze meets, his shoulders hunch and the impossible seems true. He's afraid of *me*. I'm not sure what to do with that power. Some part of me does want to hurt him, because right now, I'm not seeing the friend I thought I trusted. I'm seeing *them*. I didn't realize how much I wanted revenge for everything TNS took from me.

"Carlos is sorry too," he says, when I don't speak. "He feels guilty as shit. But that's my fault, obviously."

I blow into my tea, holding Sid's gaze with mine. "So, TNS. Is that why you couldn't get a respectable woman to marry you?"

His eyes fall from my face. "No one ever comes out and says it, but…"

"But no one wants to marry a murderer, either?" I'm probing, hoping to find out just what I'm dealing with. How deep in with them was he before he got out? "And now you want to get into government. No wonder you needed an image update."

"I meant to tell you, when we decided to do this. When you said you'd marry me, I knew I should say something, but I was so stunned you said yes, I totally forgot—"

"Scared. Don't sugarcoat it. You were scared."

"Scared shitless. I'm sorry, Kayla. I've never been a brave man. A violent one, sometimes. Never a brave one."

That's not true. Even in the short time I've known him, I've seen him choose the harder option because he knows it's the right one. But even good people have their limits, I guess. Now that I know what his is, does that change my decision?

"I won't blame you if you decide to leave," he says. Our minds must have wandered to the same place. "I'd like to think I can still help you and April out, but if it's—if I'm not someone you feel safe around—"

"I never feel safe, Sid." Now I'm the one who's lying, because for a moment, I did. As ever, I should have trusted my gut. "It's all practical for me. I still need you, so… I'm still in."

"Me too. I'm in as long as you need me."

It's tempting to let that be the end of the conversation. We're on the same page, so maybe I can justify making an escape. But then I think of what Carlos told me. *They saved our lives.* I don't doubt that's true. Why can't I make myself believe it?

I shouldn't be afraid of him. The man in front of me has more in common with a crumpled handkerchief than a bloodthirsty killer. But the way he talks about himself shows that on some level, he still believes it, too. *Violent. Unsafe.* If he believes it, I'm not crazy for worrying.

I feel sick at the thought. Using his own self-doubt to justify my fear of him is downright cruel. The night we agreed to get married, I said some awful things about how maybe the government *should* take April away if I couldn't care for her. He never agreed. Not a single time. He never let me buy into the worst version of myself. If I were a better friend, I would argue on his behalf in the same way.

I wish I could.

"Can I ask you a few questions?"

"Sure. Anything you need to know. I owe you that."

"Okay... How old were you when you escaped TNS?"

"Nineteen."

"Hmmm." That's pretty good. He rejected them about as early as one could hope.

"I didn't run a lot of missions. They scared the shit out of me. I got out as fast as I could, but... I can't say I never did things I regret. Silas, too."

"And James?"

Sid shakes his head. "James's hands are clean. TNS picked him up as a teenager, but they never let him in the field. Too much of a flight risk. He can be an asshole in his own way, but he never fired a shot for them."

"I thought you said he was the one who ended up with demerits when you got here."

"Right?" A faint smile comes to Sid's face. "I do not understand the guy. He mouthed off to Tom a hundred times worse than he ever did to anyone in TNS. I guess he knew Tom wouldn't kill him for it."

"But TNS would have?"

"Eventually," says Sid. "They beat his ass the few times he did, so he shut up. Everyone learns to keep their head low."

"Everyone?"

He's silent for a moment. Then, he reaches up and touches the side of his broken nose. "Everyone."

My vision blurs as hot tears overwhelm me. At some point in his childhood, somebody intentionally did that to him. And then he had to obey that person, or risk it happening again. I've teased Sid about his upright, rule following nature a few times, but it feels far less funny now. Between the pair of us, I don't know who TNS hurt more, but clearly, they hurt him longer.

"You okay?" he asks. "I'm sorry, I didn't mean to—"

"I'm fine. I mean, I'm not fine, but… it's not because of *you*." I wipe my eyes and make myself breathe through the anger, because I *am* still angry. At him? A little. But mostly at this awful world that put us in this horrible position. And mostly at *them*. The people who tried to ruin both our lives. "I just wish… I wish you'd told me."

"Me too," he says. "For what it's worth, I never left the mainland until we escaped on that boat with James. Never went to Vancouver Island. It wasn't me or anyone else I knew who had anything to do with Port Alberni or… well, anything else."

He gives me a quick glance, looking for confirmation of his suspicions. I guess he's heard enough about my life that he knows some kind of bullshit happened to me after Port Alberni fell.

When all is said and done, I don't know for certain TNS killed Mum and Curtis. I blame them, because I hate the alternative; that someone else murdered an innocent woman and teenaged boy without provocation, and I'll never know who or why. It's easier, pining all my anger on one villain.

But whoever that faceless, senseless villain might be, it isn't Sid.

"I believe you," I say. It's not quite as good as *I forgive you*, but it's a start.

He lets out a long, shuddering sigh. "Thank you."

I pull my knees to my chest so that I have something to hold onto, wishing, as I always do, that it wasn't my job to soothe my own aching heart. April is too young to lean on emotionally. I can't put that burden on her, even when I want to. I can't even remember the last time someone held me while I cried. It must have been all the way back when my parents...

No. That's not true. It was the night before the wedding. It was Sid.

An awful ache fills me as I realize how badly I wish I could do it again—crawl into his embrace and let someone else be the strong one. But when I look at him, I don't see a man who radiates strength, just someone struggling not to go to pieces himself. I can't beg him for comfort. Not when he clearly needs it, too, and I'm in no position to give it. So I fight the impulse to cling to him. I stay in my chair and he stays in his and we let the silence drag out between us.

He recovers first, sitting straighter, the controlled man I'm used to taking shape once more. "So, what do you need from me for this situation to work?"

A friend. To get that trust back. "I don't want anything to change. We're the same people so... same deal as before."

"Even appearing with me in public? People do know about my history. They might ask you about it."

"I'll just say you like to fire a shotgun round off before sex every night. Keeps your culture alive."

His face scrunches up. "Please don't do that."

"Oh, Sid. You really should have gotten to know me better before marrying me." *She says, as if she shouldn't have done the same thing herself.*

The joke breaks one layer of ice between us, a phantom grin spreading over his face. Does this counts as moving on? Maybe. It's good to see him smile, even if there is still a tremor in my pulse when I look at him.

"Carlos said you were asking about cooking jobs."

"Oh, yeah. He says they're hard to get."

"So? That the kind of thing that stops you?"

"I don't know." I'm used to being driven by survival, not desire. It's hard to conceive of things any other way.

"It sounds like a good idea—getting a job off the acreage, so you're not stuck with us all the time," says Sid. "There are plenty of people on this island you could be talking to who aren't paramilitary terrorist types, if that appeals to you."

"Heh." He's also trying to make light of the situation. But it rings too much of truth. "I... wouldn't mind a little space, actually."

"Of course." He rises from his chair and I realize that, without meaning to, I've dismissed him. "I'll talk to the guys. If there's ever more you want to know... you can always ask. Nothing's off the table, okay?"

"Thanks."

I return to the apartment, where I find April reading by candlelight.

"Everything okay?" she asks, setting the book down.

"Yeah." I wrap my arms around her. I might not be able to dump all my troubles on April, but she does help. During that first awful year after our mother died, April's love kept me alive. I might have given up dozens of times if I hadn't known I had a little child who needed me to hold her and sing to her. Who needed to know that, for all the bad in the world, she was still loved. And who, without thought or hesitation, always reached out to hug me back.

In some ways, her teen years have been harder. There's less of that little girl warmth about her now. But not tonight. She squeezes me back and even though the *whys* behind my grief go unspoken, I'm grateful for her support.

"The food was really good," she says, when we break apart.

"Wish I could have stomached it." All those lovely tomatoes, and I didn't get any.

"Dominick says Carlos makes that one a lot, so you'll get to try it soon."

We share a few more minutes of small talk, comparing the books we're reading. All considered, I've got a secure place to sleep, my little sister at my side, neither of us in danger of starving or succumbing to the elements any time soon. I should feel at peace.

Instead, I think of him. Who holds onto Sid when his demons chase him?

TWENTY

WHEN I FILL April in, she takes the news far better than I did. From the drop, she's all sympathy.

"That's terrible! Thank goodness they got out of there, right?"

"For sure. You're not bothered, though? You're comfortable living here?"

She snorts. "Honestly? Have you met Carlos? Can you even picture him with a gun?"

Absolutely not. But I don't need to call up a hypothetical image for Sid, James and Silas. When I point that out, she only shrugs. "Because they had a *job*. I bet they hated working for the border guard after everything TNS put them through."

Once she says it, I find myself going *oh yeah*. I never got the impression Sid liked his old job, but knowing this does put it in a new light. Salt Spring must have been eager to hire guys with combat training, even if they weren't citizens yet. And sure, those jobs pay well, but he would have been constantly reminded of where he came from.

"Still, TNS attacked Port Alberni. Obviously, it wasn't the guys themselves, but they still came from—"

"I'm sorry, Kayla, but… it's not the same for me. I wasn't even born."

Of course. This is one of those things I'll have to live with alone.

Talking with April does put some things in perspective. Mentally, I can now file Sid under *used to be an axe murderer but no worries! Will probably not axe murder me now!*

I wish I could say things go back to normal. In fairness, did Sid and I ever get a chance to establish a normal? First, I shot him, then we were unwilling housemates, then we got married. I swear there was a step somewhere in between where we became friends, but we never got to relax in that stage.

So I avoid him. And he avoids me. It's easy to do. Now that Sid has been accepted as a candidate for the next election, he spends more time in town, working on his campaign. The only time I have to see him is at dinner. Even then, it's easy enough to sit on the other side of the kitchen and keep my eyes on my own meal. I can pretend he isn't there. The illusion is only interrupted in the moments when one of the boys asks him a question and my ears prick, straining for the deep, rich notes of his voice.

One night, as he jokes with Silas and James about an old acquaintance of theirs, I'm angry all over again. There are no lurking secrets threatening to undo their trio. They're relaxed and happy in each other's company. Do they have any idea how lucky they are?

I try to tell myself that this is fine. April has a ready supply of medication, and no one is about to starve. In all material ways, my life has improved since coming to Salt Spring. True, it's dull as a wooden knife most days, but occasionally, I get a reprieve.

Twice a week, Carlos doesn't have to attend regular

classes due to his agriculture program. Instead, he stays home and helps Silas. Now that harvest is over, they're planning for the next season. They're considering investing in irrigation hose, though that's expensive, seeing as rubber needs to be scavenged from the ruins beyond Salt Spring. I know this largely because whenever Carlos is around, I eavesdrop like a fiend, eager for the moment when Silas turns to me, sighs, and says, "I guess you can have him now."

And what a time it is when I get him! We start with sauces, which he describes as "the key to covering up if the rest of your cooking is shit." So far, I seem to have the opposite problem. I'm good at making sure something doesn't burn, thanks to years of cooking with nothing but a campfire. But I can't get the lumps out of my first attempt at a roux. Dominick winces when we pass around the resulting pasta. Clearly, he remembers the "weed salad" debacle, because he has the sense not to say anything out loud.

On the day our monthly ration delivery arrives, everyone abandons their chores to go through the boxes. Most of it is late season staple crops: dried beans, flint corn, squashes, and oats. The other foods are more precious—a bundle of spinach; a pound of salt; little pouches of dried herbs; a few pounds of carrots and onions; and the last of the summer tomatoes.

One zucchini is so large, Carlos gives it a dirty look. "There's no way that's gonna be any good."

"Really?"

"They get tougher the bigger they get, and that thing's a *monster*."

"Oh, come on. You've got all the courgettes you could want." James hefts the giant vegetable over his head. "Whereas *this* is a proper marrow."

"Oh! Is *that* what a marrow is?" The great Belgian

detective Poirot was growing zucchini! I'm going to have to tell April.

"Yeah, a *right proper marrow, mate*," says Wendell, parroting James's accent.

James swings his arms, perilously close to smacking Wendell on the head with the zucchini, and Carlos hollers, "No horsing around with the food!"

James sets it down so he can tear after Wendell unencumbered. Wendell runs for his life and I laugh so hard my ribs ache.

It takes Silas joining the fray, barking orders, before anyone gets around to carrying the produce inside the kitchen. The boys quickly fall in line. James, however, picks up the zucchini and attempts to swing it like a baseball bat, only to drop it. It hits the ground hard, resulting in a massive crack.

"James!" Silas yells.

He only shrugs. "Carlos already said it wouldn't be any good. I'll feed it to the chickens."

As James trots off with the ruined zucchini, Silas throws a bag of beans over his shoulder. "That asshole goofs off more than the boys do."

"And you know that's why they love him," I say.

"Then there'll be lots of mourners at his funeral when I kill him."

I laugh at this, only to realize how strange that is a second later. Silas has been out working in the fields today, sewing a cover crop of clover to protect the beds until spring. His long hair is tied back in the same bandana he was wearing on the day when I met him. A day when he— not Sid—aimed a gun at me.

Everyone knows that April and I have found out about TNS. Since talking things out with Sid, all the other guys have addressed it in their own ways. I've put up with dozens of apologies from Carlos, who feels responsible for my messy breakdown. Young Tom asked if I wanted a hug, which I refused. Wendell thought I would find it comforting if he told me that he's a terrible shot. The DomBert brothers regaled me with a long story about their initial sanctuary host family. James gave me a high-five and said, "Isn't it cozy, knowing TNS shat on both of us?"

Except with Silas, there's been silence. And I don't care. He had more to do with TNS than James or any of the younger boys, but I don't want him to explain himself. That conversation would be so awkward. Why should either of us relive our worst memories when we could just get on with life? I'm not afraid of him; even when he jokes about murdering James, I don't take him seriously.

So why am I holding Sid to such a different standard?

"You can put the onions over here," says Silas, and I realize that I've frozen in the kitchen, consumed by my thoughts. I quickly place the bag, then head out to grab more rations.

When Sid gets home that night, I find myself staring at him over dinner. I take in the bend of his nose and the scar along his jaw. Did TNS give him that one, too? It's overwhelming, studying his face, which bears so many reminders of everything he's gone through. So I fixate on his neck, instead.

Carlos and I didn't have time to make anything fancy, too busy organizing the new food into a meal plan, so it's nothing but scrambled eggs and beans for dinner tonight. Whenever Sid takes a bite, I watch his Adam's apple slide up and down his throat with each swallow. I desperately want to reach out and touch it, as if that would help anything.

A heavy weight fills my stomach as I admit the obvious to myself—I miss him. Maybe we weren't friends for long, but our relationship clearly meant something to me. That's why his history with TNS hurt so much more than anyone else's, but also why avoiding him is making me miserable.

The ache I feel is so similar to the one that comes when I think of my parents or Curtis. Only one thing separates the experience, which is how needless this is. He isn't dead yet. If I walked up to him and asked him to give me a hug, he would probably do it.

I could have the thing I want. I don't *have* to be alone.

But as I have this revelation over scrambled eggs, I struggle to put it into words. At one point, he catches me staring. I don't look away, silently begging that he will say something and provide us with a way forward. I get a half-hearted smile before he returns to his food—and I realize that he's never going to broach the subject first. I suppose it makes sense. I'm the one who got hurt, so he's leaving the future of our relationship up to me.

That night, as April snores next to me, I resolve that I will say something. TNS already took so much from me; I can't let them take away the one friend I've made on Salt Spring. The other boys are decent enough company, but they aren't *him*.

He leaves for town before I wake up, so I spend the day psyching myself up for when he comes home. I want to ask him for a private conversation by the duck pond, though as storm clouds roll in, I worry we won't get our chance. Maybe we can talk in the apartment? Though where? He hasn't got a lick of furniture in the main areas and April will be using our room to study. And going into his room is out of the question, because... actually, I don't know why, but it is. I am not going in there.

I'm so fixated on location, I'm woefully unprepared when he comes rocketing through the kitchen door that evening. Carlos has been showing me how to caramelize onions, and I nearly drop the spoon at the sight of Sid. His usually neat hair is askew from a mix of wind and rain, his muscular chest heaving with each quick, agitated breath.

"Carlos, get out of here," he barks.

"What?" Carlos turns around, rightly confused. "We're making dinner."

"It can wait. Tom Sullivan's here."

"Shit!" I tamp down the stove. "Why?"

"Wants to check in. He came to my booth downtown to ask about you. And since you're his sanctuary case, legally he's allowed to show up if he thinks there's a problem."

"And *does* he think there's a problem?"

Sid flaps his arms weakly. "I don't know. When he asked if he could come by, I didn't dare say no."

"Why not?"

"Because the judiciary sent him our marriage certificate. He knows."

"Oh, *shit*. Carlos, get out of here." My hands are shaking as I towel them off. "How long until—"

"Maybe a minute? He's right behind me," says Sid. "James is stalling him."

There isn't time to change clothes or do anything else that might help make a good impression, so instead, I freeze while Sid gives Carlos a definitive nudge out the door.

I was already wishing that Sid and I were speaking before, but now it feels infinitely more urgent. We've got to put on a show to convince this man that we're wildly in love, and Sid knows Tom better than I do. He should be giving me direction, but the way I crashed out over TNS means he's in no state of mind to take the lead on *anything*. How's he to know I won't flip out if he tries to touch me again? This is all on me.

"We should greet him together. Show a united front." I take his hand, which is clammy to the touch. Whether it's from rain or nerves, I can't guess. My own pulse thrums as

I touch him for the first time since our wedding day. But even though I'm trembling, I have no desire to pull away, savouring the rough touch of his fingers interlocking with mine. "Come on. Let's go save James from Tom."

Once we get outside, it's clearly the other way around. James is talking a mile a minute about some girl while Tom limps down our drive, scowling more with each second.

"Hi, Mr. Sullivan!" I call out, willing myself to sound confident.

"Ms. Hollins. Or is it *Mrs. Charles* now?"

He's got my papers. He knows damn well which it is. But I've got to sound open and unthreatened. "April didn't want to change hers, and we figured I should probably match her."

"Hmmm." Tom stops to catch his breath, and I feel strangely guilty he has to walk so far before he can sit down. He looks like he's in pain. Then again, he wouldn't have had to walk anywhere at all if he hadn't decided to haunt us today.

"How is your sister doing?" Tom takes another shaky step forward.

"Fine."

"I saw she's registered at high school. Is she enjoying it?"

"Sure."

"Something beyond a single word answer would paint a fuller picture. But we can discuss that once we're inside."

"Wonderful seeing you, Mr. Sullivan!" James calls from behind us. "If you see Amy, give her a shout from me!"

"Insufferable blowhard," Tom grumbles, looking toward Sid. "Why you still choose to live anywhere near *him* is the real mystery. Though... not the one I've come to discuss."

With that, he pushes open the door to the kitchen and we're hit by the smell of onions. While Tom takes a seat and opens his briefcase, I check to make sure nothing is burning, certain he'll take the first sign of smoke as another indication I'm an uncultured barbarian.

"If you could take a seat, Ms. Hollins?"

"Coming."

I slide into the seat next to Sid, who has said absolutely nothing since Tom's arrival. At least he has the presence of mind to put an arm around my shoulders. Tom watches the gesture carefully, not giving much away. Do we look convincing, or performative? And if he determines it's the latter... what exactly will he do? Sid told me that it's hard to prove marriages are falsified, but if there's anyone with the legal means to do it, it's Tom.

"If I may make an observation," he says. "You seem more settled, Ms. Hollins."

"Oh... thank you?" By that, he probably means that I haven't yelled at him yet.

"Dinner on the hob *and* a new husband? Positively domestic."

"Carlos is teaching me how to cook."

"That's good. No, I mean it. There's no need to make that face. You clearly don't trust me, but you're more at ease among these people. Considering where we started, I would call that progress."

I don't know what to make of this little speech. He isn't wrong. I don't trust him, which is why I'm certain all these compliments are steps in a carefully placed trap.

"I offered Sid my congratulations earlier today," he continues. "I suppose I should extend them to you as well."

"Thank you."

"Pardon a sentimental old man's prying, but what about him won you over so quickly?"

"Well..."

"Tom, I'm not sure my wife feels comfortable discussing

that kind of thing with you," Sid says, his tone stern. "And it's not really within the scope of questions an immigration officer is supposed to ask."

"Under normal circumstances, I would agree with you. The judiciary sent me a record of your marriage last week. My first thought was… well, surprise, to be sure. She injured you within seconds of meeting you, Sid. That doesn't suggest marital stability. However, you volunteered so *gallantly* to rescue her from the very reasonable consequences of her actions, the thought did cross my mind that you were smitten with her. Love at first sight. Or rock."

Tom says that as if the whole idea is abhorrent. I almost want to reassure him Sid isn't that kind of idiot. Unfortunately, we're in a way better position if he thinks we did fall foolishly in love within seconds.

"It was something like that," says Sid awkwardly.

"Yeah." I should build on this narrative. We're lucky Tom is handing us an easy explanation. "Like Anne and Gilbert."

"What?" says Sid, turning to me.

"Anne Shirley and Gilbert Blythe," I say, "from *Anne of Green Gables*. She breaks a slate over his head and then he's totally obsessed with her. You haven't read it?"

"Not yet."

"Oh, it's my favourite! I'll lend it to you. Although Anne and Gilbert don't get together until one of the sequels." I only kept the first one, but April and I did find a house that had the whole series, once. Now I wish I'd held onto the rest.

"I'm sure the library can help you there. Canadian classics, after all," says Tom, his mouth twitching. "What interesting things you still have to discover about each other."

"Love isn't a list of facts. We know how we *feel*—" Sid starts, but Tom cuts in.

"Please. Save your performance for a more interested party. Like I said, I *want* nothing more than to leave well enough alone. My favourite cases are the ones I never have to think about, and you had both been silent since her arrival. No new incidences of violence, which was encouraging. I thought—hoped—that maybe Ms. Hollins was *wonderfully* integrated, and you were safely in love, and my nagging doubts were nothing but the ramblings of a paranoid mind. And then..." He reaches into his bag and tosses another file onto the table. "*This* arrived on my desk."

The papers don't have my name, but April's. From the header, it's apparent they came from the hospital. They include all the details of not only her illness and treatment plan, but also her billing information. I'm not sure what to make of it. I mean, why wouldn't Tom know all of this? He's in charge of our immigration case.

But Sid is furious. "What the hell is the hospital doing, sending this to you?"

Tom shrugs. "My office does have the right to obtain information like this. I can ask for it if I suspect immigration fraud. However, I did *not* request this file. When I asked Doctor Tremblay why he'd sent it over, he hastily apologized for the clerical error but offered no explanation for how that error happened."

"Holy shit. So you're saying it *was* a privacy breach?"

"So it would seem. The point is, *someone* suspects you only married to secure medical insurance."

"You don't have to say someone. We all know it's that shitbag doctor," says Sid.

"He did tell me about the incident with the slingshot," says Tom. "He seems to be rather... invested in this case."

"Did you tell him to mind his damn business?"

"I told him that if something like this happened again, I would have to recommend Council investigate the security of private documents at the hospital," says Tom. "I'm not sure he took me seriously. We only have two physicians on the island who trained at pre-Quake universities. Doctor Levy keeps talking about retiring and if she does, that leaves us with Doctor Tremblay. I believe he considers himself indispensable."

I don't know what to do with this news. Sid was angry with the doctor before, when I told him he suggested I could surrender April to the government. Between these papers and telling Tom about the slingshot, we've now got a pattern. Mild-mannered as he is, every step of the way, Doctor Tremblay has been undermining me.

"Why would he do this?" I finally ask. "He's been so good to April. Why would he try to ruin things for us?"

"Ms. Hollins, I try not to speculate on the inner hearts of other people. I put my trust in facts and figures. They paint a less biased picture," says Tom. "Most people, including Doctor Tremblay, agree that we should extend sanctuary services and citizenship to all children who come to our shores. But, in private settings, I *have* heard him express admiration for Wayne Donlon."

"You can't be serious," says Sid.

"Who is—" I start.

"Wayne Donlon is a guy on Council," says Sid. "If it was up to him, we'd end the sanctuary program. He says shit like, *Anyone we would want already got here years ago.*"

"*The rest are all desperate thugs,*" Tom finishes, raising his eyebrows. "He said to me once that he figures we've done our bit. We've saved *enough* people. It's up to the rest of the world to get their affairs in order."

"He can't imagine a situation where someone out in the wilds might not have heard about Salt Spring until recently. Or even what it's like working up the nerve to leave TNS." Sid shakes his head. "I'd love to see his ass get voted out this spring."

"Unfortunately, there are plenty who agree with him. He doesn't rank near the top of the ballot, but he always musters enough votes to get on Council. All we can do is try to sway the balance of power in a different direction. That's why I endorsed *you*."

"Endorsed? What does that mean?" I ask.

"It means I wrote an opinion piece for the newspaper highlighting your husband as one of our most promising young candidates." Tom scowls, as if he regrets doing that now. "So now I'm asking you, Sid… Did you put your whole campaign in jeopardy and get yourself into a sham marriage?"

Confronted so directly, Sid falls silent for a half second.

"Of course not!" I jump in.

But it's too late. Tom's face falls into his hands. "Oh, bloody hell."

"There's nothing sham about it! We're in love!" Maybe if I yell it enough, it will suddenly be true, and Sid will stop looking like he's being scolded by his favourite teacher.

"You told me you had payment." Tom levies a finger at me. "When we talked in the hospital, you said you could pay for your sister's care. I believed you."

"Well, I thought I could! How the hell was I supposed to know how much it cost? I've never used money before."

"And now you've both folded. Brilliant!" Tom throws his hands in the air. "The tiniest bit of scrutiny and you both collapse. If you're going to insist on breaking the law, could you at least be better at it?"

"Excuse me?" This doesn't seem like the kind of thing a government official is supposed to say out loud.

"I'm not an idiot, Ms. Hollins. I know your sister has diabetes. The second your marriage certificate crossed my desk, I knew what was going on," says Tom. "I would love to play ignorant. I really would. But there are people watching you, Sid. People who hate what you stand for. I understand your whole *no soldier left behind* attitude, but you can't do this. Not if you want to get on council."

"What do you mean by that?" I ask.

Tom's eyes drop to his hands. "If we annul the marriage now, there would be no damage done. It's not widely known yet. But if you carry on—"

I lunge out of my seat. "Get out of my kitchen!"

"Kayla," Sid grabs my arm, trying to pull me back.

"If you carry on, you'll be exposed! Your sister will lose her health benefits, so it won't do anyone any good. But it will also destroy any chances *you* have in the election, Sid. No one wants to see a former TNS soldier cheating the system."

"You're just scared that if he goes down, you will too," I fire back.

Tom's eyes flick over me. "Frankly? Yes. Though I would omit the *just*. You conjure up a diverse range of terrifying possibilities, Ms. Hollins. I seriously doubt either one of us knows half your story, and that concerns me."

A chill goes down my spine. He knows I lied on my papers. Well, maybe he doesn't *know*, but he suspects.

"Is there anything you want to tell me?" he asks. "Anything that would put my mind at ease?"

This is a trap. He wants to get me to admit to lying so that Sid won't trust me and will get the annulment. Obviously, it's not going to work.

"Anything I want to tell you? You're *my* immigration officer. You're supposed to be helping me. Or are you just going to tell me to surrender April to the government, too?"

"Surrender April? Why would you say that?"

"That's what Doctor Tremblay told me to do."

Tom nods. "I see. Think about what I've said, Sid. I don't want you to lose everything you've worked for."

"When I said get out, I meant it," I snap.

"I understand." Tom rises from his seat. He doesn't so much as look at me as he packs up his briefcase and hobbles towards the door.

"You're as bad as Doctor Tremblay. Worse." I can't resist letting one more barb fly. "At least *he* gave April medicine."

Tom's shoulders stiffen as he takes hold of the door handle, but he doesn't rise to my bait. "Good day, Ms. Hollins."

With that, he's out the door. The second it's shut, I slam my hand as hard as I can against the table, choking back a scream that I don't want to give Tom the satisfaction of hearing. I was doing so well, but that bastard got to me anyway. Now he's gone, I feel foolish and weak. Worse still, I look that way in front of Sid.

I know he's pissed too, but while I'm hitting things and boiling over, he's gone silent. All the anger is carefully tucked away. If he were to express it now, would it be directed at me?

"Sid?"

He lets out a slow breath. "Well. *That* could have gone better."

"I'm sorry."

"It's not your fault. I mean, it's *both* our faults. We weren't ready for him."

"No. I guess we weren't."

He's being incredibly generous, not laying the full blame at my feet. I'm not sure it even matters who's at fault. All I need from our marriage is insulin. He's the one who needs us to keep up appearances, and for a logical guy like Sid, any failure is failure. What does it matter how it happened?

"This isn't working, is it?" he says.

"But it *could* work! He caught us off guard. And he's your friend, right? It's harder to lie to friends." Until now, I hadn't known what Sid meant when he talked about his relationship with Tom, but tonight I think I got a peek. He clearly takes Tom's opinion seriously, especially about the election.

"I guess." Sid shakes his head. "But he isn't wrong, Kayla."

"No! We can do this." I grab Sid's hands, making him look at me properly. "We screwed up today, but he knew things about us that normal people wouldn't. No one has to know about the slingshot or April's insulin. You want a sweet little wife softening your image? I will do that! I will be that."

"No offence, but who would use the words *sweet little wife* to refer to you?"

"Oh, come on!" I smack his arm, proving his point, but we're both fighting back smiles. The sight gives me a shred of hope to cling to. "There must be something I can do. At the very least, I can totally make it look like I love you. You're very lovable. And if everyone sees me thinking you're great, they'll think you're great too, right?"

Those words only make his blue eyes cloud over. "Kayla, you can't even *talk* to me anymore. I'm not saying I blame you, but—"

"No." My voice cracks. He still thinks I'm afraid of him or hate him or some combination of the two.

"—if you can't trust me, then what's the point of any of this?"

"That asshole. This isn't fair." My eyes sting as tears threaten to break through.

"What?"

"I was going to talk to you tonight." I sniff against the

lump forming in my throat. "I had this whole plan. But now you're not going to believe me."

"Believe you about what?"

"We were going to go to the duck pond! But then it started raining and I thought, shit, he's not going to want to go to the duck pond in the rain. So then I was trying to think where we could talk instead, but you don't have any furniture, so—"

"What has furniture got to do with—"

"I was going to talk to you about TNS! But now you won't believe me because Tom ruined it. I was going to ask you to talk."

"Really?"

"Yes! See? You don't believe me!"

"Then pretend I do. We're at the duck pond. What were you going to say?"

A wave of fear envelopes me again. It's a chance I don't deserve, and my voice wobbles when I try to meet his eyes. "I dunno."

"You don't know." Those beautiful blue eyes drop away from mine.

"No, I do know. I… I miss you." I finally get the words out. "That was basically it. I miss you and it's making me sick. The TNS thing freaked me out, but if I've got to choose between hating them or liking you, I'm choosing you. Not just because I want to help April, but because you're the kindest man I've ever known."

Sid blinks, as if he's trying to find his way out of a spell. "Seriously?"

"Sid…" My voice shakes as I reach for something that terrifies me to admit out loud, but that I know he needs to hear. "Remember when I went running and you flipped out? Before we started talking about this whole marriage thing?"

"Yeah?"

"You were the first man—no. Other than April, you were the first *person* I've hugged since my mother died. I feel safe with you. Only you. I want that back."

"Oh." His voice is so soft, I wouldn't be able to hear it if I was more than a foot away. I squeeze his hands and in reply, his own grip strengthens, giving me courage.

"Anyway… that's all I was going to say. And that I'm sorry. I'm sorry it took me so long to forgive you. It's just, I trust people *so* infrequently. Until you kept that secret from me, it was like you were perfect. And then you weren't. I didn't know what to think."

"You've lived through a hell of a lot of terrible stuff if you ever thought *I* was perfect."

"You know what I mean."

"No. I wish I did." He sighs. "Kayla, I'm sorry, too."

I look up, suddenly terrified. What exactly is he apologizing for? Does he want that annulment Tom suggested?

"From here on out, no more secrets."

"You mean—"

"I'm a man of my word. I'm not giving up on you."

"Oh, Sid!" With that, I throw my arms around him. He's only startled for a second; then, his arms tighten around me, driving away that lonesome ache of the past week. "We'll do this right. Get to know each other, so we can trick anyone. Even Tom!"

"That might be setting the bar a little high."

"Oh, shut up. Next time you go into town, why don't I come with you? It can be, like… a super platonic friend date between two married people."

"That sounds like an incredibly normal thing to do."

"Doesn't it?" I grin. "We'll get to know each other. Favourite books. Songs. Everything!"

"I..." Sid hesitates. "I guess that would be a good idea."

"Perfect! It's a date." I release him and spin around the kitchen, feeling lighter than I have in days. "And you can show me your office and how your campaign works. Maybe we can go tomorrow? I think Carlos is at regular school tomorrow, so—Carlos! Onions! Shit!"

I make a mad dash towards the stove. A plume of smoke billows up as I expose the scorched sides of the onions. Sid breaks down with laughter and it's so contagious, I find myself joining in. I guess if I'm going to ruin his life, like Tom expects, I might as well start with his dinner.

TWENTY-ONE

I'M EAGER TO prove that I'm committed not just to our fake marriage, but also to getting Sid elected, so after eating the world's most disappointing onion soup, Sid passes me a collection of documents to read. The stack includes a modern map, a pamphlet titled *Proclamation of The League of Gulf Nations*, and the island's legal code. Both April and I spend the evening engrossed in homework.

Salt Spring Island is a miniscule dot in the larger Pacific Ocean; one stop in an archipelago of minor islands splayed out between Vancouver Island and the North American continent. Three nations inhabit this island chain or so sayeth the pamphlet. To the north of us is Penelakut, an even tinier island that controls the northern island chain. It's been a close ally of Salt Spring since the earliest days of the Quake, but operates independently due to its history as indigenous reserve lands. Post-Quake, many people from the Cowichan Tribes and other neighbouring First Nations sought refuge there rather than Salt Spring. Now, over thirty years on, they've re-established Hul'qumi'num as the official language.

To the south is the United States. More correctly, the San Juan Islands, which survived as the last major outpost of the USA. Before the Quake, they had a larger population than the Canadian islands, but that ended up being their downfall. During the massive war that followed, anywhere with an airport got the shit bombed out of it. But islands were still easier to defend against TNS and so gradually, American settlers re-established control over the San Juans. Sid says they're about a decade behind in their recovery journey relative to Salt Spring.

Smack dab in the middle, there's us. Or, to use a title that only people like Tom Sullivan would ever bother with, *Salt Spring Island and her Gulf Island Territories*. Around Salt Spring itself there's a ring of smaller islands, including Galiano, where most of the lumber mills are, and the Penders, which were designated as the agricultural hub of the new nation twenty years ago. We can thank North Pender for April's pig pancreases. Most of the nation's major services—like the hospital and high school—are on Salt Spring itself.

As Sid takes me on a walking tour of the capital city, Ganges Harbour, an impossible thing seems to be true: this tiny, insignificant island that meant so little to the pre-Quake superpowers is too damn complicated.

A light drizzle accompanies our stroll through town, but it's not enough to keep people from going about their business. Vendors line the sidewalks, hawking everything from newspapers to hot popcorn. Tarps and open tents keep the wet from spoiling the wares for sale. Sid explains that the government hasn't prioritized rebuilding malls or storefronts, so people make do with what they can cobble together. Outside one tent is a sign advertising haircuts for two dollars. A whole business devoted to cutting hair! As if a quick saw with a knife isn't good enough.

Still, I don't mind having the sights and sounds of the city to distract us. We're here with the goal of getting to know each other, but it's easiest to comment on things we see rather than manufacture a bonding experience. Indirectly, I do learn stuff about Sid. He shows me what he considers to be the best bike repair shop, his favourite place to get fish and chips, and the luxury pawn shop where—as he puts it—James blew six years of his savings on *that damn guitar.*

"But wasn't that a good thing?" I ask. "That damn guitar is my favourite thing about James."

"Yeah, *now* it is," says Sid. "But we were supposed to be saving the money for an acreage. All three of us. Silas was livid. Honestly, it's the closest we all came to falling out."

"But you didn't. How did you fix it?"

"Hmmm?"

"Come on, Sid. I can read between the lines. Obviously, *you* fixed it."

He doesn't object, but his face does screw up with discomfort. "I told Silas we owed it to him. If anyone gets to dick around with us, it's James. Though sometimes I wish the smug bastard didn't know it."

"You owed it to him?"

"Yeah."

I nearly ask what he means by that, but then the obvious answer comes to me. I don't know what role Sid played at TNS, but he must feel somewhat responsible for what happened to James. It's funny. I don't think of James as having a dark, tortured past the way Sid does, because he's such a clown, but he must. I guess some people are better at hiding it than others.

"Where's he from?" I try to gently change the topic, so that we aren't dancing so close to TNS territory. "I can't figure out the accent."

"His parents were from England. They were on vacation in the Gulf Islands when the Quake happened and got stranded here. He was born on a private yacht. You don't have to feel *that* sorry for him."

"Okay, noted. Did they ever try sailing back home?"

"Not really. There's a continent in the way." Sid sighs "James says that when he was really young, he met his grandparents on a web chat. Which is just... *crazy* to think about, since global internet was down by then. But his family was rich. They must have had some private network that didn't get destroyed as fast."

I try to picture talking with someone in Europe, but it's beyond my imagination. I've often wondered what happened to the rest of the world once mass communication fell apart. Common sense suggests there must be other people out there. We can't be the only lucky ones. However, most stories I've heard about life beyond these islands has been difficult to believe. The Grand Astrologue used to claim he got updates on his mission from a man stranded on the International Space Station. James's tale is far more within the realm of reason.

Regardless, wherever those other survivors are, none of them have the resources to cross the planet and find us. What will happen when they do? Will they be friendly, or will they want to restart the wars that ended the world? Or will we find them first?

"We shouldn't be going on about James, anyway," says Sid. "I'm supposed to be learning about you."

"Well... what do you want to know?"

"I don't know. What do you like doing for fun? Do people scavenging in the wilderness *have* fun?"

"Of course we do." I roll my eyes at him. "And you already know what I like. I read a lot. What about you? Any favourite books?"

Sid exhales slowly through his nose. "I dunno."

"Oh, you want me to guess? Is that it?"

My tone is light and teasing, yet he ducks his head, unable to meet my eye. I'm reminded of the argument we had at the library after we got married, not just because we're circling the topic of books, but because once again, I'm stumped. If he doesn't like reading, what's the big deal? I'm not going to divorce my fake husband over differing hobbies.

Then, like an echo, Tom's words yesterday come back to me.

What interesting things you still have to discover about each other.

I assumed he was being snide because Sid didn't know how much I loved *Anne of Green Gables*, but what if his remarks were meant to cut both ways? What if my disbelief that Sid hadn't read it came across as equally naïve, because…

"No." I stumble to a stop. "No, you can read. I *know* you can read. I watched you read a letter right in front of me."

"Sure, I can read." Sid's eyes track a flock of seagulls in the distance. "Slow and steady wins the race, as they say."

"You read legal documents for fun."

"*Fun* is a strong word."

"But why wouldn't you be able to…"

He once asked me if I knew how to read, and I got mad at him for thinking I was stupid. Now, I'm sick with guilt. He was asking because for him, it wasn't a default assumption.

"TNS taught some kids, but they didn't give a shit if I could read. I was five feet tall by the time I was nine. They knew what I was good for." He shakes his head. "I took night school once we got here. But I was starting from zero and working full-time. Silas still can't read."

"I'm so sorry." Impulsively, I reach for his hand. His

fingers are stiff in mine, clearly surprised by the gesture, but he doesn't let go.

"It's the main thing I worry about, going into the election. I've got a high-school education, and I had to bust my ass just to get that. There're people like Tom running who went to university before the Quake—"

"You can't compare yourself to him. You didn't get the same opportunities he did. Besides, the world's different now. You're probably one of the few people running who has lived outside of this bubble. They *need* people with your experience."

"There are plenty of people who went through the same shit I did. They're just not bull-headed enough to try this."

"*Sid.*" I jerk his wrist, prompting him to look me in the eye. "I hate Tom more than anyone, but you know he wouldn't have endorsed you if he didn't think you were capable. He's not stupid."

"I guess, but—"

"No! No *buts*. I swear, if you make me say something nice about Tom again, I'm gonna smack you."

That has a stronger effect than my pep talk. He grins. "Thanks." He gives my hands a squeeze, then drops them. "You want to grab something to eat?"

"Did we bring anything?"

"No, but the rain is picking up and I was thinking, you've probably never been to a restaurant before, right?"

"I guess I haven't."

"Great. Then let's go."

He leads me to a building covered in bright red paint. A sign outside announces that the pub was one of a handful of buildings that didn't fall during the Quake and has been preserved in its original form due to its historical significance. Even though it's midday, it's dark inside, thanks to the gloomy weather. Candles flicker on each table like we've stepped into a photograph from a pre-Quake lifestyle magazine.

"Oh!"

"Do you like it?"

"Absolutely." April and I used to scavenge restaurants for their knives and tools. But I've never seen one decked out for dining.

Sid leads me to a table by one of the windows. A view of the harbour stretches out next to us, broken up by tracks of rain streaming down the glass. I can't resist pressing a hand to the cold, clear surface, leaving a filmy handprint behind. I've never seen a sheet of glass this large and intact before.

A waiter comes to drop off menus, and it feels even more like a storybook. Everything is magical and perfect right up until I open the menu.

"Holy shit! They're charging *what* for a salad?"

"Now you know why we don't do this very often," says Sid, picking up his copy.

"We should go." Seeing the place is good enough for me. It's lovely to know restaurants exist. But Sid covers my wrist with his hand, stopping my attempt to run out the door.

"Let me treat you. Please. I want to watch you try something new."

"So you brought me here for your own entertainment?"

"Something like that. You ever had oysters before?"

"Of course I've had oysters. Nasty as hell. But... they keep you alive."

"Hmm, okay. Bad pick. Oh! Pickled beets. I'm guessing you've never had pickled beets."

"You're suggesting the gross stuff, aren't you?"

"I happen to *like* pickled beets. I'm going to order some, and you can try them if you want." He throws me a wink and my cheeks warm.

"French fries," I say, stabbing my finger on one of the

menu entries. "I've never had French fries. Or a burger. Those are supposed to be good."

"Perfect! You can put pickled beets on a burger."

"Sid!"

For all my protesting, when the food arrives, he turns out to be right. I hadn't tried pickled beets before and while I won't be rushing out to blow what little money I have on another taste, they're a pleasant mix of sweet and sour. What really impresses me are the French fries, which are oily and salty to the point of decadence. Sid also lets me try his fish tacos and the tangy coleslaw they come with.

It's everything I could hope for from my first trip to a restaurant. Delicious food, a seaside view… and a handsome guy to share it with. I've officially decided I prefer Sid's hair after the rain. I don't know why he bothers slicking it back. There's a natural wave that comes out in the wet weather. If we were actually in love, I would run my fingers through it.

I get why people used restaurants for courtship in the past. Sid Charles has never looked better than he does lavishing me with an expensive meal. But it's not just that. I've never seen him smile so much before. His cockeyed grin is out in full force as I take in every new experience. When I ask him what he's so giddy about, he only shrugs.

"I like seeing you so happy. Makes me remember what it was like when I first got to Salt Spring."

Although he's not totally trustworthy. Once I admit to liking the pickled beets, he asks our waiter to bring over some horseradish. And I—being an absolute fool—stick a spoonful in my mouth without a second thought. He laughs his head off as I gag down a full glass of water.

"I am gonna kill you for that," I wheeze, once my mouth is no longer burning.

"Oh, come on. Now you know, you can try the same trick on April."

"Are you kidding? She *would* kill me. You know... she'll be crushed when she finds out I came here without her."

"She'll have lots of chances to experience places like this," says Sid. "I'm glad it's just us. You were right. We needed this."

We. That word sends a strange buzz through me and I'm suddenly aware of his knees brushing mine beneath the table. I haven't said it out loud, because calling attention to it would only make things weird, but the longer we spend together, the more undeniable it is. This is my first date. Even if there are complicated reasons behind it, all the key ingredients are here.

Delicious food. Seaside view. Handsome man.

I'm enjoying myself, but the realization still hurts. I've been in love before, but what I shared with Curtis was simple and instinctual. There were no grand gestures. No wooing. We missed out on so many experiences. Now I can only wonder: is this what the real thing would have felt like? I try to picture a day like this, perfect in all the same ways today is perfect, but with Curtis instead. I can't quite do it. Too much of what I'm enjoying is thanks to Sid.

"You okay?" Sid's voice pulls me back to the present.

"Oh... yeah. I'm good."

"I'm sorry about the horseradish."

"No, it's not that."

"So something *is* bothering you."

Damn it, I should have chosen my words more carefully. Or I should have waited to zone out and think about Curtis somewhere private.

"Everything's wonderful, but..."

Sid nods. "I remember that part, too."

"Part of what?"

"Coming here. The survivor's guilt. That shit eats you up. Is there anything you want to talk about?"

Yes.

I'm so close to saying it. Maybe this is finally the right time, here where it's safe and we're away from the realities of everyday life. I consider telling him every story I can think of about Mum and Dad and Curtis and how I lost each one of them. This is why we came here, isn't it? To close the gaps in our story and I could fill in a big one right now. But do I want to make myself cry in a public place?

His eyes are fixed on mine. Beneath the table, his fingers slide from his knee, taking one of my hands in his. Another pulse of energy lights up my body. *We.* We're a team now. I should tell him.

The words are on the tip of my tongue.

"Sid Charles! Is that you?" A high-pitched voice comes between us with the force of an axe. We spring in opposite directions, hands and legs suddenly tucked safely around our seats.

Sid blinks, scanning the room for the source. "Pardon?"

"Ah! It's totally you!" A woman by the bar waves, hard to make out in the gloom. "Give me just a sec. I'm going to order a drink, then I'll be right over."

"Okay," Sid calls back. Under his breath, he adds, "Shit."

"Who is that?" I ask.

Sid gives me a wan smile. "Someone else running for council this year."

"Interesting! Ally or enemy?"

"Ally, technically," says Sid. "But... she's also my ex-girlfriend."

"Oh, shit."

"That's not even the worst part."

I would ask him what he means, except the woman is making her way to our table. As the light from the windows falls on her, she glimmers, even in the gloom. She's wearing gold bobby pins in her sleek strawberry blonde hair and a black cowlneck dress made of clean new wool. In other words, she looks like the kind of woman who can afford to eat at a restaurant.

"Oh! You have company. Sorry, you're like, half his height. I didn't see you," she says, laughing apologetically. "I can bother you later, Sid. Enjoy your date."

"No, come say hi." Sid rises to greet her. "You two should probably meet."

"Hello." I mimic Sid and rise from the table. This is an ex-girlfriend—does that mean I should lean into the charade? It's probably the safest course. I'm guessing he would have told a real wife about past relationships, so I smile and say, "I've heard so much about you!"

"Really?" Her hazel eyes widen. She is the sweetest, prettiest little thing I've met since coming to this island. And Sid used to go out with her? He must really be feeling the downgrade.

"Let me introduce you both properly." Sid places an arm around my shoulders, pulling me close. "Kayla, meet the famous Amy Sullivan. You can see why Tom wants us to work together, right?"

"Oh, stop!" she laughs and it's the most perfect tinkling sound I've ever heard.

It's a good thing Sid has an arm around me, because my knees buckle. He was right. Ex-girlfriend is hardly the worst of it.

Standing right in front of us is Tom Sullivan's daughter.

TWENTY-TWO

I ALL BUT black out for the next minute as Amy and Sid make small talk. Some part of me assumed Tom Sullivan was nothing but a sadistic gremlin who spent all his time ruining people's lives, but Amy is clear evidence to the contrary. Even that man has a family. I can see the resemblance now in her red hair, but it's hard to believe that anyone so cheerful could come from the same genetic stock as Tom.

The bartender calls to her and she places a hand on Sid's arm. "That's my drink. I should probably let you go, but I'll stop by the farm sometime. There're some campaign opportunities we should talk about."

"Sounds great—" Sid starts.

"Oh, don't leave on my account," I cut in. "Eat with us! You two can catch up and then I can quiz you about him."

"Kayla." Sid scowls at me, but that only makes my grin wider.

Amy's eyes dart between the two of us. "Really? Are you sure?"

"Absolutely! We'd love the company," I say, like a lying

liar who lies. "And you're the first ex I've met, so I need *all* the gory details."

Amy laughs. "I'll do my best. It just was so long ago we—actually, if I'm staying, I should save the stories for the table. I'll be right back!"

She prances back to the bar where her drink is waiting. In her absence, Sid and I whisper at each other furiously.

"What the hell? You dated Tom Sullivan's daughter?"

"Niece. But same difference. He raised her."

"Oh." It's not the same, actually. Who you're raised by says a lot about who's dead in your life and—to my displeasure—Tom Sullivan is now not only a man who has family, but one who's lost family, too.

"What are *you* doing, inviting her to join us?" Sid asks.

"*Trip to the farm*. I'm saving us from another surprise attack." I would much rather get this over with than live in dread that one of Sid's ex-girlfriends could show up at a moment's notice.

Sid huffs sharply through his nose. "Fine."

Amy returns with a chair, thanking me again for letting her join. "Talking shop is such a buzzkill, so I really appreciate it. How long have you two been dating, anyway?"

I turn to Sid with what I hope appears to be an affectionate smile, because I am truly at the mercy of the current in this conversation.

"So..." Sid starts haltingly. "I don't know if Tom mentioned, but I got my first sanctuary case."

Amy sputters into her wine. "Are you serious? She's your sanctuary seeker?"

"Yup."

"Tom never tells me anything. Confidentiality and all that," says Amy. "So, this was how long ago?"

"Ummm... six weeks?" He looks at me for confirmation, which is annoying because it's not like I know. I nod anyway. "Yeah. The wedding was two weeks ago, so in total it's been about six—"

"The *wedding*?" Amy pales.

"We just really hit it off," says Sid. "I know how it looks, but we had this special connection—"

This is bad. For all the progress we made today, we're about to flame out the same way we did with Tom. Maybe Sid would be doing better in front of a neutral party, but Amy is a particularly awful test case. For all I know, he still has feelings for her. It could even be reciprocated. Am I about to watch my fake marriage crumble in front of me?

I don't care who he shacks up with a few years from now, but for the sake of April's broken pancreas, I have got to do something to mark my territory today. I scooch my chair closer to his and grab his hand.

"By special connection, he means I hit him with a rock."

Sid turns the same colour as his pickled beets, while Amy's hands fly to her mouth, muffling her shriek.

"More! You have got to tell me more," she says, leaning forward.

"It was a total accident. I'd just come to the acreage and Carlos wanted to see how I used to hunt rabbits. Someone should have told Sid we were using the slingshots," I say. "And then bam! Just like that, Sid's got a bleeding hand and we're arguing over whether or not to go to the doctor—"

"I can totally picture it."

"And... I dunno, it's funny. But I just said to myself, I could yell at this man forever."

"Is that seriously what happened, Sid?"

"Well—"

"Babe, show her your scar."

Sid gives me a withering look, then lifts our joined hands to reveal the shining mark that may or may not have occurred in the manner I just described. But it seems to ratify my story, giving us a slap-slap-kiss vibe that our dysfunction can probably sell.

"I love it. I always knew you'd end up with someone with a bit of fire in her, Sid," says Amy. "You've got to tell me everything. Where did you come from? How are you liking the island?"

"Oh, it is so great!" I lie.

A kale and goat cheese salad arrives for Amy, but she hardly touches it, preferring to quiz me instead. The conversation is nothing short of exhausting. I give Amy a shortened version of my life, consistent with what I told Tom. Little tears prickle in her eyes when I tell her about living through the fall of Port Alberni and later my mother's death. When I mention I have a younger sister, she perks up, asking how she likes school, and is particularly delighted to learn April got an A on a math test a couple of days ago. All the studying is paying off.

"I always wanted siblings," says Amy. "But… well, it's probably for the best it was just Tom and me. How's he treating you, by the way?"

"Oh, he's great." Biggest lie yet.

"Really? That's amazing! I mean, I'm not surprised. He takes his job very seriously." But there's something to the way she says this that tells me she knows. No one is saying it out loud, but Amy Sullivan is perfectly aware that her uncle is an asshole.

"Okay, my turn. I want to know more about *you*, Amy. Sid told me you were running for office, but I'm forgetting what you do for work now."

"I'm head logistical officer at the Reinventor's Guild," she says, drawing herself up happily.

"The… what?"

"Sid! You haven't told her about the Guild?" Amy rounds on him, aghast.

Sid, who has had the luxury of silence for most of this conversation, straightens in his seat. "I guess it never came up."

"Not even when you talked about the campaign? But that's my whole platform. Innovation!" Amy sounds more distressed than she ever did asking us about our supposed romance. Maybe she isn't interested in Sid that way after all.

"Oh, I told Kayla that. I said you work in innovation."

"He did," I chip in.

"Well, you should come by the guild. If we're going to align our campaigns, it would be better if both of you know what I'm working on. I can give you a tour. You can bring your sister too, if she's interested. No, wait!" She bounces in her seat, fingers flaring into sunbursts of enthusiasm. "I'll do you one better: I'll talk to Tom. We can organize a formal tour for new immigrants and their sanctuary hosts. The branding will be perfect! Immigration and innovation all together. And with Tom there to give it some gravitas—"

"Sounds a bit contrived," says Sid.

"It's a photo op. Of course it's contrived. I've got a friend at the paper. I'll tell her about it and see what she thinks," says Amy.

"Wait, photo op?" I say. "How the hell would you take a photo?"

Amy flashes me a grin so dazzling, it reminds me of James. "Come by the guild and I'll show you."

"Hmmm." Sid scratches his chin. "I mean, I trust you when it comes to publicity—"

"As you should."

"—but Kayla and I need to talk about it. If we're involving her sister, I want April to be comfortable."

"Totally understandable," says Amy. "Crossing my fingers, though, because I am excited about this. I think

I'll head back to the office and see if I can't work out some details."

"But you've hardly touched your lunch," I say.

"Oh, I'll take it to-go." Amy waves for one of the waiters. "Honestly, I come here because you never know who you might bump into, not for the food. I forget to eat all the time."

That is the most ridiculous thing I have ever heard in my life. Choosing to skip a meal is one thing, but *forgetting* to eat? Clearly, she's never wanted for food.

Amy packs her salad up into a beaten-up plastic box which, despite its rough appearance, still seems like a luxury to me. "Sid, can I borrow you for a second? I promise, I won't take him away for long," she adds with a wink.

"Oh… sure."

Sid follows her toward the bar. I watch her place a hand lightly on his arm. The tiny gesture makes my throat clench as I wonder if I let my guard down too soon. Is she coming on to him? And if she is… what can I reasonably do about that?

He shakes his head, which plays all too well with the narrative I'm building around them. What if he's said *no* for now, but she keeps asking? What if she wears him down?

Finally, he comes back and I rise from my chair to greet him, pulling him into my arms so that Amy gets a parting view of how desperately in love we are. As his chest presses into mine, he trembles with laughter.

"What's so funny?" I whisper, watching Amy leave. "Is she on to us?"

"Not exactly. But she's a smart girl. She knows something is up." Sid pulls back from me, a wide grin on his face, despite the flush of embarrassment that colours his usually pale skin.

My heart sinks. What's so funny? I left out all the stuff about April being sick when Amy quizzed me, but we'll be in a shitload of trouble if everyone figures out why we're together.

"What did she say?"

"Well, she's trying to make sense of why I would get married to someone so quickly."

"And?"

"Kayla... she thinks I got you pregnant."

TWENTY-THREE

IT TAKES A good minute for us both to stop laughing. It's not the best-case scenario, but at least Amy didn't clock us as people who have never slept together.

After her departure, we both agree we're tired of playing pretend and want to get home. But I still hold his hand as we walk to the bus stop, just in case. Amy could pop up at any second, so there's no sense in ending the charade yet.

"You told her I'm not though, right?"

"I did, but I'm guessing I looked guilty as sin."

"Who, you?" I snort.

"She sighed and said, *waiting until there's no risk of miscarriage?*"

"Holy shit! So she actively thinks this is true?"

"So it would seem."

"Fake married and now fake pregnant. I am building quite the life here."

If it was a lie we could keep up indefinitely, I would be all for it. It's such a convenient explanation. Unplanned pregnancies are easy to stumble into. But things will look suspicious a few months from now when I don't start showing. Of course, we could tell her we had a miscarriage, but... no. My blood chills at the idea. There are some things I can't make light of.

There is another solution, of course. Sid could knock me up for real. So what if the baby comes a month late? It might even convince Tom that we like each other. But while I would do almost anything for April, everyone has a line and creating a whole ass human being to support a lie is mine.

A wagon pulls up. Sid helps me into the carriage and soon we're being whisked back towards the acreage. I allow myself to slump against his sturdy frame, because why not? I've concluded that so long as we're in public, it's safer to fasten myself to him than not. It keeps our lies consistent—but also, it feels better. While I enjoyed our little friend-date—especially the restaurant—going into town is still overwhelming and Sid's physical presence creates a nice barrier between me and that chaotic world. Thank goodness it's over.

Except... it isn't. Amy wants to parade us around town to get herself in the newspaper. Even if we don't do that, I promised Sid I would help him with his campaign.

"Sid?" We don't usually talk much on the bus, but we need to sort this out before we get home. "Are we asking April about that tour Amy wants to do?"

"You don't want to do it, do you?"

"I mean... she's your ex. Isn't it weird for you?"

He shrugs. "We broke up ten years ago. I don't think we're functionally the same people we were back then. She only dated me because it pissed off Tom."

"What?" I crane my neck so that I can look at him better. "I thought Tom liked you."

"He does now. But I was an angry, messed up kid from TNS back then. He didn't want that around his little angel. Maybe it would be different now. I don't really care. Amy is a kind, capable woman. I would love to work with her. But that's where it ends for me."

He glances at me, as if he knows I've been worrying. I find myself thinking, *give it time*. Underneath his stalwart skin, Sid Charles is a tender person. He would fall in love easily, if someone only gave him affection in return. It's tragic no one is trying to love him—which is probably why I keep imagining Amy doing just that. Someone *should* love him, but I'm here getting in the way.

The least I can do is keep up my end of our bargain. "Well… if you really want to campaign with Amy, then we can ask April what she thinks."

"Thanks." Sid smiles. "I think it would be a good test run, before we do larger campaign events. A smaller, more controlled crowd full of people already on our side."

"You figure Tom is still on our side, then? Even if you don't divorce me?"

Sid sighs. "I hope so. But I could ask Amy to leave him off the guest list, if you really want me to."

"No. That will tip her off that things are bad between us."

There's a pause that lasts long enough, I think we've fallen into our typical bus silence. But then Sid says in little more than a whisper, "She would understand."

That's what I was scared he would say. I've got nothing against Amy herself, aside from that she didn't finish her salad. But as far as I'm concerned, she's guilty by association, even if no one can choose their family. Anything we tell her could worm its way back to Tom.

"I need to get used to being around him, anyway."

"Okay," says Sid, squeezing my shoulder, which gives me a pleasant buzz. We really are becoming the team we hoped to be.

Secretly, I'm praying April objects to this whole plan before it gets off the ground.

WHO DO I think I'm kidding? April is thrilled by the idea. Unlike me, she has heard of the Reinventor's Guild already. It's come up during her science classes.

"Kayla, we've got to do the tour!" Her eyes are massive. "They do so many cool things there! Everyone else got to go on a field trip last year, but I *missed* it. I've missed everything! But if I can get a tour with one of the directors—"

"Don't worry. She seemed super keen on it."

"This is so amazing! Thank you!" She hugs me and then, to everyone's surprise, throws her arms around Sid. Afterward, April goes spinning off around the empty living room and Sid and I stare at each other, no doubt wondering the same thing. Does she even know how incredible what she did was? What it means?

She's safe. My sister feels safe.

It takes a while for Amy to work us into her schedule, but a week or so later, the special day arrives. She sets up the tour on a weekend so that April can come without missing school. The three of us get off the bus just before we reach town, then follow Sid up a gravel path strewn with a carpet of maple and oak leaves. As we crest the top of the hill, we come face to face with a large barn. A high-pitched whining noise alerts me that something more than cows wait inside.

"What the hell is that?" I ask.

"Power drill, probably," Sid says.

"Power? So electric?"

"Yup. The Reinventor's Guild is one of the few places on consistent wiring."

"Amazing!" April crows.

I spot Amy standing by a shed adjoining the main barn. A small crowd is gathered behind her, but her red hair stands out. She's wearing the same, sharp black dress as before, but this time I also notice the polished high-heels on her feet. Next to her, a woman holds what looks like an old cellphone. I can't imagine what it's for—until she holds it up in front of us as we march up the hill. "Say cheese."

Is this the camera Amy was so excited about? I guess it's impressive that there's enough spare electricity on Salt Spring to run a cellphone at all, but how do they get the photos off it and into the newspaper? They can't still have working printers, can they?

"You're here! And this must be the lovely April I've heard so much about," says Amy, offering hugs and handshakes as we join the circle.

"You've heard of me?" April goes slightly white.

Amy nods. "Kayla says you're doing very well in school."

"I mean, I try to. I've got a lot to catch up on."

"There's no shame in that. Sid, have you met the Wongs? They're hosting another sanctuary case."

Amy deftly moves through the crowd, forcing everyone to shake hands and smile at each other. It isn't a large group. People who immigrated within the last year have been invited, along with their sanctuary hosts, if they have them. There are two families who have recently immigrated from the San Juan islands and a woman who moved here from Penelakut. Only one other person is a sanctuary case—a skittish, white-haired man who eyes both April and I with suspicion. A small part of me wants to grab his hands and whisper, "Same, old timer," but for obvious reasons, neither of us do. The Wongs seem to be the people hosting him. They shake Sid's hand as Amy tells them all about how our chance encounter at the restaurant inspired this whole afternoon.

I'm a little surprised there are so few of us. Amy's talk of making it a big event convinced me this would be a huge production, but I guess this is a more realistic view of what immigration would look like thirty-two years after the end of the world. Sid has mentioned that ten or twenty years ago, it was a lot more people. Whole groups showed up begging for refuge at once. But we're far enough out now that people are either settled within their own nations or dead.

I don't mind, of course. A smaller group suits me. Best of all, there's one face I don't see.

"Where's Mr. Sullivan?" April asks, invoking the devil's name.

"He'll be here soon. Bradley is driving him up," says Amy.

"Bradley?" Sid says. "Bradley who?"

"Patterson."

I can't help noticing that Amy is no longer meeting Sid's eye.

"*Bradley Patterson*? Is he hosting a sanctuary case?"

"No, but I met him for drinks, and he said he would drive Tom. You know how his leg gets."

"And then is he *leaving*?"

"Sid... he wants to form a coalition."

"No. Amy, you already know how I feel about this."

"But why not?" She grabs his arm, pulling him away from the larger group. I drift in their direction, curious. Not that I understand what they're talking about. "We've already started one. We've got you and me and Uncle Tom. If you can stomach that—"

"Patterson is different. You know he is."

"How? Why? He doesn't have to be."

I would very much like to know that, too.

I get my answer when their argument is cut short by a pair of horses trotting up the hill, towing a wagon. Nay, a *carriage*. This is easily the most elegantly appointed vehicle I have seen since coming to Salt Spring, with tassels dangling from the corners of the enclosed box. I make out Tom Sullivan through a window, sour-faced as usual, but the real sight to behold is the man driving the buggy. He's wearing a black fedora, patent leather shoes and a tailored suit that somehow puts Amy's dress to shame.

"Bradley! You made it." Amy rushes forward. "And thank you for bringing Uncle Tom."

"It wasn't any trouble," says the man, getting down from the carriage seat. "I like driving. Does me good to get outside."

"No..."

I turn at the sound of April's voice. She's staring at the carriage too, but her face is so pale, it reminds me of when she was still sick.

"What is it?" I ask her.

"It's... it's nothing." She blinks furiously. "I just thought... it's nothing."

Normally, I would press for further details, but the arrival of our last two guests means Amy is eager to get the tour started and the woman from the newspaper starts snapping photos again. Sid's hand clenches around mine as the man in the fedora strolls up to us.

"Sid Charles! And this must be your wife. Amy told me all about you."

"*Bradley.*"

"Hi." I hold my hand out for him to shake, since Sid seems incapable of doing that.

"It's good to see all of you." Tom Sullivan gives me nothing but a curt nod. My pulse jerks as he strides past, and I wonder if Bradley Patterson can feel it through my trembling fingers. Wanting something to focus on other than Tom, I look up at Bradley. He's not a bad-looking man. He doesn't have the sheer presence of Sid, or the magazine swagger of someone like James, but I would guess he's a couple of years younger. There's a boyish charm to him. His hands look so soft, I wouldn't avoid him if I came across him the wilds. Which is to say, I'm certain I could kick his ass if I needed to.

"And... April, was it? I think my sister goes to school with you," says Bradley, turning to her.

"Oh. Does she? I'm still learning everyone's names," says April, unconvincingly. "Especially last names."

"I imagine so. You're in a mixed education stream, yes? So you'll have lots of students to meet across all the grade levels."

"Something like that," mutters April.

"But that's nothing to be ashamed of. Getting into Grade Ten at all is impressive for a girl who grew up a Wildling. You must be *very* proud of her, Mrs. Charles."

"Oh, sure. Proud as can be."

Well, *now* we're on the same page. Bradley may look harmless but he's clearly a pretentious prick. No wonder Sid hates him. And I'm guessing based on April's horrified reaction to his carriage that his sister sucks just as much as he does—though luckily there are no signs of another surprise guest.

Bradley takes off his fedora and pulls a small hand mirror out of his pocket so that he can fluff up his hair.

"Welcome everyone!" Amy beams at her small audience, and April shoulders her way to the front of the group. "I'm Amy Sullivan, head logistics officer at the Reinventor's Guild, one of the bedrocks of our community on Salt Spring. People come here because we promise them both the future and the past. Medicine, electricity, plumbing. We make those promises to you, but living up to them isn't easy. The necessities of yesterday are the luxuries of life today. But here, we're putting in the work to help create that beautiful, comfortable future all of us deserve. All of *you* deserve.

"One of you asked me recently, how does a photo get in the newspaper these days? Well, step inside and let's find out. This is where the magic happens!" She pulls a large key out of her purse and unlocks the door behind her. "Please keep to the marked walkway inside. We don't want to get in the way of the engineers and scientists."

"Scientists…" April whispers the word and my heart strains. Is this something she's dreamed of? How did I not know that? The idea that she managed to keep anything to herself during all those years in the woods makes me feel inadequate. Then again, why would she ever mention a dream like that? It would have been impossible. Like dreaming of toilet paper.

April and Amy lead the way into the massive barn and the whirling cries of machinery intensify. This is hardly the science lab I saw illustrated in children's books—no twirly tubes or beakers filled with mysterious substances. That doesn't make it any less impressive. Amy points us to the most powerful working furnace in the Pacific Northwest. The artisans surrounding it are bent over workbenches, smoothing out moulds for a variety of projects. Gears for water turbines, rudder blades for boats, letters for the printing press that keeps the newspaper running. They also create mounts that an artisan can use to insert a woodblock, which is how they make prints. In other words, that photographer is only taking pictures for references images. If the newspaper wants to print any photos, they'll need someone to meticulously carve the image before it can go through the press.

Up next is an area stationed by someone dressed like a traditional scientist. She wears a protective coat, gloves, and goggles. A massive collection of plants, rocks, and bits of seaweed surround her. Right now, she's grinding a lump of dried clay to a fine powder.

"This is our chemistry department. They work on fertilizer blends, so quite a few of our employees are in the test field out back. We're also getting *very* close to lightfast ink."

April nods as if this makes a lick of sense. My gait stiffens as we follow Amy to the area where a dozen people are operating tools that survived the Quake. I let the strange words tumble by me: *table saw, power drill, angle grinder, nail gun.*

Until now, I hadn't realized how ambitious the island is. They're not satisfied with survival, but instead are looking to some future where life resembles the riches of the past. I should be impressed—and yet I can't help thinking, *isn't this how the world ended*? Progress at the expense of all else? Do we *need* all these inventions?

Or are these just more of the Grand Astrologue's opinions rattling around inside me? He had to find some way to justify keeping us in that tiny compound, tending goats. We were avoiding the *evils of the modern world*. He picked and chose from a wide variety of religious beliefs and cultural traditions, trying to convince us that everyone from Buddha to Jesus agreed that things had gone too far. Fossil fuels, big pharma, the Canadian government. Every one of them accelerated us into catastrophe as they chased nothing but progress, progress, progress. It was our job to simplify things and take humanity back to its roots. Men tending goats in the pasture. Women spinning wool at home.

The memories make me shiver. Yet I can't chase his voice

out, because maybe—in a small way—the science agrees with him. All the wars and plagues that buckled humanity wouldn't have gotten their hooks in without the help of global warming. Mum told me that our Quake was one of many humanitarian crises before everything fell apart. There was always some far-flung place suffering in the news—waves of refugees forced off the vanishing coastline of Bangladesh. Global markets flying into chaos as blackouts worsened in China and Shanghai flooded. Hurricanes battered the American Southeast until Mickey Mouse himself had to flee Florida. Whole Pacific islands were swallowed by the sea. Even with our earthquakes and tsunamis, we got lucky out here because of the steep cliffs of our beaches.

I'm being paranoid. A couple mitre saws hooked up to solar cells is not the same as a billion people fighting over oil—but where is the line? The world ended in increments, too.

A large hand lands on my shoulder. Sid hovers over me, his expression gloomy. "I'm sorry."

"What?"

"We shouldn't have encouraged this. And I *know* you're uncomfortable."

"I'm fine." I whisper back, determined to do a better impression of pretending that's true. "It's just… a lot. A lot of noise. A lot of people."

"I can't believe she invited Bradley Patterson. He doesn't have a thing to do with the Guild. He just wants to slide into as many photos as possible leading up the election."

"But isn't that what you're trying to do?"

Sid falls quiet, which shouldn't be noticeable in the general din of confusion inside the shop. The old man is currently trying to grab one of the power drills and Amy's typically tinkling laughter goes several notes shriller as she tries to redirect him. Not far away, Tom Sullivan has a file out and is scribbling away. Personally, I'm grateful. April and I are easily the best-behaved Wildlings here. But Sid is so upset, it sours any sense of accomplishment I might have enjoyed. This whole day was meant to help Sid's campaign and now he's worried that Bradley Patterson is stealing his thunder.

That Bradley Patterson is stealing his Amy?

"The difference," says Sid slowly, "is that Bradley Patterson doesn't care about anything. The only reason he's running for office is because he's got a shitload of money and his mother expects him to. Because apparently, they don't have enough control over the island already."

"Oh."

"And Amy wants to align with him. I'm not saying it's a terrible idea. He's running more ads in the paper than any other candidate. But there could be consequences down the line."

"Like what?"

"Right now, a council runs the island. It's a lot like the local elections that existed before the Quake. We've got a mayor and thirty-two council positions. There are a few rules about how many need to come from each of the islands. We get half of them; the outer islands get the other sixteen. But aside from that, people mark their five favourite candidates, turn in their ballots and the people with the most ticks get in. It's simple. Since we're all against each other, no one really gangs up."

He sighs dramatically. I'm missing the tour now, but I just don't have the same level of interest as April does in Salt Spring's attempts to resurrect the chicken pox vaccine. Plus, Sid, clearly needs to get this off his chest.

"But the nation is growing, so… people are talking about changing things. We might go back to a parliamentary system someday. It would make it easier to ensure everyone has regional representation, and I'm not against that. But you just know that if we do start cutting things up into ridings, we're going to end up right back in political parties. It's already happening a little. Tom has council friends on the other islands whom he doesn't directly compete with. He writes opinion pieces for the paper endorsing them."

"He did that for you, too."

"He did. I think he wants to be ready in case the change happens. I can live with being in the same political party as Tom. He's kept the immigration department alive on his own for years. But Bradley? You should see the ads he runs. He'll have one that's going on about *protecting our way of life* one week, then one about *building a welcoming nation* the next. He's just throwing shit at the wall, seeing what sticks. He doesn't care. Why should any of us trust someone who flip-flops on everything? Who's to guess how he's going to vote once he gets in?"

"Hmmm." I'll need to read up on parliamentary government back at home, but I get the gist of where he's coming from. At the very least, I know how awful it is when people are telling you to trust someone who you know is bad news. "If he isn't committed, then maybe he's pliable? Maybe you and Amy can shape him into someone you can work with?"

"Maybe Amy can. I'm not touching Bradley Patterson."

"You might not have a choice," I say.

He sighs, which seems about as good a place to leave the conversation as any. Besides, the tour is wrapping up. Both the reporter and Amy are making their way through the crowd, asking people how they enjoyed themselves. To her credit, Amy seems busy handing something to April, so the reporter reaches Sid and I first.

"Sid Charles and Kayla Hollins?" she reads off a small sheet. "Do you mind if I record this conversation?"

"Not at all," says Sid, so I also nod.

"Great." She pulls out her phone again, but instead of pointing the lens at us, turns one end toward our mouths so that it can pick up our voices through the din of people talking. "You're running for council this coming spring, right Mr. Charles?"

"Yes. I am."

"Would you say that you see yourself as in-line with Ms. Sullivan's work here? She told us that she's hoping that if she gets onto council, she'll be able to allocate more government resources towards the Reinventor's Guild."

"Ms. Sullivan and I would be in agreement on that, yes," says Sid. "I'm familiar with her work. She's done a lot to direct investment into practical solutions for our nation. Improved wind turbines. Modular housing designs. She played a major role in spearheading those projects."

"And do you see yourself as playing a role in all of this? Or is this strictly Ms. Sullivan's area?"

"Well, like she said earlier, the main reason people come to Salt Spring is because we offer a better quality of life. I know that played a huge role in my decision to escape TNS. There's a promise we make people when they come here. We've got a duty to keep it. My focus would be advocating for advancements and solutions that make a higher quality of life accessible to all."

"Thank you."

I expect her to head towards Bradley Patterson, who is clearly hovering at the edge of our conversation, but instead she turns the phone toward me.

"Kayla Hollins. You're a recent immigrant here. Would you say the nation is keeping its promises to you?"

"Oh... um. Yeah. Sure."

"Sure?"

"Sure."

"So you think there's room for improvement?" she presses.

I stare at her, wide eyed. I don't get the impression people will like it if I complain about their island. Especially when April would be toast without their stupid insulin.

Luckily, Sid saves me from having to come up with a nuanced answer. "There's always room for improvement. That's why we need people in government committed to working for our citizens," he says.

"Yeah, what he said."

"I see." The reporter looks over her shoulder at April. "Your sister seemed enthusiastic about the tour. Do you think today inspired her? Are we looking at the birth of a future scientist?"

"I dunno. Maybe?" When the reporter looks disappointed yet again, I stammer on. "I mean, this wasn't something we even thought about before. We were in the woods. Surviving. It's a totally new world for her."

"Perfect." She lowers her phone. "And not a moment too soon. My battery is dead."

From the corner of my eye, I see every inch of Bradley Patterson deflate, including his voluminous hair.

"Will this seriously be in the paper?" I ask, now that I know her phone is off.

"Maybe. It's a nice human-interest story. Might spruce up the election coverage," she says. "Good luck, Mr. Charles."

She goes to speak with Bradley, even if her phone is in her pocket now, and I grin up at Sid. "So? How'd we do?"

"Good, I think."

"I'll take it."

Maybe I don't suck at being his wife after all.

As if he can read my thoughts and wants nothing more than to sow doubt in them, Tom Sullivan's voice cuts through the crowd. "Well done today, Ms. Hollins." He's smiling in that smug, satisfied way of his. "Let's see how long we can keep this up,"

Keep this up. Maybe he's only referring to my marriage with Sid, but I think again of my sanctuary papers, which I regret lying on more each day. Back when I made that choice, I didn't think April and I would need to stay on the island. I didn't think what we said mattered. If Tom ever gets proof that I falsified them, then he'll... Actually, that's part of the problem. I have no idea what he'll do. And it's not like I can ask Sid about it either, when the trust between us is so fragile. We've only just moved past TNS.

But I'm not letting Tom steal my confidence. I can keep this up all day. I loop an arm around Sid's waist and go up on my toes. It takes him a second to realize what I want him to do, but eventually he bends down enough that I can peck him on the lips. Our first kiss since I learned about TNS.

Take that, Tom Sullivan.

I land on my heels to see Tom rolling his eyes.

TWENTY-FOUR

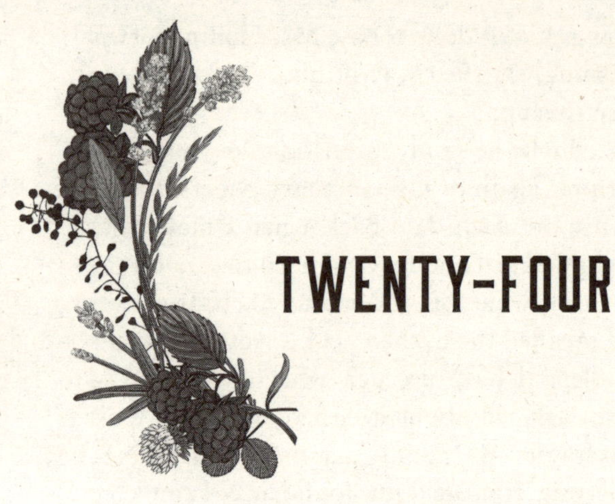

"I CAN'T BELIEVE how long she talked to me," says April, who is still giddy during the bus ride home. "Like, she could have gone back to shmoozing with the reporter lady, but instead she talked to *me*."

"And why shouldn't she? You were the most interesting person there," I say. But honestly, I am grateful for Amy Sullivan. I wouldn't have expected someone who hustles as hard as she does to notice how much this meant to April. Ever since finding out she dated Sid—and that she's Tom's niece—I've been on a constant see-saw, trying to decide if I like her. Today, she's in my good books.

"Ms. Sullivan says they run a summer program for high-school students," says April. "Doing it really helps your chances of getting an apprenticeship at the guild after graduation. She says if I can get my math up, I should apply next spring."

"That's amazing! And you totally will. Didn't you get an A on that test?"

April huffs. "Kayla, that was on factoring. We were coving stuff that kids here learn in Grade Four. Grade

Four! I am so far behind, it hurts. In regular math, they're adding exponents to polynomials."

"What's an exponent?"

"Exactly." She looks down at a pamphlet Amy gave her, describing the program the guild ran this past summer. "I need a whole plan of attack. Would you mind if I stayed late at school a few nights a week? Sometimes there's a teacher on duty to give tutoring—maybe if I got some, I would catch up faster."

"Oh... um..."

"I think that's a great idea," says Sid.

"Thank you!" April squeals.

"Hold on, I'm still deciding. He's not your big sister."

Sid places a hand over his heart. "And here I thought I was. You wound me, Kayla."

"Ha ha ha. I'm not saying no. I just want to think about it." I still dislike the idea of April spending any more time separated from me than she absolutely needs to. But the way she lit up during the tour is undeniable.

"Why? What's the big deal?" Sid asks.

"She's still my responsibility."

"Her pancreas is my responsibility. I say her pancreas can go."

"Please, Kayla?" April stares at me with that wounded bird expression that made me march us miles across Vancouver Island looking for passage to Salt Spring. I really would be a bitch if I don't let her chase this new dream.

I grunt. "Fine. But not every night. I hardly get to see you anymore."

"I promise it will be worth it! Thank you so much!" She gives me a tight squeeze, like she used to as a little girl. Too soon, she's back to her pamphlet, flipping to the page that most interests her. "They've got a lot of different specialties you can take. I like the idea of chemistry. I could design new drugs for people someday. Maybe rediscover synthetic insulin."

Maybe. She's got a whole life ahead of her to try.

Still, I can't shake my unease as we arrive home. I stopped worrying about the school trying to brainwash her weeks ago. Her math booklets are too boring to possibly be trying to woo her into some dark cult. And I know if she wants to be successful on this island, she needs a good education. So how come I feel oddly disappointed?

April heads straight to our bedroom to study. Meanwhile, I stand listless in the living room, growing grumpier by the second.

"Why don't you have any furniture?" I ask. "It would be nice having somewhere to sit down."

"Well, there's the kitchen," says Sid, closing the door to the apartment.

"Everyone uses the kitchen! People can just show up whenever." I tilt my head towards the bedroom, which April has already commandeered. "There's nowhere for me to be alone."

Sid's brow furrows. "I thought you said you don't like being alone."

"Shut up."

"No, I'm being serious. Are you okay?"

"Everyone likes being alone sometimes. I was just talking out of my ass."

"You said people only want to be alone because they have to be," says Sid, not buying my flippant explanations. "Are you feeling unsafe?"

The question is so direct, I'm not sure how to answer it. I look over my shoulder at April, but she's so engrossed with the pamphlet, I don't think she's listening to any of this. "No. I don't think that's it."

"Oh. That's good, then?"

"Sure. New shitty emotion unlocked. It's everything I've ever dreamed of."

"Kayla—"

"I'm going for a run. Tell Carlos I'm sorry I can't help with dinner. And don't panic, big guy." I punch him lightly on the arm.

"I won't." He serves me the same face most people make when they bite into an unripe blackberry. "You told me where you're going this time."

Running for the sake of running. It's almost as absurd as paying for a haircut or taking a salad home uneaten. But for some reason, this one comes naturally to me. I miss the long open roads on Vancouver Island. I miss the empty space I had to traverse to find food or water. There was a purpose to all the running then, but here, in this place of ease and comfort, I miss the feeling of my muscles aching and sweat dripping down my spine.

With each slap of my feet against gravel, it's like I'm grounding my body in an earlier version of myself. The Kayla of two months ago was never tortured with discontent. There was always something that needed to be done; always a teenaged girl who depended on me for life. Now, I've arrived at the greatest success a parent can hope for: April doesn't need me anymore. Not like she used to.

My sister wants to be a scientist. I should be thrilled and on one level, I am. Look at her, taking after our mum. They got so few years together, but her influence is still there. It's poetic, even. In hindsight, I guess I was more Dad's child. I work with my hands. I take care of what needs doing. Except even Dad had a passion. No one carved more beautifully than he did. I wish I'd been able to keep more of the things he made.

I slow to a walk as the ugly emotion I didn't dare name back in Sid's apartment swells inside me. It's not just that

April is outgrowing me. I'm jealous of her. Where was I at fifteen? Stumbling around the woods, grieving my father's death. I still had Mum and Curtis then, but my life was so small. It still is. I never got to have big, teenaged dreams. I survived. That's all I ever dared to ask for. Now, I'm living that same small life in a place that offers April so much more.

It's telling that I never had this internal crisis while living in Astolia. Really, I wasn't that far off April's age when we left. We weren't at risk of starving while we lived there. At some point, shouldn't I have wanted something more? I try to remember the conversations I shared with Beth-Anne, the closest I ever got to bearing my unfettered heart.

Every morning, we would go to the goat pen and pick neighbouring does to milk. Under our breath, we would whisper all the things we knew the adults didn't want us to say. Often, I told her stories Mum had read to me back in Port Alberni, though we had to depend on my memory for the details. One time, I was telling her *The Wizard of Oz* and she asked me what a twister was. Since I didn't know, I just told her it was like a tsunami. Close enough, right?

Other days, we talked about the future. I wanted to get married. I wanted to have kids. I wanted to be able to read books without hiding them at the bottom of my bag, *just in case*. Only that last one hints at any ambitions that weren't predetermined for me. And by some metric... I guess I've already achieved most of them now. Look at me. Winning at life yet again.

Beth-Anne, I remember, was more specific in her dreams. The Grand Astrologue had already made a deal with her father. She was promised to Alan, a guy who was already in his twenties when we were thirteen. He was waiting for her to *come of age*, a turn of phrase that now makes my skin crawl.

Once—only once—I remember her saying, "You know what would really be the best? Getting to fall in love and choose my husband."

The wind picks up, making my shirt stick to my sweaty skin. I need to go home and wash up before it gets too late. April will kill me if I fall asleep smelling like this in the bed we share.

"YOU COULD TAKE night classes. Finish your high school diploma, if you want to."

I shouldn't have told Sid about this. He doesn't understand mindless complaining. He's immediately jumped into fix-it mode, each suggestion more overwhelming than the last.

"That's your thing, not mine. Next you're going to suggest I run for office."

We're writing letters. Sid asked for my help getting word about his campaign out to constituents, since my penmanship is significantly more legible than his. James used to help him with tasks like this, but Sid says he always had to check them for sex puns, so I'm a clear improvement. I've been writing the same message over and over—*Do you have concerns about healthcare accessibility on our island?* The task is repetitive enough that we both got bored. He asked if my run the other night helped me feel better, and soon I was rambling about envying April's ambitions.

Big mistake. He's got no sense of when to leave well enough alone.

"You could see if the agriculture department needs your expertise in foraging," he suggests as he presses a wax seal over one of the completed letters.

"I'm not working for the government." I'm not putting

myself through another interview like the one with that asshole in charge of the border guard.

"Not even as a border guard? If you want to make money—"

"I don't want anything, Sid! That's the point."

"You like cooking."

This isn't the first time he's brought that up. I grind my molars as I start yet another letter.

Do you have concerns about healthcare accessibility on our island?

"Carlos lived with Mrs. Buckerfield for years. I almost took you to her café when we went out to eat. But I thought it might be too much pressure. Now I'm thinking I should have introduced you sooner."

"You don't have to do anything! I'm just bitching."

"You're scared."

"You're pushy."

"It's okay to be scared, Kayla. You're starting over here. I remember when I came here—"

"You remember that you had... *concerns about health-care accessibility on our island*?" I hold one of the letters up in front of my face. "If so, Sid Charles wants to hear from *you*."

"When I came here, I felt lost for a while—"

"That's probably because you don't own any furniture. No landmarks."

"Would you stop changing the topic?"

"Nope." I pass him the finished letter. "Look, I know you're trying to be nice, but it isn't helping. I'm not *there* yet."

"You're never going to get *there* if you don't do anything about it."

"Carlos is teaching me," I snap. "And why does something have to be my job, just because I like it?"

"It doesn't, but if you're not happy, shouldn't something change?"

"You know what? You're right. I like cooking. I'm complaining about nothing. I'm sorry I bothered you. I'll shut up about it now."

"That's not—" But I throw him a glare, and he relents. "Fine! Never mind. You are impossible."

It takes all my self-control not to reopen the argument just so I can have the last word. This feels—obnoxiously—like a real marriage. I can hear my parents in our voices, arguing behind closed doors about the Grand Astrologue and whether living in Astolia long term was safe. Only Sid and I are mad at each other over much stupider things. Aren't we lucky? We've got all the petty annoyances of marriage with none of the make-up sex.

"I'm sorry," he says suddenly. "You just wanted someone to listen to you, didn't you?"

I shove another stack of letters in his direction. "Yes. I did."

"I'll try to do better next time."

"Thank you."

"Just—please don't stop talking to me again. Back when you were scared of me—"

"Hey, it's okay." I place a hand over his, hoping it reassures him. "I'm sorry too. I promise I won't ice you out like that again, okay? But... sometimes I need time to think about things before I'm ready to talk about them. Or try to solve them."

He nods, twisting his fingers into mine like he does when we're out in public. "I'll try to remember that. But... it was Hell, Kayla. I never want to be someone you're afraid of."

"I'm not afraid of you. We're still figuring this out. We're going to have arguments."

"True."

His thumb slides across my knuckles, caressing them and drawing a soft hum of pleasure from me. It might have taken us a while to get here, but I *do* feel better. Maybe he's better at listening than I gave him credit for.

"Well… we should probably get back to these letters," he says.

"Oh! Absolutely." I pull my hand from his as an unsettling thought occurs to me.

We hold hands all the time when we're out in public. Obviously, some things are going to turn into habits. But the fact remains that tonight, we did not have an audience. We reached for each other anyway.

I've done a decent job of stowing my heart away. A weaker woman would have ripped his shirt off him by now, I'm sure of it. For instance, this morning, Sid took a break from his campaign and stayed home to help on the acreage. The compost piles needed turning one more time before winter sets in. Sid spent several hours forking over the layers of leaves, dead summer plants and kitchen waste, working up a sweat. Maybe I watched as he took off his button down and tied it around his waist, nothing but a tank top remaining. Maybe he even caught me staring and asked, "What are you looking at?"

I smirked at him. "I was just thinking that a guy built like you is going to be absolutely wasted sitting behind a desk."

He laughed and went right back to work. Every roll of his shoulders or twist of his wrist caused a cascade of ripples, like waves bumping up against the contour of a jagged, gravel beach. Like the waves, they teased at something far greater. His body is a vast ocean I've yet to explore.

And I never will. I value Sid as a friend, but there are certain lines I'm not willing to cross. For one thing, April needs us to stay together long enough for her to become a full citizen. I can only imagine what a mess it would be if Sid and I got involved, only to want to break up, except *oops!* We're married. I can't go anywhere for at least two years. Even without April to consider, I wouldn't do that to Curtis. I promised I would always love him, and I still do.

But as Sid seals another letter shut and I think about his campaign—about the people who might want to prove we have a sham marriage and ruin everything for both of us—sometimes, it feels like we're ignoring the obvious solution.

It would be so easy to convince people that I'm in love with Sid if I actually was.

TWENTY-FIVE

AS AUTUMN WINDS to a close, I help Silas plant garlic bulbs in the cool soil. Carlos comes home from school one day, giddy with news. One of his classmates has a barn cat with new kittens, who is supposed to be a very good mouser. After a few rounds of cajoling, everyone agrees he can have one of the kittens, so long as he can keep it from bothering Wendell's allergies. Each night, the sun sets earlier, so we move our meals inside. James's guitar echoes off the walls of the kitchen every evening.

One of those nights, I finally meet Silas's boyfriend. Roger has bushy hair and round-framed glasses that immediately make me like him. He hugs me on sight, because we're the two "in-laws," which is hilarious, since our situations aren't comparable: Silas and Roger aren't temporary. There's an easy, time-won affection between them that I learn goes back five years, when Roger tried working as a medic for the border patrol and got assigned to their team.

"It was a total bust," he says with a laugh. "I was a nervous mess. Don't know how these guys did it."

"But something good came of it, right?" I say, serving

up carrots caramelized in honey. Carlos and I have been hard at work again.

"Meh. I guess."

Silas rolls his eyes.

On the other end of the spectrum, James scuttles by with a girl I've never met before. I've seen him tow three girls home since arriving: a leggy brunette named Jen; a giggly blonde who I never got the name of—and now this girl, who has a black bob. She introduces herself as Alison, but declines sitting down to dinner. James drags her away once he's snagged cheese and bread from the kitchen.

The next person to bang through the door is April, hair sticking to her face thanks to the rain. When she spots the large crowd gathered around the table, she stops, scanning the room like a rabbit caught in crosshairs.

"Hey, you're home late," I say. Tonight was one of her days staying after class for tutoring, but she's usually home before supper. I was trying to decide how worried I should be and if we needed to establish a curfew for her.

"I know." She marches around the table, not looking at me, but making a beeline for Sid, who looks up when she taps him on the shoulder. "Can I talk to you?"

He stares at her, slightly bewildered. "Sure?"

"I mean in private. Can we talk upstairs?"

His eyes slide to me. I give him a nod, and he rises from his chair. As they go outside, every head at the table follows them.

"Are they close?" Roger voices the question on everyone's mind.

"Umm... sort of?" I slide fried ham onto the table to go with the glazed carrots. "They're both pretty independent. I wouldn't say their paths cross a lot."

"And is school going well for her?"

"Yeah, I think so." Except, do I? April talks about school

a lot, but it's all circumscribed into her study regime. I took that to be a good sign, but school is more than tests and assignments. Most of what I remember about Port Alberni's classroom is my time with Mom. In Astolia, the lessons were so rudimentary, it was my classmates that stuck out to me. Those are an important part of school, too.

"I mean, teenagers never really tell you anything," Roger chuckles, giving me an out.

"Right?" I sure as hell never told my mother I was sleeping with Curtis. Sometimes I like to picture them in Heaven together, her giving him a disapproving glare when their souls are exposed to the cosmic consciousness and she realizes what we shared.

But I never thought about April hiding things from *me*. She didn't when we were in the woods. Why would she? I was all she had. I was her mother, sister, best friend, you name it. What if someone else is taking that friend role in her life now?

It would be for the best. Or at the least, it would be more like what life looked like pre-Quake, and everybody tells me I'm supposed to want that for her—to live an echo of the past.

I try to be talkative. With Sid off with April and James bedding whatever her name was, we've been whittled down to the younger crew, plus me, Silas, and his boyfriend. We all know how well Silas does carrying the social obligations, so someone has to engage Roger.

Try as I might, I keep looking toward the door, wondering when April is going to come back. What secrets could she want to tell Sid instead of me?

When my paranoid behaviour becomes impossible to ignore, Roger gives me a weak smile. "It's probably not anything serious."

"Yeah." I try to laugh. "It's probably…"

A muffled shout reaches my ears. *Sid.* Both my pulse and my body leap, so I'm already at the door when it bursts open. April is in the lead, cheeks flaming. She pushes past me with a hard thrust of her shoulder.

Sid shakes a finger at her. "Hey! That is *not* how you treat your sister, young lady."

April's back goes rod straight, her hands balling into fists. One of which, I realize, is holding a piece of paper.

"Sid, calm down. It's okay." I hurry to her side. "Something going on?"

"*You* have to sign this." She shoves the piece of paper at me so hard, it's like a punch in the stomach.

"Have to sign wha—" I unfold the page, and the words die on my lips.

Dear Mr. Charles and Ms. Hollins,

I am writing to inform you that April Hollins was involved in an altercation today, where she struck another student. Behaviour of this kind is not tolerated at Gulf Islands Secondary School and as such, she is required to attend detention following classes from November 13th – November 17th.

We require your signature as her legal guardians to certify that you have been informed of the situation.

It goes on, describing what I need to do if I want to consult with a member of staff and how the actions they take might escalate if she repeats this behaviour, but I'll have to go over the details another day.

"April, what the hell?" I round on her. "This is why you—did you ask Sid to sign this and not show me?"

"You don't have to scream about it. He wouldn't do it."

"*April!*" On a certain level, I'm impressed. She's embarrassed and did her damnedest to make it so that only Sid had to know. But my mind is reeling. April has a temper, but she's never been physical in how she expresses herself. Hell, I used to wish she had more fight in her. That kind of thing is useful out in the woods.

But we aren't in the wild anymore. Society's standards for tameness are different from mine.

"What happened?"

Her fists tighten, and it dawns on me how public our setting is. I grab her by the wrist. "Let's talk upstairs. Roger, I am so sorry—"

"Oh, you're fine," he says, but like everyone else, he's obviously incredibly uncomfortable.

"I'll be up later tonight," Sid says.

"Sure. Thanks. Grab food before we go, April. You need to eat."

"I know!" she snaps, taking out the measuring cup she keeps in her knapsack to control her portions before ladling carrots and ham onto a plate. "I know how to manage my own body!"

"I never said you didn't." The sooner we get out of this room, the better.

Once we're in our bedroom, I give her time to administer an insulin dose and start her meal. Her hands are shaky, the needle drawing a prick of blood, when usually she's so slick nothing shows on her arm after she's done. I don't interfere, except to tell her how much honey I used per pound of carrots so she can enter all of it into her dose computations. Someone should tell her math teacher about this, and he'll pass her in an instant. Geometry can't be more important than the things she needs to calculate every day.

I wait for her to finish eating, so we both have a chance to cool off. When she's done, I take a steadying breath. "I'm only asking because I care about you. What happened?"

She sets down her fork, balancing an empty plate on her knees. "I hit someone."

"But why? I thought you were studying."

"I was." She presses her hands into her eyes. "That's all I ever do. I was in the school library, studying."

It sounds terribly lonely. "And?"

"And when I got up to go, Gia Lawson was waiting outside for me. Some of the other girls put her up to it, I think. I don't know how anything works." She sniffs hard. "But they were standing down the hall. Maria Patterson and Cirie Gagnon and… I didn't see everyone. At first, I thought it was just Gia, until they started laughing."

"What did she do to you?"

"You wouldn't get it!" April lurches up from the bed, and her plate nearly topples off her knees. Not for the first time, I want to tell Sid to buy some more furniture, but this isn't my apartment. For now, I take the plate and cutlery off her lap and set it on the floor where she won't break it by accident. "You've never dealt with any of this."

"Hey! I was fourteen when we left Astolia. I've been to high school." Sort of. "There were class politics. Girl drama. All that stuff. You can tell me."

April gives me a withering glare. "Did all the kids make fun of you for being a Wildling with a weirdo sister who married her sanctuary host, too?"

My mouth falls open. "Excuse me?"

"Gia was asking me…" She clears her throat and holds her hands up to make scare quotes around the next words. "If I was a *big slut too* and sleeping with Carlos, since that's what my sister did the second she got here."

My heart and face burns for this poor girl. My girl. "How did they know about—"

"Maria Patterson." April buries her face in her knees. "Her older brother is that douchebag who came in the carriage to the guild tour. He must have learned about you guys and then… rumours, I guess."

"The little shit." I'm not sure if I mean Maria or Bradley. I have half a mind to punch either one in the face now, too.

"And—and when I told her you weren't sleeping together, they…" She gasps for air, close to tears again. "They laughed! They laughed even harder and called you a tease and—and Gia kept saying the word *cockblock* and I didn't know what that meant, so I hit her in the face. I slapped her as hard as I could, then everyone screamed and…" Her eyes are wild as she looks at me. "How was I supposed to *know*? How was I supposed to know telling them would make it worse? It's stupid! It's so stupid. Like, first they were calling us sluts, and then when I tried to fix it—"

"April." I wrap my arms around her, pulling her off the chair. "I'm so sorry. You didn't hit enough of them."

"I don't want to hit *anyone*!"

"I know." I rub my hand in circles over her back. "Which is why I can joke about it. You're not going to do it again, right?"

"Of course not!" April pushes me away, swallowing back the few tears she let herself cry. "They're never going to let me into that summer program now."

"You don't know that. You're assuming the worst."

"But it isn't fair. I'm not the problem! I'm…" She rubs her face. "I want to go to bed."

"Sure. In a minute." I smooth her hair. "What about the other girls? Did they get in trouble?"

"Gia did. Not the rest. The other girls sold her out the second the principal asked them. *Gia was so mean! We don't know why she did it!* And like, all they actually did was laugh. The teachers couldn't pin any of it on them. None of it's fair."

"You're right. It's not." I wish I had words of wisdom to give her, but I'm starting to wonder if she's right. I don't know how to relate to this experience. Astolia had its problems, but friends weren't one of them, at least for me. Beth-Anne was the most popular girl in the whole colony, and since I had her on my side, no one messed with me.

Beth-Anne.

"Maybe if you can make one good friend at school?" I say. "Someone you could team up with, so it's harder for them to pick on you? You don't have to get along with everyone, but one person—"

She snorts. "That's what Sid said. But not everyone gets a Silas."

She buries her face in her pillow. I wonder why she picked Silas as an example instead of Beth-Anne. Then it hits me: I've never mentioned her. We both have so much to grieve already, I never wanted to afflict her with more loss. I rarely talk about what we left behind when we escaped Astolia, Beth-Anne included.

As I look around the sparse but safe walls of our apartment, the thought makes me uneasy. What happened to Beth-Anne after I left?

ONCE MY PARENTS found out that my teachers had asked us to lie about the reproductive fitness tests, they began planning. What was to stop the Grand Astrologue from dragging me behind a shed one day and handing me over to some man without telling my father? It had long been obvious he didn't respect my mother's opinions, but we'd convinced ourselves Dad was our shield. Now that the illusion was gone, my parents started squirrelling away haunches of goat meat and bags of turnips.

Some of our neighbours agreed to come with us, including Curtis. That was when I first took notice of him. Up until then, he'd just been another boy in the year below me at school. Now, he was someone brave enough to run away. Resistance popped up around us all at once—an awareness that life had never been what it should be in Astolia, and we had been wrong to excuse it. It seemed everyone had been following the Grand Astrologue out of fear, rather than conviction, and would gladly leave if given the chance.

So I told the one person I couldn't bear to leave behind. I told Beth-Anne.

At first, she hesitated. Astolia was all she'd ever known, the world beyond the hills where we pastured the goats a foreboding mystery. But there were plenty of tantalizing things in the future I painted for her. She wouldn't have to marry Alan. She wouldn't have to hide picture books from sight, to be read only in secret.

"If enough of us go," I whispered as we milked our goats, "maybe we could start our own colony. Do it the right way, with my mom as a teacher and everything."

"That would be perfect." Her hands, usually so nimble, slowed. "But how would we defend ourselves against TNS? Do your parents have guns?"

"Probably not." They were harder to sneak off with than goat meat.

Beth-Anne began milking furiously again "My dad's a guard. He could get us guns. He could protect us."

For about an hour, I was sure we'd solved the problem. If there was one thing that scared me about leaving Astolia, it was running afoul of TNS without any means of defence. After we finished the chores, I raced home, so proud of our solution. I told Dad what Beth-Anne had said and how we would have guns thanks to her father, and... well, looking back, it's obvious what went wrong.

Everyone was a rebel waiting for a reason to fight in my childhood mind. It never occurred to me that the Grand Astrologue chose his guards carefully.

I'll never know if Beth-Anne told her father. We didn't risk it. The minute my parents knew the plan had leaked, they grabbed what little we had stockpiled and made a break for it.

If Dad had made it out alive, would the rest of my story be different? Mom tried to assure me it wasn't my fault. *Never blame yourself for the terrible things someone else does.* And even if he had survived Astolia, our camp was discovered by another hostile group three years later. I've always assumed it was TNS, but I'm not actually sure, because April and I weren't there for the attack. Dumb luck is all that saved us. There's no guarantee Dad would have fared any better.

Even with my mother's reassurances, I still feel guilty. No, worse: some part of me blames Beth-Anne. Why else would I never mention her to April?

Sitting in the quiet of Sid's home, it seems obvious that it wasn't her fault either. She never asked for a father she couldn't trust to protect her.

I pick up April's empty plate and leave her to sulk alone in our room. The dish still smells of glazed carrots. An image creeps into my mind of Beth-Anne, ten years older than I last saw her, eating the same mushy turnip stew, living in a hut with Alan and his goats. For years, I've thought of her as one of my dead, because it's easier than admitting the truth.

Odds are, she's still trapped there.

TWENTY-SIX

EVENTUALLY, SID COMES upstairs. It's a relief to be free from my own mind, so I rush toward him, which he takes as a sign that I need a hug.

"You okay?"

"*I'm* fine. I just…" The scent of him hits me as I wrap my arms around him, struggling for words. "We came here for her. *I* don't have to like it, but if April doesn't…"

"School is hard. She'll get through it." He pats my shoulder. I take that as a hint I should let go before I make it weird. "We should talk to the principal, though."

"*We?*" I assumed I would have to go in, but Sid's participation never crossed my mind. "You don't have to do that."

"We're both her legal guardians."

"In name only."

"Do you not want me there? I could help. Dom got into a lot of fights growing up, and his sanctuary hosts hated dealing with it, so I've had practice."

"Of course I would love the help, it's just…" I already owe him so much.

As if sensing the reason for my reticence, Sid grimaces.

"It wouldn't all be to help you out. One of the kids involved is Bradley Patterson's little sister. I would like to know what's going on at the school. If she runs her mouth again—"

"Oh, shit." I hadn't stopped to think what this could mean for Sid's campaign. What if April and I put it in jeopardy? "Do you think he'd do something?"

Sid shakes his head. "I don't know. He was friendly enough at the guild tour, but like I said, he's wishy-washy in his positions. He wants to work with us now, but I doubt we're his *only* options. What if instead of allying with us, he decides he'd rather just knock us out of the race entirely? And if he found proof we have a sham marriage—"

"And April told those girls we aren't sleeping together."

"Exactly."

"Well... Well, what do we do?"

Sid lets out a sigh that belongs to an apostle overlooking the sins of the world. He draws a crumpled letter out of his pocket. "I pulled this out of the recycling."

"What is..." The answer appears soon enough. Personal, embossed stationary, the words *Patterson Family* adorning the letterhead, greets my eyes.

How's it going, Sidney?
    I've been thinking about our chat the other day. You simply must give me a chance to pick your brain about campaign strategy. That tour you and Amy cooked up was sheer brilliance. If you've got time next week, you and your charming wife must visit for—

"You're kidding. Bradley Patterson sent us a dinner invite, and you threw it away without showing me?"

"He's *not* the kind of ally I care about courting."

"Is your name even short for Sidney?"

"Nope."

"Huh." I trace my fingers over the embossed roses at the top of the paper. This must have been kept in storage since the Quake. How perfectly pretentious. "So… if we go to dinner with these people, what do you think will happen?"

Sid shakes his head. "At this point? Not a clue. We're lucky he sent the letter before April started smacking kids around. I doubt he'd do it now."

I know what he means by that. This branch is the one thing we can grab onto before plummeting over a waterfall. After all the trouble we've caused Sid, it's the least I can do. "I'll come, but…"

"But?" he leans forward, uneasy.

I run my thumb across the flowers and try not to be intimidated. "I need a new dress."

SID AND I craft the most glowing, enthusiastic letter we can. *So wonderful meeting you, Bradley! Kayla admired your coach and can't believe she'll get the chance to see your home! We would love to share dinner!*

I will admit, I may have overdone it on the punctuation.

Then, for a week, we wait for Bradley's reply. If he's sending one. Even if he does, there's a chance it will just tell us to jump off a bridge. Luckily, another sheet of rose paper does arrive, giving us a date, time, and bearing the telling little line, *and why don't you bring April, too? Maria is so eager to get to know her better. Hope you don't mind, but I've invited Amy Sullivan along too.*

"*Invited* Amy?" sighs Sid. "What do you want to bet she talked him into it?"

"You think she would?" I ask.

"It's a chain. If I go down, Tom looks like an idiot for endorsing me, then Amy is way too deep in Tom's branding, so she falls next—"

"Right. Guess I'll tell April."

She is less than enthusiastic about the idea.

"I'm not going to that snake's house!" April shrieks.

"You think you have a choice in this?" I snap. "Just be glad you're getting a new outfit."

And April is at least pleased about that. Sid gives us a whole ten dollars to spend on clothes—a standard week's wages—though we soon discover we could be spending far, *far* more on even one outfit. But after rummaging through the exchange for a while, we manage to find something. I get a dress covered in red polka dots whereas April picks a—frankly—boring brown skirt. They both only need a little mending, which I spend the next couple of days doing.

Before the dinner, I follow Sid around the acreage like a hawk, making sure he doesn't smoke. We already know we're going to have to kiss at some point tonight. How else are we going to sell Bradley on our very legit romance? But I would rather not taste ash every time.

"You know I only smoke when I'm stressed, right?" he barks at me. "And this is not helping."

"Is that the pattern? Because you smoked all the time when we first met—oh."

No one is in a good mood by the time we pile onto the bus, heading towards the northern end of the island. I've never visited this area before. As we approach St. Mary's Lake, Sid points at a line of acreages. "That's the old golf course the Pattersons sold off."

"The what?"

"Maria's family used to own a golf course before the Quake," says April, who must have heard about this at school. "The government bought it off them to make farms."

"And they accepted money? There wasn't anything to buy back then."

"Not yet." Sid shrugs. "But Bradley's mother was smart enough to wait. She started a bank twenty years ago. If you want to get funding to do anything on Salt Spring and the government won't pay for it, you go to the Pattersons."

I nod. I'm not sure I understand this perfectly, but one thing is clear. If anyone has the power to ruin things for us, it's these people.

The sun is setting by the time we reach the estate, long shadows painting the road. We walk down a winding driveway to reach their property. Fewer trees have been logged to create farmland here, and they block out the moon. My grip tightens on Sid's hand.

The gravel path opens up to reveal a three-storey home with a massive veranda. More than the size of the house, it's the number of lights that stuns me. I've seen plenty of broken-down mansions, but light costs resources. Candles burn in every window. The front walk is rigged with lanterns that wink happily in the evening gloom. Some even have solar cells built into them.

I point at one illuminating the front walk. "I thought the government took all those."

Sid grunts. "Not much the Pattersons don't have."

I'm trying to wrap my head around what the limits of that might be when a man comes to the door to take our jackets. For a wild moment, I think they have their own butler like some long dead lord, but it turns out this is a service provided by the catering company. My head goes right back to spinning, because apparently catering still exists.

We're shown inside, where there's a grand oak staircase

and a crystal chandelier rigged with a dozen candles. It's incredible how little the place looks like the deserted mansions April and I looted in high-end communities on Vancouver Island. The pictures are still hanging on the walls, their frames polished instead of broken down for firewood. A china vase of poppies sits on an end table. All the furniture matches.

We're led upstairs to where a crowd has gathered around a brick fireplace. Every other guest can afford to wear wool, not scavenged clothes like the ones April and I bought at the exchange. The colours are muted, due to the limited range of dyes available these days, but there's a polished newness about everything. So *that's* why April wanted something brown. Me and my polka dots are clearly out of fashion.

Bradley's mother nods as we enter. She sits in a chair by the fire, eating crab cakes and talking to an old man who Bradley introduces as the mayor of Galiano Island. A few other distinguished faces ring the circle, but I hardly catch any names. They're a who's who of who-gives-a-shit as far as I'm concerned, but Sid's face pales in a way that communicates they're important. Government types, maybe. Or business leaders. I can't be sure, but if Mrs. Patterson controls the main bank, I can only assume people are itching for a chance to sit down to dinner with her.

"We had to double up events. We've always got someone coming and going," says Bradley with a laugh. His hair is waxed upright, and he's dressed in a starched hemp shirt. "Mother can't rearrange her schedule much. We'll be in the second dining room. Hope you don't mind."

"Of course not," I say. If we're being slighted, it's not like people of our station have a right to object. I'm relieved I won't have to eat with these people, but I feel their eyes following us as we file out of the main dining room. Mrs. Patterson's friends might not think we deserve to be included in their circle, but we're worthy of gossip. Instinctively, I latch onto Sid and pray it looks like we're in love.

Once we reach the second dining room, two more guests are waiting for us. A sullen girl, who must be Maria Patterson, and Amy Sullivan.

"Kayla and Sid! It's so good to see you!" She hugs me first, then makes her way down the line, ending on April. "And how's my future scientist doing?"

"Oh... I'm—um..."

When April can't form a sentence, it hits me that there might be someone she's even more embarrassed about disappointing than me.

"Did I tell you, Maria? April came on a tour of the Guild with me. I think you two have a lot in common. You're both so bright."

"Yeah, you said something about it." Maria doesn't turn to look at anyone. She has lush, pin-straight dark hair that probably involves ironing every morning. April keeps begging us to get an iron so she can do the same, but considering we don't even bother using one for clothes, it seems frivolous to me. Or did, until standing in this place.

It's like we've stumbled into a Jane Austen novel, where trivial things matter a great deal. This resembles the distant past more than the years immediately preceding the Quake, what with the candlelight and the comedy of manners we're all engaged in.

The caterers bring out a round of crab cakes and Bradley recites the latest polling numbers, complimenting Sid on how high he's ranked. After the guild tour, the paper did run a short story. Not one with any pictures, but pulling quotes from both Amy and Sid.

"That's the kind of publicity you can't buy. Amazing stuff," says Bradley.

"Thanks. It was nice collaborating on something." Sid raises his wine glass towards Amy and she mirrors him, big smile lighting up her face. "That's kind of the dream, isn't it? That we're all going to get into government and be able to work together?"

"To be sure," says Bradley, raising his glass too.

My heart sinks as I realize what Sid is doing. In light of our recent disasters, he's weighed his options and decided he needs to offer Bradley what he wants. What did Amy call it before? A coalition.

"Don't you wish the vote would just happen tomorrow? We could all get it over with and—" Amy starts, but Bradley cuts in.

"That's because *you're* a shoe-in. I don't mind a few more months to bolster my numbers." He leans out of the way as the caterers place the next course, a salad of kale and hazelnuts, on the table. "What about you, Sid?"

"What about me?" He's barely touched his food.

"What would you do if the vote happened tomorrow? Assuming you got in. Anything you two would do to... celebrate?" His eyebrow cocks.

Here we go.

I drape an arm across Sid's shoulders, fishing out one of the stories we brainstormed. "We've been talking about going on a trip. I want to see America. Sid told me there are places in the San Juans where you can see all the way to Mount Rainer."

"Things will be busy after the election. America might have to wait," Sid says.

"Oh, come *on*. If we're imagining the perfect scenario, then I want to go somewhere with you. It would be romantic." My hand slides up to his neck to play with his fine hair. He tenses under my fingers, but I don't relent.

A second later, his hand falls on my shoulder, the next

step in our choreography. "Well. I'm sure we'll think of something."

It's as good an excuse as any, so I lean in for a peck. Maybe it's the hint of danger lacing the air tonight, but my heart skitters at the warmth of his mouth against mine.

"I think it's a lovely idea," says Amy, eager for everyone to get along. "I wish I had someone to celebrate with."

"Aw, Ames. I didn't know you were looking for company." Bradley nudges her playfully and she erupts into giggles.

"Oh, stop!" she squeals. I sincerely hope she means those words literally. Maybe I've been giving her too much credit. Maybe this woman isn't as brilliant as everyone claims she is.

But her attention—or maybe the wine— has put Bradley in a good mood. "Well, I think it's wonderful you two found happiness so quickly. See, Maria?" He turns to his younger sister. "I told you. You shouldn't believe everything you hear at school."

The girl's cheeks flush, and she stares deliberately down at her meal. If Bradley is making a show of chastising his sister in front of us, I probably need to do something similar. I laugh and say, "Oh, I'm sure whatever happened was a misunderstanding. If April had remembered to use her words, Maria would have known what was going on."

Bradley gives an appreciative chuckle. April stares daggers at me. But when dinner ends and we break off into smaller groups, I think we might have struck the right balance. The girls wander off together, whispering furiously. I catch Maria saying something that sounds like *"they're all full of bullshit."* I have to supress a smile.

Nothing bonds people together quite like ragging on the same enemy.

TWENTY-SEVEN

AFTER DINNER, BRADLEY takes us out to the veranda, where a few visitors from his mother's party have spilled over. Sid and I wander the crowd, making introductions and small talk. The whole evening is exhausting, but even if he complains about Bradley Patterson, coming was the right choice for Sid's campaign. He secures an invitation to a future town hall meeting and has a long conversation with the Mayor of Galiano about the lumber trade. All the while, I smile and clutch his arm, ever the adoring wife.

Best of all, whatever threat Bradley posed seems to have been neutralized. The more he drinks, the more freely he talks, but at least he's a cheerful drunk. Better yet, he's one who is on our side.

"The more I think about it," he says loudly, forcing all the guests to be his personal audience, "the more I think, I say *yes*! We *do* need immigrants. We're building a new nation, here! It's like when they built the railway. You need *people* to build a railway."

My grasp of Canadian history isn't the most thorough, but even I know the labour practices that built the transcontinental rail aren't what anyone wants to be replicating in the modern age. But at least he's seeing some value in Sid's own positions.

"You ever seen the railway, Sid? Is it still there?"

"You mean the CPR? Yeah. It's still there. We…" Sid looks awkwardly around at the others, who have leaned in. It's not like they don't know who he is or where he came from. He's public about it in his campaign. But it's hard to guess how stories about TNS will be received. Still, Bradley is asking directly, and this is his party. "We used to run marching drills on it."

Bradley lights up and soon has dozens more questions about Sid's life. Not so much the sordid details of being a child soldier, but where he went. Bradley has vacationed on the San Juans, but the one thing money can't buy in today's world is the safety to leave these islands. He's rapt as Sid describes places as far away as the Okanagan. I could participate if I wanted, since I've been across the entirety of Vancouver Island, but the thought makes me sad in a way I can't afford to unpack right now. Bradley Patterson's world might be filled with sights and tastes I've never experienced, but this place is undeniably smaller than what I used to have.

Sid seems to have the conversation well in-hand, so I wander away once I've finished my drink. The veranda wraps all the way around the house, until it opens over a sheer cliff. It's a steep drop to the ocean below, water dark as the night and sighing like a sleeping giant. I've only been alone a few minutes when soft footsteps approach. I turn, expecting April, but Amy Sullivan draws up to my side.

"Mind if I join you?"

"Oh…" I don't know if I should be wary or not, but it would be rude to refuse. "Sure."

"Thanks. Even I need a break from all that, sometimes." She nods toward the partygoers we left behind. "You're doing amazingly, by the way. I don't know how you manage it."

"You don't think I'm smart enough to talk to those people?" I ask, failing to keep my tongue in check.

Amy doesn't get angry or defensive. She leans against the cedar railing and breathes in the ocean. "You were living in the woods two months ago. Sid threw you to the wolves here, but you're killing it. I'm jealous. It took me thirty years to figure out how to talk to these people."

"You don't think of yourself as one of them?"

"Maybe I am. I don't know. Tom—my uncle, I mean— he doesn't like the Patterson crowd much. Finds this all… excessive."

"Please, do not make me agree with your uncle on something. Shit! I mean…"

Amy only laughs. Sid did tell me she would understand if I said I disliked Tom. "So he *has* been giving you the gears. I'm sorry."

"Not like it's your fault."

"He means well, but he's like a lot of old-timers. Shell-shocked. Convinced the world is going to end all over again if he doesn't do something to stop it. I keep telling him to get a therapist, but you try having that conversation with a sixty-two-year-old man."

"Hmmm."

"You shouldn't worry, though. From what I've seen, you and April are doing fine. And Tom will see that. He always does, eventually."

"Thank you." I'm sure Amy is being sincere, but she doesn't know certain things about me that Tom does. To my annoyance, I have a flash of empathy for him. I showed up on his island and shot his friend. No wonder he wanted to string me up by the heels. Can I really pretend I wouldn't have done the same in his position?

"Can I ask you something, Amy?"

"Go right ahead."

"Sid seemed surprised Bradley followed through on his dinner invitation. Did you have a hand in that?" I ask both because I'm curious and because I don't want to talk about Tom.

Amy shrugs. "Maybe. I might have reminded Bradley that Sid is good for his image."

"Really? How?"

"Because everyone thinks the Pattersons are snobs."

"Because they are."

"Of course! But that's terrible for politics. Bradley wants people to think he's approachable. I told him that if he attacked Sid, it might come out that his younger sister was bullying a poor immigrant girl at high school—"

"Holy shit, you said that to him?"

"I don't believe in mincing words behind closed doors." She throws me a wink.

"Well... thank you. I mean it." Amy might have done it just to protect her own political prospects, but the result is the same. Honestly, she's done more to help me than her uncle has, and that's his *job*.

"Speaking of not mincing words... back at the guild tour, your sister was really interested in the medical research. I talked to Maria, and she says April carries needles at school. She has diabetes, doesn't she?"

Sid has told me Amy is smart and resourceful, but seeing it in action is a little terrifying. Beneath the frothy, bubbly exterior is hard, weathered stone.

"So?"

Amy shakes her head. "That's why you came, isn't it? To get her healthcare? Is it why you married Sid, too?"

"I love him," I say without hesitation. "That's why I married him."

Amy nods. "Two things can be true at the same time."

"What?" I expected an attack of some kind, but this was not it. Despite myself, I'm completely flustered. "No. I don't—"

"Kayla, you don't have to justify anything to me. I don't care what you guys do. Well, I *do* care, but I mean…" She taps a hand on the railing. "I care about Sid. He's a good man. If he wasn't so damn broody, I probably wouldn't have dumped him."

"Broody? I wouldn't really call him—"

"See? You're already more patient with him than I was," she says with a laugh. "Just promise you won't hurt him, okay?"

"My relationship with Sid isn't your business."

"I guess that's fair." She steps away from the railing. "I won't tell Bradley about April. I think he's on our side but, well… some things are better left secret."

"Am I supposed to thank you for that?"

"No." She sighs. "I know you don't trust me. But so long as you're good to him, I'm on your side, okay? Whether you like me or not. Just don't hurt Sid."

With that, she walks back toward the lights of the party. I stare after her retreating form, my breath growing more ragged as the full force of the conversation settles in. She knows. Those damn Sullivans. Our secret is in their hands and there's nothing I can do about it.

I grab hold of the railing, suddenly weak at the knees as my brain scrambles to find a solution. What's she expecting to get from us by keeping our secret? Is she going to ask for a favour? Make Sid do what she wants, once they're in office? Ironically, the one thing she did ask of me is the only one I'm certain isn't her true motive. Why would she worry about me hurting Sid? I can't hurt him. He doesn't love me, and she knows that now.

Sid's heavy tread jerks me out of my thoughts. I look up to see his wide shoulders blocking out the noise and glow of Bradley Patterson's world. I let go of the railing and collapse into his arms, praying this will ground me and stop the mounting panic attack that might otherwise take over.

"Hey. You okay?" he asks.

"No."

"Shit. What happened? Amy said you needed me, but—"

"*Amy*?!" I cry her name out, then regret it. I don't want to draw anyone else from the party while I'm shaking like this. Quieter, I ask, "Amy sent you?"

"Yeah."

"Sid, she knows. She figured out everything about April and now she *knows*."

Sid's body goes rigid against mine. It's all too much to bear, so I bury my face into him, grateful for the chorus of ocean waves that help to drown out my stuttering lungs. As I choke back sobs, his grip tightens around me.

"Hey, it's going to be okay. Did she say she would tell anyone?"

"No. She said she wouldn't."

"Okay. Then we're okay."

"No! We are *not* okay. None of this is okay." I look up at him, angry enough to regain control of my voice. "You expect me to trust her because you do?"

"Well..."

"How?" I demand. "How am I supposed to trust her?"

"Amy's been helping us so far. She gave April that tour. She's helped smooth things over with Bradley—"

"But what if she betrays you? What if someone tells you you're safe and then one day—"

"I don't know! How does anyone trust anyone? At some

point, you decide to believe them," says Sid. "Because as scary as it is, it's worse being alone."

Is it? I'm drowning in company these days, but I've never felt more anxious. I would be crashing out if I didn't have Sid to hang onto. My arms slide from his waist to his neck, drawing him downwards, so that his spine curls around my body, enveloping me.

"You told me once that you trust me." Sid's voice is right by my ear. "If you can't believe her, then maybe you could believe me? I wouldn't put us into this situation if I didn't think it would be okay."

He reaches up to cradle my face. As one of his rough, calloused thumbs wipes a stray tear off my cheek, I gasp, and my nose fills with the scent of cedar trees and ocean waves and him. His breath is warm against my chin as he waits for my response. But words fail me. I answer him the only way that makes sense anymore.

I've never kissed him like this before. My mouth is eager and intentional. As his lips part, I'm hit by the taste of red wine and finally appreciate Bradley's insistence on opening a good bottle. My arms tighten around him, forbidding any escape. Not that he tries. His thumb presses into my spine, steering me like he did when we danced at our wedding so that I fit more snuggly in his arms.

I want nothing more than to dissolve into him. Breaking apart long enough to breathe is a chore; every second I spend separated from that glorious mouth is a total waste. I've never needed someone like I need him. The feeling roaring up inside of me is so much more urgent than anything I experienced in my youth.

He pulls away, and I whimper. "Don't stop."

"Do you trust me?"

"Yes."

"Do you want me?"

"*Yes.*"

"Good."

And then his mouth is on me again, tracing my collarbone. My hands ball up fistfuls of his hair and I groan out his name.

So this is what it's like to live through an earthquake. This is what it's like to have your whole world break apart and then be caught in the aftermath of tsunami waves, each more powerful than the next.

My hands shift again, caressing the length of his body, coming to rest at his waist. Without thinking, I hook my thumb around a button in his shirt. His stomach twitches as my hand finds its way to bare skin and suddenly, he goes still. He pulls away from me. I'm about to demand why, but then I hear the distant guffaws of the party. It's like surfacing above water as my ears clear and I become aware of the rest of the world.

My eyes dart over my shoulder, but we're still alone, obscured by a curtain of dark. We haven't embarrassed ourselves in front of anyone. Maybe it would be better if we had. Everyone at the party would be gossiping about how Sid Charles can't keep his hands off his new wife. No one would think this was a sham marriage.

The straps of my dress have fallen off my shoulders and my hand is splayed across his stomach without a single person to bear witness. The only reason he stopped, I realize, is that we're not alone *enough*. If this had happened at the apartment, I know where it would go next. I should be in his bed right now.

I let go of him. He's quick to tuck his shirt back into his pants, while I hastily readjust my dress.

"Yeah, sorry. That was… here." He touches my face, cleaning up a smear of beetroot lipstick.

"Thanks. Let me get you." My finger runs across the

lips I just had against mine. Touching him there again, it takes all my strength to keep my head above water. Sid Charles is an ocean waiting to suck me under.

What did I just do? And why the hell didn't he stop me?

Sid's eyes are wide, transfixed. "Kayla... I didn't mean for that to happen. But—"

"We'll talk about it at home."

"Sure."

We don't hold hands as we walk back to the party. When the night is over and we're on the bus, I make sure April is sitting between us. Once we're home, I head straight to bed, ignoring Sid's attempts to get my attention. It's all I can do to make myself feel in control. Otherwise, I'm going to start screaming.

It turns out, Amy was right. I can hurt Sid. But I can also hurt myself.

Two things can be true at the same time.

TWENTY-EIGHT

I WAKE APRIL up in the middle of the night, thrashing from my nightmares. It hasn't been this bad since Curtis and Mum died. She grumbles about having school in the morning, so I apologize and climb out of bed.

Instead of trying to sleep again, I dig through my bag until I find the cedar heart Curtis carved for me. I still remember the night I came back from trapping squirrels to find it resting on my bedroll. It was a perfect gift. My dad used to make them when he was alive, and Curtis knew how badly I missed him. He did his best to replicate the gesture, but the lines were rougher. I press the carved heart to my lips and do my best to conjure him up.

No matter how hard I try, images of Sid interrupt. Dancing with him on our wedding day. His hand finding mine beneath the table at the restaurant. Most of all, I drift back to our kiss tonight. How did I not see that coming? There have been warning signs for weeks, our touches growing more frequent and casual. Even that first time I kissed him, when I told myself it was simply to prove that I could do it, shouldn't I have been suspicious? It was so easy. So natural. I've wanted him for a long time now, even if I wouldn't let myself acknowledge it.

The only question I'm left with is how deep this thing goes. Physically, the answer is obvious. My eyes have been lingering on him since the first day we met. Tonight, there wasn't a single moment I wanted him to stop. Even now, I feel crazy, sitting on the floor of my bedroom when I know he's just down the hall. I could have him. He's my husband, damn it.

But that's part of what makes this so terrifying. He's not someone I can have a spontaneous tryst with. We're already tied together, and we need that connection to be stable until April and I get full citizenship. What if this is all some side effect of faking our romance? I forced myself to be comfortable with him for April's sake, and now my hormones are so confused, they're running amok.

What if in a few months, the passion fizzles? I hate the prospect of resenting him, unable to rely on our friendship to keep me sane. Worse still, what if we mess around and suddenly have another reason to stay together, even if we don't want to? I remember Amy's first theory about us: that we got married because of an unplanned pregnancy. That could still happen. Birth control isn't what it used to be.

My mind spins out over this hypothetical future. No matter how much he wanted to, I know he wouldn't leave me. Not if we had a baby. And I'm such a mess, it would be irresponsible of me to take the kid and leave him. We'd be stuck with each other for another eighteen years. Maybe more, if we relapsed and more popped out.

Shit, I am spiralling. There are no babies, Kayla. Remember? That's the thing I never got to have. Instead, I got April. She's the only one I owe anything to. And for everyone's sake, it needs to stay that way.

The floorboards outside my room creak. Someone is pacing back and forth on the other side of the door, no doubt trying to decide if it's safe to knock. I shouldn't let him wake April, so I get up and open the door.

I'm not ready for the sight of him. Not the way he towers inside the doorframe or the fact that he's in nothing but a worn-out t-shirt and shorts. His eyes are bloodshot, making it obvious he hasn't been able to sleep either. When he sees me, his breath catches, eyes wandering over my tank top.

"Hey..." My voice is wispy.

He leans away from the doorframe, allowing me enough room to step around him. Carefully, he shuts the door. I'm mesmerized by every movement. The way the veins in his arm twist with the motion of his wrist. The way his shoulders roll when he turns to face me. The way his Adam's apple moves when he sees me in the dark, staring right back at him.

Here we are. Alone again.

I could have him.

I can't have him.

"Kayla—"

"We can't do this, Sid." I sputter out. "I'm sorry. I am *so* sorry, but I've got to keep things steady. For April."

He swallows. There's no hint of surprise on his face, but the disappointment is palpable. "You're sure that's what you want?"

What I *want*? Sometimes life isn't about what we want. But saying that out loud will only encourage him.

"You *promised*," I say. "You promised when you married me, you were fine with sex being off the table."

"Yeah... I did." He runs a hand through his hair. *My* fingers should be there. "I just didn't know how bad this was going to fuck me up."

"I'm sorry." I reach for him—then stumble backwards when I realize what I'm doing. Shit, I was so close to touching him. Tonight, that's all it would take. Maybe once we've had a chance for the initial rush to die away, I'll be able to hug him again, but right now? Contact of any kind is a one-way ticket to his bedroom.

"I shouldn't have kissed you. This is my fault, and I'm sorry," I repeat. "I don't even know why I did it. I'm still in love with Curtis. I fell in love, and I lost him. One time. That's all I've got in me."

I can't tell if I'm lying or not. I've believed it for so long, how can it not be true? But the words sound hollow. The truth is probably much simpler.

I'm not too in love to move on. I'm too scared.

"I want you, Kayla," says Sid, and I lean forward, doubting my own decision. "I'm not going to lie. I want you. But... you're right. I made you a promise. And no matter how much I want you, I couldn't live with myself if I hurt you."

I let out a shuddering breath. "Thank you. All I want is to keep being friends. You mean so much to me, I just can't—"

He holds up a hand. "You don't need to keep apologizing. We both screwed up. We were just... caught off guard. We'll be ready next time."

"Next time? There isn't going to be a next time!"

"I meant next time we have to go to some political event together."

"Oh." Right. *That.* "When will next time be?"

"I got invited to a town hall next week. Usually, candidates bring their partners to things like that." He folds his arms across his chest. "Do you think you'll still be able to—"

"Yeah. Sure. I can fake it." A little too well, apparently.

"Great. Then we'll be ready." He nods, then heads for his room. Once his door is shut, I collapse against the nearest wall, sliding slowly down until my butt rests on the floor. I did it. I stopped us from doing anything stupid. Now I've just got to stop feeling like absolute dogshit.

TWENTY-NINE

THE NEXT MORNING, April is in high spirits, and the stars be praised for that. Her ongoing high school drama makes for a wonderful distraction and apparently, the Patterson party was a smashing success for her. Once dinner ended, she and Maria hung out together, since what else was there for them to do? All the adults were busy schmoozing.

"—and you'll never guess what she told me! It's perfect," she crows.

"Oh! Are you two friends now?" I ask, blithely hopeful.

"Who cares about that? I have ammo. She kept asking about Carlos. That's what started it, remember? She made Gia ask if I was sleeping with Carlos. Well, it turns out *Maria* has a crush on him. Do you know how much power she's handed me?"

"April, no—"

"I've basically stamped my ticket to her lunch table. I made it clear Carlos and I are just friends. *Close* friends. And no one's gonna mess with me if Maria Patterson is trying to earn an invite to *my* house."

"You are downright Machiavellian."

"I'm free. That's what I am."

"You still have a week of detentions to serve out, Little Miss *Free*."

April only shrugs.

Once the dust has settled, April turns out to be right. The sad irony is that the girl April slapped—Gia—ends up with nothing. Whatever increased popularity she might have hoped for by doing the Patterson girl's dirty work goes to April, who quickly joins their circle. Maria Patterson even shows up at the acreage a few nights later, under the pretext of helping April study for an upcoming test. They come up into the apartment, giggling madly over something that happened on the way in, only for Maria to draw to a stop as she surveys the room.

"Where's all your stuff?"

"Right? Sid doesn't own *anything*." April grabs the girl's hand and drags her to the bedroom we share. "C'mon. We can just sit on the bed."

"But then we're going downstairs for dinner, right? Everyone eats together, right?"

"Yeah. *Carlos* makes most of the food!"

They both burst into laughter, and I decide I don't need to sit around listening to this. Besides, I've got nowhere to read with them in the room. I head downstairs.

Carlos isn't in the kitchen yet, so I get started mincing carrots, celery and onions into a soffritto by myself. The next steps come easily, as I render lard in a pan, then tip the vegetables in to sauté. Next come the shrimp Wendell bought in town this morning. Once a golden rim forms along each side, I take the aromatics and shrimp off the heat, reserving them in a bowl. Now for the hard part. I add a little more lard, then whisk in flour, until a golden paste forms at the bottom of the pan. Gradually, I top it off with cream and grated cheese. From there, it's small adjustments. Parsley, basil, oregano. A dash more salt.

Finally, it's time to grab the pasta that I rolled out earlier in the morning and drop it into a pot of salted water. A splash of pasta water goes into the sauce, making it glossy and fluid. With all the components prepped, it's nothing but assembly. Pasta. Sauce. Shrimp. It all gets a quick mix over the heat, flavours warming and melding into each other. By the time Carlos stumbles through the door, all that's left to do is send him back out to gather everyone else.

James arrives first, guitar over his back. "You did that by yourself?"

"Yeah. Guess I did."

"Well. I will gladly eat my words *and* that."

"Eat your words?"

He shrugs. "Silas and I were taking bets on if you would ever stop burning things."

I smack him hard in the arm, which only makes him laugh. As I place the finished pasta on the table, he starts strumming the opening notes of *Alice's Restaurant*. The other guys file in, Carlos and the girls arriving last. Everyone says nice things about the meal, though I think the best compliment is the fact that Maria doesn't mention it at all. Nor does she look secretly disgusted.

Knowing she might gossip about anything that happens at our house, I purposely sit next to Sid. It's been a while since the disastrous Patterson party, and though things are still awkward, we've made an effort to chit-chat around the acreage. We can't risk another situation like the day Tom caught us unprepared. Still, Sid stiffens when I run a hand along his shoulders, tracing little circles down his back.

"What are you—"

"Maria, April. How's the math going?" I say, smiling vaguely in their direction.

The girls give a chorus of "fine," both far more focused on dinner and talking to Carlos, who looks very confused by whatever it is he's been caught in. Sid, however, has wised up. His gaze lingers on Maria for a second; then, he slings an arm around the back of my chair. I try to ignore the thrill of his touch.

For a while, we eat in silence, letting the comradery of the others wash over us.

"This really is good," he says, once his bowl is almost empty.

"Thanks."

"You keep getting better. If you wanted…" He trails off, no doubt remembering how little good it does to suggest I try something new. Guilt pinches me as I wonder if he was right. Am I just afraid of everything that could make me happy?

"Town hall tomorrow," I say, trying to keep the small talk going. "You ready?"

"Yeah. I think so. You?"

"Of course. All I've got to do is stare at you and tell people you're wonderful. I can do that."

He narrows his eyes, and I smirk. Even pissed off, he's so endearing. The temptation to kiss him dances through me, but Maria isn't paying us any attention, so it would be wasted effort. I'll save it for tomorrow, when he needs a wife.

Anticipation and dread colour every bite I take of my meal.

WE DO NOT get off to a good start the next evening. I put on the same dress I wore to Bradley's party, only with a cardigan thrown over so I look a bit more conservative.

When I step out, ready to go, Sid is waiting for me, nursing a cigarette.

"Oh, come on! You know we're going to have to kiss tonight."

"It's not like it has to last long," he says, which makes me think this isn't a stress smoke. He's being deliberate. Fine. Great. Isn't he considerate, making himself less appealing?

"Whatever, let's just go."

The meeting is in an old community hall not far from Salt Spring's largest natural harbour. It's a prime location for anyone who wants to visit from the other gulf islands like Galiano and Pender.

I don't recognize anyone, which becomes even more distressing when I realize that the chairs set up on the stage are for the candidates. I'm expected to sit in the audience.

Sid moves towards the stage but my grip tightens on his hand. His face morphs from confusion to empathy when he notices the way I'm eying the crowd. There must be two hundred chairs set up, including a reserved spot for a newspaper stenographer. In all our discussions about the town hall, I never considered how daunting it would be to sit alone in public, surrounded by hundreds of people.

Sid squeezes my hand sympathetically, then leads me a few rows back to where an old woman wearing a boiled wool hat is seated. She is not who I would have picked to approach—her mouth is set in a deep frown and the bags under her eyes give a look of perpetual misery. Her expression doesn't improve when Sid's shadow falls on her. If anything, the scowl intensifies.

Sid nods to her, not that it helps. "Good evening, Mrs. Buckerfield."

"Yes?"

"I don't know if you remember me, but I'm Sid Charles—"

"I remember." She turns to look at the stage.

"Wonderful." How Sid keeps smiling, I'll never know. "Forgive me for imposing, but my wife wanted to meet you. She keeps asking who taught Carlos all those wonderful recipes, so I had to introduce you."

"Oh! You raised Carlos?" I ask.

Her gaze snaps to me. She scans my simple outfit and unruly curls, trying to decide what a girl like me means, standing next to him. "I didn't realize you got married, Mr. Charles," she says at last.

"We did." I put an arm around his waist, both to steady myself and in hopes that it makes us look like a happy couple. "I know I shouldn't pick favourites out of the boys, but if I've got one, it's Carlos. He taught me your flapjack recipe the other day. They were incredible."

"That boy had *such* potential." She sighs, and I understand why she's been so frosty with us. It's impossible not to love Carlos. I can't blame her for being gutted that he picked his TNS crew over her. "How is he, then? Good to hear he's still cooking."

"He's wonderful."

"Would it be all right if Kayla sat with you? She's been meaning to ask about your café," says Sid.

My head whips round to him. What the hell is he doing? But I can't make a stink about it right now. Not when the whole point of coming here tonight is to make Sid look good.

On the other hand, arguing with him in front of strangers while sexual tension simmers beneath the surface *would* make us look very married. But he's already heading for the stage, so without any other option, I slide into the seat next to Mrs. Buckerfield.

"Your husband isn't running, is he?"

"He is."

"Hmmm." She's polite enough not to directly insult him in front of me. "And I suppose you're here supporting him?"

"Of course. We'd be lucky to have him on council."

She chuckles, eyes still fixed on the stage. "Naturally, *you* would think that. Not that it's a bad thing. We all see the good in those we love. It's very *Beauty and the Beast*, isn't it?"

If anyone is beastly, it's me. But that fairy tale ends happily and has some moral about appearances being deceiving, so I don't argue. This is what I'm here for. To humanize him. I try to play my role and turn an adoring face to where he's seated on stage. It at least saves me the trouble of talking to Mrs. Buckerfield.

There are twenty-four candidates presenting their positions tonight. More than that are running, but not everyone gets invited to these town halls. It's a pretty big deal that Sid scored an invite, so I really should pay attention. But man, this shit is boring. My eyes glaze over as one person after another takes their turn.

As a well-respected incumbent member of council, Tom Sullivan is given one of the first slots of the night. He hobbles up to the podium to applause. "Good evening. It has been my pleasure to serve this island for thirty-five years and with your blessing, I would be honoured to do so for another four."

Thirty-five? His tenure predates the Quake. Indeed, his speech reveals that he served the island when it was a tiny regional office affiliated with the capital of British Columbia. Back then, he was an unelected civil servant, since there were enough people to separate out governments into those who administered the law from those who voted on its policies. With the Quake, things had to change, but he adjusted.

He served the island through its transition to earthquake

decimated danger zone, to defending its borders from TNS after Canada's collapse, to prosperous final bastion of civilization. His leg was wounded during his time in the navy, back when TNS tried to invade Salt Spring. He oversaw the Land Redistribution Act, that turned most private property into farmland. He was on the committee that drafted the first sanctuary laws, reopening Salt Spring's borders twenty-three years ago. He *is* the Council.

He doesn't say much about his upcoming platform. He doesn't have to, with a lifetime of service behind him. I'm one of the few people who doesn't clap at the end.

Sid's turn is right after his, as if to signal their alignment, but there is markedly less applause when he takes the stage. This is his first time addressing an audience of this size and he's an unknown. But he's well prepared, not even looking at his notes as he gives a carefully rehearsed speech.

"As someone who wasn't born here, there is no doubt in my mind that Salt Spring Island is a special place," he begins. "When I came here, I felt for the first time in my life that I had control over what happened to me. That I had the potential to lead a good, long life. To me, there is nothing that is more important than to offer that opportunity both to our citizens and to those who are seeking refuge within our borders."

He manages to weave in all sorts of positives as he talks about immigration and sanctuary laws: how welcoming policies encourage newcomers to share their knowledge with our community; how population growth is aided, encouraging faster recovery; how we become more secure when members of groups like TNS defect to us. It stuns me, hearing him mention them so casually, as if he isn't knotted up over their role in his life. He ends by reiterating his first point. Where we are is special. Being safe and being free—those are special things. But they shouldn't have to be.

He's said this to me so many times, but hearing him voice these ideas in a public forum, I wonder more than ever: can it be true? Are we, collectively, safe? Not a single person in this room can control whether our island is rocked by another megaquake. Or if TNS attacks tomorrow. No matter what we want to believe, life doesn't offer guarantees. But people need to believe their choices matter, I guess, or they aren't likely to vote.

The speeches wear on. Some of the other candidates do okay. Honestly, I start to zone out. I do notice when Bradley Patterson gets up, because his hair is waxed into a ridiculous pompadour and his speech consists of name-dropping relatives who have told him all about *what this island needs.*

There's another name I vaguely recognize—Wayne Donlon—though I can't place why for the longest time. His speech starts off as boring as anyone else's, but my ears prick when he suddenly breaks into a rant about how lenient our government has become.

"We aren't doing enough," he says, "to protect ourselves against the threat of TNS. There are people out there who want to destroy everything we've worked for."

And then he has the nerve to look directly at Sid before carrying on. So this is the guy Doctor Tremblay likes. He's damn lucky I don't have my slingshot anymore, standing boldly in front of me like that, throwing insults at my husband. Once he finishes, I don't hear a lot of people clapping, but the few who do are enthusiastic. It makes my toes curl.

The very last candidate to participate is Amy Sullivan, looking as perfect as the day I met her. Her shoes are made of new leather. Her nails are buffed to the luster of an oyster shell. She flashes the audience a dazzling smile and begins her speech.

"I am pleased to announce my candidacy for Council of Salt Spring Island and her Gulf Island Territories. I offer a proven record in public service, beginning with my tenure as Chief Logistical Officer of the Reinventor's Guild. During my time there, our island saw a seventeen per cent increase in available electricity, a thirty per cent expansion in our water catchment facilities, and the development of modular designs for residence construction that have since been implemented throughout the islands."

She really is a lot like Tom. Tom, with a glaze of honey to make her more digestible. When her speech ends, she gets more applause than anyone else, ending the evening on a high note. I'm clapping too, mostly because I don't have to listen to any more speeches. Not that this is over. My job has just begun.

"Excuse me, Mrs. Buckerfield." I bid goodbye to my companion, who is still frowning at the stage.

"You can tell your husband he did well enough," she says—words in the form of a compliment, while lacking the substance thereof. No wonder Carlos left her as soon as he could.

"Thank you, I will."

As I reach the stage, Sid is shaking hands with the other candidates. Gradually, others join the mix, including the stenographer. I spot a woman kissing one of the speakers on the cheek and decide to make that my line of attack too. Sid is deep in conversation with a woman of about Tom's age. I think she's a current council member—something I would probably know with certainty if I had paid better attention. Whatever.

I wait until there's a natural break in what they're saying about crop yields, then slide my hand along his arm. He twists to look at me and I grin like a woman in love. That's what I'm here for, right? I'm so good at this.

"I have it on excellent authority that you exceeded expectations."

His smile is so sincere. "Really?"

"Not mine, though. I always knew you would be perfect." I go up on my toes, intending to hit his cheek, but Sid leans in as well so I end up pecking him right on the mouth. He's barely there—long enough for me to get a whiff of his earlier cigarette—and yet my damn stomach still somersaults. I wobble as I sink back to my heels.

Luckily, Sid takes over, because my brain is busy leaking out my ears. "Rachel, have you met my wife? Kayla, this is Rachel Bromley. She serves in the Department of Fisheries and Natural Resources."

"Lovely to meet you." She extends a hand, which I barely have the presence of mind to shake. I'm busy fighting with a fantasy where I drag this man outside and flatten his body against a wall with mine.

They start talking again, and a business owner who sailed over from North Pender to hear the speeches walks up. More handshakes, more platitudes. I lose track of the number of times Sid says the words *have you met my wife*. My cheeks ache from smiling. I spot the same reporter who interviewed us at the Reinventor's Guild tour snapping photos with her phone camera in between peppering candidates with more questions.

It's almost an hour before the hubbub dies down enough that Amy Sullivan has time to greet us. Her face burns as bright as her red hair. No doubt she's riding high off her success. Before either of us can say anything, she's thrown her arms around Sid in a hug.

"Wasn't tonight brilliant? You did great, Sid. Tom sends his compliments too, but his leg was bugging him, so he went home."

Thank goodness for that. I'm so sick of him taunting

me with that smug grin of his whenever we see each other. Like he's just *waiting* for the right time to strike.

Amy lets Sid go—and stuns me by embracing me with the same enthusiasm. I'm hit in the face by rose-scented perfume. "And it's so good to see you again, Kayla."

"Yeah, you too." I think I might even mean it. I still don't love the fact that she knows so many of my deep, dark secrets, but ever since I kissed Sid, I've been forced to confront the idea that she was right about us. That maybe means she was sincere that night too, when she asked me not to hurt him.

Am I hurting him? I can't tell anymore.

"You were great tonight," says Sid. "Perfect, really."

"Thanks." She shrugs. "Tom says I didn't have enough personal content, because of course I had to have done *something* wrong."

"You sure you want to work in the same office as him?" Sid asks.

"You sure you do?"

They both laugh. I half-heartedly join in, but I don't have much to offer. Soon, they're arguing about which candidates they think performed best, and my opinion is irrelevant. It stings more than it should. It's not my fault that I don't understand this world, and Sid has never tried to make me feel guilty about it. But watching them, I'm struck by how little I fit with him. Even if we both started out as immigrants, even if we both come from messed up backgrounds, he's one of *them* now. It feels so ridiculous that he ever kissed me or said he wanted me. He could do so much better. He *deserves* so much better.

They're interrupted when the haircut belonging to the Patterson family wanders into the conversation with an invitation to join him and a few other *select people* (seriously, this guy) for drinks at a nearby pub. Amy crows with delight and even Sid is enthusiastically agreeing. Looks like he's getting over his dislike of Bradley after all. But I know I can't take another second of this, so instead, I make a dramatic display of yawning.

"That all sounds lovely, but I think I'm going to head home. Have a good time, babe." This time, I move quickly so that I do land the kiss on his cheek. I release his hand and start walking towards the exit.

"Bradley, Amy, would you please excuse me for a second?"

They both mutter agreement and Sid runs up behind me. I quicken my pace, wanting to be outside before we boil over.

"You want to go home now?" Sid asks.

"Yes."

"Fine," he sighs, falling into step, but I speed up even more.

"I said *I* want to go home. You don't have to. Go out with your friends."

"Kayla, I'm not leaving you."

"Why not?"

"Because it's late and you don't know this end of the island—"

"I'm not a child, Sid! You don't have to babysit me. Just go. Honestly? I would rather you did."

That draws him to a standstill. "What?"

"I did what I promised tonight. I posed as your wife, gave you someone to show-off. I'm done." I continue walking toward the bus stop. "I did my job, now you can do yours. Go out with your friends. Have a drink. Smoke a cigarette—"

"You're still mad about that?"

"I'm not mad about anything! You've got a right to live your own life, same as me."

"I don't want to go anywhere without you," he says, drawing close again. And unfortunately, I have now reached the bus stop. I have no excuse to keep walking.

"Well, I'm not going out to dinner with Bradley Patterson."

"Sure! Fine. So we go home."

"No, *I* go home. *We* don't need to do anything!"

"But we're a team. And we just had an amazing night. If I'm going to celebrate with anyone—"

"We can't *celebrate* together."

"I didn't mean *that*," he says. "You told me you want to stay friends. Friends still celebrate each other's victories—"

"I can't. Not tonight. I... I'm sorry."

A wagon trundles up to the bus stop and I've never been so relieved. I pull myself onto the step, but Sid won't leave me be, waiting for his turn to board. Frustrated and desperate, I spin around on the step and plant my mouth against his. It only lasts a second, but I make no attempts to hold back every raw and aching thing I'm feeling.

My mouth breaks from his and I push him, hard, away from the wagon.

"Don't you dare follow me." My voice trembles.

As the wagon pulls away, I watch the waves of confusion and anguish break over his face. What have I done?

One kiss, and I've lost the only friend I had on this island.

THIRTY

ON THE BUS, I realize I can't go home. That's where he'll expect me. He'll come to my door and make me talk to him and then I'll have to explain that it's over. We can't be friends. We can't be lovers. We can't be anything to each other. And I am not brave enough to face that conversation yet.

I hop off when I reach Ganges town. Nothing is open, but I think I like it better that way. A large moon hangs overhead and it's so quiet, I can pretend the city is abandoned. This could be another ghost town like the ones I used to wander through on Vancouver Island. The night is mild for so late in autumn and so I decide to just walk the streets like I might have before coming here.

It's easy enough to stay awake through the night.

Gradually, everyone else wakes up and ruins my perfect solitude. But even as the city comes alive, I keep wandering. Eventually, I end up at the exchange, rubbing my eyes and pretending it's because of the dust.

A table in the back features a recently discovered jewellery cache. Everyone *ooohs* and *aaaahs* over a gold choker, a silver bracelet, and a matching set of garnet earrings, necklace, and ring. I check for my mother's pearl earrings, but I don't spot them. Maybe they've already sold.

I drift to the furniture section of the hall and stare at a red velvet sofa with a hasty patch job on each cushion. I still don't have any money besides what was left over from April's first batch of medicine, but I find myself testing it, seeing how I like it. Irrationally, I want it. I want to take it home and shove it into one of the barren corners of the apartment.

I try to imagine what it would be like to snuggle close to Curtis on it, and then I'm crying, because I can't picture it. I don't remember what he felt like anymore; in so many ways, Sid has already overwritten him. I'm sick with guilt. Would it be better for me to bid Curtis goodbye? To truly move on with someone else? I'm so miserable right now; is there anything left to ruin if I take my chances and tell Sid I want to be with him?

Because I do. I would give anything to have him here on this damn couch with me.

"Everything all right, ma'am?"

I brush away tears to find a salesman with a pinched brow standing a few feet away.

"Oh... yes, sorry." I rub away the evidence of my breakdown. "I... um... I like this couch. I think I'll bring my husband by to see it tomorrow."

"Would you like us to hold it for you?"

"Yes. Yes, hold this couch." I don't care if he does, but I need some way out of this conversation. I hop up and speed walk away from the furniture as fast as I can, the salesman's voice chasing me.

"Ma'am! Under what name?"

Well, that went terribly. I could visit the library, but I didn't bring any books to trade in for new ones. I wrack my brain for something else I could be doing, but what even is there?

I hate to admit it, but Sid's right. I've been living my life afraid and as a result, I don't have a life outside of April or the acreage. Nothing has prepared me for making choices based on anything other than survival. Everything about me faces backward toward the past.

I shouldn't go anywhere important with my eyes red from crying. But something about standing in the middle of dozens of busy people, buzzing about the exchange on their own personal missions while I have no idea what to do with myself, makes me snap. Who knows if it's bravery or desperation? After a bit of asking around, I get directions toward Mrs. Buckerfield's café.

The porch is built from bits of driftwood. Strings of seashells rim the roof, and the outdoor seating area has a view of the ocean. A chalkboard near the front door advertises a daily special of goat cheese omelettes.

Garlic and dill perfume the air inside. The place is like a dream. There's a high counter like the ones I saw inside of abandoned mall food courts, and displayed on it is a tempting array of scones, slices of pie, and cheese sticks. Mrs. Buckerfield must have some way of purchasing wheat, because our rations don't allot enough for all the goodies on display.

This could be a picture book. A memento of the world at its best.

A bright faced girl steps up behind the counter, smiling at me. "Can I get you anything?"

"I... I'm not sure. Is Mrs. Buckerfield in?"

"She takes Thursdays off, but I can tell her you came by. Is there a name I can give her?"

Thursday. Right. I know what that is, I think.

"Tell her Kayla came by. Kayla..." I almost say my real last name, before realizing it will mean nothing to her. "Kayla Charles. And, um... Carlos said I should try one of the scones."

He did. A long time ago. He said he could never get the batter as fluffy and light as hers.

"Carlos? Oh, well then, you've got to try his favourite!"

The girl picks out one decorated with the last of the summer blackberries and I pay an exorbitant dollar for it. But within my first bite, it's worth it.

It's hard to justify spending resources on something that brings only pleasure. Eating this scone has not increased my odds of survival. But it's beautiful, in the same way a sunset over the ocean is, or the smell of rain on raw cedar. And unlike so many things that make me happy, nothing about it conjures up dark memories of those I lost in my past. It's new and remarkable and entirely rooted in this place.

I savour every crumb, chasing the traces around my plate with my finger. When I return the dish to the girl at the counter, she flashes me the kind of grin that can only come from someone who already knows the answer to their question. "Good?"

"It was wonderful." My heart thuds. I know I need to say something more. But I'm not bold enough to ask. I'm so beneath this place—a wild girl tasting the best civilization can offer her. "Does… Mrs. Buckerfield offer cooking classes?"

"Sure," says the girl. "I'm not sure when she'll run another set, but maybe when you come by again you can ask her? And you should bring Carlos. She *always* says yes to Carlos."

"Maybe I'll do that." A hopeful bubble lifts my heart. The classes might cost something, but I'll cross that bridge later. For now, it's enough to know they exist. Maybe April isn't the only one interested in going back to school.

"Thank you," I say to the girl. "Truly. I needed this today."

"Aw, it's no problem." She has the sweetest, prettiest smile. "You're Sid's wife, then?"

"Yeah, that's me."

"That's so great. I'm Becca. Say hi to James for me!"

Why am I not surprised? She does look like one of James's girls. He always goes for these delicate beauties, slinking up to the acreage with him for who-knows-what carnal nonsense. It's a minor miracle there aren't a million copies of him running all over the island, but that's James for you. Lucky bastard.

I feel miles better as I leave the café. Nothing about this fixes my situation with Sid, but at least I can go home and say I did it. I talked to someone and started planning something new. I practically deserve a second scone for my bravery. Except I have to save my money. Until I've got my own income, I can't be silly with it. April might grow out of her current clothes and need something new and how would I take care of that?

At the thought of April, I think of one more thing I could do. We got a letter a couple of days ago saying she's due another batch of insulin which Sid or I can pick up when it's convenient. I haven't been back to the hospital since we first came to the island, but I find it easily enough. The same Desk Lady who helped me on that day so long ago is seated at the reception. She perks up when she sees me.

"What brings you to Emergency today, hon?"

"Oh… sorry, I'm just here to get a prescription. Should I be somewhere else?"

"It's fine for now. We've got a pharmacy at the other end of the building, but I can take care of you," she says, with a wink. "Isn't this a treat for me! I haven't seen you in an age."

"I'm surprised you remember me."

"Are you kidding me? That's the most excitement we've had here in a while." She beams. Excitement is not the word I would use to describe my confused rampage through the hospital, but I'm grateful she found it entertaining rather than terrifying. "And then I heard from Doctor Tremblay you got your sister's medication under Sid Charles' name!"

"Um… yes." Doctor Tremblay sure does love to gossip about my business—one more bit of evidence of those privacy breaches Tom told us about.

"I always wondered why no one snatched him up sooner. Those border guards come in an awful lot, but it's been a while since he's been around. Heard he's running for office, so I guess he's moving up in the world! That's attractive. Shame about the broken nose, of course, but—"

"There is nothing wrong with his nose." An objectively untrue statement, but I can't help feeling protective of Sid.

"Gives him character, doesn't it?" Desk Lady leans in, her voice a conspiratorial whisper. "By the way, this is where you come when you find yourself on the nest. We'll set you up with a midwife real quick."

"Is there any chance you can get me April's medicine? *Please*?"

"I'll just tell Riley you're here. You wait for me."

The hospital is quiet, with the occasional person passing as they scurry between hallways. Nurses with clipboards. Doctor Tremblay. He gives me a quizzical glance as he hurries by and I smile back, daring him to say anything. Of course, nothing happens. That sneaky bastard is too much of a coward to mess with me in public.

Eventually, a nurse comes out with a tall man following her, his fair hair thinning in the back. He's clutching a paper bag, much like the one April's insulin comes in. He has a star tattoo on the back of his hand. Something about him is so familiar, the hair on my neck stands on end.

"If you have any issues with your dosage, come back as soon as you can," the nurse says. "I know it's difficult to make the trip to the island, but—"

"God willing, I'll be here," he says with a laugh and again, there's the grating sense of familiarity. Did I see him at the town hall? Or maybe at the Reinventor's Guild? I can't think of anywhere else I've met people on Salt Spring.

Then his gaze swings round and we lock eyes. His brow furrows, as if he's experiencing that same déjà vu, unable to place me. Face to face, he crystalizes into someone I know all too well.

My eyes drop as he turns back to the nurse. I'm trapped inside a hallucination. This can't be real. My mind refuses to interpret this as real, even as he continues talking, his voice growing more and more recognizable. "Does Pat need to sign me out?"

"She should. I don't know where she went." The nurse cranes her neck down the hall. "Oh! There she—"

"Pardon me, hon. I was getting something for Mrs. Charles. Oh, that you, Gord? Leaving us already?"

Gord. I grip my seat to keep from tilting out of my chair. It's such an ordinary name; it tumbles through my mind like a stone. Gord. Gordon. I focus on breathing evenly, so that I don't draw his attention again. I can't give this man another reason to look at me. All that's protecting me are eleven years and the fact that Pat used Sid's last name, not mine, when she brought the medicine out. Funny, how we've both hidden behind false names.

I never knew him as Gord. I never knew him to dress in a sweater and jeans, either. His hair is a decade greyer since the last time I saw him. He shouldn't look so ordinary. He shouldn't be named Gord.

The Grand Astrologue stuffs his prescription into his bag. "Do I owe you anything?"

"No, Astolia's accounts are squared away already," she says. "The goats you turned in last May should tide you over for a while."

Goats. The goats we had to give as sacrifice to show our commitment to his mission? The goats he said represented the constellation Aries and also tied back to the old law of Israel? He really did pick and choose from whatever tradition he wanted, but it was supposed to prove something —that we were obeying the old ways of the Earth, which all secretly agreed, when you thought about it hard. Agreed that goats were worth something.

No shit they are. They're worth medicine.

"Perfect. Thank you, Pat." He gives a slight bow, like an old-fashioned gentleman.

He tries to look at me one more time, but I keep my head ducked, playing with my hair as if I'm lost in thought. The nurse says something to Pat, which is a relief, because it keeps them busy until Gord—Grand Astrologue of Astolia—is out of the door and beyond earshot. By the time the nurse leaves and Pat calls me over, no one else is there to hear my name.

"Kayla, I got that insulin."

"Thanks." I rise from my seat on tilting legs. "So... that man said he was from somewhere?"

"Oh, yes. Astolia." Pat passes me my bag.

"Astolia," I repeat, hoping to sound like I'm trying to familiarize myself with a new word. "I've never heard of it. Is it like Penelakut or America or…?"

"Oh no, I don't think that place is half as big," says Pat. "They're a smaller colony. Campbell River area, I think? It's really something they're still around, considering how TNS runs amok on the big island."

"Wow." There's a small chance this isn't bad news. Maybe there's some non-ominous reason for the Grand Astrologue coming here. Maybe the time they attacked him was all a big misunderstanding and they've all made up. Then he realized how stupid it was locking people off from the modern conveniences of Salt Spring. I left over eleven years ago. I was what... fourteen? Things could change in that time.

But *goats*. Things could still be the exact same.

"Has that colony been around a long time?" I ask. "I never ran into them in the wilds."

"Rotten luck for you. I think they've been around a while." She scrunches her face, considering my question. "Been coming by the hospital as long as I can remember. And I've been working here for over twenty years."

Twenty years. The entire time my family was there, he was nipping off here whenever it suited him, warning us all that if *we* ever met these people, they'd kill us. And no one on this island did a damn thing to stop him.

"Thanks for the medicine." I take the bag and retreat toward the door.

"See you in a month!" says Pat merrily.

No, she won't. Because no place that lets that man in can possibly be safe.

THIRTY-ONE

"YOU ARE MAKING no sense." April raises a textbook to obscure my face.

"April, I know what I saw! He's been coming here for over twenty years. Pat told me herself." I'm not sure how I expected this to go, but April's resistance is understandable. The words spill out of me anyway. They have to. I don't know how much time we have to run. "We need to leave. It isn't safe!"

"No, Kayla, *you* aren't safe!" She snaps the book shut, heat flushing her cheeks. "I can't leave here. I can't!"

"We could. I figured it out." I grab her hands, desperate to make her understand. "We'll go to Penelakut or America. We could still visit here from those places. Or order your insulin. We could get it, even if we're living there—"

"Stop being a paranoid idiot and think for two seconds! He didn't recognize you."

"He might. He might put together where he knows me from—"

"He isn't going to care! What do you think he'll do? Cart us back there? We would expose him. He's got no reason to want us to come with him. If we all ignore each other, it's going to be fine."

"The whole island is a problem! How can we trust people who work with Astolia? How can we—"

"What makes you so sure they know what's going on there?" she demands. "If the Astrologue is lying to everyone in Astolia, what makes you think he's telling the truth to Salt Spring?"

Damn it. There is nothing more frustrating than having a younger sister who is smarter than I am. I don't have a good rebuttal for that, except that my gut knows she's wrong. If we don't move now, he'll get us.

"April, we can't risk it. We can't."

"Sid is in politics. Why don't you ask him?"

"I can't." Not after everything I've put him through.

"Why not?"

"Because he wouldn't understand! I never told him about Astolia or—"

"He's not going to care if you grew up in a cult. His was, like, ten times worse." April tosses her ponytail over her shoulder. "Whatever. If you don't want to ask him, I will."

"No! What if he lies—"

"For fuck's sake, Kayla, listen to yourself! He isn't going to lie to us." April swears so rarely, the outburst shuts me up. "He never has. You know that."

"I..." I don't know what's wrong with me. Or what to do. Or where we're safe anymore. I want to run. I want to steal the knife from the butcher block in the kitchen. But I can't force my sister to believe me. "Fine. Fine, I'll talk to him."

"Sure, go ahead, if you like. I'm still asking him myself."

"I said I would talk to him."

"I want to hear it from him myself. You..." April shakes

her head, and it dawns on me: she's more afraid of me lying to her than him. "I don't understand you anymore."

With that, she reopens her textbook, heedless of the knives her words drive through me. My sister. My own baby sister doesn't trust me.

I can't stay in this room. It feels as though the walls of our apartment will crash in and bury me. On instinct, I pack my bag. There isn't much to gather—just a few clothes and books scattered around the bedroom. Most of our survival supplies are still packed. I always knew this day would come and that we would need to run again.

I'll scout a route. While I wait for April to understand the danger we're in, I'll come up with a plan. That way, when we run, we'll know where we're going. It's how we did it in the old days and how we need to do it now.

I head outside, walk toward the road and then…

As I reach the end of the drive, the panic clutching my chest squeezes harder. I might not feel safe here anymore, but it's even worse out there. I could walk toward the coast if I wanted, but then what? There are stockades around every accessible point, plus constant patrols, keeping me in as much as they keep TNS out.

I hurry back into the acreage, my breath coming easier when I see the house and Wendell splitting wood by the back stoop. I give him a wide berth, avoiding conversation as my head continues to swirl. I circle the whole property— chickens, toolshed, beehives, berry bushes. Every so often, I come across a break in the fencing that would make a good escape route. I mark each spot in my mind.

But what good is any of this? April won't follow me. How can I ever protect her if she won't follow me?

Finally, I give up and collapse by the duck pond, pressing my face into my knees. There, the real reason for all my fretful pacing becomes obvious, because while running around the farm might not have done any practical good, it kept the memories at bay.

I stare across Sid's duck pond and wonder if in some other universe, there's another version of myself who came here at the age of fourteen with her parents. A girl who got to go to a real school and watch her sister grow up without the stress of being her caretaker. Would I have chosen Curtis, if we'd had the option of meeting hundreds of other people? Or one day, would I have gone to the exchange and seen a trio of young men, recently returned from the border patrol, and spotted Sid leading them?

Neither story is likely. A third Kayla would exist. A girl I can't even imagine, except that I suspect she's happier than I am. A girl who got to keep all the people who mattered most to her. Mum, Dad, Curtis, even...

"Kayla?"

A shudder steals down my spine. I look over my shoulder and see Sid staring back, unsure if I want him to approach. After my behaviour last night, I can't blame him for keeping a healthy distance. It's almost enough to make me regret what I do next, because I can't be certain I won't hurt him again.

"Sid." My arms reach out, beckoning. A few hours ago, I'd convinced myself even *he* could be lying to us, but in the flesh, my fractured heart sees something different. In many ways, love is nothing but a survival mechanism, something we use to manipulate people into helping us. My throbbing pulse identifies him not as a foe, but as my last chance for defence. If I can make him love me, he'll have to protect me.

"You disappeared again."

"I know."

"You scared the shit out of me when you didn't come home. And the worst part is, I didn't know if I would make it worse by looking for you."

"I'm sorry."

He takes a single step forward. "April said we needed to talk?"

At least she gave me a chance to explain things to him. Maybe I haven't lost her completely. I flex my fingers, arms still outstretched, and sure enough, he slides a hand into one of mine. I pull him closer, letting heat flood my body, bidding goodbye to all the other lives I might have lived. This one, with him, is the only one left.

I tug at him, trying to make him sit. "You were right about me."

"What do you mean?"

"Cult trauma. All of that. I'm screwed up. And… I don't know if it's going to get any better. I saw someone today. Someone I thought I escaped a long time ago."

That gets his attention. Whatever awkwardness might exist between us, it's less important than what I'm hinting at.

He sits next to me on the bench, and when I tuck myself against his side, there's only a second's pause before he gives in and puts his arm around me. "Go on," he says, voice soft.

I could kiss him. But I hold off, knowing I need to get this out first. I twine my arms around his waist and let the closeness anchor me. "I was born in Port Alberni," I say. "I lived there until I was nine, when TNS attacked."

His stomach muscles stiffen, but he doesn't pull away.

"After that, my parents were desperate to find somewhere safe to live. Mom was pregnant, so… we headed east and joined the next colony we found. Astolia."

"Astolia?" he repeats.

"Heard of them?"

"Yeah, but…" There's nervousness in his voice. "They're a cult?"

"What have you heard about them?"

He shrugs. "Fledgling colony. One of the few on Vancouver Island that hasn't gone down to TNS, so… Council tries to support them. No one's ever said anything about them being a cult. But they're really well fortified for only fifty people, so—"

"Fifty people?" I look up at him. "That's the estimate they give for Astolia? Just fifty people?"

"That's what Council reported when they took a tour of it a few years back," says Sid.

"Shit." It wouldn't be hard to make it look true for a day or two. During the summer, most of us led the goats quite far from the colony to pasture on the surrounding hills. If they timed a visit from Salt Spring correctly, there would be no reason for most of the population to know about any alliance. How perfect.

"Were there more than that when you were there?"

"Well over six hundred."

"*Six hundred*? Crammed into that tiny compound?"

"Have you been?" I ask.

"No, but I've seen the specs. I try to keep up with all our international partners. So, what happened to you?"

I wish I didn't have to answer. But how can I expect him to trust me without the full truth? I start at the beginning, with April's birth and how for a moment, we thought we might be safe. I talk about Beth-Anne and herding goats and how I started hating turnips. It doesn't seem so bad. Not until I tell him about the Grand Astrologue. And the "attacks."

TNS, they told us, was always waiting. Practically once a month, there would be gunfire on the hills, and we would all have to huddle inside the compound for safety. The Grand Astrologue would lead us in chants until the shooting stopped and miraculously, we were safe. That gets under Sid's skin more than any other detail I've shared.

"TNS did *not* have enough bullets to waste them on one random colony, over and over again."

"Yeah," I say. "I would love to know what they were actually shooting at."

"I'm sure they were firing blanks. Though how they had that much powder to burn..." He shakes his head. "TNS made us use that shit sparingly. It's possible to melt down bullets and cast more, but a lot harder to manufacture proper, modern gunpowder."

"Probably should have thought of that when we were still there." I had my suspicions back then, but it seems so obvious now that it was part of the manipulation. The Grand Astrologue excelled at the theatre of fear.

Eventually, I get to the end of the story. Our escape. How my father died protecting me from people who wanted to hand me over to be someone's teenaged wife. Sid's grip tightens around my shoulders. I tell him how the day we broke out of the compound, my dad held back the guards so Mum and I could keep running. Curtis managed to squeak past too, tying his fate to ours for a few years. I go all the way to the end, describing our time in the wilderness. And finally, I reach the second attack.

"When I really think about it, I'm not even sure it was TNS," I say. "Just... people with guns. April and I managed to avoid the whole thing. Sometimes I think... TNS wouldn't have killed Mum. She wasn't that old. Early forties. Young enough that someone might have wanted her for... you know. But if Astolia found them, and me and April weren't there? They would have wanted to punish her. They would have..."

"Kayla." He wraps his other arm around me.

I cling to him, my eyes screwed shut as I go on. We're getting to the worst part. The bit I've never said out loud, not even to April. The death I can hardly acknowledge.

"April and I got away. We lost most of our supplies and almost starved, but we made it. But... only us. A couple weeks later, I miscarried."

The hand stroking my hair goes still. "You were..."

"Just a couple months. Curtis knew, but no one else. We were trying to find the right moment, because we knew my mum wasn't going to be thrilled when she found out. A pair of stupid teenagers, thinking we were old enough to..." I swallow hard, but there are fewer tears to repress than one might think. It's always been the thing I couldn't cry about. There was no one to share it with. No way to connect to the life I lost before it ever began. "I wanted that baby, Sid. I know it doesn't make sense. I couldn't have kept me and April alive while pregnant. It was all for the best, but I wanted it. I wanted some piece of him. Of them. Of what we lost. It didn't seem fair that I couldn't even save the life inside of me. I couldn't do anything."

"Fuck." He doesn't say much, but it's enough. I'm so unaccustomed to sharing the story, I don't think I could have listened to comforting sermons on the topic anyway. "I wish—I wish I could fix it for you."

Something between a sniff and a laugh emanates from me as I shift in his arms to lean against his side. "It is what it is."

"Have you talked to anyone about this?"

"That's literally what we're doing right now."

"I mean like counselling."

I wrinkle my nose. "You mean like a... therapist?"

"Yeah, exactly."

I've read about them in books. They were something of a fixture in pre-Quake communities. But I can't picture what they did or how it would help. I barely managed to talk about this with Sid.

"It's not like you have to do it tomorrow," he says,

sensing my hesitance. "But therapy helps more than you think. I had to do it when I came here. It's mandated for former TNS members; part of the rehabilitation program. I fought against it for the first few months, but eventually, stuff they said started to break through. If nothing else, it helped me figure out how to keep going."

"I can't tell anyone, Sid. I didn't mention Astolia on my papers. I'll get another demerit."

"Therapists have to keep patient confidentiality."

"And you *believe* them?"

The silence that follows reassures me he's not foolish enough to trust a promise blindly. "I think so," he says, lukewarm but hopeful. For all his crabbiness, Sid is inherently optimistic.

"I'm not telling anyone." Sid opens his mouth to argue with me further, but I shake my head. "I'm sorry. I can't do it. Telling you was bad enough."

"How are we going to expose what's going on in Astolia if you don't say anything about it? I can't go up to Council spouting a bunch of hearsay."

I spring away from him. "You want to tell *Council*?"

"Well, we should, shouldn't we? If there are people suffering there—"

"You *can't*. If they figure out I'm here, they'll come for me and April, or Council will send us back or—"

"Kayla, they won't."

"I have demerits! If I get more, they'll suspend my sanctuary papers and then—"

"You're my *wife!*" he shouts over my panicking prattle. That word reverberates through my bones. "If you don't want to say anything, that's fine. I won't make you. But they can't carry you away, because you've got a legal right to be here. We're married and—"

"Are we?" I thread my fingers through his, taking his left

hand, then his right, in mine. It feels like the right moment. I've spilled my guts about Astolia. The only lingering question is whether he'll stand by me. "Are we *really*?"

He struggles to clear his throat. "I... I don't know."

"You know all the worst parts of me, Sid Charles." I let my voice drop, low and husky, no longer trying to mask my desire. "Do you still want me?"

He leans in and rests his forehead against mine, so tantalizingly close. "More than anything. But what if—"

I'm done with the what ifs and maybes. This time, when I kiss him, there's nothing left to restrain me. Speaking about Curtis severed my last tether to him. For years, the memory of being loved sustained me, but it's not enough anymore. I need this. Like air and water and food, this is essential to my survival.

Sid pulls me into his lap and I let my body melt against his. My mouth roves over his face, kissing his jaw, his cheek, his uneven nose. I want to be touching all of him. The clothes separating his skin from mine bunch uncomfortably between our bodies. I snake my hands beneath his coat, then find my way to the hem of his shirt to touch his stomach. He growls as he moves to kiss my shoulder, and his own hands find their way into my blouse. Buttons pop and he digs his thumb into my navel. A whimper escapes me. I go back to his mouth for more, but a second later, he breaks away.

"We—we need to..."

"Please don't stop," I beg. None of my demons can threaten me when he's holding me and that makes his touch the most precious medicine I've ever tasted. "I'm sorry about before. You were right. I was scared, but I've always—"

"I mean..." He clears his throat, struggling to regain control. "Maybe we should... take this inside?"

"What? Oh!" I push against his shoulders, stunned. I've

always fumbled my way into intimacy without thinking about any kind of preparation like setting. Curtis was a summer child's romance, but maybe I've grown beyond that now.

"You know…" A small amount of Sid's chest hair pokes above the neckline of his shirt, and I tug at it playfully. "I've never done it in a bed before."

"Holy shit." He lets out a nervous laugh. He's flushed from his forehead to his neck. "Well… I'm excited to be your first for something."

He tries to ease me off his lap so he can stand, but I tighten my legs around him, so he rises with me clinging to his body like a possum to a tree. He scoops an arm beneath my ass so that I can hang on him more comfortably, then gives me a withering look. "Kayla. We can't walk in like—"

"Like what?" I ask, right before cutting him off with a kiss. Despite his protests, he leans in, mouth open and wanting. This man is helpless against me and I love it.

He could probably carry me up to the apartment like this, but eventually, I concede and straighten so that my feet hit the ground. I almost tip over when I touch earth, as if I've been in a canoe on the ocean for too long and forgotten how to stand without the sway of his body to anchor me. An anxious bubble forms in my chest. Standing on my own two feet reminds me how frightening the world beyond him is. Astolia and everything it represents is closer than it's ever been.

I grab Sid's hand, dragging him towards the house. As we draw closer, I spot James coming over the hill. I drop Sid's hand. It's not that I'm ashamed to be with him—but whatever is happening between us is so new and tenuous, I don't want anyone's input on it yet.

James's gaze flicks from my red eyes to the open buttons on my shirt. He smirks in a way that says we haven't fooled him one bit. "Carlos wanted someone to grab you two for dinner. But... Kayla, I can see you're still upset about whatever it was and Sid... you've got a lot of files to go over, I guess?"

"Go jump in the sea, James." Sid grabs me by the shoulders and steers me up to our apartment. I'm trembling with a mixture of horror and laughter as we get the door open.

"Oh, you're welcome. No need for gratitude at all!"

"Wait, James!" I place a hand on Sid's arm, halting him. "Is April down there?"

"She came down a few minutes ago, yes."

"Tell her everything's okay, all right? I'm lying down, but... everything's okay." Is that true? I can't tell. I'm not interested in dragging us off this farm anymore. If anything, this is the one safe place left in the world.

"I'll keep her away as long as I can." He winks, and I am equal parts relieved and mortified that a secret like this is in James's hands.

He disappears into the kitchens. When I turn back to Sid, there's a thoughtful pinch to his brow.

"You sure you want to do this?"

I grin, remembering the morning we left for our wedding. "*I'm* not the one who is going to back out."

THIRTY-TWO

DESPITE MY EARLIER bravado, my heart thuds ominously following Sid into his bedroom. I've lived with him since the wedding, but never set foot inside. It isn't big. Most of the space is taken up by the bed, which is large for one person, but necessary, considering his height. Aside from that, there's a cedar chest that holds his clothes and doubles as a bench, and a window that lets in a cloudy beam of moonlight. It isn't late, but the sun sets so early in November, night has already set in.

But at least it has a bed. I was frankly starting to wonder if he owned anything. "Why haven't you decorated your house?"

Sid bends down to open the cedar chest. "What?"

"They've got so much stuff at the exchange! Pictures, rugs, couches. I saw a big red couch I liked today." Had a good breakdown on it too, but let's skip that part. "You could do anything with this place."

He looks up at the naked walls. "Yeah... I guess."

"So why haven't you?"

"I'm not sure I know how. I bought a table once, but

I got rid of it a few days later. It feels make-believe most of the time. Like… moving toys around in a dollhouse." His response startles me. After twelve years, I would have thought he was settled here. As if sensing my thoughts, he adds, "At least I'm not still living out of a knapsack."

"Hiking pack," I say.

"Is there a difference?" He draws up so that he's standing in front of me. The air between us is charged with heat, but we don't reach out. Not yet.

"Hiking packs are bigger. Fancier. Like the king-sized bed of backpacks." Everything I'm saying is so stupid, but I can't stop smiling. Even as Sid's face takes on its usual, serious bent, I can't stop beaming at him like a firefly.

"Kayla." He places a hand on my arm, and I let my hands travel up his chest. His pulse races against my palms. "I made you a promise when you came here."

"You seriously didn't bring me all the way up here to *not* take me to bed, did you?"

"No, I'm not saying that. I'm saying…" As he struggles for words, I realize this is one of those rare moments when his guards are down. If I ever want to see him clearly, I have to listen.

I try to be tender instead of hungry as I reach up and touch his face. "Saying what?"

"I don't want you to regret me. If you wake up tomorrow and come to your senses, and it turns out that I've hurt you by doing this…"

It's too awful to let him go on. "Sid." I take him into my arms, pressing him close. "I know I don't deserve it, but *please*. Please have faith in me. I want to be with you. Please don't punish me for making mistakes."

"*Punish* you?" he says disbelievingly.

"I… I know you don't want someone as messed up as me, but—"

His face contorts with confusion. "When did I ever say—"

"Same night you promised not to sleep with me. You said I came from a weird sex cult and you didn't want anything to do with that."

A dark shadow passes over his face. "I shouldn't have said that."

"No, I deserved it. And it's true. But if you give me a chance—"

"Kayla, I know this is a shitty excuse, but I said that because I was trying to convince myself it didn't matter that you didn't want me. I was asking you to marry me without telling you I was ex-TNS. I knew I would never deserve to touch you. I was trying to talk myself into thinking it was okay that you wanted nothing to do with me, even though I was falling for you."

His words stun me for half a second. Then I burst forth like a breaking damn. "But I treated you like shit!"

"I never said I had good taste."

I slam an angry fist into his chest, but that only makes the grin wider on his face. He wraps a hand around each of mine.

"You shot me with that rock and I was done. I'd never met someone so fearless." He weaves his fingers into my curls. As his thumbs press against the nape of my neck, I slide my hands up his chest to rest on his shoulders. "And it would kill me if I became the one thing you were afraid of."

"I'm afraid of a lot of things, Sid." That much must be obvious after today. "But not you. Never you."

His mouth meets mine and I let the taste of him take over me. For the first time, we go slowly. Desperate as I am to be with him, I also don't want to miss a single sensation. I take my time rolling up the hem of his shirt, revealing his stomach, the thin trail of pale hair leading downward from his navel to his jeans. His chest shudders as I reach it, and I'm stunned for a moment by the breadth of his ribs heaving under my hands. Our lips break apart and I teeter backward until he catches the small of my back, my fists still clutching his shirt.

"If we do this…" His eyes don't look like themselves, blue swallowed up by the dark of his pupils. "If we do this, there's no going back. No… whatever our deal used to be. If we do this—"

"It becomes real. I know." And it's a bad idea. At this point, I've known him for a little over two months. It's not enough to build a marriage on. But that's what we'll be if we go through with this—legally bound, physically consummated. Husband and wife. Married, in every conventional sense of the word. I should not be sleeping with him. But I can't take the longing or the loneliness anymore.

He must agree this is insane. The cold, logical part of him must be driving all these questions. But he kisses my forehead, drawing my eyes up to him. "Do you trust me?"

A smile breaks over my face as I recognize that question. "Yes."

He kisses the side of my neck. My eyes close.

"Do you want me?"

"*Yes.*"

"Good."

He helps me peel his shirt over his shoulders. His hands slide into the few buttons on my blouse that are still fastened. It drops to the floor behind me and cold air pricks my skin, driving me forward into the warm mass of his body. It's happening. It's *actually* happening. Belatedly, it hits me how long it's been since I did any of this. Should I be worried about screwing it up? Curtis and I weren't exactly discerning lovers. We only had each other. What if Sid is expecting something more sophisticated than I know how to give? But then his hand threads beneath the clasp of my bra and it's so wonderful to be touched there again, the worry melts away.

It's been too long since I let myself be close with someone like this—yet I can't think of anyone I would have wanted to share myself with in those empty years other than him. If I have any regrets, it's only that we didn't do this sooner.

I pull away so that I can back up and seat myself on the foot of his bed, finally getting a good look at him. All I can think is *holy hell, I'm a lucky girl*. His chest is even paler than the rest of him, which shouldn't surprise me, but it still amazes me how brown my tanned skin looks against his. His pecs are well defined, with fine, blonde hair spread across them. It's soft against my palms when he bends close to me.

I press my hands against his clavicle. Even when he's trying to be slow and gentle, the sheer force of his body is intense, and I lie back on the bed, grateful for the support of the mattress. I scooch back, making room as he climbs over me, and then we're hooking fingers into each other's jeans.

He takes a moment to simply look at me, lying exposed with my back against his pillows. "How are you even real?" he murmurs—and if I could find the strength to speak, I would return the compliment.

But he doesn't seem to mind my breathless silence. His smile is so wide, it pulls at the scar near his ear. "There isn't a single inch of you I haven't thought about touching."

"Oh. Then I guess you better get to work."

"Gladly." He kisses my stomach. Then his hands slide down my side, scooping around my breasts, caressing my stomach, tickling the inside of my thigh. His hand lingers there, sending a shuddering wave through me. No part of me wants for attention. I pull one of his hands close to

me—the one that still bears the scar from my slingshot—
and kiss it. It's the best way I know how to say thank you.

But he's not done with me yet. Far from it.

"You ready?" he murmurs, and I nod, as certain as I
can be.

To my amazement, he has a lambskin condom in the
cedar chest. It makes me recklessly giddy. As soon as he's
ready, I pull him toward me, eager to finally feel the weight
of his body against mine.

We meet, and my breath catches. This might not be my
first time, but it's been so long since anyone has touched
me like this. Light pulses through me as he takes me in
his arms; presses his mouth against my cheek, my neck,
my breast. As he skates lower down my stomach, his name
comes tumbling out of my lips. "*Sid.*"

"Yes?" His voice rasps against my ear.

I don't actually have anything to say. There are no
words for this feeling coursing through me. Despite the
cold night, everything is on fire. The press of his hand over
my wrist. The way his mouth traces the curve of my neck.
We find a rhythm together, our bodies rocking, causing a
squeak in his mattress as we dig into each other.

All I want is to dive deeper into the swell of this feeling.
No matter how long we go or how my body tightens
around him, I want more. And then, all at once, I'm
drowning. I gasp for air as wave after wave breaks over
me. His breath is hot against my shoulder. My fingers dig
into his hips as I try to steady myself, stay grounded to this
moment that is at once too much and the only thing that
could ever be enough. Soon, I'm crying out his name and
he's gasping mine, until we both unfurl together, like sails
bound for a foreign land.

Finally, we come apart, though we never stop touching.
He rolls to my side, and I wrap my arm over his shoulder,

keeping him close. His hair sticks up at odd angles thanks to my roving hands, but it's so much softer than mine, I can't stop playing with it.

Once we've both caught our breath, he pulls me close again, so that our stomachs press together. "Hey," he whispers.

I burrow my face in his neck, deliriously happy.

"Did you want to go back to your room with April tonight? Or did you want to stay—"

"You had better not be kicking me out, Sid Charles."

"I'm not." He laughs. "But she will notice if you don't come back. I wanted to let you know I'll be okay, either way."

"Okay? What would you prefer?" I ask, more anxious than I dare admit. If this was a one and done thing for him, I'll be furious, heartbroken, and will push him out the second storey window.

His grip tightens against my back. "I would have thought you could guess."

I grin, then plant a kiss on his mouth. "I think I'll stay. But on one condition."

"Oh, we're back to putting conditions on our relationship, are we?"

"Definitely this one."

"And what is it?"

"You have to go down to the kitchens and get us some food. I am *not* missing Carlos's huevos rancheros again because of you."

He rolls away, laughing so hard it shakes the bed and me and it seems, in my eyes, the whole world. Because he is the world. All my hope and happiness are wrapped up in him.

It isn't smart. It isn't safe.

I can't help it.

THIRTY-THREE

SID MANAGES TO go downstairs and get food without drawing too much attention. The kitchens aren't close to his bedroom, so no one heard us—small mercy—and since the boys are used to deferring to Sid, no one asks questions. When he turns up with our shares of the meal, he does note that James gave him a few eyebrow waggles, but for now, we're still in that honeymoon bliss of no one else knowing.

It doesn't last long. We share one, glorious, private night together eating eggs, indulging in each other when we like, and fall asleep curled into one another's arms. And then in the morning, it's over.

April bangs on Sid's door at the crack of dawn. I groan and lean deeper into his chest.

"*Kayla?*" April's voice is frantic on the other side. "Are you in there?"

Sid starts to stand, but I pull him back into bed.

"No, let me." I don't particularly want to deal with her, but this is also more my responsibility than his. I grab a shirt from the floor and throw it on before opening the door.

Even though I'm sure she's expecting it, April gasps when she sees me standing in the doorframe, wearing nothing but one of Sid's shirts that swoops across me like a dress.

"Morning." I give her a wry smile.

"You have *got* to be joking!" April stamps her foot. "I send him out to talk to you about Astolia and you end up like this? What is wrong with you?"

I shut the door behind me before Sid can be subjected to more of her sniping. "Why do you even care? You got what you wanted. We're not going anywhere."

"You're joking. *Please*, tell me you're joking." She pulls my shoulder, but I only grunt and push past her toward our shared room. She's on my heel, still bleating like a wounded goat. "You're supposed to divorce him in two years!"

"Well, if he knocks me up, I'll lose a demerit, and then we can be out of here in one."

"*What*?!"

"Calm down! I'm kidding." I glower at her as I grab my bag, still fully packed from my half-hearted escape attempt last night. "Well... sort of. I *would* lose the demerit if we had a kid, but we're obviously not going to do that yet."

"Yet?!"

"I don't know, April! I married him, okay? I married him for you and I slept with him for me. Is that so hard to wrap your head around?"

"So when it goes to shit, whose fault is it going to be? Mine or yours?" Tears brim in her eyes.

I would feel bad for her if she weren't being a total asshole right now. "Thanks for the vote of confidence." I shoulder past her.

"Where are you going?" she demands.

"Back to him. Congratulations. You've got your own room."

"I never asked for this, Kayla! I never asked for any of this."

She has a right to be upset. I spent a lot of time blaming myself for my parents' choices, and I hate that I'm putting her through this, no matter the reason. It would have been smart if we'd waited so April wouldn't associate our relationship with my earlier breakdown. But I've had so many since moving to this damn island. I'm not waiting for some distant day when I'm emotionally stable enough to deserve a relationship. April can prise whatever shreds of happiness I still feel out of my cold, dead hands.

I slam the door on her and come face to face with Sid, whose eyebrows shoot up. He's half dressed, and my cheeks flush, as if I haven't just spent a night tangled up with him in far less. He buttons up his shirt, watching my reaction carefully. "Everything okay?"

"It will be." I swing my hiking pack in front of me, worried I might be overstepping, but already committed. "Can I stay with you going forward?"

"Sure," he says. I sigh and drop the pack on the floor. He raises a hand and points at it. "But only if you unpack. I'm not tripping over that every time I walk through my own room."

"Back to putting conditions on our relationship?"

"Absolutely." He steps around the bed and kisses me before opening the door. "You unpack, and we'll get you that couch you want."

"Really?"

"I'm mad at you too, Sid!" April's voice careens against my ears as she catches sight of him in the doorway.

He shakes his head at me. "To be continued."

The door shuts and I'm alone in his room. *Our* room. I collapse onto the bed, pressing his cotton shirt I'm wearing against my skin. It smells of homemade soap, a hint of cigarettes, and nothing has ever felt so comfortable. We're getting a couch. I need to unpack.

Holy shit.

I have a husband.

SID GOES INTO town and buys the red couch from the exchange. He had to ask around, but luckily it was the only red couch on the floor, so he found it. It immediately brightens the apartment and makes it look like someone might live here by choice. He also surprises me by buying a small shelf, because he noticed April and I were keeping our books in piles on the floor. I'm stunned by the thoughtfulness of the gift for about two seconds, then I screech and fly into his arms. I'm kissing him all over again, this time in full view of my scowling sister.

I set the shelf up in the main living room, proudly arranging my small collection of books and the few knick-knacks I considered worth dragging around with me for over eleven years. A handful of wave-worn sea glass. My mother's old perfume bottle. Even the carved heart from Curtis. Sid has the nerve to call them *dust collectors*, but I think he secretly likes it.

We transfer my cooking equipment into the kitchen downstairs, including an old bugle from Port Alberni. April and I used it to signal to each other over long distances in the woods, but in its first life, it was used for announcing mess times. Carlos takes to blowing it around the acreage every time a meal is ready, until Dom and Albert forcibly wrestle it away from him, which escalates into a fight that Sid and Silas have to break up. After that, everyone is banned from touching the bugle, which is looking more dented after its foray into active duty. It hangs above the stove, out of reach.

The winter rains arrive in full force. Silas strings a tarp over the beehives to keep them safe from a typhoon that leaves the fields waterlogged for days. We trap as much of the rain in barrels as we can, and Sid starts working on a long-term budget to install catchment pipes along the roof of the homestead.

I teach Carlos how to identify wood blewits and a handful of other mushrooms that last past the first hard frost. When the foraging gets too lean, I hack into one of the cedar trees that came down during the typhoon to access its soft inner bark. With that, I start twining cordage, weaving baskets, and generally keeping myself busy. It's amazing how similar it is to the winters April and I shared in the wilds, only she's at school now and I'm on the acreage.

I tell Sid I went to the café; I've never seen him light up so quickly. He asks me when I think I might go in again, and I say that I'm waiting until Carlos has time to spare. That way, I'll get a better reception when I ask Mrs. Buckerfield about classes. That satisfies Sid for now, but I know I'll have to think up a different excuse eventually.

Spending my days surrounded by strangers in town is out of the question.

The acreage is different. The acreage is safe. Sid and the boys have total control over this place—if anyone from Astolia showed up, I'm confident Sid could squish their brains with his bare hands. But every time I approach the perimeter of the acreage, a choking grip seizes my throat and stops me from going further.

This place barely accepted me, yet the Grand Astrologue walks around freely. They took my knives and slingshot. They took every means I had of defending myself, then let monsters roam their streets. Sid and the boys have sentimental reasons to protect me and April, but the rest of Salt Spring Island can go to hell for all I care.

One day, I try to work up the nerve to bus into town to get new books from the library, but every time I load up my bag, I can't breathe. It isn't worth it. Instead, I wait until April has lost the will to be stony towards me, then hand her my overdue books. She turns them in after school. No one ever questions why I didn't go myself.

When she comes home later that day, I check to see if she picked up anything good, but the only new books she has are on pre-Quake Canadian history and post-Quake Salt Spring Island. In the past couple of months, she's managed to scrape her mathematical knowledge up to a passable level, so she's moved onto another class she's close to failing.

"They want me to memorize the capitals of the provinces. It's so stupid! Who needs to know where Fredericton is?" she demands, cracking a book open and hunkering down on her bed. "I told Mrs. Patel that I've been to Victoria and it's just some useless, fancy hotel that sunk into the ocean. No one needs to know where it was."

"And what did she say?" I ask, thumbing through the handbound volume on post-Quake Salt Spring Island, my back against the wall of my old room.

"That I should respect the past." April rolls her eyes. "You're lucky you don't have to go to school, Kayla. You'd be in trouble constantly."

"Hmm." I flip another page. "Can I borrow this? I should know something about history or whatever, in case Sid needs me to help him write something else for his campaign."

"Sure, if you like."

For a few minutes, I skim a section on how the island was remodelled to be more self-sufficient following the Quake. I wish there were pictures, but I guess those are tougher to print now that most illustrations rely on woodcut blocks. Still, I would love to know what this place looked like four decades ago, when people lived in absurd, single-family boxes that cost a fortune to heat and cool individually and—

"Do you love him?"

April's question jolts me out of my reverie.

"Who?"

"Sid, of course." Of course. "I mean, you *seem* happier. But is it just the sex, or do you love him?"

I should have seen this coming. If my sister is no longer furious with me, naturally, that means questions. The thought of answering gives me that same, clenched feeling I get when I near the road out of the acreage, so I do my best to dodge her. "I *am* happier."

"But you were so firm about not sleeping with him. And I thought he promised you he wouldn't—"

"I like him, April. He…" I have to say something to shut her up. Would claiming I love him do the trick? Would it be true? "He makes me feel safe."

She nods slowly. "Good."

"Yeah, it's really good." *Safe* matters more than love, when you think about it. *Safe* keeps people alive. *Safe* is what we need right now, because the Grand Astrologue could appear at any minute.

"So long as you're not freaking out about the Astolia thing anymore."

"Exactly."

She still doesn't get it, but I'm tired of arguing with her about Astolia. She doesn't remember it well enough to know how horrible it was.

"I couldn't handle it if you were doing this for me or something like that."

"How on earth would me sleeping with Sid be about you?"

"I don't know! I don't know what kind of deal you two made. If he asked you to—"

"He didn't ask me to do anything."

April stares at me like she's seeing a stranger. Maria Patterson must be getting in her head again; back when she tried to defend my honour, she said we weren't sleeping together and now whoops, we are. I don't care if a group of teenaged girls calls me a slut, but April is young enough to think labels like that matter.

I place a hand over her wrist, hoping she will listen to me. "Sid would never pressure me into a relationship. I thought you trusted him."

"Well... I used to. I guess I could again." She lets it drop, but from the line of her frown, I know she still has doubts. She can smell that I'm lying about something, but can't figure out exactly what. It makes the room feel tight around me, so I snap the book shut and head out.

In the living room, Sid is seated on the red couch, scowling at a newspaper. I push the last of my conversation with April from my mind and curl up next to him. Without looking up, he puts his arm around me—the casualness of the affection is strangely thrilling. What we have doesn't require thought or focus. It's automatic.

That night, I just as easily join him in his bed. A storm rages outside; we rely on the pounding of rain against the roof to drown us out. We're making up for lost time these days, as if that first, needlessly chaste era of our marriage haunts us. There's something incredible about getting used to the feel of him, knowing he'll give me what I want. I find myself wondering which answer to April's question is the truth. Maybe I do love him. Maybe it is just the sex. Does it even matter?

Afterward, I lie next to him in a haze, mesmerized by the sound of water banging against the shingles. Nights like this used to make April and me miserable, especially if we hadn't found a ruined house to shelter in. Tonight, the opposite is true. I've never felt safer, despite the storm keeping us indoors.

My skin is slick. Heat pulses through my abdomen. I stretch my bare legs against the thick, wool blanket that covers our bed, delighting in the fuzz.

Sid reaches out to stroke my hair. "So… tomorrow."

"Yeah?" My eyes drift closed.

"You ready?"

"Mmmm."

"Main debate topics are going to be economic growth and innovation. Amy's going to be the obvious standout with all her years working on the Reinventor's Guild."

"What?" I raise my head from the crook of his arm.

"There's another town hall tomorrow," he clarifies. "We talked about this. Are you feeling up to it?"

I vaguely remember it coming up. I even remember agreeing to go, because that was easier than admitting I couldn't leave the acreage if I wanted to. Now, my speechless pause says far more than I'd like.

Sid rolls on his side so he can look at me better. He trails a hand down my spine, coming to rest in the curve between my chest and hips. "I've never seen someone at a Council election who wasn't from the island, if that helps."

"It's fine. Of course, it's fine." My words come out in a rush. "I'm happy to come."

"Thanks. I like having you there," he says, still stroking my hip. "It's nice knowing there's someone in my corner."

He's not asking for much. Just for me to show up and clap when he speaks, reminding people of a domestic scene that died out with the Quake. Maybe even before then. But it doesn't matter. This is about appearances. Plus, Sid will be there the whole time. There's nothing to worry about.

But when the time comes to leave the next day, I'm shaking so hard I can't do the buttons up on my shirt. I collapse onto the bed, breathing hard in an attempt to calm myself down.

No one from Astolia will be there. That's true. But Tom will. I should be thrilled by that idea, since I no longer have to fake liking Sid. We could be gleefully affectionate, until even he concedes that our marriage is real. But I'm sure he knows that wasn't my only lie. Even in the comfort of my bedroom, I feel those cold, pale eyes on me, cutting around, trying to draw out a truth that could get both me and Sid in trouble. I can't go. I can't face him. My papers are a mess. He could suspend my sanctuary case with enough demerits, no matter what Sid says.

Sid knocks on the door. The waver in my "out in a minute!" must give me away, because he comes in. He takes one look at me, half dressed and white as a blizzard, and that's it.

"Why don't you get some rest?" He bends to kiss me on the forehead.

"No, I'm coming. I said I'd be there. And I'll be—"

"We'll try again next time."

"Sid, wait—" But I can't follow him without a shirt on, and he needs to catch the wagon into town, so what are either of us to do? He's gone within minutes and I'm still not ready.

I slam the door to our room shut, furious with him and myself, because he knows. I'm still broken. I'm still the problem that was foisted onto him. Soon, he'll tell April, or she'll figure it out on her own, and the two people I care most about will realize that I've become the things I've always most despised.

Weak. Useless. Defenceless.

THIRTY-FOUR

FOR YEARS, APRIL was the fearful one. She was the girl who couldn't hack it exploring abandoned malls, even though we needed to for survival. She used to close her eyes before she fired her slingshot, so terrified of seeing the blood when it struck an animal. Of course, her shots never did. You can't hit much with your eyes closed.

I made up the difference. I killed enough for both of us. I went into ruins and pulled out supplies. I did every shitty thing I needed to in order to keep us alive, and when she got sick, I made the call to bring us here.

So how is it that this place broke me?

I watch April claw her way through mathematics and new classmates, but I can't leave this farm without crumpling like newspaper. When Tom said I wasn't cut out for civilization, I thought he believed I was too dangerous to fit into society. I forgot wild animals usually bite out of fear. The world beyond the acreage is monstrous and I have nothing to defend myself with. So I curl up on the bed like a hermit crab retreating into its shell and wonder when the sounds in the walls will stop haunting me.

When Sid comes home, he hushes my apologies and says things went fine. It makes it worse. I already know I've let him down and don't deserve his kindness, but I must look too fragile to handle criticism. What am I supposed to do to convince him otherwise? Beg him to yell at me?

I don't know what to say, so I turn my back to him on the mattress, shutting down any further conversation. We fall asleep next to each other, but not touching for the first time since I moved into his room.

By the time morning comes, I feel slightly better. Sunlight is a marvellous thing. I've gotten very good over the years at pushing my dark moods away once daylight greets me. Never mind that the only reason I'm awake before the others is that I barely slept. I drizzle extra honey into breakfast and put on my brightest smile.

Wendell looks unnerved when he tastes the porridge. "Sid's gonna get after us for using so much of the honey."

I ignore him and gather up three bowls, plus a kettle of mint tea, and carry the lot upstairs to our apartment. I have it all nicely set out on the bookshelf when Sid finally emerges.

"I made breakfast." I gesture to the display. "Thought we could eat up here. It's cozier."

"Feeling better?" he asks.

"We need a table. How do you not own a table?"

"Well, there wasn't much point, living alone."

"Sure, but you're not alone anymore." I point to where I've pushed the seashells and perfume bottle out of the way to make room for bowls and cups. "And coasters! Do you think the exchange has coasters?"

"I don't know. You want to go check it out?" It's a small dig, and if he were a stupider man, I might think it was unintentional, but Sid watches me with a wary eye. I don't know why he's taking issue with me being nice to him this morning, instead of when I was sulking all night, but I decide not to dignify it with an answer.

"Morning, April!" I call as my sister shuffles out of her room. He exhales sharply through his nose, but he must understand that I don't want my shit dragged out in front of my sister.

I try not to notice the way he broods at me over his tea while April tries to convince me that her history teacher is the most sadistic woman known to humankind, all because of a pop quiz yesterday.

After April leaves for school, I make a point of not talking about last night and Sid has the decency to follow my lead. Maybe this problem can fade away. Give it enough time, and I'm sure I'll get over my cowardice. I'll attend the next town hall and we'll never, ever have to talk about that night where I couldn't bring myself to leave the house for no good reason.

Sid heads outside to work with the rest of the guys as they attempt to build a rain catchment system out of a mishmash of old piping. I help Young Tom butcher chickens, so we don't have to feed the males through the winter. It's a productive day. A good day. We're back to normal.

But in the evening, right as Carlos and I have started slicing up vegetables for a bean and mushroom casserole, Albert runs into the kitchen with a message.

"Kayla! You've got a visitor."

"What?" My knuckles whiten against the knife. *Visitor.* The word rings more like *intruder* in my ears. What the hell is someone doing on the acreage, looking for me?

I squeeze the knife, reminding myself of its weight. It isn't large, but if someone from Astolia is here, it's better than nothing.

"Yeah, Sid's out talking to her, but she asked for you," says Albert.

She? That rules out the Grand Astrologue, but I don't trust any strangers. I glance between Albert, who is waiting expectantly for me, and Carlos, who hasn't looked up from the mushrooms. April, Sid, and the boys are the only people I've talked to for weeks. Why would anyone come to see me here? There's no one else I know or trust.

"Should I tell her to come inside?" Albert asks.

"No." If she's dangerous, I can't let her inside the house. A surge of adrenaline pulses through me as instincts I haven't used since my time in the wilds rage back to life. "I'm coming. Stay back here, Albert."

"Um... okay?"

I surge through the door, brandishing the blade and find...

Amy.

Amy Sullivan, talking to Sid.

They turn, and Amy's eyes pop when she spots me—a blinking, knife-wielding idiot, arm frozen in a raised battle stance, as if I were going to war, not greeting a woman in a pant suit. All the fight I built up vanishes. The knife falls from my hand. "Amy—I mean, Miss Sullivan," I sputter.

"Hi, Kayla." She waves tentatively, smiling that pretty, perfect smile of hers. "It's so good to see you. Sid invited me for dinner and—"

"You didn't tell me that." I round on him, heat flooding my cheeks. "Why didn't you tell me we were going to have company?"

"I tried to—" he starts, but Amy waves her hand, cutting him off.

"Oh, he told me to swing by when I could get the time off. There wasn't a specific date." She punctuates her explanation with a nervous laugh. "Sorry, is tonight a bad night? I can go. If you want, I can—"

"No. No, of course not. Please stay." I smile so hard

my teeth grind together. "Why don't you wait for us in the kitchen. I need to have a word with my husband."

She turns to Sid, eyes wide, but he nods. "If you don't mind, Amy?"

"No… of course not." She slides a piece of strawberry blonde hair behind her ear and walks towards the kitchen door where Carlos is poking his head out with a curious expression.

I grab Sid's arm and drag him into one of the fields. It cuts into my ability to yell at him—Silas and a few of the other guys are still working outside—but it's the closest we can get to private right now. "You at least could have told me about an open invitation!" I snarl at him.

"I planned to! I didn't know she would come today," he hisses.

"*Planned*? Did something get in the way of this *plan*?"

"Oh, don't give me that bullshit. I'm not the one who's been avoiding conversations. You shut me down when I tried to talk about last night, so forgive me if I thought it would be better to wait a day or two so that *you* might consider talking about it."

It is so bloody awful, arguing with someone who has reality on their side. My face burns with a mixture of embarrassment and rage. "Why did you invite her? I came at her with a knife. Do you have any idea how mortifying—"

"She was worried about you. She asked."

Another, even more horrifying thought crawls down my spine. "Did you tell her about me? About the things I told—"

"No. Not really."

"*Not really?*" That adverb is doing a lot of work and none of it is good.

"She asked why you didn't come last night, and I told her you had a rough day. That's it."

"And then she shows up? The next day?" I press, disbelieving. "You told her a hell of a lot more than that."

"I didn't! Her uncle works in immigration. You're not the first person to move here and have… stuff to sort through." He's struggling to put things diplomatically. "People don't need to know how the shit got on your boots to smell it. I'm sorry, all right? I would have told you she might swing by, but you wouldn't talk to me—"

"Fine. Whatever. I get it. I'm the one being illogical." I throw my arms in the air. "Why don't we go inside and have dinner, then?"

"Kayla, that isn't what I said." He puts a hand on my shoulder, but I knock him away. "Please. I'm trying to help."

"When I asked you for help, Sid," I say pointedly, "inviting strangers into the only place I feel safe wasn't what I had in mind."

The colour drains from his face. Against all odds, it seems I've won this fight. "I'm sorry," he murmurs.

Amy is sitting in the kitchen with her hands clasped tightly while James regales her with some story about over-hearing the island's white-tail deer going into rut last week. The poor woman looks ready to pass out from discomfort.

"James, move." I push him to the side. "She came to see me, so I get to sit next to her."

"Well, I am not one to get in between female friendships." James gallantly slides down the bench, making room. How did he even know she was here? He was nowhere near the kitchens when she arrived. He must have some special organ for sniffing out female pheromones. He grins his usual smarmy grin. "I dated twins once, you know. Worst mistake of my life."

"Thank you," Amy whispers. Mercifully, this means we'll have something to talk about other than my issues or the fact that Sid and I obviously had an argument.

Harassing James really is the perfect cause for women to rally behind.

Sid and I had an argument. We hadn't done *that* since we started sleeping together, either.

I push the thought away, determined to perform normality. "All those years in TNS and dating twins is the worst thing you've ever done?"

James shrugs. "I wasn't responsible for any of their shit."

What I wouldn't give to live with this man's unbridled confidence.

Dinner is relatively pleasant. If anyone does a poor job of acting natural around Amy, it's Sid, who doesn't stop sulking until I kick him under the table. He rallies and starts a conversation with Amy about trade deals with Penelakut and America. Apparently, there's a big negotiation going on with the San Juans over their limestone deposits. Both are fiercely opinionated on the subject.

"What do you think they want? More access to the hospital, of course," Amy says. "I don't know why Council is stalling—"

"Because we've barely got enough medicine to keep our own people alive," he counters.

"We could manufacture more if we could build more permanent structures. Cement, glass, fertilizer. It's all connected, Sid. It *matters*."

"You just want them to repair the road to the south island."

"Can you blame me? Biking that thing is hell."

I wish I could join in, but I've barely cracked that book on Salt Spring's history. I want to like Amy, but I find myself reminded again that she's the type of woman Sid should have married: someone who mirrors his political aspirations and has her life together. He's not doing anything wrong with the way they're talking. I don't think discussing lime deposits counts as flirting, but a horrible sense of inadequacy snakes into me nonetheless. I'm still angry with him, but I slide my hand into his beneath the table, trying to reassure myself.

After dinner, Amy taps me on the shoulder. She inclines her head toward where Sid and the boys have started washing dishes. "They look busy. Care to go for a walk with me?"

"Oh. I should probably help out—"

"No. You and Carlos cooked." Amy grabs my arm and steers me out the door. "Anyone who has to clean up after they've cooked dinner for their family is suffering a great injustice and you will never convince me otherwise."

"The duck pond is nice," I say, mostly to be sure she doesn't try to drag me toward the road.

"Sure. We can head that way."

I feel bad when her nice black shoes sink into the muddy paths down our back field. The main road has better drainage. Still, if she wasn't ready to get dirty, she shouldn't have come to the countryside today.

"This place is beautiful," she says, surveying the misty bank robing the cedars at the eastern edge of the property. "I'm glad they got this place. Must be a load off Sid's mind."

"Yeah, he seems…" I trail off, realizing I don't actually have the best idea how he's feeling right now. Probably like I've screwed everything up for him.

"He's lucky you showed up. Their occupancy rate was pretty low for a property with so many units," she says. "Are you doing well, though? Are you happy here?"

"Of course I am."

"Of course."

I don't know what response she's expecting. She's always

been kind to me, but she's still the niece of my immigration case worker. And let's not forget, my husband's ex-girlfriend. Like hell am I giving her anything to report back with.

"I guess I find myself worrying about you because... well, they're a good group of guys but there *are* a lot of them," she continues. "It must be a little lonely with no other women."

"I've got my sister."

"I know, but she's still a kid," Amy points out. "I might be overstepping, but... if I have my facts straight, you haven't lived with other people for a long time. Like, you've never had female friends."

"I did. Back in..." Astolia almost rolls off my tongue along with Beth-Anne's name.

"Port Alberni? But you were a child back then." She fills in the blanks for me and I let myself nod. It's close enough to the truth.

"I mean... in fairness, I haven't had friends of either gender since then, so the boys are an improvement in my books."

"True." She gives a half-hearted laugh. "What I'm saying is, if you need someone to talk to, I would be honoured. I really would. Yesterday, I went to tell Sid how well-written his speech was, and he said you practically wrote it for him."

"I wouldn't say that. We did dictation." I don't know which way to look to avoid the earnestness of her large, hazel eyes, but eventually settle on a mallard preening his feathers on the other side of the pond.

"It still meant a lot to him. He... look, he's not always great at spelling things out, but he cares about you. That much is obvious."

I'm sure she means all this kindly, but it's hard not to

hear the implication that she thinks she knows him better than I do. "Yeah, I know."

"And… he's worried about you."

"I know."

"So, if you ever need anything—"

"Amy, I appreciate you coming out, but if talking to me is a favour to my husband, you don't need to worry about me."

"I—I'm so sorry. That's not what I meant at all." Her face falls, a flush spreading across her cheeks. She's practically mimicking Sid an hour ago. Wouldn't they be peas in a pod together?

"Like I said, I've got the boys. I can always ask James about rutting deer if I get lonely."

"Heh." There's still colour in her cheeks, but at least she acknowledges my joke. "Let me try this again: Sid doesn't ask for things. I would like to think we're friends, but he sure as shit never asks for my help. Not even with his campaign, when we're supposed to be working together. He's an absolute ox."

I almost counter that it isn't true; his stubborn streak folds the moment he cares about someone, because for all his walls and gruffness, he's driven by hope and love.

But Amy carries on. "That's why I was so surprised when he asked me to come by. I thought, that girl must mean the world to him."

My chest tightens. Sid and I have skirted naming our feelings for each other. Maybe that's silly. I don't think it's possible to have "casual sex" while married, so we clearly mean something to each other. The guy carted a couch home for me on the basis of nothing but one off-hand comment. It's obvious he's in deep.

You've clearly got a lot of trauma. I have no interest in dealing with that.

He told me not to believe what he said that night—but I can't stop proving that I'm screwed up. If he's begging Amy to deal with me instead, doesn't that show he knew his own mind all the way back then?

I never should have slept with him. Not the first time and definitely not the next. Why the hell did I think things would be better if I slept with him?

"Anyway..." Amy stammers awkwardly. "Maybe he is the common factor between us, but I would still like to be friends. Anyone he loves is worth knowing."

"Don't say that." I cannot imagine this conversation going any worse, though she does keep thinking up new ways to top herself. "If that was true, he would say it himself."

"I mean... I think he probably—"

"He would." And so long as he doesn't, I don't have to confront what love would mean for us. For him. Roped to a miserable, dependent shut-in. Neither of us got into this situation for love. All it would do is trap us. Him with me. Me with this version of myself. "I... I should go. Check if they need help with the dishes."

Amy brushed off this excuse only a moment ago, but she's clever enough to realize that I want an escape. From her. From me. Even from him. The lifeline I caught hold of after spotting the Grand Astrologue slips from my grip as I realize who I would be pulling below water with me.

I have to find some way to break away from Sid before I drown him.

THIRTY-FIVE

WHEN I RETREAT to the room I used to share with April, Sid is distraught. He bangs on the door—and to make matters worse, April lets him in, then abandons me, so I have to face my heartbroken husband on my own. You can't count on teenagers for anything.

I press my face against the mattress, the sheets already sticky with my tears. I can't look at him. Forget leaving the farm, I don't know how I'm ever supposed to leave this bed again.

It's not even Astolia I'm thinking about anymore. It's every fucked up thing I've done since lighting the signal fire.

Shooting Sid with my slingshot.

Running around the hospital, trying to break down doors.

Cussing out an old man who walks with a cane.

Knocking the wooden spoon out of Wendell's hand.

Sobbing on a couch in the middle of the exchange.

Trying to convince April to abandon the only place that can keep her alive.

Greeting Amy with a knife.

Along with these memories comes a gallery of stunned faces, as if each person was shocked to discover I wasn't as human as I looked. Maybe I'm not. Humans are supposed to be social animals, craving the support of a community. Instead, I'm terrified of everything that's supposed to make me happy. This place might have saved April, but it's crushing me.

"Kayla." Sid's hand is warm as it wraps over my shoulder, large and firm. I'm not strong enough to push him off. "I'm sorry. I'm so sorry. I shouldn't have tried to fix things or... I thought you might want a friend, you know? But I should have asked you first. I should have—"

"You *should* have picked Amy."

"You're kidding, right? I thought we already..." He lets out a hollow laugh. "I don't *want* Amy. I want you. I love you."

There it is. Strange, how such beautiful words can cut so sharply.

I curl into the mattress. "You shouldn't. Why the hell would you ever choose me when you deserve a normal—"

"Don't talk about yourself that way."

"It's true!" I'm angry enough that I roll over so I can yell at him without the mattress swallowing my words. When I look up, I'm confronted by his face, leaning over me, eyes shining like blue skies I could fly up into if I had wings. It leaves me breathless for a second, until I swallow back the last of my tears and go on. "You've been—I mean... you're perfect."

"Holy shit, *no*."

"You are! You're perfect and I can't even love you the way you deserve."

There. I said it.

His knees buckle as he sits next to me on the bed. "So...

you don't love me," he finally says, blue sky eyes shuttered by clouds.

"I can't." My voice sounds a thousand leagues away. "I don't know how."

"You love April," he says.

"You know that's not the same."

"Isn't it? Because I know it's not the sex thing. You're okay with *that*." His voice rises and I flinch. Not because I'm afraid of him anymore, but because it's clear I did what Amy warned me about. I hurt him. "So it's just the love part. Why, Kayla? Why can't you love me?"

"I don't know!" How can I even put this into words? There's no good explanation, because a normal person wouldn't be reacting this way. "I just can't. I've lost too much. I can't live a normal life because I can't make myself believe it's real. It's too late. I'm too scared."

"Of me?"

"Of everything."

He nods. For a long time, we're both silent, the space between our knees wider than a canyon formed by an earthquake.

"Is it because of TNS?" he asks finally.

"Them. Astolia. Everything."

"Shit." His hands shake as he runs them back through his hair. "I'm so sorry. I knew we shouldn't have..." He chokes on his words. "I knew I reminded you of them, but I still—"

"What?" I straighten, startled. "No, what the hell? It's not your fault."

"You just said it was."

"No, I didn't!"

"You said you were too scared of me."

"No! That's not what..." I mentally play back what we just said to each other and realize where I went wrong.

"I'm not afraid *of* you. I'm afraid of losing you. Loving you and then… having that ripped away."

His eyes flick back to mine. "But you said—"

"The problem isn't you! It's never you. How…" I brush the tears from my face and try to see us from his point of view. "How could you possibly think *you're* the problem?"

"Come on. My people killed your family, Kayla. If you never wanted to see me again—"

"I already told you that could have been Astolia. That could have been anyone. And even if it was TNS, you're not one of them anymore. How many times do I have to spell this out? You should know by now…" The realization hits me. "Nothing I say is going to fix that, is it? You can't help thinking everything is *your* fault, no matter how long ago it was."

"Oh shit, you sound like my therapist." Sid rubs his temples, a weary sigh filling his lungs. "Yeah. Something like that."

"But it's been twelve years. How are you—after twelve years…" It never goes away. That should be the most depressing thought in the world, because if he's still reliving the horrors of his youth, what are the chances I'll ever put away mine? I'm afraid of losing people. He's afraid of hurting them. Instead, it fills me with wonder, because through it all, he's still here.

Still himself. Still, for his faults, willing to love me.

"I'm not Amy's kind of person. I don't even know how to imagine a life with someone like her. I don't own a table. Twelve long, shitty years and I don't own a table." He gives me a wan smile. "The best twelve, shitty years of my life."

"And what about before that? The worse years?" When he doesn't respond right away, I rephrase my question. "You never told me about how you grew up."

I place my hand over his. A pulse rages through the thin skin of his wrist. "It's been a long day. Maybe—maybe we can talk about this another night—"

"Sid, you promised. You promised I could ask about it whenever I wanted."

"I also promised I would never sleep with you," he points out.

"Yeah, well… keep stalling and that might come true yet."

That draws a laugh out of him, and a sliver of courage warms my chest. I thread my fingers through the cornsilk texture of his hair. "Please."

His eyes fall away from my face. "I don't want you to think less of me."

"I know." I rest my head against his shoulder, hoping the power of my touch is enough to reassure him. "But you're never going to believe I won't judge you for it unless you tell me."

What if the reason I don't know how to be happy with him is because I haven't ever held the full weight of his grief? For so long, I've been drowning in my own darkness, but the idea of his doesn't pull me down the same way. For once, maybe I can be the person in the lifeboat, offering him a hand up.

"You've already done so much for me. Please. Let me be here for you."

He bends lower, pressing his forehead against mine. I could stay this way forever, I think, right before he begins to speak.

"I've only shot three people myself," he says. "But I've helped kill far more."

THIRTY-SIX

SID CHARLES WAS born a year after the Quake. A shit time, if ever there was one, to enter this world. People were dropping like flies, trying to avoid disease, war, crumbling infrastructure and whatever else might be killing them on a given day. It was a hard time to survive as an adult, let alone for babies.

Growing up near Vancouver, he has vague memories of the sea wiping out the Fraser Valley as oceans incurred and flooding got worse each year. People headed for the mountains around the city, where TNS reigned supreme. He can't remember his parents. He doesn't know if he was born in the group or not. All he knows is that by the time he was old enough to speak and respond to orders, he was bigger than any of the other kids his age, and that made him worth investing in.

"It was the same with Silas," he says. "He was tall. They placed their bets on kids who were healthy. They started us young. First few years, it's drills and athletics training. I worked my ass off. Gave them whatever they wanted. I was a good soldier, so I got treated well. They had stuff they would give us if we made top of class, saved from pre-Quake times. Candy, when we were kids. As we got older, condoms. And cigarettes." He waves the one he just lit in front of me, scowling. I decided, given our topic, to let him smoke, since he needs something to ease his nerves. It did necessitate moving from April's room to ours, so she wouldn't come back to a smoke-filled room.

"So that's when this started." I say, tapping the cigarette.

"Yeah. I was ten when they started handing me these. Silas kicked the habit once we got here, but I haven't. Just one more way they tried to keep us loyal. Addicts are easy to push around." He stumps it out against a metal tray, as if trying to find new resolve to resist their influence. "But I hardly needed an excuse to be loyal. I gave them everything.

"When they introduced guns, I wasn't a natural shot, so I spent months doing extra practice because I knew I was in trouble if I didn't improve. I couldn't be one of those grunts they risked on the frontlines of away missions. I had to make officer. I had to be top of class. They made me spar with kids five years older than me. One broke my nose, but I was proud, because I knew they couldn't get rid of me if I took a beating from a boy twice my size and got back up. That was my whole childhood. Taking shit every single day so they would think I was worth keeping alive."

"So why did you leave? If you were one of the loyal ones, what changed?"

Sid runs his hand over his chin. "Silas and I both made the officer track. We started running missions once we turned sixteen, but we always were partnered with older officers. They were mentoring us. I got tapped for instructing the younger classes. I was so excited, because that meant one day, I wouldn't have to go on missions at all. Not that I said it out loud. That kind of coward shit was a great way to get sent on a suicide run. But it meant one day, I would be safe. Evan—the one who was training me—used to pull me aside and ask my opinion when we found groups with younger kids in the field to see if I thought they were worth rehabilitating.

"One day, we found a father and son living on a boat docked too close to shore. We managed to board them. The kid was fourteen; it wasn't clear if we could re-educate him into TNS or not. Evan asked me my opinion and I remember saying, keep him. Then we'd have someone who knew how to sail. Most of TNS was terrible at it. Their navy got wiped out during the war with Salt Spring a few years earlier, so that kid was useful. He was James."

"James!" I'm happy for a split second.

"Then Evan shot his dad."

"Right." It's too early for this story to have any happy endings.

"He didn't integrate well, but he's not stupid. He followed orders to stay alive. Always stared at me across the mess hall like he wanted to strangle me. I tried not to think about it. And then... a few years later, we found a group from Salt Spring."

His eyes are hollow, seeing the ghosts of the people they caught. The ones who led him here. "It was an expedition team, trying to scavenge supplies from the mainland. Well armed, but we had the numbers and we whittled them down. I'd heard of Salt Spring before, obviously. I always thought they were like us: another place trying to hold onto enough power to stay alive. It never occurred to me things could be different there. But one of the men had glasses."

"Glasses?" I repeat.

"I know, right? Glasses. It was that simple. I'd never seen anyone wearing glasses before. After he was shot, I took them and put them on my face and everything went blurry. Evan laughed at me; explained what they were for. And I stared at them thinking… these people fix *eyes*. They know how to do that, and we don't. When I went back to my tent that night, Silas was sobbing. It took a while before he calmed down enough to explain why. He said he'd seen two of the men kiss each other goodbye before they were shot.

"You know how TNS is. A lot of it started from people trying to recreate some version of the past before people like Silas were allowed to exist out loud. My best friend had been faking interest in women his whole life just to get by, and at that point I thought, *shit*. Shit, we can't do this. If someone finds out, they might shoot Silas, and if I stand up for him, they'll shoot me. The choice was simple. I could turn in my best friend, or I could run."

"So you went to James," I say.

"We went to James." Sid nods. "We had the whole thing figured out. We would get ourselves onto a boat and James would sail it to Salt Spring, where we would surrender. But he didn't trust us because… well, obviously, he didn't trust us. He thought we were trying to bait him into something, to expose that he was really a traitor. So he told us he would only take us if we got him a gun and we brought some other kids with us, because he figured we might risk him, but we wouldn't risk *them*.

"So I came up with a plan. I told Evan that James had agreed to start teaching some people how to sail, but he wouldn't work with senior officers. Just kids. It was this whole back and forth until finally, command agreed, and we held a contest for the younger classes. The top student of each one would get the chance to learn about the boat with James. We weren't allowed to go anywhere, of course. We weren't supposed to be under sail. But James taught me and Silas enough that we were able to sneak supplies aboard. He told us how to get things ready, without making it look different, so he could pull up the mainsail in less than a minute and get us underway.

"So we held the contest. We picked the winners. I remember when Albert won a slot, we fudged the results so that Dominick got in too, because it seemed cruel, breaking up blood brothers. There was this whole ceremony, that all the youth classes had to attend. Evan came down to the dock with a couple of the commanders and then..." He shrugs. We both know what's coming next. "Silas led the winning boys below deck, then locked them in. James pulled the sails. Everyone was screaming. I noticed Evan put his hand on his sidearm. It was his favourite gun. The one with pearl handles. I shot him."

"Sid..."

"The other officers were slower getting their guns up. I picked them off, too. One, two, three. But the first bullet was Evan.

"People ran, looking for some way to stop us, but there wasn't anyone else ready to sail. No one else was armed. My record was spotless, Kayla. No one saw it coming. So... one day, I saved five kids because for nineteen years, I never gave anyone a reason to think I would be anything other than a good soldier."

I tighten my grip around his arm, thinking the story is over. And while it's true that the worst part is done, there's still more.

"I can't blame Council for thinking we were bad news. We were three heavily armed teenaged boys with a bunch of screaming children we'd literally kidnapped. They took the kids and threw the three of us in jail. Eventually, all our stories lined up and they realized that the reason the boys were freaked out was because I'd shot TNS officers, not because I'd threatened any of them. So after a few months, we got transferred to the sanctuary program. And... now we're here."

I lean my head against his arm and try to picture every-thing he has skipped over. The years of working for the border guard, trying to build not only a life for himself, but everyone he dragged here along with him. Pieces of their history that I've already learned make more sense, like James blowing his savings on a guitar and Sid insisting they forgive him. Or how Sid stepped in to handle the issues at the high school, when teenaged Dominick started acting out. Twelve years of small steps, atoning for the life he led before he came here.

I wonder when, if ever, he'll forgive himself.

"Then last year, Tom reached out to me," Sid says. "Just after we got the acreage. He said he had a new sanctuary case from TNS. He wanted to meet me. He'd been on the docks when we sailed away, when he was only a kid. Said we gave him the courage to try and escape one day himself. And as he was giving me a hug and saying thank you, it hit me... it *was* worth it. And maybe if there was someone with my story in government, even more people out there would hear about it. Then they might try to come here too."

"That's why you want to get into government?"

"One of the reasons. There are a lot. No one talks about it, but TNS is dying. The cracks were already showing while I was there. There aren't enough smaller groups to prey on anymore. Not enough stuff to scavenge. They've got loads of land, but not a lot of experience farming. A few years from now, they're either going to fall apart, and Salt Spring will get waves of refugees, or they'll get their shit together. Either way, we're going to have to deal with them. If that happens, I would rather we get ready to make peace. I'm done shooting people. Who's to say we would be firing at anyone other than a kid like Silas or me?"

"Forgive TNS? That's asking a lot of people."

"Maybe not forgive them. But there's got to be a better

path forward than constant skirmishes with them. That's why I want to be on Council. I talk about immigration now because in the long run, I want to avoid a war." He twists his dead cigarette between his fingers. "Now that we're here, I don't want to lose this."

"But you'll be a public figure if you get on Council. You're not afraid of people higher up in TNS recognizing you, considering how you left?" I hardly have enemies compared to him. All I did was run.

"Of course I am." His voice is soft. "But I'm not doing it for them."

Unbidden, a bright, pretty face framed by blonde hair rises into my mind's eye. Beth-Anne. Perfect, beautiful, doomed Beth-Anne. I've got every right to be afraid of the Grand Astrologue and everyone else that helped support that regime, just like Sid fears the people he betrayed in TNS. I would give anything to never see Astolia again. But is that true of every person there? What if Beth-Anne had the chance to come here?

Guilt clutches at my heart as I realize that Sid, in my position, would try to save her.

And there's only one way to help the people stuck there.

"How many demerits do you get…" I swallow, terrified of the question about to breach my lips. "… if you admit you lied on your sanctuary papers?"

Sid shakes his head. "I don't know. I never did."

"And you've never talked to anyone who…"

He shrugs. "I think it's on a case-by-case basis."

"Say I wanted to speak up. Say… say there was someone from Astolia who might come, if they knew I was here. Would it be worth it?"

"I think…" Sid runs his fingers through my hair. "That you'll always wonder if you could have helped them if you don't."

My head is nodding before I've even made up my mind. "You'll come with me?" My voice cracks like tumbling shale.

"Every step of the way."

"I don't know how long it will take. I can't even leave the..." I swallow back the foam in my throat. "But I don't want him to win."

"Then let's take that shitbag down."

It feels good when laughter finally releases the tears from my eyes. It feels even better to collapse against Sid's chest and have his arm wrap around me. When I squeeze the water from my eyes, I picture Beth-Anne.

"Hey." I twist in his arms so that one of my knees slides in between his legs. His arms shift to my waist. "If I get more demerits, that might mean we get to stay married a bit longer."

"Think you could handle that?" He pulls me toward him.

A breath catches in my throat as I stare up at him. My safe harbour. "I don't think I could survive anything else."

"Me neither."

He bends to kiss me, and all those feelings I tried to push away bloom like a dandelion. Deep-rooted, and impossible to get rid of, but bright. Sunshine yellow and seeded with a thousand wishes. That peculiar blend of cigarettes and pine holds command of me as I breathe him in. My heart, pressed close against his, thrums like a ballad on James's guitar.

When we break apart, I want to go straight back, but more than desire fuels me tonight. There's one other truth I need to speak into existence.

"I don't want to get divorced, Sid." It tumbles out of me as I brace my hands against his chest. "I want to stay here and have this be my home. I want to live with you and—and I want kids. I want Carlos to teach me how to make pastry and I want to grow mushroom logs and I want so many things. I think I want a life."

"Woah, were kids in that list?"

Shit, maybe I said too much. "Yes. At some point."

"Oh. Okay."

"Okay? Is that it?" My face burns.

"No. That's not it." He cups one of my cheeks in his hand. "I love you, too."

"I—I should have said that."

"You did."

"Sid Charles, I love you." The moment the words are spoken, the feeling grows, the truth becoming brighter the louder I let it live.

"And I love you."

This time when we kiss, nothing else needs to be said. I lean back into the pillows, drawing him with me. Our movements are slow and deliberate, a testament to the belief we share that we can afford to take our time. A lifetime together opens up in front of me, and while I'm still learning what the exact shape of it will be, I know he'll be a central part of it.

I don't know if I deserve to be loved like this. It seems too incredible that a world filled with terrible pain has also given me the chance to belong somewhere again. Perhaps there will always be whispering doubts that this could be taken away, but no matter how cruel fate may one day be, I find myself hopeful. There will always be something about the world that is worth loving. And even if joy isn't permanent, neither is its end. Like pine seeds after a forest fire, there will always be something that grows where pain once was.

And so I love him.

And so the world carries on.

THIRTY-SEVEN

I **WISH** I could say that I wake up the next morning and march straight into town, ready to storm Astolia. I wish change came that easily.

I start by walking April to the road and sitting with her before she takes the bus into school. As we wait for the wagon, I give her a shortened version of the story Sid told me about TNS and how that led into our discussion about Astolia. And for the first time, I tell her about Beth-Anne.

April takes it all in with a frown. "Do you really think we'll get in trouble?"

"We?"

"I mean… we *both* lied to them."

"Shit." I forgot about that. April still has a demerit on her papers for *lengthy unknown affiliation*, too. Would telling someone we lied put her access to insulin in jeopardy? "If you don't want me to, then—"

"No," she says firmly. "For once in your life, don't worry about me."

It's so hard not to, even facing her steely gaze. Why

does she have to be so desperate to grow up? But maybe she's right. The greatest gift I can give her is letting go.

"Okay."

"Good." She nods sharply, not the least bit afraid. Trusting Salt Spring's promises always has come easier to her than me. "I'm glad you and Sid finally talked about everything. It definitely explains a few things."

"Like what?"

"Mostly why James is such a cocky bastard."

I burst with laughter. "You're right. He must love rubbing in the fact that he was never a true TNS kid."

"I wonder why he stuck around with Sid and Silas once they got here."

"I don't." I look down the path toward the comfort and safety of the farm. I'm growing antsy, sitting out in the open so long, but I'm also proud. It's more than I've managed to do for a long time. "I don't wonder about it at all."

"Yeah, but I don't think James was shagging either of them. Granted, I don't know for sure," says April. "But your case seems a little different."

I shrug. "Maybe it is."

"Maybe?"

I'm unsure how April will react to the next thing I need to tell her. She might scream at me for being irresponsible, but hopefully, with time she'll realize how deeply I've considered my choice. "Sid and I... we've decided that whatever happens with this demerits situation, we're not splitting up once you and I get citizenship. I'm staying with him."

"And am I supposed to stay here as well?" she asks. "Forever?"

"You..." There's an excellent chance she's testing me to see how quickly I freak out at the thought of her having independence. "Once you're legally an adult and have a job, that will be entirely up to you."

A smile plays on her lips. "I thought *you* were supposed to get a job."

"I am a grown ass woman with a whole acreage to care for," I remind her. "But... maybe. I would like to find something here that's just mine."

"Yeah. Me too. Maria already knows she wants to be a teacher." April looks down at her shoes. "I'm just trying to survive this school year."

"Hey. You're going to be a scientist, remember? No selling yourself short." I nudge her arm, and she flushes at the reminder of her real ambition. I'm never letting her forget what she promised herself. She deserves to live a life as brilliant as she is. "What did you get on that math test, by the way? The one Maria helped you study for?"

She rolls her eyes at me. "Kayla, that was weeks ago."

"Well, I apologize for being wrapped up in my own shit back then. So, how did you do?"

She flicks her ponytail behind her shoulders. "I got an A. Of course."

Finally, the bus comes, and I'm free to head back to the acreage. I spot Sid and Silas chopping back the last of the dead tomato plants. Wendell and Dom are tossing a football back and forth. James is gathering eggs while one of the hens pecks at his shoelaces and Carlos is by the herb garden, picking sage leaves for tonight's stew. His new kitten is perched on his shoulders, rubbing her face into his ear.

A word I've rarely used for the places I've lived sings through my bones. *Home.*

"THERE ARE PROVISIONS for abuse survivors." Amy scribbles in a pre-Quake spiralbound notebook. "No one is expected to disclose abuse upon applying for sanctuary, so Tom can't assign you demerits for choosing to do it now. What you're describing seems to qualify, but..."

"There's a *but*?" I ask.

For a brief second, the law seemed sane to me. Sid and I agreed it would be best to get another opinion before I approach Council with what I know about Astolia. Amy was the safest person to tell, since she already knows a few of our secrets and—most importantly—isn't Tom.

The three of us sit together around a very ugly table Sid picked up from the exchange. It's hard, plastic patio furniture, misshapen on one side due to melting against a fireplace at some point. He admitted that he chose it "because it was cheap"; I'm suddenly glad he never bought much furniture before I came here. He promised we could return it in the morning if I come with him. I'm starting to wonder if the table was a ploy to get me into town with him again and damn it, it might work.

Still, it's easier to talk with somewhere to set our mugs, papers, and Amy's large collection of pens. They're all black. I have no idea why she needs so many.

Amy pushes one pen back and picks up another. "The issue is that we have a long-standing relationship with Astolia. Or *thought* we did. They're not a major trade partner, but they passed the human rights check years ago." I open my mouth to protest, and Amy holds up a hand. "I know! I know they faked it. Sent a whole bunch of people away before we could see how cramped the living conditions were. I'm not saying your accusations aren't true. They add up, if you ask me. But..."

"But it's our word against theirs?" Sid says.

"Exactly." Amy sweeps a hand out.

"Hmmm."

"And it could hurt your platform, Sid, if people think you're throwing accusations around but can't substantiate them. Not to mention, you've built a lot of your campaign on working closer with foreign partners and immigrants."

I know we invited her over to give us the brutal truth, but I struggle not to resent her for it. There shouldn't be problems. I know what I experienced. I turn to look at Sid, arms folded tightly over my chest. "So… do you want me to shut up about it?"

"No," he says, but I can hear the worry in his voice. "But… it would be nice if we had evidence. Is there anything you can think of that might help?"

"Help do what? If no one wants to believe me—"

"Trigger an investigation of the colony," says Amy. "Convincing Council to do something like that will require reasonable doubt that they're the ones lying. Not you."

I wish I was facing demerits instead. A slap on the wrist for hiding my past sounds easier to handle than people doubting my story. Evidence? All the scars I carry are internal.

"I didn't bring anything from there," I say. "But I can give names. I can list whole families of people who should be there."

"That would be a start." Amy adds another note. This black pen produces a thinner line than the one she was using earlier, giving her notes the illusion of headings and subheadings. "Though they could easily deny the existence of those people. I think it would help once we're investigating them, but triggering the investigation is the issue."

"Well… I don't know. What do they do when they visit the island?" I ask.

Sid shrugs. "From what I understand, not a whole lot. They're technophobes."

"Ugh, we had one come by the guild and, like, sprinkle holy water on our door." Amy shivers at the memory. "He was given a warning. Haven't seen him since."

"And that's not weird enough?" I ask.

"Well, not if they stopped once they were asked. So long as they aren't harassing anyone, it's all personal belief," says Sid.

"But they use the hospital. They never let us touch modern medicine, but they *use the hospital*." I fume with frustration. "That shows they're inconsistent, doesn't it?"

"Like I said, I think your story makes sense," says Amy. "But the hospital is about the only thing they do use, and I can understand making an exception from their standpoint."

"The hospital..." The one place on the island with regular contact with the Astolians. If there's any dirt to be had on them, it's there. "Do they keep records there? Of the people who visit them from outside Salt Spring?"

"Legally, they're required to keep documentation for all their patients," says Amy.

"Then that's it! If there's something shifty going on, won't it show up in their records? Maybe there are patterns." I'm not sure what we might find, but we have to start somewhere. "They couldn't bring any obvious medicine back to Astolia, like April's needles. What if there are conditions they let go untreated? Stuff like that?"

"There might be, but isn't it going to be the same problem as with the government?" Sid says, looking between me and Amy. "Those records are private, so without a good reason to look at them, no one is going to—"

"Pasteurization." Amy's eyes have gone wide. "I know what we can tell the hospital. Or at least, if we combine it with Kayla's story, we might have a compelling case."

"Really?"

She sets her pen down, flaring her fingers out in excitement. "A few years ago, there was a salmonella outbreak in Astolia. We must have had half a dozen cases come over, all at once. Afterward, the hospital concluded it was due to unpasteurized goat's milk."

"It *would* be goat's milk," I say.

"The hospital contacted the Reinventor's Guild, asking us to put together some tools that would help Astolia set up basic pasteurization. I even wrote a support document all about the long, ancient history of heat-treating wine, so that they wouldn't get their panties in a twist about the technology aspect, but it didn't matter. They said they didn't have the funds for the proposal. Back then, I believed them. I mean, all they've got are goats. But that probably wasn't the reason, was it? They couldn't let people suspect they learned *anything* from us."

"Yes! That's exactly what would have happened." It's official. I love Amy Sullivan.

"But would that be enough? Walking up to the hospital and saying Kayla thinks they're creeps and you agree, because they won't pasteurize their milk?" Sid asks.

"Maybe," says Amy. "It's worth a try."

"And I think I know who we need to hit with our story to get results," I add.

"You do?"

"Sure." Desk Lady. The hero this story needs. I don't even mind Doctor Tremblay and his loose lips anymore, because he's clearly primed the whole hospital to bend the rules. "When you need someone to break confidentiality, you go to the gossipiest bitch you know."

WHEN WE GO into town at last, it's for a double feature. Buy a new table, take down a cult. Ever since coming to this island, I've struggled to know what my purpose is here or what I wanted, especially once April's needs were taken care of. It's incredible how much braver I feel now that I want something again. Beth-Anne. I'm doing this for Beth-Anne.

No, I'm doing it for me. Because I want to see her. Because maybe I don't have to let go of everything in my past.

Sid and I walk toward the hospital together, my pace slowing as I near the drive until we're at a standstill. The last time I visited, the world crashed in on me. Statistically, I know the odds are low that the Grand Astrologue will be here again, but he was once. Once is enough to give me pause.

Sid squeezes my hand. "Do you want to start by going to the exchange? Work our way up?"

"No," I say. "I was thinking… Actually, I was thinking I would rather talk to Pat alone."

His eyebrows fly upwards. "You sure that's a good idea?"

Not really. But I nod anyway. "I'm trying to get her to gossip with me. You might kill the mood."

"Take that back. I can be a gossipy bitch if I like," says Sid, but his sad smile says he knows the real reason I want to do this alone. I need to prove to myself that I can. "I'll be waiting outside."

His fingers slip from mine and I break into a run. A slow, purposeful walk would be more dignified, but it's starting to rain. In a way, I'm grateful. I'm eager to get beneath any roof, making the warm hospital sound like a good idea right now.

When I reach the door, I notice that pine boughs have been tied to the doorframe, along with sprigs of holly, red berries burning bright in the grey December rain. The sight puzzles me, until a faded memory from all the children's books I used to flip through with April surfaces in my mind. *Christmas*. It's Christmastime.

Are we going to put a tree up at the acreage? Do Sid and the boys give each other presents? I haven't prepared anything, but I would like to. Does James know any of the old songs they used to sing? Already, I can picture us sitting around with the guitar, eating cranberry sauce or... whatever it is they do at Christmas. I'm making this fantasy up as I go, but that's half the appeal of a holiday, isn't it? Making up your own traditions? I push the door to the Emergency department open, strangely comforted.

Pat the Desk Lady is seated at her desk, eating a bagel, and waves enthusiastically when she spots me. "Well, if it's not my friend the Wildling!"

Still not my favourite word. I grit my teeth and smile.

"Mr. Charles came by for your sister's medicine last week. She's not due for more, is she?" Pat asks, setting her lunch aside.

"Um, no. I'm not here about her." I glance around the waiting room in what I hope is a conspiratorial manner. I grip the envelope Amy passed me, detailing the pasteurization equipment the Reinventor's Guild drew up for Astolia all those years ago.

"You aren't here for Emergency care, are you? Pregnancy doesn't fall under that, by the way. Just routine—"

"I'm not pregnant."

"Oh." She deflates.

"I wanted to ask you a question, since you seem to know *everyone*, Miss..." Too late, I realize I never learned her last name.

"Moore. Pat Moore. Everyone calls me Pat, though. And like you said, I do mean everyone!" She chuckles delightedly, and I think we're back on track.

"There was a man who came here the other day," I say, thumbing the pages. "It was over a month ago, but maybe you remember? He said he came from this place called Astolia—"

"Oh, yes! Well, I can't give out patient details of course, but—"

"You don't have to, Pat. I know him. I never thought I would see him again, until he was there that day."

She straightens, clearly surprised. "But you're a Wildling. How d'you know Gord?"

I slide the envelope from Amy across to her. "In Astolia, he made us call him the Grand Astrologue. And my family did everything we could to escape him."

"But why would you—"

"If you have time, I think I might be able to explain."

It's an emergency department. There are other things she should be doing. But as her eyes dart between me and the packet, I know I've won her curiosity. At the very least, she seems to be entertaining the idea that I might be crazy. And from her point of view, crazy is *interesting*.

"Of course, hon." She motions for me to grab one of the waiting room chairs and take a seat by her. "What is it you want to tell me?"

THIRTY-EIGHT

THERE IS ONE more person I have to tell the truth to before we put our whole case in front of Council. Tom Sullivan. Immigration officer and asshole extraordinaire.

Of everyone I've trusted with this secret, he is the one who has the most power to make my life hell. Amy promised me that disclosing abuse was not required when I applied for sanctuary, and Pat assured me of the same thing. If he's a prick about this, I can contest any demerits he tries to assign. But with a demerit on my papers already, the thought tickles in the back of my brain: who would the judiciary believe?

"Maybe you should knock me up first," I say to Sid three days before Christmas, as we're hanging evergreen branches around the acreage. A letter has arrived from the hospital and with it, we think we have what we need to convince Tom. But there's still so much at stake, it's hard to rest easy. "Then I would have a clean record."

"Don't you *dare*." April calls from the bottom of the ladder, while Sid throws me a skeptical look. "If you do something that stupid—"

"I don't think these are the right circumstances to—" Sid starts.

"Holy shit, guys! I'm kidding!" I drop a branch on Sid's head, then slide down the ladder.

"Are you, though?" comes a distant voice.

"Not helping, James!" Sid and I shout back in unison. All we get is a cackle from the other side of the farmhouse, where James is setting up a tree for us to decorate with painted pine cones and seashells. He's put the Lady Liberty crown on top, because of all his silly hats, that one looks the most like a star.

The next day, Sid and I head into town. The hospital was one thing, but I decide I would rather have him with me to face Tom. Complaining about him is one of the great, unifying creeds of our marriage, so it only feels right walking into City Hall together and heading toward the immigration department for our appointment.

It's awful how open the area around Tom's office is. I wonder if this is really what Sid wants—to pore over papers in a renovated grocery store. It's not a glamorous place, and I try to let that give me courage. The people in charge of this island aren't lounging in luxury like Bradley Patterson. They're overworked, ordinary people like Tom.

He fetches a couple of chairs for each of us and then extends his hand to shake, though neither of us take it. Sid, because I've got a vice grip on his right hand, and me, because I have not forgiven Tom for anything.

Sid cracks first, putting out his left hand, which Tom switches hands to receive. "Good to see you, Tom."

"Yes. Very nice." He gives us both a false smile. "To what do I owe the visit?"

"Kayla wanted to talk to you." Sid nudges me forward, but I don't relinquish my hold. The solid mass of him is the only thing keeping me from bolting.

"Does she? Then why don't you take a seat, Ms. Hollins."

As we sit, Tom opens the files that govern my life here on Salt Spring. "So, what brings you here today? I should let you know, I received a note from the secondary school about a month ago that your sister had served detention for an altercation with another student. You're not worried about her, are you?"

"No. I think she's okay."

"Then why *are* you here?"

"I…" I look down at my hands, which slide against each other in my lap. "I need to update something on my papers. The line about last known zone of origin. It wasn't Port Alberni. It was eleven years ago, in Astolia."

Tom straightens in his chair. "Astolia has provisional ally status. You *can't* put that on sanctuary papers. You would have to immigrate through some other mechanism or—"

"And has anyone ever done that?" I ask. "Have you ever had immigrants from Astolia?"

"Not to my knowledge," he says. "But that isn't to say—"

"It is." I pull a document from my bag, signed by Pat Moore. I hold it out to him, while I rattle off the monologue I memorized. "During the twenty-three years Salt Spring Island has had contact with Astolia, the hospital has only seen twenty-six individual patients and never treated anyone of Astolian origin with Salt Spring citizenship. Nineteen of these patients have been adult men. Three were adult woman. Four were infants below the age of three. There has never been a child old enough to remember a visit to the island who has checked into the hospital."

"How did you get this?" Tom flips through the multi-page document, his face rippling with shock. "This should be confidential information—"

"All names and private information have been removed. So it isn't." I lean forward and point out the line on the document stating exactly that. Right before the signature of Doctor Levy, who luckily hasn't retired yet. Once Pat heard my story, she knew immediately which physician would be the most likely to help us.

"Surveying legal records of our alliance with them, they've also been assigned provisional allyship for longer than the recommended ten years, as outlined by the charter. But they're yet to agree to a more thorough evaluation of the colony, which would be required if they wanted to advance to full participation in the League of Gulf Nations," adds Sid. That's been his job for the past couple of weeks— gathering whatever legal backing he could find through the library and City Hall records to bolster our case.

"I'm aware of *that*," says Tom. "We've been trying to arrange a day with them, but they're a superstitious bunch. They keep going on about choosing a spiritually meaningful day to—"

"Superstitious? They're a cult!" I can't hold it in any longer. "They're a cult and my family had to run away from them when I was fourteen so they couldn't marry me off!"

Tom does a double take, looking between Sid and me. "And how did that turn out for you?"

"Oh, go to Hell, Tom!" Sid shouts. "Do you trust me or not?"

"When it comes to your judgment around this woman? Not remotely," says Tom. "But... I am looking at something signed by the hospital. It *does* give one pause. What makes you say they're a cult?"

"Well... they're probably spewing propaganda about this place right now," I say. "That's why the hospital hasn't seen any children. That's why they don't bring many women in. Only the people the Grand Astrologue trusts get to come here. The numbers shouldn't look the way they do. The moment the hospital pulled the information, they knew something was wrong. Doctor Levy recommends pulling services to Astolia until a thorough investigation into the living conditions and size of the population can be conducted."

"And you want me to… to what?" He shuffles the pages of the medical recommendations between his fingers. "Instigate an international incident?"

"No. I'm going to do that." I don't think my words reassure him. "What I'm asking is for you to listen. So that no one can think I'm lying when they ask you."

He lowers the papers and looks at me, eyes no longer squinting and critical. "Well. Go on, then."

"I… I guess I'll start when Port Alberni fell," I begin.

Tom never interrupts. He might prompt me, if my pace slows, but none of his cutting remarks shorten my story. Of all the times I've told my tale, this is by far the worst. It's like I'm rattling off statistics, my whole life reduced to numbers. If I try to gloss over something, Tom's questions are to the point. How old was I when they measured the girls at school for reproductive fitness? How old was April when we left? How many individuals do I remember?

At least with him, I get to end before I reach the death of my mother and Curtis. I let the story trail off with my family wandering the woods, with the implied addendum that only April and I survive.

A long pause follows as he rifles through the pages from the hospital, reviewing Doctor Levy's statement again and again. Finally, he sets it aside and picks up his copy of my sanctuary papers. My heart is in my throat as he begins writing notes on it.

"Congratulations, Ms. Hollins," he says. "I'm amending your application. You will be free to apply for full citizenship in January, once you've reached the four-month anniversary of coming to the island."

I straighten in my chair, sure I misheard him. "Excuse me?"

"I'm recommending you for a fast-tracked path to citizenship, which I suggest you take."

"You can do that? This whole time, you could—"

"Yes and no." Tom throws a hand up in the air. "It's my department. I can make exceptions in exceptional circumstances. But fast-tracking the wife of someone I endorsed for election in the newspaper? Someone might think I'm handing out political favours. That's a risk we must take."

"But why would you—"

"Because I believe you." He locks eyes with me. For the first time, I notice that they're almost as blue as Sid's. "If what happened to you is still going on, this needs to be dealt with swiftly."

"Oh." I should say thank you, but I'm too overwhelmed.

"So come January, we'll finalize your citizenship. Following that, you can speak to Council about this situation and the hospital's findings. That way, if this stirs up any trouble from Astolia, they'll be unable to request your repatriation." He passes back my files from the hospital and the amended papers, all demerits struck and marked as resolved. "And you two can finally free yourselves from this… situation." He gestures vaguely at where Sid's hand is resting on my knee. "If it pleases you."

"It does not," says Sid, sourly.

"Bloody hell. I knew it." Tom squeezes his eyes shut.

"Tom, thank you, I…" I gaze at the words printed at the top. *Exemplary participant. Recommended for immediate admittance.* "I don't understand. I lied on my papers."

"Everyone lies on their papers. Especially Wildlings."

Tom shrugs, as if this is the most obvious component of his job.

"I didn't," says Sid.

"Yes. Neither did Silas. It was the most disconcerting thing about dealing with you," says Tom with a laugh. "Everyone *else* lies. Not everyone admits it. You aren't the first to grovel in my office over some secret you kept when you first arrived here, Ms. Hollins."

That spikes my anger again. "Why didn't you tell me that before?"

"I tried asking you once. For my trouble, you told me I was worse than the doctor who wanted to see your sister taken from you."

"Oh."

Tom's face pulls into a thin smile. "I decided to wait and hope you came forward of your own accord."

Was that the right approach? I'm sure he could have done better in some regard. People always can. But for the first time, it's clear that he never had a vendetta against me. Even when he wanted to throw me in jail, I had—admittedly—shot a friend of his unprovoked. Maybe he isn't even an asshole. Maybe it was just easy to imagine him as one, because every time I saw him, I was reminded of all the lies I was telling. He never bought my bullshit. Of course that scared me.

In a strange way, that makes him a lot like Sid.

"Thank you, Tom. Thank you for everything."

"Of course." He nods appreciatively, and I realize, I finally managed to do that thing Sid told me the islanders wanted: be grateful. The thought disgusts me, except when I think about it... I am. I'm happy to be here. I'm on an island with medicine for my sister, a bureaucrat who wants to protect me from Astolia, and a man who loves me.

As Sid and I leave City Hall, the chill of outside

surprises me, and I pull my coat tight. My breath clings to the air in a vaporous puff as the rain thickens to snow. Great, globby flakes of it fall from the clouds to melt against the pavement.

And it's beautiful. Here, where it's safe, for the first time in my life, snow is beautiful.

"Look at it," I whisper.

"This is gonna mess up the roads," Sid grunts, and a laugh bursts out of me.

"Grumpy much?"

"Well… no. I don't think so. We're on the same page, right? About your impending freedom?"

That tiny hint of doubt makes me love him even more. He'll never take me for granted. I'm too wonderful to him. I hope he knows I feel the same way about him.

But I am nothing if not obnoxious, so I swoop in and place my hands against his chest. "Of course. I promised not to leave until you get elected."

"Very funny, Kayla." He takes my hands in his and bends over me, so that his height and wide shoulders shelter me from the cold.

Bicycles whisk by us, as ordinary life goes on in all its incredible complexity. I can't move, too overwhelmed. The gratitude I felt back there wasn't so much for Tom and his policies, but for the man in front of me. For him.

I kiss his fingers. "Thank you."

"I didn't do anything."

"I mean for everything. For standing by me when they asked about the slingshot. For marrying me. For…" I choke as I think of those awful first days on the island and then again, when I was too broken to leave our home. "For wanting me when no one else did."

"Kayla." He threads a hand behind my neck. "That was all you, too."

"I don't see how."

"You…" He isn't a crier. But something is caught in his throat. I understand the feeling all too well. "You *trusted* me. No one's ever looked at me and expected me to be the good guy before. No one until you. I don't know how I can ever deserve—"

"Don't talk that way. You don't have to earn me." At that, I go up on my toes and kiss him. He holds me like he's trying to make sure I don't escape. Like this is a dream we could wake up from. When I rock back on my heels, I slide my hand into his so I can pull him toward our bus stop. "I'm here for good."

He grins. "That's all I wanted to hear you say."

"Come on, worrywart." I tug him forward, anxious to be back in the quiet and familiarity of the acreage. "Let's go home."

THIRTY-NINE

I'M NOT SURE at what point life slips into the kind of *happily ever after* that used to end the children's books April and I scrounged from collapsed homes. I never knew how to picture that when life was nothing but a smear of survival. If I lived happily ever after, what would be the illustration the author used to communicate my bliss?

I can name a few moments.

Like Christmas Day. April and I give bracelets we wove from cedar to all the boys and Sid surprises me with a fabric box. Inside are my mother's earrings.

"But how did you...?" I scream, and throw my arms around his neck while he laughs.

"After we got married, I went to the hospital and reworked the billing so it was in my name. They gave me a full refund." He grins. "Headed to the exchange right after."

"But they must have cost more than I sold them for."

He shrugs. "You need to get your ears pierced."

As it turns out, on Salt Spring Island, even Santa Claus is real.

Then there's the day April and I are granted full

citizenship. We celebrate by surprising April with her own bicycle. She shrieks in terror when James lets go of the seat for the first time and suddenly, she has to rely on her own momentum to stay upright. That day is perfect, too.

And I'm not quite sure I would call it *happily*, but life does seem like it will be at least *better* ever after on the day Council grants our petition to revoke Astolia's provisional ally status, with a full investigation to come. And yes, okay. I admit it. I am happy when the Grand Astrologue— or should I say, *Gord*—spots me watching the hearing. He starts cursing when he recognizes me and tries to make his way toward me, only to be caught by the island guard. And, *oh* does it feel *delicious* when the mayor declares that this makes the decision easier.

That night, I wake up gasping, cold with sweat, trying to make sense of where the nightmares came from, but Sid's hand is there, steadying me. Helping me find the right pace for my heartbeat.

No one told me that about happily ever after. It can still have sleepless nights and days where I admit, that yes, my husband is right. I need to start therapy. So I finally go and talk to someone who helps me make sense of myself. And just like how all Wildlings lie on their papers, apparently most of us also have issues left over from—how does she put it? *My time disconnected from a safe environment.* She even says it's normal that I reacted so negatively to my first taste of safety, because my body wasn't used to living without a crisis. I had years upon years of unprocessed pain waiting to burst out of me when I got here. It's nothing to be ashamed of, she says. It stings to clean a wound before it heals.

It's worth putting up with those days, because in March, the election comes. Amy makes Council, because of course she does. But so does Sid. His involvement in the Astolia situation reassured voters that he was someone with a balanced view on human rights and immigration and all that government shit. Tom, as my brave sponsoring immigration officer, played a role in the success too, so he also gets in with a landslide. The newspaper even makes him and Sid pose together for a photo—not that it will actually go in physical papers, but Amy says they have a database on a computer somewhere that holds onto important records of the island's history, in case there's a distant day when they can print the images. Our victory matters enough that it's going to be saved there.

As people come to shake Sid's hand and congratulate him, a few throw me winks and say they would have voted for me, if they could.

"Oh, believe me. No one wants someone with my mouth in government," becomes my refrain. "And honestly, I would get bored."

When Mrs. Buckerfield hears this line, she blinks in surprise. "Well, what is a brave girl like you doing with herself so she doesn't get bored?"

"Well... not a lot. But I really like to cook."

"Do you? Why haven't I seen you at my place, then? Bring Carlos by. He never visits."

"O-okay." I can't fight the grin on my face.

But none of those moments beat today. It's a little over a year since I first arrived on the island. I've been given the day off work from the café to help with the pandemonium on the acreage. Dom has agreed to move into the spare room in Albert's unit so we can open one of the apartments to another family—sanctuary seekers. They asked for us in particular.

It's merry chaos. Outside, Silas is hastily constructing a goat pen, not easy in the autumn rain. April has instructions to pick up any books she can find on animal husbandry from the library after school, while Carlos rearranges the kitchen, as a generous ration upgrade was dropped at the farm to accommodate the newcomers.

I'm helping to transfer Dom's rock collection to its new lodgings. James, Young Tom, and Wendell are carting in furniture for a woman and three children.

"We really don't have to worry about them liking it. This is more space than they're used to," I say, boxing up another geode, then attempting to heft the collection into my arms.

"Kayla, for the last time! You're not supposed to be lifting things!" James rushes to pull the box out of my hands.

"It's, like, ten pounds!"

"Twenty!"

"If you don't let me do this, DeLuca, I will whip your ass!" The box teeters against my belly, which has started to make itself prominent. Five months prominent.

I had a few rough days during my first trimester—a mixture of fear that I might lose this baby too, and guilt about having a child with someone other than Curtis. But more often than not, I feel so lucky. I'm due in February.

James throws his hands up in surrender. "Far be it from me to call your judgment into question."

"*Thank you.*" I do my best to stride away with purpose, but between the box and my condition, it's more of a victory waddle.

I step outside, meaning to head straight to Albert's—but then I spot them coming up the drive. I drop the box and it clunks to the ground. I shouldn't be trusted with heavy objects at the best of times.

"Beth-Anne!" I sprint towards her, James's voice chasing me.

"You shouldn't be doing that, either!"

I don't pay him any attention. In front of me is a woman my age, her golden hair falling loose from a sensible bun. She walks tentatively onto the acreage, a small girl's hand in hers. Behind them are a pack of five goats, which an eight-year-old boy drives forward with a thin willow branch. Bringing up the rear is Sid, carrying the baby.

"Kayla Hollins." She says my name so softly, reverent. "As I live and breathe. It's really you."

"Can I hug you?" I want to, desperately. I found out she was alive months ago, after Astolia conceded to Salt Spring's terms. In order to maintain access to the hospital and other island services, they have to allow regular visits from the League of Gulf Nations, including a medical practitioner, to assess the entire population. I wanted to go and see her myself, but Astolia made it clear that my husband and I aren't invited.

Last month, Beth-Anne decided to take Salt Spring up on the offer to apply for sanctuary, which was extended to any colony members who were kept from knowing about the so-called alliance for all those years. Most didn't accept. Either they've been there too long to see straight, or it feels too much like home to them. It isn't for me to judge.

Beth-Anne grins and opens her arms. I reciprocate and find the one thing that feels better than letting go of the past. Holding on. "I got your letters," she says.

"I'm so glad."

"Doctor Levy had to sneak them in. But she said you were happy. She said…" She trails off, looking around the freshly harvested fields, and the boys popping up to wave at her. "By Aries, you've got a lot of space here."

"You're going to love your apartment." I slide my arm through hers. "There's a big room for you, and a whole second one for the kids."

"Rafe, take the goats to that tall man over there. He

seems to want them," she says to her son, and the boy drives the flock toward Silas. Beth-Anne looks at me, expression wary. "Your husband says they'll want the kids to go to school? All day?"

"All day,"

"Well, that's a long time." Her eyes drift over the acreage again, resting on the house. I wonder if I looked this spooked the first day I arrived. Scratch that, I was worse. "I guess they need it, though, to live in a place like this? It's so *big*."

It's tiny, really. A single island in an ocean of unknowns. But it's enough.

"Who's ready for the grand tour?" James strides forward. He's under strict orders not to flirt with her, but even when he's not trying to sleep with a beautiful woman, James is perpetually friendly. I let him get away with it.

Especially because two seconds later, Dominick pushes him out of the way. "It's *my* old place! I get to show it to her!"

"Hope you like overgrown boys," I whisper, and she laughs.

"I do. I like men best when they're still boys."

I nod. Maybe her sanctuary papers say why she came without her husband. Maybe it's a pleasant reason, like he's dead. I'll wait for her to explain when she's ready. It's clear that she's here for a fresh start, and if there's one thing I've learned since coming here, it's that change takes time.

"I like your husband." She nods in Sid's direction, who is gingerly setting her youngest down so that she can pull at a dandelion she spotted. "He's a nice man."

"I like him, too."

He perks up, as if he just caught us talking about him, looking slightly embarrassed. I give Beth-Anne a parting squeeze, then skip toward him. He pulls me into a hug and a handful of papers press against my back—probably the sanctuary documents for Beth-Anne's family. This time, the whole process went through the right government offices, instead of happening hastily in a hospital waiting room.

"She says you're great," I say. "Which I have to agree with. You look pretty okay holding a baby."

"Trying to get practice in while I can," he says.

"Just so you know, though—you're not allowed to marry her. Not even if she asks nicely. That's the rule."

"As I explained to Tom, that is *not* going to be our policy with sanctuary seekers going forward."

"He's still on your ass?"

"Worse than ever. It's the closest he gets to the concept of friendship."

I laugh, before realizing two things—one, I might pee a little if I'm not careful. And two, Beth-Anne is waiting for me. I can catch up with Sid later tonight.

And catch up we do. After we've eaten together with our new family. After we've sat around the fire, James playing his guitar. After I've guided Beth-Anne back to her apartment, because the music brought her to tears and she needs a moment alone. After the kids are in bed and April is cursing at a worksheet on the quadratic formula and Carlos has dampened the fire in the stove.

After all of that, I curl up next to Sid and we swap stories. Mine involve purchasing children's beds at the exchange. His describe the commotion at City Hall when the boat from Astolia arrived. Four families came all at once. We haven't had a refugee situation like that since the early days after the Quake and the government is a-twitter about it.

Once the words are caught up and there's nothing left to say, we simply exist together. He kisses me, gentle as his hand slides over my swollen belly, flutters of small limbs dancing against a father's hand.

It's not quite what I would call a storybook ending. But it is happiness. And it is ever after.

And it means the whole world.

THE END

ACKNOWLEDGMENTS

First, I'm grateful to this book itself. *All We Have Left* was born from the ashes of a writing slump. It had been an awful year, where I kept having to tell my agent I didn't have anything for her to sell. She was marvellously understanding, but I was disappointing myself, if not her. As is often the case, the solution lay in pretending no one would ever read my next novel. I worked up the nerve to draft something completely self-indulgent, publishing industry be damned, and suddenly the words came rushing back. So thank you, Sid and Kayla, for rescuing me from my own neurotic brain.

And thank you (naturally) to Penelope Burns, who took the news that I had abandoned the previous project we agreed on in stride. You gave such thorough editorial support to a book that desperately needed it. Drafting a whole book in two months—it turns out—gives you not so much a book as a promising pile of goo.

I'd like to think that goo was in *slightly* better shape when it crossed Katie Dent's desk at Titan Books. I'm incredibly grateful for not only your enthusiasm for the book, but your sharp eye for how it could be improved. You have been so steady through all the ups and down of the past year. I'm proud of this story we got to create together and all you've done to make Titan Books my continued home.

As this is my second book with Titan, I also want to thank the wider team, especially Bahar Kutluk and Katharine Carroll. Few people have had more fun publishing a book than I did when *Death on the Caldera* launched. You made incredible things happen for me and now I sing the praises of the Titan marketing and publicity team everywhere I go. And of course, a shout-out goes to Rufus Purdy, the first to welcome me into the Titan fold.

I'm lucky enough to have lots of friends who help me grow as a writer. As usual, I wouldn't be here without my Writer's Alliance. Eliza, Ipuna, Jennifer, Diana, Molly, Cass, and Kristine—you guys are rockstars. I can't wait for the day I get to hold all your books. And a huge thank you goes to my buddies from Discord—both Book Club and The Prose Pros—who cheered this book on from its earliest, goopiest form.

A special shout-out goes to Bori Cser, who reached out when I needed a friend and became this book's biggest advocate. You helped me see this story as something with genuine potential. To Risto Snow and Miranda Leavitt, thank you for reading the earliest, clumsiest version of this book and giving such helpful notes. Finally, to Julie Leong, I feel so lucky that I get to be your friend. Thank you for sharing sci-fi/fantasy writer summer camp with me! I hope we can do it again soon.

I only wish I could have spent *more* scenes describing the unparallelled beauty of the Pacific Northwest. Thank you to the camp counselors, master gardeners, sailing instructors, and countless others who helped me fall in love with these islands. What a joy it is, to call this place home.

But most of all, thank you to my family. To Colton, who is stuck with me now. To Andrew, who inspired so much of this story. To Jessica, my singing and dancing partner in crime. To Katie, expert berry picker. To Matt, who can reach the berries Katie can't. To Dad, who built me garden beds. To Mum, who still holds me when I need to cry. And to all the nephews, nieces, cousins, uncles, and aunts who fill my life—the world is always worth saving and you are the world to me.

May we treat this world with the reverence it deserves.

ABOUT THE AUTHOR

EMILY PAXMAN is an author and artist from Vancouver Island in beautiful British Columbia, Canada. She's a huge fan of gardening, cats, watercolour painting, and several other hobbies that befit an octogenarian. She has her Master's of Fine Arts in Creative Writing from Chatham University, has written for indie video game company Wizard Games, and splits her time (unevenly) between creating comics and writing novels. You can read her webcomic, Neptune Bay, on Webtoon. Her debut novel, *Death on the Caldera*, was published by Titan Books.

Follow Emily on Bluesky: @emmypax.bsky.social;
and on Instagram: @emmypaxman